Genometry
Edited by Jack Dann & Gardner Dozois

Edited by Jack Dann & Gardner Dozois

Edited by Terri Windling

GENOMETRY

EDITED BY
JACK DANN & GARDNER DOZOIS

ACE BOOKS, NEW YORK

GENOMETRY

An Ace Book / published by arrangement with
the editors.

PRINTING HISTORY
Ace edition / January 2001

The Penguin Putnam Inc. World Wide Web site address is
http://www.penguinputnam.com

Check out the ACE Science Fiction & Fantasy newsletter
and much more on the Internet at Club PPI!

ISBN: 0-441-00797-X

ACE ®
Ace Books are published
by The Berkley Publishing Group,
a division of Penguin Putnam Inc.,
375 Hudson Street, New York, New York 10014.
ACE and the "A" design are trademarks
belonging to Penguin Putnam Inc.

PRINTED IN THE UNITED STATES OF AMERICA

10 9 8 7 6 5 4 3 2 1

CONTENTS

PREFACE

Here on the edge of the twenty-first century, we also stand poised on the brink of a revolution that may change everything about our world as deeply and pervasively as did the Industrial Revolution, and perhaps even as profoundly as did the Neolithic Revolution that changed us from wandering bands of hunter-gatherer nomads and gave us agriculture and towns: the Genetic Revolution.

Bioscience—genetic technology—may be the science that will shape our lives in the most significant ways during the twenty-first century, probably having an even more significant impact than the evolution of computer technology has had in the closing decades of the twentieth. Already, we've seen our daily lives changed by early manifestations of genetic technology, sometimes in behind-the-scenes ways that we hardly recognize. Everyone has heard about the controversy about cloning raised by the production of Dolly, history's most famous sheep, but fewer realize that similar bioscience is behind the development of human-derived insulin and a dozen similar drugs on the cutting edge of medicine, or that they *already* live in a world where organisms created in a laboratory can be patented, or where genetically altered foods are available in every supermarket.

And this is just the thin edge of the wedge. Just ahead, perhaps in the next few decades, are changes driven by bioscience and genetic technology that will transform our daily lives almost beyond recognition, and perhaps even change *us* beyond recognition, that could change forever our ideas about what it means to be human. All our definitions of what makes a human being *human,* all of our "eternal verities," all of the deep truths about human nature that have remained fundamentally the same since we came down from the trees at the dawn of time, all may be about to melt like snow—or, perhaps a better analogy, become molten and reshapable, like hot plastic, into any pattern we desire.

The prospect is both exhilarating and deeply terrifying.

Wonders and terrors await us ahead that, from our current perspective, are almost unimaginable.

In the anthology that follows, some of the world's most expert dreamers take their best shot at imagining those coming wonders and terrors, doing a better job of pointing out the pitfalls and promise, the marvels and horrors, of the coming (hell, already almost *here*!) Genetic Revolution than you're going to be able to find anywhere else. So, to buffer yourself from the oncoming tsunami of culture shock as well as anybody *can* be buffered, and also, not at all incidentally, to have a great time reading some of the most entertaining, colorful, and wildly inventive cutting edge speculations that science fiction has to offer, turn the page, while you're still recognizably human (do you think you'll still have *fingers* twenty years from now?), and enjoy!

(For more speculations about how the Genetic Revolution will reshape our society and ourselves, check out the Ace anthologies *Immortals, Clones, Nanotech, Hackers,* and *Future War.*)

GENOMETRY

THE INVISIBLE COUNTRY

Paul J. McAuley

Born in Stroud, England, in 1955, Paul J. McAuley now makes his home in London. A professional biologist for many years, he sold his first story in 1984, and has gone on to be a frequent contributor to Interzone, *as well as to markets such as* Amazing, The Magazine of Fantasy and Science Fiction, Asimov's Science Fiction, When the Music's Over, *and elsewhere. He is considered to be one of the best of the new breed of British writers (although a few Australian writers could be fit in under this heading as well) who are producing that sort of revamped, updated, widescreen space opera sometimes referred to as "radical hard science fiction." His first novel,* Four Hundred Billion Stars, *won the Philip K. Dick Award, and his acclaimed novel* Fairyland *won both the Arthur C. Clarke Award and the John W. Campbell Award in 1996. His other books include the novels* Of the Fall, Eternal Light, *and* Pasquale's Angel, *two collections of his short work,* The King of the Hill and Other Stories *and* The Invisible Country, *and an original anthology coedited with Kim Newman,* In Dreams. *His most recent books are* Child of the River *and* Ancients of Days, *the first two volumes of a major new trilogy of ambitious scope and scale,* Confluence, *set ten million years in the future. Currently he is working on a new novel,* Life on Mars.*

Here he takes us to a haunted future London in which nearly every aspect of daily life has been transformed almost beyond recognition by biological science and genetic technology—but where many of the old, cold choices you need to make in order to survive remain unsettlingly familiar. . . .

Cameron was discharged from the black clinic with nothing more than his incubation fee and a tab of painkiller so cut with chalk it might as well have been aspirin. Emptied of the totipo-tent marrow that had been growing there, the long bones of his thighs ached with fierce fire, and he blew twenty pounds on a pedicab that took him to the former department store on Oxford Street where he rented a cubicle.

The building's pusher, a slender Bengali called Lost In Space, was lounging in his deckchair near the broken glass doors, and Cameron bought a hit of something called Epheridrin from him.

"Enkephalin-specific," Lost In Space said, as Cameron dry-swallowed the red gelatin capsule. "Hits the part of the brain that makes you think you hurt. Good stuff, Doc. So new the bathtub merchants haven't cracked it yet." He folded up his fax of yesterday's *Financial Times*—like most pushers, he liked to consider himself a player in the Exchange's information flux—and smiled, tilting his head to look up at Cameron. There was a diamond set into one of his front teeth. "There is a messenger waiting for you all morning."

"Komarnicki has a job for me? It's been a long time."

"You are too good to work for him, Doc. You know there is a place for you in our organization. There is always need for collectors, for gentlemen who have a *persuasive* air."

"I don't work for the Families, OK? I'm freelance, always will be."

"Better surely, Doc, than renting your body. Those kinky cell lines can turn rogue so easily."

"There are worse things." Cameron remembered the glimpse he'd had of the surrogate ward, the young men naked on pallets, bulging bellies shining as if oiled and pulsing with the asynchronous beating of the hearts growing inside them. The drug was beginning to take hold, delicate caresses of ice fluttering through the pain in his legs. He looked around at the dozen or so transients camped out on the grimy marble floor and said loudly, "Where's this messenger?"

A skinny boy, seven or eight years old, came over. All he wore were plastic sandals and tight-fitting shorts of fluorescent orange waterproofed cotton. Long greasy hair tangled around his face; his thin arms were ropey with homemade tattoos. A typical mudlark. Homeless, futureless, there had to be a million of them in London alone, feral as rats or pigeons, and as little moved. He handed Cameron a grubby strip of paper and started to whine that he hadn't been paid.

"You've a lot to learn, streetmeat," Cameron said, as he deciphered Komarnicki's scrawled message. "Next time ask me before you hand over the message." He started for the door, then turned and knocked the shiv from the boy's hand by pure reflex.

The blade had been honed from the leaf of a car spring: when Cameron levered it into a crack in the marble floor it bent but would not snap. He tossed it aside and the boy swore at him, then dodged Cameron's half-hearted cuff and darted through the broken doors into the crowded street. Another enemy. Well, he'd just have to take his turn with the rest.

Lost In Space called out, "Your soft heart will get you in trouble one day, Doc."

"Fuck you. That blade was probably all that poor kid had in the world. Sell a working man a couple more of those capsules and save the opinions."

Lost In Space smiled up lazily. "It is always a pleasure doing business with you, Doc. You are such a regular customer." The diamond sparkled insincerely.

Cameron checked his gun harness out of storage and hiked around Wreckers Heaps to Komarnicki's office. The shantytown strung along the margin of the Heaps was more crowded than ever. When Cameron had lived there, his first days in the city after the farm, after Birmingham, there had still been trees, even a little grass. The last of Hyde Park. No more. Naked children chased each other between tents and shanty huts, dodging around piles of rubbish and little heaps of human shit that swarmed with flies. Smoke from innumerable cooking fires hazed the tops of the Exchange's far-off riverfront ribbon of glittering towers, the thread of the skyhook beyond. Along the street, competing sound systems laid overlapping pulses of highlife, rai, garage dub, technoraga. Hawkers cried their wares by the edge of the slow-moving stream of bubblecars, flatbed trucks crowded with passengers, pedicabs, bicycles. Occasionally, a limo of some New Family or Exchange vip slid through the lesser vehicles like a sleek shark. And over all this, ad screens raised on rooftops or cantilevered gantries straddling the road or derelict sites glowed with heartbreakingly beautiful faces miming happiness or amazement or sexual ecstasy behind running slogans for products that no one on the street could possibly afford, or for cartels only the information brokers in the Exchange knew anything about.

A couple of mudlarks were stripping a corpse near the barricades at the southern corner of the Heaps. Riot cops guarding the gibbets where the bodies of a dozen felons hung watched impassively, eyes masked by the visors of their helmets, Uzis slung casually at their sides. They stirred the usual little frisson of adrenaline in Cameron's blood, a reflex that was all that was left of his days on the run, a student revolutionary with an *in absentia* sentence of treason on his head. But he was beyond the law now. He was one of the uncountable citizens of the invisible country, for whom there were only the gangs and posses and the arbitrary justice of the New Families. Law was reserved for the rich, and fortress suburbia, and the prison camps where at least a quarter of the population was locked away, camps Cameron had avoided by the skin of his teeth.

Inside the barricades, things were cleaner, quieter. The plate-glass windows of Harrods displayed artful arrangements of electronics, biologics, the latest Beijing fashions. Japanese and Brazilian businessmen strolled the wide pavements, paced by tall men in sleeveless jackets cut to show off their fashionably shaped torsoes—like a blunt, inverted triangle—and the grafted arm muscle and hypertrophied elbow and shoulder joints. Some had scaly spurs jutting from wrists or elbows. A league away from Cameron's speed. He relied on his two meters and muscles shaped by weight-training, not surgery, to make a presence. Consequently, he got only the lesser members of visiting entourages, translators, bagmen, gofers: never the vips. As Lost In Space had said, he was getting old. And worse than old, out-of-date. Even though Komarnicki's protection agency had never been anything but a marginal affair just one step ahead of the law, Cameron was hardly getting any work from it anymore.

Komarnicki's office was in a Victorian yellow-brick townhouse in the warren of streets behind the V&A, as near to Exchange as he could afford, three flights up stairs that wound around a defunct lift shaft at least a century old. Cameron swallowed another of the capsules and went in.

Komarnicki was drinking rice tea from a large porcelain cup, feet up on his steel and glass desk. A fat man with long white hair combed across a bald spot, his gaze shrewd behind old-fashioned square-lensed spectacles. "So you are here at last," he said briskly. "Doc, Doc, you get so slow I wonder if you can anymore cut the mustard."

"Next time try employing a real messenger."

Komarnicki waved that away. "But you are here. I have a special job for you, one requiring your scientific training."

"That was another life. Twenty years ago, for Christ's sake." In fact, Cameron had hardly started his thesis work when the army had been sent in to close down the universities, and besides, he had been too involved with the resistance to do any research.

"Still, you are all I have in the way of a biologist, and the client is insistent. He wants muscle with a little learning, and who am I to deny his whim?" Komarnicki took his feet off the desk. Tea slopped over the rim of his cup as he leaned forward and said in a hoarse whisper, "All he wants is backup at a meeting. Nothing you haven't done before and good money when the deal goes through. You get your usual cut, ten percent less agency fee. Plenty of money, Cameron. Maybe enough for me to pay for my heart."

"Your body would probably reject a human heart," Cameron said. It was well known that Komarnicki had the heart of a pig, a cheap but safe replacement for his own coronary-scarred pump, and was buying a surrogate human heart on an installment plan from the same black clinic which had rented space in Cameron's bones. It was also well known that Komarnicki was an artist of the slightly funny deal, and this one seemed to have more spin on it than most. Running flack for a simple meeting was hardly worth the price of a human heart, and besides, what did biology have to do with it? Cameron was sure that he wasn't being told everything, but smiled and agreed to Komarnicki's terms. It wasn't as if he had any choice.

The client was a slight young man with a bad complexion and arrogant blue eyes, and long hair the dirty blond color of split pine. You wouldn't look at him twice in the street, wouldn't notice the quality of his crumpled, dirty clothes. A loose linen jacket, baggy raw cotton trousers crisscrossed with loops and buckles, Swiss oxblood loafers, the kind of quality only a cartel salary could pay for, but rumpled and stained by a week or more of continuous wear. He was a defector, a renegade R&D biologist on the run from his employers with bootlegged inside information, the real stuff, not the crap printed in the *Financial Times*. The kind of stuff the New Families paid well for. *Dangerous* stuff. His name, he said, was David Holroyd. He kept brushing back his long blond hair as he walked beside Cameron along the street and explained what he wanted.

"There's a meeting where I get paid in exchange for . . . what I have. Only I don't really trust these people, you see?" Nervous sideways smile. His eyes were red-rimmed, and he held himself as though trying not to tremble. "It could be that I'm being followed, so maybe you should drive me around first. I have plenty of cash. What sort of biologist were you?"

"Molecular biology. Enzyme structure. That was all a long time ago."

The young man grimaced. "I guess it will have to do."

"I'd rather not know anything," Cameron said. Holroyd's nervousness was affecting him. There was something not quite right about the young man, hidden depths of duplicity. "It's dangerous to know too much."

Holroyd laughed.

The cash was in US dollars. It took a whole sheaf of wrinkled green notes to pay for half a day's hire of a bubblecar. For a couple of hours, Cameron weaved in and out of crowded Picadilly, looped around Soho. They weren't being followed. He parked the bubblecar at a public recharger near the arcades of Covent Garden and tipped a mudlark to look after it.

They drank cappuccino in one of the open air cafes, and

since his client was paying, Cameron devoured half a dozen ham and cheese sandwiches as well. He needed all the protein he could get; it was hard to keep up his muscle-bulk while living a knife-edge from the nirvana of total poverty.

Holroyd was beginning to sweat, even though he had left his jacket in the bubblecar. His cup chattered in its saucer each time he set it down, and his eyes darted here and there, taking in recycling stalls piled with everything from cutlery to crowbars, food stalls swarming with flies, big glass tanks where red-finned carp swam up and down, the ragged half-naked children running everywhere through the milling crowds. After a while he began to talk about kinship, the way organisms recognized siblings and mates. "We've this crocodile in the basement of our brains, know it? The limbic cortex. The archipallium. All the later mammalian improvements are jerry-rigged around it. It snarls and grumbles away beneath our consciousness, hating the new situations that the cortex keeps throwing up. It needs appeasing. That's what social ritual is all about, trying to fool the paranoid crocodile that strangers are okay, they're not a threat. When ritual breaks down you get murder, war. All this is old theory, right, but I see it all around me. Those kids running around. I mean, who looks after them."

"The mudlarks? They have to look after themselves."

"Yeah. The way I was brought up, I know all about that." Holroyd's coffee cup rattled in its saucer. "Ever hear about the Ik?"

Cameron had, but didn't say so. He was there for whatever the client wanted. If the client wanted to fuck a donkey or direct his very own snuff video, Cameron was there to go fetch the boy or girl or whatever, to make sure he got an animal that was retrovirus free. And he would probably do it, too. He had given up making moral judgments long ago. In his line of business, they were an unaffordable luxury.

So while Holroyd talked about this African tribe whose ethical system had broken down entirely after they'd been displaced from their homeland and their way of life, children running wild, old people dying for want of care, Cameron faked attention and watched the crowds and thought of what he could do with the fee and now and then glanced at his watch. It was more than three hours since he and Holroyd had left Komarnicki's office.

"I think I'll have to arrange a new meet," Holroyd said at last.

"If they were expecting only you, I might have queered the pitch."

"You make me feel safe."

They walked back through the crowds to the hired bubble-car. Halfway there, Cameron glimpsed a shabbily dressed man pawing at the vehicle, and he started forward just as the hatch swung up. Holroyd caught his arm and in that moment the man and the bubblecar vanished in a sheet of flame that blew across the crowded street.

"Mau-mau," Holroyd said distinctly, and then his eyes rolled up and he fainted.

For three days after the assassination attempt, Cameron tended his dying client in a room that Komarnicki sometimes used for his less salubrious deals. It was in what had once been a hotel at the western edge of Wreckers Heaps, an area that Cameron knew all too well: the Meatrack. The building's concrete panels were crumbling and stained with the rust of steel underpinnings; its cantilevered balconies hung at dangerous angles or had fallen away entirely; its rooms had been subdivided with cheap pressed-fiber panels. Their room was scarcely wide enough for the stained mattress on which Holroyd sweated passively in the fetid heat, but at least it had a window, and Cameron kept it open for any chance breeze. The cries and conversations of prostitutes and the muffled throb of the sound systems along the Bayswater Road drifted through it day and night, punctuated every hour by the subsonic rumble of a capsule rising into orbit along the skyhook. It was said you could buy anything anytime in the Meatrack, even love. It never slept.

Cameron had been through Holroyd's pockets as a matter of course. Nothing but a bunch of useless credit chips, a fat roll of dollar currency notes, and a stack of canceled airline dockets, none more than a week old, that detailed a weird round-the-world itinerary. Bancock, Macao, Zanzibar. Cairo,

Istanbul, Leningrad. Geneva. Manchester. No sign of any stolen data. Maybe it existed only inside Holroyd's head.

The biologist grew weaker by the hour, feverish and unable to eat, sometimes vomiting thin green bile. Lack of complicated template proteins in his diet, a dependency to ensure his loyalty, had triggered an RNA virus lodged in his every cell.

There was no cure for it, he said, but Cameron needed him to stay alive, long enough at least to tell him what he had stolen. It was the dream ticket, the chance, the way out. Cameron had been without a chance for so long that he was determined not to let it go. He washed away Holroyd's fever-sweat with expensive filtered water; helped him to the stinking toilet every other hour. He bought black-market antibiotics to counter secondary infection, antipyretics and a tailored strain of *E. coli* to ease the symptoms of general metabolic collapse, a sac of glucose and saline which he taped to the renegade biologist's arm. Once it had settled its proboscis into a vein the thing pulsed slowly and sluggishly, counterpoint to the frantic flutter of Holroyd's pulse in his throat, but it didn't seem to do much good.

"I thought I might have lasted a little longer," Holroyd said, with a wry smile. He looked very young, there on the bed. His blond hair, sticky with sweat, was spread around his white face like a dirty halo. "I've always had this tendency to overestimate what I can do. Part of my training." Sold into service by his parents at the age of eight, he'd be brought up a company child, selected for research, running his own laboratory by age fifteen, his own project by twenty. That project was why he had run, because it had worked too well. Holroyd was vague on just what the project had been about, but Cameron gathered that it had been intended to produce some kind of indoctrination virus, a way of infecting workers with loyalty rather than crudely enforcing it. Holroyd had gone beyond that, though precisely what he had produced wasn't clear.

"I tried it on rats first. It was a major operation keeping them in their colony afterwards, we had to sacrifice them in the end. That's when I knew it wasn't safe to let the company have it. I came up out of the streets. I remember what that was like. Having nothing to compete with, always dependent, always running scared. That's the way it would be with everyone, if I'd let the company keep it. It would be like a new species suddenly arising, a *volk*. Luckily, my bosses didn't want it used on people until a kink had been put in it to limit its spread. The way they kinked my metabolism. So I took it out under their noses before it got near a bioreactor."

"Tell me what it is," Cameron said, leaning close to Holroyd. "Quit talking around it and just tell me straight."

Holroyd was staring past him at the cracked ceiling. "What are you going to do, hurt me again?"

"No, man. That was a mistake. I'm sorry." He was, too. He had begun to care for Holroyd, something beyond simply keeping him alive just long enough. Care for him in a way he hadn't cared for anyone since the farm, since losing Maggie.

Looking down at his big, square hands, knuckles scarred and swollen, Cameron said, "I know you want me to understand what you did. And I want to know."

"You'll get it." Holroyd's smile was hardly there, a quiver. "You're already getting it."

Cameron bit down his frustration. He was pushing forty; maybe this was his last chance. This, or ending up in some alley with mudlarks ripping off his clothes before he had even finished dying. "If it's made you so smart, how come you can't figure out a way to cure yourself?"

"It doesn't make you smarter. I thought I *explained*—" Holroyd broke off, racked by a rattling cough that turned into a spasm of vomiting. After a while, paler than ever, he said, "I knew they'd send the mau-maus after me, so I changed my pheromone pattern, kept a vial of my old scent signature. It was in the jacket. I broke it when we were driving around. I was pretty sure one of them would pick it up and follow it to its source. Let them think I'm dead . . ." Suddenly he was blinking back tears. "I suppose a lot of people were caught. In the explosion."

"Half a dozen killed, twice that hurt. Mostly after the cops turned the whole thing into a riot, not in the explosion. There never was going to be a meeting, was there?"

"You're catching on. Appropriate, really, the mau-maus. The virus that transforms their rinocephalum, the place in the

brain which controls the sense of smell? Prototype of part of
my thing. Use it on lobotomized criminals, replace the marrow in their long bones with TDX. They reach the locus of the
scent . . . Well, you saw. Comes from an old colonial war,
back in Africa last century. Guerrillas used to train dogs to eat
under vehicles, then they'd send the dogs out into Army compounds, only with explosives on their backs, triggered by a
length of bent wire . . ."

There was a measure of unbreakable will in Holroyd, like
a steel wire running down his spine. Sometimes when he ram-
bled feverishly he came close to explaining, but always he
stopped himself. His blue eyes would focus and he would
clamp his mouth. He would turn his head away. It was like a
game he was playing, or some kind of test.

Of course, Cameron could have walked away. The thought
returned whenever he went out to get something to eat at the
food stalls, pushing his way through the prostitutes thronged
up and down the Bayswater Road. Many had been so radically modified that you couldn't tell what sex they were; a
good proportion didn't even look human. The brief clothing
of others clung to graphically enlarged male or female geni-
tals, sometimes both. One had an extra set of arms grafted to
his rib cage; another sat in a kind of cart like a beached seal,
leg stumps fused together, flipperlike arms crossed on his
naked chest. Clients walked on the far side of the road, in the
shadow of the Heaps, only a few looking openly at the sexual
smorgasbord on display. Most of the business seemed to de-
pend on a kind of mutual ESP. Occasionally, a black limo
would be drawn up, a beefy bare-armed man or woman standing beside it and scanning the crowd for their employer's
choice.

This throng of human commerce brought Cameron back to
himself after the confines of the room. He could think about
what he had gotten himself into. The prize was unknown. Perhaps it would not even be worth anything. And the chance that
Holroyd's owners would find their hiding place increased
asymptotically with every hour that passed. But something
other than logic compelled him. Carrying his little package of
noodles or vegetable stew, he would return to Holroyd with a
measure of relief. He found himself caring about the dying

man more and more, and he had not cared for anyone since the fall of Birmingham.

Holroyd had got him to talk about his past; in the long watches of the evening, the dying biologist lay as still as a wax figure while Cameron mumbled over memories of university and the barricades, the commune farm he'd helped set up afterwards in the hills of North Wales. There had been a price on his head, and rather than continue the fight he had dropped out, a luxury he had not regretted then. In place of futile bloody struggle there had been misty days of shepherding, learning karate. Always the rush of the stream at the bottom of the steep valley, the squeak of the handmade turbine fans which trickle-charged the batteries. A peaceful span of days in the midst of a civil war. Until the night the machines came, squat lumbering autonomic monsters grubbing up the byres and barn, knocking through drystone walling, flattening the wooden turbine-tower.

The next day, the commune had split what little they had saved and had gone their separate ways. Cameron had managed to get as far as Birmingham with Maggie, but then he had lost her in the riots, his last glimpse of her by the falling light of a flare, across a street crowded with refugees. The smell of burning or the rattle of gunfire always brought that memory back. Much later it occurred to Cameron that no one had known the commune was there, that the machines were simply carrying out some central plan of reforestation. All over the country, gene-melded pines were being planted to produce long-chain polymers for the plastics industry. But at the time it had seemed like a very personal apocalypse.

"I understand," Holroyd said. "The way it is with the combines, most of the world is invisible, not worth thinking about. So we don't. Now I've changed, I know. I begin to know." Tears were leaking from his eyes as he stared fixedly at the ceiling. "I saw a way to break the cycle open, you see, and I grabbed it. Or maybe it grabbed me. Ideas have vectors, like diseases, ever think that? They lie dormant until the right conditions come along, and then they suddenly and violently express themselves, spread irresistibly. The rats . . . never could figure out whether they were trying to escape, or if they were driven from within by what I'd given them . . . Oh Christ. I didn't realize that caring would hurt so much."

Later that night, Holroyd didn't so much wake as barely drift into consciousness. His voice was a weak unravelling whisper, so that Cameron had to bend close to understand. His breath stank of ketones. "I've a culture. Dormant now, until it gets into the bloodstream. A gene-melded strain of *E. coli,* MIRV'd with half a dozen sorts of virus. Gets into lympho-cytes, makes them cross the blood/brain barrier, then kicks the main viruses into reproductive gear. A day, two days, that's it. Some bacteria remain in the blood, spore-forming vector. Breathed out, excreted. Any warm-blooded animal. Spread like wildfire."

"And what does it do? You still haven't told me."

"At first I thought of bonding, pheromonal recognition. But bonding, the pack instinct, is the cause of the trouble. And the committee running the center were real enthusiastic about the idea, so I knew I had to take the opposite direction. You know about kinship?"

"The way animals recognize their relations. You talked about it."

"Yeah. One of the viruses turns that into a global function. You recognize everyone as a brother or a sister. It makes you want to make other people happy, to care for them. It gets into the base of the brain, downloads information into cells of the hypothalamus. Subverts the old lizard instincts, the crocodile in the basement. Are you following this?"

"I think so." Holroyd's voice was very weak now; Cameron was kneeling over him to catch every precious word.

"Infected cells start to produce a variant of an old psy-choactive drug, MDMA. What they used to call Ecstasy. A second virus gets into the neurons, makes them act as if they've had a dose of growth hormone, forces them to grow new synapses. That and the MDMA analog kicks in a higher level of awareness, of connections. The way everything fits together, could fit together . . . You'll see." Holroyd clawed at Cameron's arm. "I want you to take it now, before it's too late."

There was a false varicose vein in his leg. Cameron dug it

out with his pocketknife, first sterilizing the blade in a candle-flame.

Later, Cameron went out to buy breakfast noodles, pushing past a shabby blank-eyed man on his way into the building in search of thrills. As always, Bayswater Road was busy with prostitutes and prospective clients. Every one of the gallery of grotesques dragged at Cameron's attention, vibrant with implied history. Every one an individual, every one human.

It was then Cameron knew what had happened to him—and at the same time flashed on the blank-eyed client. Maumau. Had to be. He turned just as the window of the room where he had left Holroyd blew out. A ball of greasy smoke rolled up the side of the building, and Cameron began to run, dodging through the crowds that thronged Bayswater Road.

Things were coming together in his head, slabs of intuition dovetailing as smoothly as the finest machine parts. If they had known where to find Holroyd, then they'd be after him, too. Or after the short soft length of tubing, bloated with spore suspension. He headed straight into Wreckers Heaps.

Ragged piles of scrap machinery threaded by a maze of paths always turning back on themselves. There was no center, no heart. Gene-melded termites had reared their castles everywhere, decorated with fragments of precious metals refined from junked machines: copper from wiring; selenium and germanium from circuits; even gold, from the lacquer-thin coatings of computer sockets. Glittering like the towers of the Exchange. Sharecroppers picked over the termite castles, turned in the fragments of refined metals for Family scrip. Mudlarks ran wild, hunting rats and pigeons. Nominally owned by the Wasps, the Heaps was a place where even the code of the streets had broken down. No man's land, an ideal hiding place because no one would think of hiding there. It was too dangerous.

Cameron had a contact in the Heaps, a supervisor called Fat Tony. They'd done each other a few favors in the past, and Fat Tony was happy enough to let Cameron borrow part of his stretch in exchange for most of what was left of Holroyd's roll of dollars. He waddled alongside Cameron as they walked down narrow aisles between heaps of rusted-out cars. Useless shit, Fat Tony said, cheap pressed steel not worth the trouble of reclaiming. His hair was slicked back, pulled into a tight ponytail; despite the heat, he wrapped a tattered full-length fur coat around his bulk.

"I need to talk with the Wasps," Cameron said.

"What's that to me?"

"This is their turf."

"This is *my* goddamn turf, man. They might own it, I run it. This thing between you and me is strictly private because if the Wasps hear I'm renting, they'll cut my fucking nose off. I won't tell."

"That's good to know. Where is this place I'm renting?"

Fat Tony turned a corner, ducking awkwardly beneath the end of a bus that tilted on half a dozen mashed down Fords. "Right here, man. Right here."

It was a circular space roughly a hundred meters across, floored with compacted ashes and scrap, one side cut by a long channel of oily water that reeked of long-chain organics. "Don't fall in," Fat Tony said, standing at the very edge, the metal toes of his knee-length biker boots over the rim. "They used to render down organics from the junkers here, tires, plastic trim. All round here we got the cars that were left stranded when the petrol run out, no place else to take them in the city, nothing to move them further. I'm like a fucking industrial archeologist, you know." He spat towards the murky water, wiped his chin. "Hell's own soup of bugs in there. Strip you to your bones in a second."

Cameron watched a little kid walk by on the far side. A string of dead pigeons dangled down the boy's smooth mud-streaked back, wings flopped open. "Listen, I really need to talk to the Family."

Fat Tony turned away from the water. "Happens the Wasps want to talk with you too," he said. "Seems all sorts of people are after your ass, Doc. What's the score?"

Cameron pressed one of the man's hands between both his own. "You'll see soon enough. One more thing. I want to buy anything the kids catch in here."

"You want food, I can arrange it. You needn't eat rats."

"Not to eat. Anything they bring me has to be alive."

• • •

The contact for the Wasps was a smooth-skinned boy with only the faintest wisp of a mustache, no more than fifteen. He lounged in the back of the electric stretch with studied cool, looking at Cameron from under half-closed lids. He wore a white linen suit, white sneakers. No socks. He said, as the stretch pulled into the traffic, "I hear the Exchange is after you. A contract going all the way across the water. It'll cost you real money to help you out."

"I appreciate that. There's enough for all of us. Are you interested?"

The kid held out a hand with a languid gesture, and the big bodyguard who was driving reached around and put a little glass tube into it. The kid sniffed at it, held it out, and it was taken back. The spurs on the bodyguard's wrists were tipped with black polycarbon. The kid said, "From what I know of it, it'll give us the clout to take over the other Families, maybe even put us into the Exchange. Of course I'm interested."

"What you can do with it is down to you," Cameron said. "I can set up a demonstration."

"Real soon. Your ass is on fire, from where I stand."

"Let me worry about that. But if I'm not left alone until the meeting you'll never see what I have to sell."

"For streetmeat, you have sass. I dig that." The kid's laugh was like fingernails drawn down sharp metal. "Okay, we'll meet on your terms. Now, let's deal."

The stretch circled the perimeter of Wreckers Heaps half a dozen times while Cameron talked with the kid. When at last it stopped and Cameron climbed out, the outside air seemed to him like pure oxygen, for all the heat and stink of the street. The stretch had smelled of bad money and worse promises. As he watched it pull away, he knew at last what Holroyd had meant, about the pain of connections, and he mused on it all the way to the place where he had once lived.

Cameron knew better than to walk into the old department store, so he sent a mudlark around the corner to fetch Lost In Space. "Oh my man," the pusher said, when he saw Cameron. "Doc, you are bad news all over town."

"I just need to talk with the people who own your deckchair."

"You're dealing? That's keen, Doc." They stood in the doorway of a shop, Lost In Space shifting from one foot to the other, his tongue passing over his lips with a lizard's flick. For an instant, Cameron saw clear to the roots of the man's life. The filthy crowded room where he'd grown up in the constant smothering company of a dozen brothers and sisters and a despairing mother, childhood innocence withering in the fire of his pride, pride which had driven him to be different when he couldn't begin to define what he really wanted, when all he had was pride, and his fragile armor of vanity and indifference . . .

"I'm dealing," Cameron said. "Something big enough to promote you out of that deckchair, if you want to help me."

There was a derelict huddled in a nest of rags in the far corner of the doorway, asleep or dead. Lost In Space spat in his direction, unsettled by Cameron's tender gaze, and said, "It'll take maybe an hour."

Cameron thought of all he had to do before night fell. "It had better be quicker."

Komarnicki wasn't answering his office phone, but Cameron had already worked out where his former employer was likely to be. He got into the black clinic by offering to incubate more mutated marrow, slipped out of the confusion of reception and sprang door after door along a row of office cubicles until he found a white laboratory coat that didn't fit too badly.

Komarnicki was in intensive care, a guard at the door and a screen flagging vital signs above his head. Cameron waited until the guard went to use the toilet and then walked straight in.

Komarnicki lay naked on the bed, his flabby chest a shield of vivid purple bruises, slashed by a raw, ridged scar. Gene-melded sawfly larvae lay along it, jaws clamping the incision closed, swollen white bodies glistening with anti-inflammatory secretions. Cameron sat down beside him, and presently he opened his eyes.

"You're a ghost," he said wearily. "Go away, Cameron."

"I'm real enough. Want me to pull open your chest to prove it? What did they pay you, apart from a heart?"

"Nothing else. They explained about Holroyd. I wasn't

going to get his fee, so it seemed fair. I took a guess at where you were hiding him, and they got his scent from the couch in my waiting room. It was just business, you understand. I've always liked you, Doc."

"I've got what they want. I can make a deal, cut you in too. Ten percent, for old time's sake."

"You don't make deals with them. They don't operate like the New Families. You're streetmeat, Cameron. Even if you give it to them, they'll take you. And don't you tell me what it is, either. I don't want to know. That kind of knowledge is dangerous—"

Cameron had caught Komarnicki's hand, as it edged towards the buzzer on his bedframe. After a moment, Komarnicki relaxed. He had squeezed his eyes shut. Sweat glittered on his pink face. Cameron leaned close and said, "I'm not going to hurt you. Just tell them I'll deal, OK? I'll call you later." Cameron set down Komarnicki's limp hand and smiled at the guard on his way out, impervious in his white coat.

At Wreckers Heaps, the mudlarks had delivered all Cameron had asked for, and after he had paid them with the last of Holroyd's dollars and set things up, there was nothing left for him to do but wait. He sat near the arm of scummy water, watching silver beads shuttle up and down the almost invisible thread of the skyhook beyond the shining towers of the Exchange, letting sunlight and the invisible flux of the Exchange's trade fall through him, until it was time.

He had arranged to meet with both the Wasps and the Zion Warriors at sunset. With half an hour to go, he called up Komarnicki and told him where he was. And then he sat back and waited.

He did not have to wait long. Soon there was the rattle of gunfire in the south, and then a series of flares rose with eerie slowness against the darkening sky. All around him, stacks of junked vehicles began to groan and shiver, dribbling cascades of rust: someone was using a sonic caster. Cameron sat still in the middle of the clearing, in a bucket seat he'd taken from one of the cars, imagining the hired fighters of the Exchange and the war parties of the two Families clashing amongst the

wreckage of the twentieth century. Exchange fighters out-
numbered, Family members outgunned. Smoke billowed up
from an explosion somewhere near the perimeter. Soon after,
the gunfire stopped. One by one the sound systems that circled the perimeter of the dump started to broadcast their competing rhythms again. Cameron sighed, and allowed himself
to relax.

The electric limo glided into the clearing twenty minutes
later, its sleek white finish marred by the spattered stars of
bullet holes. The teenage negotiator was ushered out by his
massive bodyguard. "I know I'm a little late," the boy said
coolly, "but I nearly had an accident."

"You're later than you think," Cameron said, looking past
the boy at the junk heaps across the channel of stinking water,
where he knew sharpshooters must be taking up positions.

"I got all the time in the world," the boy said, his smile as
luminous as his white suit, and motioned to the bodyguard.

The tall burly man crossed to where Cameron was sitting
and without expression patted him down, pulled his pistol
from his harness, showed it to the boy. "It's empty," Cameron
said.

"Your mistake," the boy said. "Let's go."

The bodyguard put his hands under Cameron's armpits and
effortlessly pulled him to his feet.

And then everything went up.

The pressure switch had been sprung when Cameron's
weight had been taken away. It closed the circuit which ig-
nited the cartridge loads, shredding the mesh covering the wa-
tertank where Cameron had caged what the mudlarks had
brought him. Pigeons rose into the dark air in a vortex of
wings. The bodyguard's attention flickered for a second and
Cameron punched him in the solar plexus. The man staggered
but didn't let go of Cameron. For a moment they teetered at
the edge of the water, and then Cameron found the point of
leverage and threw the man from his hip. The bodyguard
twisted awkwardly and fell the wrong way, flailing out.
Cameron danced back (one of the man's spurs drawing blood
down his forearm) as the man hit the lip of the drop and rolled
into the water, screaming hoarsely before disappearing beneath the oily surface.

Cameron sprang on the boy and whirled him around as a
shield. "I'll let you drive me out of here," Cameron said, but
the boy, limp with shock, was staring down at the red spot of
a laser rifle-guide centered on the left lapel of his white jacket.
Cameron wrestled him into the car in a clumsy two-step,
slammed the door and slid behind the wheel as bullets rattled
on the armor.

The boy pressed hard against the corner of the passenger
seat as Cameron drove down the winding alleys that threaded
the junk-piles. At last he said, "Whatever it is you're doing,
I'm impressed, OK? But there's still a chance to make your
deal."

"There never was going to be a deal. I just canceled things
out, that's all. The Exchange and the Families. Hang on now."

The gate was ahead, armed men running towards it from
both sides. Cameron floored the accelerator and swerved between two flatbed trucks, pedestrians scattering as the limo
shot through the gate. Then it was weaving through dense
traffic and the armed men were lost in the crowds. Cameron
said, "I'm sorry for all the hurt I caused, especially your bodyguard. He was only doing his job, and I meant for him to land
on dirt."

"You stop now, I can help you," the boy said.

Cameron laughed. "Oh no, it's too late for that. Holroyd
took it all round the world, but I want to play my part, too. I
ran away one time. No more. When the universities were
closed down, when knowledge was finally transformed into a
commodity, I should have done more to try and stop it. I can
remember when there was free exchange of ideas, and now
most of the cartels' energies are spent on security against
piracy. But that won't do them any good now, not against five
billion data pirates."

"You're rapping like a crazy man. I bet you never even had
the stuff."

"I had it all right. You saw it go." Cameron pulled the limo
over and switched off its motor, leaned across the seat. The
boy's wide eyes looked up into his, centimeters away. "I
turned pigeons and rats into vectors," Cameron told him. "If
you want what I had, you'll have to catch them. Doves would
have been more appropriate, but I had to make do." And then

he kissed the astonished boy on the lips and slid out of the limo and vanished into the crowds.

Afterwards, Cameron lived on the street, restless for change. The Exchange must have found out what had happened; suddenly there was a bounty on rats and pigeons. But it only served to spread the caring sickness through the mudlarks, and within a week it was irrelevant. The rats had gotten too organized to be caught by ordinary means, but suddenly there were weird devices all through Wreckers Heaps, eye-bending topological conundrums of rusty mesh that mesmerized rats and drew them into their involuted folds. Mobile traps like tiny robot shopping carts careened after rats and pigeons, multiplying like sex-crazed von Neumann machines. When they had run out of prey they started raiding the street markets for trinkets and bits of food, and then sleek machines armed with a rack of cutting tools starting hunting *them*. After that the sickness must have gotten into the water supply, for infection seemed to take off on an asymptotic curve. There was a sudden boom in ingenious, horrible murders—one night two dozen eviscerated riot cops were found dangling from the Knightsbridge gibbets—and then crime plummeted. Graffiti went the same way, and one by one the sound systems fell silent.

One day a young mudlark stopped Cameron in the street. After a moment Cameron recognized Komarnicki's messenger. The little kid was clean now, wore a shirt several sizes too big for him and had a canvas pack slung on his shoulder. He was heading out he said, a lot of people had that idea. Divide up the conglomerate farms, grow food again.

"Out or up," the boy said.

They were at the northern edge of Wreckers Heaps. Amongst abandoned shacks, people were working on what looked like a small air dirigible, a hectare of patched white fabric spread on the ground amid a tangle of tethering cables. The boy looked past them at the skyhook, still there beyond the irrelevant towers of the Exchange. Looking at the boy looking at the skyhook, at the door into orbit, Cameron thought about what Holroyd had said about vectors. Maybe humans were just the infection's way of spreading beyond the

Earth's fragile cradle, the Galaxy like a slow-turning petri dish, ripe for inoculation. Maybe it was his thought, maybe the infection's. It didn't matter. It was all one now, no longer an infection but a symbiosis, as intimate and inextricable as that with the mitochondria in his every cell.

The boy was smiling at Cameron. "I heard you were around here. I just came to say thanks, for what you did back then. What are you going to do? You could come with us, you know."

"Oh, I've already done that stuff, in another life. Who told you about me?"

"I heard from an ex-pusher who heard from some muscle who got it from the kid who was right there. Everyone knows, man. Luck, now."

"Luck," Cameron said, and the boy grinned and turned and headed on down the street, a small brave figure walking into a future that everyone owned now.

Cameron watched until the boy was out of sight. The dirigible was beginning to rise, its nose straining against the people who were hauling back on the anchor ropes. Cameron strolled over to give them a hand.

THE KINDLY ISLE

Frederik Pohl

Here's a wise and gentle story by one of science fiction's best-known authors, one that takes us to a friendly island paradise that is perhaps a little too good to be true . . .

A seminal figure whose career spans almost the entire development of modern SF, Frederik Pohl has been one of the genre's major shaping forces—as writer, editor, agent, and anthologist—for more than fifty years. He was the founder of the Star series, SF's first continuing anthology series, and was the editor of the Galaxy group of magazines from 1960 to 1969, during which time Galaxy's sister magazine, Worlds of If, won three consecutive Best Professional Magazine Hugos. As a writer, he has several times won Nebula and Hugo Awards, as well as the American Book Award and the French Prix Apollo. His many books include several written in collaboration with the late C. M. Kornbluth—including The Space Merchants, Wolfbane, and Gladiator-at-Law—and many solo novels, including Gateway, Man Plus, Beyond the Blue Event Horizon, The Coming of the Quantum Cats, and Mining the Oort. Among his many collections are The Gold at the Starbow's End, In the Problem Pit, and The Best of Frederik Pohl. He also wrote a nonfiction book in collaboration with Isaac Asimov, Our Angry Earth, and an autobiography, The Way the Future Was. His most recent books are the novels O Pioneer!, The Siege of Eternity, and The Far Shore of Time.

I

The place they called the Starlight Casino was full of people, a tour group by their looks. I had a few minutes before my appointment with Mr. Kavilan, and sometimes you got useful

bits of knowledge from people who had just been through the
shops, the hotels, the restaurants, the beaches. Not this time,
though. They were an incoming group, and ill-tempered.
Their calves under the hems of the bright shorts were hairy
ivory or bald, and all they wanted to talk about was lost luggage, unsatisfactory rooms, moldy towels and desk clerks
who gave them the wrong keys. There were a surly couple of
dozen of them clustered around a placatory tour representa-
tive in a white skirt and frilly green blouse. She was fine. It
was gently, "We'll find it," to this one and sweetly, "I'll talk
to the maid myself," to another, and I made a note of the name
on her badge. Deirdre. It was worth remembering. Saints are
highly valued in the hotel business. Then, when the bell captain came smiling into the room to tell me that Mr. Kavilan
was waiting for me—and didn't have his hand out for a tip—
I almost asked for his name, too. It was a promising beginning. If the island was really as "kindly" as they claimed, that
would be a significant plus on my checklist.

Personnel was not my most urgent concern, though. My
present task was only to check out the physical and financial
aspects of a specific project. I entered the lobby and looked
around for my real-estate agent—and was surprised when the
beachcomber type by the breezeway stretched out his hand.
"Mr. Wenright? I'm Dick Kavilan."

He was not what I expected. I knew that R. T. Kavilan
was supposed to be older than I, and I took my twenty-year
retirement from government service eight years ago. This
man did not seem that old. His hair was blond and full, and
he had an all-around-the-face blond beard that surrounded a
pink nose, bronzed cheeks and bright blue eyes. He didn't
think of himself as old, either, because all he had on was
white ducks and sandals. He wore no shirt at all, and his
body was as lean and tanned as his face. I had dressed for the
tropics, too, but not in the same way: white shoes and calf-
length white socks, pressed white shorts and a maroon T-
shirt with the golden insignia of our Maui hotel over the
heart. I understood what he meant when he glanced at my
shoes and said, "We're informal here—I hope you don't
mind." Formal he certainly was not.

He was, however, effortlessly efficient. He pulled his open

Saab out of the cramped hotel lot, found a gap in the traffic,
greeted two friends along the road and said to me, "It'll be
slow going through Port, but once we get outside it's only
twenty minutes to Keytown"—all at once.

"I've got all day," I said.

He nodded, taking occasional glances at me to judge what
kind of a customer I was going to be. "I thought," he offered,
"that you might want to make just a preliminary inspection
this morning. Then there's a good restaurant in Keytown. We
can have lunch and talk—what's the matter?" I was craning
my neck at a couple we had just passed along the road, a
woman who looked like a hotel guest and a dark, elderly man.
"Did you see somebody you wanted to talk to?"

We took a corner and I straightened up. "Not exactly," I
said. Somebody I had once wanted to talk to? No. That wasn't
right, either. Somebody I should have wanted to talk to once,
but hadn't, really? Especially about such subjects as Retroviridae and the substantia nigra?

"If it was the man in the straw hat," said Kavilan, "that was
Professor Michaelis. He the one?"

"I never heard of a Professor Michaelis," I said, wishing it
were not a lie.

In the eight years since I took the hotel job I've visited more
than my share of the world's beauty spots—Pago-Pago and
the Costa Brava, Martinique and Lesbos, Bernuda, Kauai,
Barbados, Tahiti. This was not the most breathtaking, but it
surely was pretty enough to suit any tourist who ever lived.
The beaches were golden and the water crystal. There were
thousand-foot forested peaks, and even a halfway decent wa-
terfall just off the road. In a lot of the world's finest places
there turns out to be a hidden worm in the mangosteen—bribe-
hungry officials, or revolutions simmering off in the bush, or
devastating storms. According to Dick Kavilan, the island had
none of those. "Then why did the Dutchmen give up?" I asked.
It was a key question. A Rotterdam syndicate was supposed to
have sunk fourteen million dollars into the hotel project I had
come to inspect—and walked away when it was three-quarters
built.

"They just ran out of money, Mr. Wenright."

"Call me Jerry, please," I said. That was what the preliminary report had indicated. Probably true. Tropical islands were a bottomless pit for the money of optimistic cold-country investors. If Marge had lived and we had done what we planned, we might have gone bust ourselves in Puerto Rico . . . if she had lived.

"Then, Jerry," he grinned, turning into a rutted dirt road I hadn't even seen, "we're here." He stopped the car and got out to unlock a chain-link gate that had not been unlocked recently. Nor had the road recently been driven. Palm fronds buried most of it and vines had reclaimed large patches.

Kavilan got back in the car, panting—he was not all that youthful, after all—and wiped rust off his hands with a bandanna. "Before we put up that fence," he said, "people would drive in or bring boats up to the beach at night and load them with anything they could carry. Toilets. Furniture. Windows, frames and all. They ripped up the carpets where they found any, and where there wasn't anything portable they broke into the walls for copper piping."

"So there isn't fourteen million dollars left in it," I essayed.

He let the grin broaden. "Look now, bargain later, Jerry. There's plenty left for you to see."

There was, and he left me alone to see it. He was never so far away that I couldn't call a question to him, but he didn't hang himself around my neck, either. I didn't need to ask many questions. It was obvious that what Kavilan (and the finders' reports) had said was true. The place had been looted, all right. It was capricious, with some sections apparently hardly touched. Some were hit hard. Paintings that had been screwed to the wall had been ripped loose—real oils, I saw from one that had been ruined and left. A marble dolphin fountain had been broken off and carted a few steps away—then left shattered on the walk.

I had come prepared with a set of builder's plans, and they showed me that there were to have been four hundred guest rooms, a dozen major function areas, bars and restaurants, an arcade of shops in the basement, a huge wine cellar under even that, two pools, a sauna—those were just the sections where principal construction had gone well along before the

Dutchmen walked away. I saw as much of it as I could in two hours. When my watch said eleven-thirty I sat down on an intact stone balustrade overlooking the gentle breakers on the beach and waited for Kavilan to join me. "What about water availability?" I asked.

"A problem, Jerry," he agreed. "You'll need to lay a mile and a quarter of new mains to connect with the highway pipes, and then when you get the water it'll be expensive."

I wrinkled my nose. "What's that smell?"

He laughed. "Those are some of the dear departed on the island, I'm afraid, and that's another problem. Let's move on before we lose our taste for lunch."

Kavilan was as candid as I could have hoped, and a lot more so than I would have been in his place. It was an island custom, he said, to entomb their dead aboveground instead of burying them. Unfortunately the marble boxes were seldom watertight. The seepage I had smelled was a very big minus to the project, but Kavilan shook his head when I said so. He reached into the hip pocket of his jeans, unfolded a sweat-proof wallet and took out a typed, three-page list.

I said he was candid. The list included all the things I would have asked him about:

Relocation of cemetery	$350,000
New water mains, 1.77 miles	680,000 (10-inch)
	790,000 (12-inch)
Paving access road, 0.8 miles	290,000

But it also included:

Lien, Windward Isles Const. Co.	1,300,000
(Settlement est.	605,000)
Damage judgment, Sun/Sea Petro.	2,600,000
(Settlement est.	350,000)
Injunction, N.A. Trades Council	
(Est. cost to vacate	18,000)

The total on the three-page list, taking the estimated figures at face value, came to over three million dollars. Half the items on it I hadn't even expected.

The first course was coming and I didn't want to ruin a good lunch with business, so I looked for permission, then pocketed the paper as the conch salad arrived. Kavilan was right. It was good. The greens were fresh, the chunks of meat chewed easily, the dressing was oil and vinegar but with some unusual additions that made it special. Mustard was easy to pick out, and a brush of garlic, but there were others. I thought of getting this chef's name, too.

And thought it again when I found that the escalope of veal was as good as the conch. The wine was even better, but I handled it sparingly. I didn't know Dick Kavilan well enough to let myself be made gullible by adding a lot of wine to a fine meal, a pretty restaurant and a magnificent view of a sun-drenched bay. We chatted socially until the demitasses came. How long had he been on the island? Only two years, he said, surprising me. When he added that he'd been in real estate in Michigan before that, I connected the name. "Sellman and Kavilan," I said. "You put together the package on the Upper Peninsula for us." It was a really big, solid firm. Not the kind you take early retirement from.

"That's right," he said. "I liked Michigan. But then I came down here with some friends who had a boat—I'm a widower, my boys are grown—and then I only went back to Michigan long enough to sell out."

"Then there really is a lure of the islands."

"Why, that's what you're here to find out, Jerry," he said, the grin back again. "How about you? Married?"

"I'm a widower, too," I said, and touched my buttoned pocket. "Are these costs solid?"

"You'll want to check them out for yourself, but, yes, I think so. Some are firm bids. The others are fairly conservative estimates." He waved to the waiter, who produced cigars. Cuban Perfectos. When we were both puffing, he said, "My people will put in writing that if the aggregate costs go more than twenty percent over the list we'll pay one-third of the excess as forfeit." Now, that was an interesting offer! I didn't agree to it, not even a nod, but at that point Kavilan didn't expect me to. "When the Dutchmen went bust," he added, "that list added up to better than nine million."

No wonder they went bust! "How come there's a six-million-dollar difference?"

He waved his cigar. "That was seven years ago. I guess people were meaner then. Or maybe the waiting wore the creditors down. Well. What's your pleasure for this afternoon, Jerry? Another look at the site, or back to the Port?"

"Port, I think," I said reluctantly.

The idea of spending an afternoon on the telephone and visiting government offices seemed like a terrible waste of a fine day, but that was what they paid me for.

It kept me busy. As far as I could check, the things Kavilan had told me were all true, and checking was surprisingly easy. The government records clerks were helpful, even when they had to pull out dusty files, and all the people who said they'd return my calls did. It wasn't such a bad day. But then it wasn't the days that were bad.

I put off going to bed as long as I could, with a long, late dinner, choosing carefully between the local lobster and what the headwaiter promised would be first-rate prime rib. He was right; the beef was perfect. Then I put a quarter into every fifth slot machine in the hotel casino as long as my quarters held out; but when the light by my bed was out and my head was on the pillow the pain moved in. There was a soft Caribbean moon in the window and the sound of palms rustling in the breeze. They didn't help. The only question was whether I would cry myself to sleep. I still did that, after eight years, about one night in three, and this was a night I did.

II

I thought if I had an early breakfast I'd have the dining room to myself, so I could do some serious thinking about Val Michaelis. I was wrong. The tour group had a trip in a glass-bottomed boat that morning and the room was crowded; the hostess apologetically seated me with a young woman I had seen before. We'd crossed paths in the casino as we each got rid of our cups of quarters. Hair to her shoulders, no makeup—I'd thought at first she was a young girl, but in the

daylight that was revised by a decade or so. She was civil—
civilly silent, except for a "Good morning" and now and then
a "May I have the marmalade?"—and she didn't blow smoke
in my face until we were both onto our second cups of coffee.
If the rest of her tour had been as well-schooled as she it
would have been a pleasant meal. Some of them were all
right, but the table for two next to us was planning a negli-
gence suit over a missing garment bag, and the two tables for
four behind us were exchanging loud ironies about the bugs
they'd seen, or thought they had seen, in their rooms. When
she got up she left with a red-haired man and his wife—one
of the more obnoxious couples present, I thought, and felt
sorry for her.

Kavilan had given me the gate key, and the bell captain
found me a car rental. I drove back to the hotel site. This time
I took a notebook, a hammer, a Polaroid and my Swiss Army
knife.

Fortunately the wind was the other way this morning and
the aromatic reminders of mortality were bothering some
other part of the shoreline. Before going in I walked around
the fence from the outside, snapping pictures of the unfin-
ished buildings from several angles. Funny thing. Pushing my
way through some overgrown vines I found a section of the
fence where the links had been carefully severed with bolt-
cutters. The cuts were not fresh, and the links had been rubbed
brighter than the rest of the fence; somebody had been getting
through anyway, no doubt to pick up a few souvenirs missed
by his predecessors. The vines had not grown back, so it had
been used fairly recently. I made a note to have Kavilan fix
that right away; I didn't want my inventory made obsolete as
soon as I was off the island.

One wing had barely been begun. The foundations were
half full of rain water, but tapping with the hammer suggested
the cementwork was sound, and a part where pouring had not
been finished showed good iron-bar reinforcement. In the finished wing, the vandalism was appalling but fairly superficial
in all but a dozen rooms. A quarter of a million dollars would
finish it up, plus furnishings. Some of the pool tiles were
cracked—deliberately, it seemed—but most of the fountains

would be all right once cleaned up. The garden lighting fixtures were a total writeoff.

The main building had been the most complete and also the most looted and trashed. It might take half a million dollars to fix the damage, I thought, adding up the pages in my notebook. But it was much more than a half-million-dollar building. There were no single rooms there, only guest suites, every one with its own balcony overlooking the blue bay. There was a space for a ballroom, a space for a casino, a pretty, trellised balcony for a top-floor bar—the design was faultless. So was what existed of the workmanship. I couldn't find the wine cellar, but the shop level just under the lobby was a pleasant surprise. Some of the shop windows had been broken, but the glass had been swept away and it was the only large area of the hotel without at least one or two piles of human feces. If all the vandals had been as thoughtful as the ones in the shopping corridor, there might have been no need to put up the fence.

About noon I drove down to a little general store—"Li Tsung's Supermarket," it called itself—and got materials for a sandwich lunch. I spent the whole day there, and by the time I was heading back to the hotel I had just about made up my mind: the site was a bargain, taken by itself.

Remained to check out the other factors.

My title in the company is Assistant International Vice President for Finance. I was a financial officer when I worked at the government labs, and money is what I know. You don't really know about money unless you know how to put a dollar value on all the things your money buys, though, so I can't spend all my time with the financial reports and the computer. When I recommend an acquisition I have to know what comes with it.

So, besides checking out the hotel site and the facts that Kavilan had given me, I explored the whole island. I drove the road from the site to the airport three times—once in sunlight, once in rain and once late at night—counting up potholes and difficult turns to make sure it would serve for a courtesy van. Hotel guests don't want to spend all their time in their hotels. They want other things to go to, so I checked out each of the island's fourteen other beaches. They want entertainment at

night, so I visited three discos and five other casinos—
briefly—and observed, without visiting, the three-story ve-
randahed building demurely set behind high walls and a
wrought-iron gate that was the island's officially licensed
house of prostitution. I even signed up for the all-island
guided bus tour to check for historical curiosities and points
of interest and I did not, even once, open the slim, flimsy telephone directory to see if there was a listing for Valdos E.
Michaelis, Ph.D.

The young woman from the second morning's breakfast
was on the same tour bus and once again she was alone. Or
wanted to be alone. Halfway around the island we stopped for
complimentary drinks, and when I got back on the bus she
was right behind me. "Do you mind if I sit here?" she asked.

"Of course not," I said politely, and didn't ask why. I
didn't have to. I'd seen the college kid in the tank top and cut-
offs earnestly whispering in her ear for the last hour, and just
before we stopped for drinks he gave up whispering and
started bullying.

I had decided I didn't like the college kid either, so that
was a bond. The fact that we were both loners and not preda-
tory about trying to change that was another. Each time the
bus stopped for a photo opportunity we two grabbed quick
puffs on our cigarettes instead of snapping pictures—smokers
are an endangered species, and that's a special bond these
days—so it was pretty natural that when I saw her alone again
at breakfast the next morning I asked to join her. And when
she looked envious at what I told her I was going to do that
day, I invited her along.

Among the many things that Marge's death has made me miss
is someone to share adventures with—little adventures, the
kind my job keeps requiring of me, like chartering a boat to
check out the hotel site from the sea. If Marge had lived to
take these trips with me I would be certain I had the very best
job in the world. Well, it is the best job in the world, anyway;
it's the world that isn't as good anymore.

The *Esmeralda* was a sport-fishing boat that doubled as a
way for tourists to get out on the wet part of the world for fun.
It was a thirty-footer, with a 200-horsepower outboard motor

and a cabin that contained a V-shaped double berth up forward, and a toilet and galley amidships. It also came with a captain named Ildo, who was in fact the whole crew. His name was Spanish, he said he was Dutch, his color was assorted and his accent was broad Islands. When I asked him how business was he said, "Aw, slow, mon, but when it comes January—" he said "Johnerary"—"it'll be *good.*" And he said it grinning to show he believed it, but the grin faded. I knew why. He was looking at my face, and wondering why his charter this day didn't seem to be enjoying himself.

I was trying, though. The *Esmeralda* was a lot too much like the other charter boat, the *Princess Peta,* for me to be at ease, but I really was doing my best to keep that other boat out of my mind. It occurred to me to wonder if, somewhere in my subconscious, I had decided to invite this Edna Buckner along so that I would have company to distract me on the *Esmeralda.* It then occurred to me that, if that was the reason, my subconscious was a pretty big idiot. Being alone on the boat would have been bad. Being with a rather nice-looking woman was worse.

The bay was glassy, but when we passed the headland light we were out in the swell of the ocean. I went back to see how my guest was managing. Even out past shelter the sea was gentle enough, but as we were traveling parallel to the waves there was some roll. It didn't seem to bother Edna Buckner at all. As she turned toward me she looked nineteen years again, and I suddenly realized why. She was enjoying herself. I didn't want to spoil that for her, and so I sat down beside her, as affable and charming as I knew how to be.

She wasn't nineteen. She was forty-one and, she let me know without exactly saying, unmarried, at least at the moment. She wasn't exactly traveling alone; she was the odd corner of a threesome with her sister and brother-in-law. They (she let me know, again without actually saying) had decided on the trip in the hope that it would ease some marital difficulties—and then damaged that project's chance of success by inviting a third party. "They were just sorry for me," said Edna, without explaining.

Going over the tour group in my mind, I realized I knew

which couple she was traveling with. "The man with red hair," I guessed, and she nodded.

"And with the disposition to match. You should have heard him in the restaurant last night, complaining because Lucille's lobster was bigger than his." Actually, I had. "I will say," she added, "that he was in a better mood this morning. He even apologized, and he can be a charmer when he chooses. But I wish the trip were over. I've had enough fighting to last me the rest of my life."

She paused and looked at me speculatively for a moment. She was swaying slightly in the roll of the boat, rather nicely as a matter of fact. I started to open my mouth to change the subject but she shook her head. "Do you mind letting your shipmates tell you their troubles, Jerry?"

I happen to be a pretty closed-up person—more so since what happened to Marge. I didn't know whether I minded or not; there were not very many people who had offered to weep on my shoulder in the past eight years. She didn't wait for an answer, but went on with a rush: "I know it's no fun to listen to other people's problems, but I kind of need to say it out loud. Bert was an alcoholic—my husband. Ex-husband. He beat me about once a week, for ten years. It took me all that time to make up my mind to leave him and so, when you think about it, I seem to be about ten years behind the rest of the world, trying to learn how to be a grown-up woman."

It obviously cost her something to say that. For a moment I thought she was going to cry, but she smiled instead. "So if I'm a little peculiar, that's why," she said, "and thank you for this trip. I can feel myself getting less peculiar every minute!"

Money's my game, not interpersonal relationships, and I didn't have the faintest idea of how to react to this unexpected intimacy. Fortunately, my arm did. I leaned forward and put it around her shoulder for a quick, firm hug. "Maybe we'll both get less peculiar," I said, and just then Ildo called from the wheel:

"Mon? We're comin' up on you-ah bay!"

The hotel site looked even more beautiful from the water than it had from the land. There was a pale half-moon of beach that reached from one hill on the south to another at the northern end, and a white collar of breaking wavelets all its length. The water was crystal. When Ildo dropped anchor I could follow the line all twenty-odd feet to the rippled sand bottom. The only ugliness was the chain-link fence that marched around the building site itself.

The bay was not quite perfect. It was rather shallow from point to point, so that wind-surfing hotel guests who ventured more than a hundred yards out might find themselves abruptly in stronger seas. But that was a minor problem. Very few tourists would be able to stay on the boards long enough to go a hundred yards in any direction at all. The ones who might get out where they would be endangered would have the skills to handle it. And there was plenty of marine life for snorkelers and scuba-divers to look at. Ildo showed us places in under the rocky headlands where lobsters could be caught. "Plenty now," he explained. "Oh, mon, six years ago was *bad*. No lobster never, but they all come back now."

The hotel, I observed, had been intelligently sited. It wasn't dead center in the arc of the bay, but enough around the curve toward the northern end so that every one of the four hundred private balconies would get plenty of sun: extra work for the air-conditioners, but satisfied guests. The buildings were high enough above the water to be safe from any likely storm surf—and anyway, I had already established, storms almost never struck the island from the west. And there was a rocky outcrop on the beach just at the hotel itself. That was where the dock would go, with plenty of water for sport-fishing boats—there were plenty of sailfish, tuna and everything else within half an hour's sail, Ildo said. The dock could even handle a fair-sized private yacht without serious dredging.

While I was putting all this in my notebook, Edna had borrowed mask and flippers from Ildo's adequate supply and was considerably staying out of my way. It wasn't just politeness. She was obviously enjoying herself.

I, on the other hand, was itchily nervous. Ildo assured me there was nothing to be nervous about; she was a strong swimmer, there were no sharks or barracuda likely to bother her, she wasn't so far from the boat that one of us couldn't have jumped in after her at any time. It didn't help. I couldn't focus on the buildings through the finder of the Polaroid for more than a couple of seconds without taking a quick look to make sure she was all right.

Actually there were other reasons for looking at her. She was at home in the water and looked good in it. Edna was not in the least like Marge—tall where Marge had been tiny, hair much darker than Marge's maple-syrup head. And of course a good deal younger than Marge had been even when I let her die.

It struck me as surprising that Edna was the first woman in years I had been able to look at without wishing she were Marge. And even more surprising that I could think of the death of my wife without that quick rush of pain and horror. When Edna noticed that I had put my camera and notebook away she swam back to the boat and let me help her aboard. "God," she said, grinning, "I needed that." And then she waved to the northern headland and said, "I just realized that the other side of that hill must be where my old neighbor lives."

I said, "I didn't know you had friends on the island."

"Just one, Jerry. Not a friend, exactly. Sort of an honorary uncle. He used to live next door to my parents' house in Maryland, and we kept in touch—in fact, he's the one that made me want to come here, in his letters. Val Michaelis."

III

Ildo offered us grilled lobsters for lunch. While he took the skiff and a face mask off to get the raw materials and Edna retreated to the cabin to change, I splashed ashore. He had brought the *Esmeralda* close in, and I could catch a glimpse of Edna's face in the porthole as she smiled out at me, but I wasn't thinking about her. I was thinking about something not attractive at all, called "bacteriological warfare."

Actually the kind of warfare we dealt with at the labs wasn't bacteriological. Bacteria are too easy to kill with broad-spectrum antibiotics. If you want to make a large number of people sick and want them to stay sick long enough to be no further problem, what you want is a virus.

That was the job Val Michaelis had walked away from.

I had walked away from the same place not long after him, and likely for very similar reasons—I didn't like what was

happening there. But there was a difference. I'm an orderly
person. I had put in for my twenty-year retirement and left
with the consent, if not the blessing, of the establishment. Val
Michaelis simply left. When he didn't return to the labs from
vacation, his assistant went looking for him at his house.
When the house turned up empty, others had begun to look.
But by then Michaelis had had three weeks to get lost in. The
search was pretty thorough, but he was never found. After a
few years, no doubt, the steam had gone out of it, as new lines
of research outmoded most of what he had been working on.
That was a nasty enough business. I wasn't a need-to-knower
and all I ever knew of it was an occasional slip. That was
more than I wanted, though. Now and then I would spend an
hour or two in the public library to make sure I'd got the
words right, and try to figure how to put them together, and I
think I had at least the right general idea. There are these
things called oncoviruses, a whole family of them. One kind
seems to cause leukemia. A couple of others don't seem to
bother anybody but mice. But another kind, what they called
"type D," likes monkeys, apes and human beings; and that
was what Michaelis was working on. At first I thought he was
trying to produce a weapon that would cause cancer and that
didn't seem sensible—cancers take too long to develop to be
much help on a battlefield. Then I caught another phrase:
"substantia nigra." The library told me that that was a small,
dark mass of cells way inside the brain. The substantia nigra's
A9 cells control the physical things you learn to do automatically, like touch-typing or riding a bike; and near them are the
A10 cells, which do something to control emotions. None of
that helped me much, either, until I heard one more word:

Schizophrenia.

I left the library that day convinced that I was helping people develop a virus that would turn normal people into psy-
chotics.

Later on—long after Val had gone AWOL and I'd gone my
own way—some of the work was declassified, and the open
literature confirmed part, and corrected part. There was still a
pretty big question of whether I understood all I was reading,
but it seemed that what the oncovirus D might do was to mess
up some dopamine cells in and around the substantia nigra,

producing a condition that was not psychotic exactly, but angry, tense, irresponsible—the sort of thing you hear about in kids that have burned their brains out with amphetamines. And the virus wouldn't reproduce in any mammals but primates. They couldn't infect any insects at all. Without rats or mice or mosquitoes or lice to carry it, how do you spread that kind of disease? True, they could have looked for a vector among, say, the monotremes or the marsupials—but how are you going to introduce a herd of sick platypuses into the Kremlin?

Later on, I am sure, they found meaner and easier bugs; but that was the one Michaelis and I had run away from. And nobody had seen Val Michaelis again—until I did, from Dick Kavilan's Saab.

Of course, Michaelis had more reason to quit than I did, and far more reason to hide. I only made up the payrolls and audited the bills. He did the molecular biology that turned laboratory cultures into killers.

The lobsters were delicious, split and broiled over a driftwood fire. Ildo had brought salad greens and beer from Port, and plates to eat it all on. China plates, not paper, and that was decent of him—he wasn't going to litter the beauty of the beach.

While we were picking the last of the meat out of the shells Edna was watching me. I was doing my best to do justice to the lunch, but I don't suppose I was succeeding. Strange sensation. I wasn't unhappy. I wasn't unaware of the taste of the lobster, or the pleasure of Edna's company, or the charm of the beach. I was very nearly happy, in a sort of basic, background way, but there were nastinesses just outside that gentle sphere of happiness, and they were nagging at me. I had felt like that before, time and again, in fact; most often when Marge and I were planning what to do with my retirement, and it all seemed rosy except for the constant sting of knowing the job I would have to finish first. The job was part of it now, or Val Michaelis was, and so was the way Marge died, and the two of them were spoiling what should have been perfection. Edna didn't miss what was going on, she simply diagnosed it wrong. "I guess I shouldn't have dumped my

troubles on you, Jerry," she said, as Ildo picked up the plates
and buried the ashes of the fire.

"Oh, no," I said. "No, it's not that—I'm glad you told me."
I was, though I couldn't have said why, exactly; it was not a
habit of mine to want that kind of intimacy from another person, because I didn't want to offer them any of mine. I said,
"It's Val Michaelis."

She nodded. "He's in some kind of trouble? I thought it
was strange that he'd bury himself here."

"Some kind," I agreed. "Or was. Maybe it's all over now."
And then I made my decision. "I'd like to go see him."

"Oh," said Edna, "I don't know if he's still on the island."
"Why not?"

"He said he was leaving. He's been planning to for some
time—he only stayed on to see us. What's this, Friday? The
last time I saw him was Tuesday, and he was packing up then.
He may be gone."

And he was. When Ildo deposited us at the Keytown dock
and the taxi took us to the apartments where Michaelis had
lived, the door of his place was unlocked. The rented furniture
was there, but the closets were empty, and so were the bureau
drawers, and of an occupant the only sign remaining was an
envelope addressed to Edna:

> I thought I'd better leave while Gerald was still
> wrestling with his conscience. If you see him, thank
> him for the use of his space—and I hope we'll meet
> again in a couple of years.

Edna looked up at me in puzzlement. "Do you know what
that part about your space means?"

I gave the note back to her and watched her fold it up and
put it in her bag. I thought of asking her to burn it, but that
would just make it more important to her. I wanted her to forget it. I said, "No," which was somewhat true. I didn't *know*.
And I surely didn't want to guess.

By the time we were back on the boat I was able to be cheerful again, at least on the surface. When we docked at our own
hotel Edna went on ahead to change, while I sent Ildo happily

off with a big tip. He was, Edna had said, a pretty sweet man. He was not alone in that; nearly everyone I'd met on the island was as kindly as the island claimed; and it hurt me to think of Val Michaelis going on with his work in this gentle place.

We had agreed to meet for a drink before dinner—we had taken it for granted that we were going to have dinner together—and when I came to Edna's room to pick her up she invited me in. "The Starlight Casino is pretty noisy, Jerry, and I've got this perfectly beautiful balcony to use up. Can you drink gin and tonic?"

"My very favorite," I said. That wasn't true. I didn't much like the taste of quinine water, or of gin, either, but sitting on a warm sunset balcony with Edna was a lot more attractive than listening to rockabilly music in the bar.

But I wasn't good company. Seeing Edna off by herself in the bay had set off one set of memories, Val Michaelis's note had triggered another. I didn't welcome either train of thought, because they were intruders; I was feeling almost happy, almost at peace—and those two old pains kept coming in to remind me of misery and fear. I did my best. Edna had set out glasses, bottles, a bucket of ice, a plate of things to nibble on, and the descending sun was perfect. "This is really nice, Marge," I said, accepting a refill of my glass . . . and only heard myself when I saw the look on her face.

"I mean Edna," I said.

She touched my hand when she gave the glass back to me. "I think that's a compliment, Jerry," she said sweetly.

I thought that over. "I guess it is," I said. "You know, I've never done that before. Called someone else by my wife's name, I mean. Of course, I haven't often been in the sort of situation where—" I stopped there, because it didn't seem right to define what I thought the present "situation" was.

She started to speak, hesitated, took a tiny sip of her drink, started again, stopped and finally laughed—at herself, I realized. "Jerry," she said, "you can tell me to mind my own business if you want to, because I know I ought to. But you told me your wife died eight years ago. Are you saying you've never had a private drink with a woman since then?"

"Well, no—it has happened now and then," I said, and then added honestly, "but not very often. You see—"

I stopped and swallowed. The expression on her face was changing, the smile softening. She reached out to touch my hand.

And then I found myself telling her the whole thing.

Not the *whole* whole thing. I did not tell her what the surf-board looked like, with the ragged half-moon gap in the side, and I didn't tell her what Marge's body had looked like—what was left of it—when at last they found it near the shore, eight days later. But I told her the rest. Turning in my retirement papers. The trip to California to see her folks. The boat. The surf-board. Marge paddling around in the swell, just before the breaker, while I watched from the boat. "I went down below for just a minute," I said, "and when I came back on deck she was gone. I could still see the surfboard, but she wasn't there. I hadn't heard a thing, although she must have—"

"Oh, Jerry," said Edna.

"It has to do with water temperatures," I explained, "and with the increase in the seal population. The great white sharks didn't used to come up that far north along the coast, but the water's a little warmer, and there are more seals. That's what they live on. Seals, and other things. And from a shark's view underwater, you see a person lying on a surf-board, with his arms and legs paddling over the side, looks a lot like a seal. . . ."

I saw to my surprise she was weeping. I shouldn't have been surprised. As I reached forward and put my arms around her, I discovered that I was weeping, too.

That was the biggest surprise of all. I'd done a lot of weep-ing in eight years, but never once in the presence of another human being, not even the shrinks I'd gone to see. And when the weeping stopped and the kissing began I found that it didn't seem wrong at all. It seemed very right, and a long, long time overdue.

IV

My remaining business with Dick Kavilan didn't take long. By the time Edna's tour group was scheduled to go home, I was ready, too.

The two of us decided not to wait for the bus to the airport. We went early, by taxi, beating the tours to the check-in desk. By the time the first of them arrived we were already sitting at the tiny bar, sipping farewell piña coladas. Only it was not going to be a farewell, not when I had discovered she lived only a few miles from the house I had kept all these years as home base.

When the tour buses began to arrive I could not resist preening my forethought a little. "That's going to be a really ugly scene, trying to check in all at once," I said wisely.

But really it wasn't. There were all the ingredients for a bad time, more than three hundred tired tourists trying to get seat assignments from a single airline clerk. But they didn't jostle. They didn't snarl, at her or each other. The tiny terminal was steamy with human bodies, but it almost seemed they didn't even sweat. They were singing and smiling—even Edna's sister and brother-in-law. They waved up at us, and it looked like their marriage had a good shot at lasting awhile longer, after all.

A sudden gabble from the line of passengers told us what the little callboard confirmed a moment later. Our airplane had arrived from the States. Edna started to collect her bag, her sack of duty-free rum, her boots and fur-collared coat for the landing at Dulles, her little carry-on with the cigarettes and the book to read on the flight, her last-minute souvenir T-shirt . . . "Hold on," I said. "We've got an hour yet. They've got to disembark the arrivals and muck out the plane—you didn't think we'd leave on time, did you?"

So there was time for another piña colada, and while we were drinking them the newcomers began to straggle off the DC-10. The noise level in the terminal jumped fifteen decibels, and most of it was meal complaints, family arguments and clamor over lost luggage. The departing crowd gazed at their fretful replacements good-humoredly.

And all of a sudden that other unpleasant train of thought bit down hard. There was a healing magic on the island, and the thought of Val Michaelis doing the sort of thing he was trained to do here was more than I could bear. I hadn't turned Michaelis in, because I thought he was a decent man. But damaging these kind, gentle people was indecent.

I put down my half-finished drink, stood up and dropped a bill on the table. "Edna," I said, "I just realized there's something I have to do. I'm afraid I'm going to miss this flight. I'll call you in Maryland when I get back—I'm sorry."

And I really was. Very. But that did not stop me from heading for the phone.

The men from the NSA were there the next morning. Evidently they hadn't waited for a straight-through flight. Maybe they'd chartered one, or caught a light flight to a nearby island.

But they hadn't wasted any time.

They could have thanked me for calling them, I thought. They didn't. They invited me out to their car for privacy—it was about as much of an "invitation" as a draft notice is, and as difficult to decline—while I answered their questions. Then they pulled out of the hotel lot and drove those thirty-mile-an-hour island roads at sixty. We managed not to hit any of the cows and people along the way. We did, I think, score one hen. The driver didn't even slow down to look.

I was not in the least surprised. I didn't know the driver, but the other man was Joe Mooney. Now he was a full field investigator, but he had been a junior security officer at the labs when Michaelis walked away. He was a mean little man with a high opinion of himself; he had always thought that the rules he enforced on the people he surveilled didn't have to apply to him. He proved it. He turned around in the front seat, arm across the back, so he could look at me while ostensibly talking to his partner at the wheel: "You know what Michaelis was working on? Some kind of a bug to drive the Russians nuts."

"Mooney, watch it!" his partner snapped.

"Oh, it's all right. Old Jerry knows all about it, and he's cleared—or used to be."

"It wasn't a bug," I said. "It was a virus. It wouldn't drive them crazy. It would work on the brain to make them irritable and nasty—a kind of personality change, like some people get after a stroke. And he didn't just try. He succeeded."

"And then he ran."

"And then he ran, yes."

"Only it didn't work," grinned Mooney, "because they couldn't find a way to spread it. And now what we have to worry about, we have to worry that while he was down here he figured out how to make it work and's looking for a buyer. Like a Russian buyer."

Well, I could have argued all of that. But the only part I answered, as we stopped to unlock the chain-link gate, was the last part. And all I said was, "I don't think so."

Mooney laughed out loud. "You always were a googoo," he said. "You sure Michaelis didn't stick you with some of the stuff in reverse?"

I hadn't been able to find the entrance of the wine cellar, but that pair of NSA men had no trouble at all. They realized at once that there had to be a delivery system to the main dining room—I hadn't thought of that. So that's where they went, and found a small elevator shaft that went two stories down. There wasn't any elevator, but there were ropes and Mooney's partner climbed down while Mooney and I went back to the shopping floor. About two minutes after we got there a painters' scaffold at the end of the hall went over with a crash, and the NSA man pushed his way out of the door it had concealed. Mooney gave me a contemptuous look. "Fire stairs," he explained. "They had to be there. There has to be another entrance, too—outside, so they can deliver the wine by truck."

He was right again. From the inside it was easy to spot, even though we had only flashlights to see what we were doing. When Mooney pushed it open we got a flood of tropical light coming, and a terrible smell to go with it. For a moment I wondered if the graveyard wind had shifted again, but it was only a pile of garbage—rotted garbage—long-gone lobster shells and sweepings from the mall and trash of all kinds. It wasn't surprising no one had found the entrance from outside; the stink was discouraging.

No matter what else I was, I was still a man paid to do a job by his company. So while the NSA team was prodding and peering and taking flash pictures, I was looking at the cellar. It was large enough to handle all the wines a first-class sommelier might want to store; the walls were solid, and the temperature good. With that outside door kept closed, it would be no problem to keep any vintage safely resting here. The Dutchmen shouldn't have given up so easily, just because they were faced with a lot of lawsuits—but maybe, as Dick Kavilan had said, people were meaner then.

I blinked when Joe Mooney poked his flashlight in my face. "What are you daydreaming about?" he demanded.

I pushed his hand away. "Have you seen everything you need?" I asked.

He looked around. There wasn't a whole lot to see, really. Along one wall there were large glass tanks—empty, except for a scummy inch or two of liquid at the bottom of some of them, fishy smelling and unappetizing. There were smaller tanks on the floor, and marks on the rubber tile to show where other things had been that now were gone. "He took everything that matters out," he grumbled. "Son of a bitch! He got clean away."

"We'll find him," his partner said.

"Damn right, but what was he doing here? Trying out his stuff on the natives?" Mooney looked at me searchingly. "What do you think, Wenright? Have you heard of any cases of epidemic craziness on the island?"

I shrugged. "I did my part when I called you," I said. "Now all I want is to go home."

But it wasn't quite true. There was something else I wanted, and that was to know if there was any chance at all that what I was beginning to suspect might be true.

The next day I was on the home-bound jet, taking a drink from the stew in the first-class section and still trying to convince myself that what I believed was possible. *The people were meaner then.* It wasn't just an offhand remark of Kavilan's; the hotel manager told me as I was checking out that it was true, yes, a few years ago he had a lot of trouble with help, but lately everybody seemed a lot friendlier. *Val Michaelis was a decent man.* I'd always believed that, in the face of the indecencies of his work at the labs . . . having left, would he go on performing indecencies?

Could it be that Michaelis had in fact found a different kind of virus? One that worked on different parts of the brain, for different purposes? That made people happier and more gentle, instead of suspicious, paranoid, and dangerous?

I was neither biologist nor brain anatomist to guess if that could be true. But I had the evidence of my eyes. *Something* had changed the isle from mean, litigious, grasping—from the normal state of the rest of the world—to what I had seen around me. It had even worked on me. It was not just Edna Buckner's sweet self, sweet though she was, that had let me discharge eight years of guilt and horror in one night. And right here on this plane, the grinning tour groups in the back and even the older, more sedate first-class passengers around me testified that something had happened to them. . . .

Not all the first-class passengers.

Just across the aisle from me one couple was busy berating the stewardess. They didn't like their appetizer.

"Langouste salad, you call it?" snapped the man. "I call it *poison*. Didn't you ever hear of allergy? Jesus, we've been spending the whole week trying to keep them from pushing those damned lobsters on us everywhere we went. . . ."

Lobsters.

Lobsters were neither mammal nor insects. And the particular strains of Retroviridae that wouldn't reproduce in either, I remember, had done just fine in crustaceans.

Like lobsters.

V

The NSA team caught up with me again six months later, in my office. I was just getting ready to leave, to pick Edna up for the drive down to Chesapeake Bay, where the company was considering the acquisition of an elderly and declining hotel. I told them I was in a hurry.

"This is official business," Mooney's partner growled, but Mooney shook his head.

"We won't keep you long, Wenright. Michaelis has been reported in the States. Have you heard anything from him?"

"Where in the States?"

"None of your business," he snapped, and then shrugged. "Maryland."

I said, "That would be pretty foolish of him, wouldn't it?"

He didn't respond, just looked at me. "No," I said, "I haven't heard anything at all."

He obviously had not expected anything more. He gave me a routinely nasty look, the whatever-it-is-you're-up-to-you-won't-get-away-with-it kind, and stood up to go. His partner gave me the routinely unpleasant warning: "We'll be watching you," he said.

I laughed. "I'm sure you will. And don't you think Michaelis will figure that out, too?"

That night I told Edna about the interview, though I wasn't supposed to. I didn't care about that, having already told her so much that I wasn't supposed to about Michaelis's work and my suspicions. There was a lot of laws that said I should have kept my mouth shut, and I had broken all of them.

She nibbled at her salad, nodding. We were dining in the hotel's open-air restaurant; it was late spring, and nearly as warm as it had been back on the island. "I hope he gets away," she said.

"I hope more than that. I hope he lives and prospers with his work."

She giggled. "Johnny Happyseed," she said.

I shook my head slightly, because the maitre d' was approaching and I didn't want him to hear. He was a plump young man with visions of a career at the Plaza, and he knew what I was there for. He was desperately anxious to make my report favorable. The hotel itself was fine. It was the top management that was incompetent, and if we bought it out there would be changes—as he knew. Whether he would be one of the changes I didn't yet know.

So when he asked, "Is everything satisfactory, Mr. Wenright?" he was asking about more than the meal. I hadn't been there long enough to have made up my mind—and certainly wouldn't have told him if I had. I only smiled, and he pressed on: "This is really a delightful old hotel, Mr. Wenright, with all sorts of marvelous historical associations. And it's been kept up very well, as you'll see. Of course, some improvements are always in order—but we get a first-class clientele, especially in the softshell crab season. Congressmen. Senators. Diplomats. Every year we get a series of seminars with Pentagon people—"

Edna dropped her fork.

I didn't, but I was glad to have him distracted by the necessity of clapping his hands so that a busboy could rush up at once with a fresh one. Then I said, "Tell me, isn't it true that the crabbing has been very poor lately? Some sort of disease among the shellfish?"

"Yes, that's true, Mr. Wenright," he admitted, but added eagerly, "I'm sure they'll come back."

I said, "I absolutely guarantee it." He left chuckling, and wondering if he'd missed the point of the joke.

I looked at Edna. She looked at me. We both nodded.

But all either of us said, after quite a while, was Edna's, "I wonder what kind of seafood they eat in Moscow?"

CHAFF

Greg Egan

Looking back at the century that's just ended, it's obvious that Australian writer Greg Egan was one of the big new names to emerge in SF in the nineties, and is probably one of the most significant talents to enter the field in the last several decades. Already one of the most widely known of all Australian genre writers, Egan may well be the best new "hard-science" writer to enter the field since Greg Bear, and is still growing in range, power, and sophistication. In the last few years, he has become a frequent contributor to Interzone *and* Asimov's Science Fiction, *and has made sales as well to* Pulphouse, Analog, Aurealis, Eidolon, *and elsewhere; many of his stories have also appeared in various "Best of the Year" series, and he was on the Hugo Final Ballot in 1995 for his story "Cocoon," which won the Ditmar Award and the Asimov's Readers Award. His first novel,* Quarantine, *appeared in 1992; his second novel,* Permutation City, *won the John W. Campbell Memorial Award in 1994. He won the Hugo Award in 1999 for his novella "Oceanic." His other books include the novels* Distress *and* Diaspora, *and three collections of his short fiction,* Axiomatic, Luminous, *and* Our Lady of Chernobyl. *His most recent book is a major new novel,* Teranesia.*

Here he takes us to the steaming jungles of South America for an unsettling and hard-edged story that explores some of the same sort of territory as Conrad's Heart of Darkness—*but then throws away the map and takes us into a whole new uncharted territory, into a world completely reshaped by radical bioscience, a world full of both promise and menace, for a glimpse of what may be the future of humanity. . . .*

El Nido de Ladrones—the Nest of Thieves—occupies a roughly elliptical region, 50,000 square kilometers in the western Amazon Lowlands, straddling the border between Colombia and Peru. It's difficult to say exactly where the natural rain forest ends and the engineered species of El Nido take over, but the total biomass of the system must be close to a trillion tonnes. A trillion tonnes of structural material, osmotic pumps, solar energy collectors, cellular chemical factories, and biological computing and communications resources. All under the control of its designers.

The old maps and databases are obsolete; by manipulating the hydrology and soil chemistry, and influencing patterns of rainfall and erosion, the vegetation has reshaped the terrain completely; shifting the course of the Putumayo River, drowning old roads in swampland, raising secret causeways through the jungle. This biogenic geography remains in a state of flux, so that even the eye-witness accounts of the rare defectors from El Nido soon lose their currency. Satellite images are meaningless; at every frequency, the forest canopy conceals, or deliberately falsifies, the spectral signature of whatever lies beneath.

Chemical toxins and defoliants are useless; the plants and their symbiotic bacteria can analyse most poisons, and reprogram their metabolisms to render them harmless—or transform them into food—faster than our agricultural warfare expert systems can invent new molecules. Biological weapons are seduced, subverted, domesticated; most of the genes from the last lethal plant virus we introduced were found three months later, incorporated into a benign vector for El Nido's elaborate communications network. The assassin had turned into a messenger boy. Any attempt to burn the vegetation is rapidly smothered by carbon dioxide—or more sophisticated fire retardants, if a self-oxidizing fuel is employed. Once we even pumped in a few tonnes of nutrient laced with powerful radioisotopes—locked up in compounds chemically indistinguishable from their natural counterparts. We tracked the results with gamma-ray imaging: El Nido separated out the isotope-laden molecules—probably on the basis of their diffusion rates across organic membranes—sequestered and diluted them, and then pumped them right back out again.

So when I heard that a Peruvian-born biochemist named Guillermo Largo had departed from Bethesda, Maryland, with some highly classified genetic tools—the fruits of his own research, but very much the property of his employers—and vanished into El Nido, I thought: At last, an excuse for the Big One. The Company had been advocating thermonuclear rehabilitation of El Nido for almost a decade. The Security Council would have rubber-stamped it. The governments with nominal authority over the region would have been delighted. Hundreds of El Nido's inhabitants were suspected of violating U.S. law—and President Golino was aching for a chance to prove that she could play hard ball south of the border, whatever language she spoke in the privacy of her own home. She could have gone on prime time afterwards and told the nation that they should be proud of Operation Back to Nature, and that the 30,000 displaced farmers who'd taken refuge in El Nido from Colombia's undeclared civil war—and who had now been liberated forever from the oppression of Marxist terrorists and drug barons—would have saluted her courage and resolve.

I never discovered why that wasn't to be. Technical problems in ensuring that no embarrassing side-effects would show up down-river in the sacred Amazon itself, wiping out some telegenic endangered species before the end of the present administration? Concern that some Middle Eastern warlord might somehow construe the act as licence to use his own feeble, long-hoarded fission weapons on a troublesome minority, destabilizing the region in an undesirable manner? Fear of Japanese trade sanctions, now that the rabidly anti-nuclear Eco-Marketeers were back in power?

I wasn't shown the verdicts of the geopolitical computer models; I simply received my orders—coded into the flicker of my local K-Mart's fluorescent tubes, slipped in between the updates to the shelf price tags. Deciphered by an extra neural layer in my left retina, the words appeared blood red against the bland cheery colours of the supermarket aisle. I was to enter El Nido and retrieve Guillermo Largo. Alive.

• • •

Dressed like a local real-estate agent—right down to the gold-plated bracelet-phone, and the worst of all possible $300 hair-cuts—I visited Largo's abandoned home in Bethesda: a northern suburb of Washington, just over the border into Maryland. The apartment was modern and spacious, neatly furnished but not opulent—about what any good marketing software might have tried to sell him, on the basis of salary less alimony.

Largo had always been classified as *brilliant but unsound* —a potential security risk, but far too talented and productive to be wasted. He'd been under routine surveillance ever since the gloriously euphemistic Department of Energy had employed him, straight out of Harvard, back in 2005—clearly, too routine by far . . . but then, I could understand how 30 years with an unblemished record must have given rise to a degree of complacency. Largo had never attempted to disguise his politics—apart from exercising the kind of discretion that was more a matter of etiquette than subterfuge; no Che Guevara T-shirts when visiting Los Alamos—but he'd never really acted on his beliefs, either.

A mural had been jet-sprayed onto his living room wall in shades of near infrared (visible to most hip 14-year-old Washingtonians, if not to their parents). It was a copy of the infamous Lee Hing-cheung's *A Tiling of the Plane with Heroes of the New World Order,* a digital image which had spread across computer networks at the turn of the century. Early 90s political leaders, naked and interlocked—Escher meets the *Kama Sutra*—deposited steaming turds into each other's open and otherwise empty braincases—an effect borrowed from the works of the German satirist George Grosz. The Iraqi dictator was shown admiring his reflection in a hand mirror—the image an exact reproduction of a contemporary magazine cover in which the moustache had been retouched to render it suitably Hitleresque. The U.S. President carried—horizontally, but poised ready to be tilted—an egg-timer full of the gaunt hostages whose release he'd delayed to clinch his predecessor's election victory. Everyone was shoe-horned in, somewhere—right down to the Australian Prime Minister, portrayed as a public louse, struggling (and failing) to fit its tiny jaws around the mighty presidential cock. I could imagine a few of the neo-McCarthyist troglodytes in the Senate going apoplectic, if anything so tedious as an inquiry into Largo's defection ever took place—but what should we have done? Refused to hire him if he owned so much as a *Guernica* tea-towel?

Largo had blanked every computer in the apartment before leaving, including the entertainment system—but I already knew his taste in music, having listened to a few hours of audio surveillance samples full of bad Korean Ska. No laudable revolutionary ethno-solidarity, no haunting Andean pipe music; a shame—I would have much preferred that. His bookshelves retained for sentimental reasons, and a few dozen musty literary classics and volumes of poetry, in English, Spanish and German. Hesse, Rilke, Vallejo, Conrad, Nietzsche. Nothing modern—and nothing printed after 2010. With a few words to the household manager, Largo had erased every digital work he'd ever owned, sweeping away the last quarter of a century of his personal archaeology.

I flipped through the surviving books, for what it was worth. There was a pencilled-in correction to the structure of guanine in one of the texts . . . and a section had been underlined in *Heart of Darkness*. The narrator, Marlow, was pondering the mysterious fact that the servants on the steamboat—members of a cannibal tribe, whose provisions of rotting hippo meat had been tossed overboard—hadn't yet rebelled and eaten him. After all:

> No fear can stand up to hunger, no patience can wear it out, disgust simply does not exist where hunger is; and as to superstition, beliefs, and what you may call principles, they are less than chaff in a breeze.

I couldn't argue with that—but I wondered why Largo had found the passage noteworthy. Perhaps it had struck a chord, back in the days when he'd been trying to rationalize taking his first research grants from the Pentagon? The ink was faded—and the volume itself had been printed in 2003. I would rather have had copies of his diary entries for the fortnight leading up to his disappearance—but his household computers hadn't been systematically tapped for almost 20 years.

I sat at the desk in his study, and stared at the blank screen of his work station. Largo had been born into a middle-class, nominally Catholic, very mildly leftist family in Lima, in 1980. His father, a journalist with *El Comercio,* had died from a cerebral blood clot in 2029. His 78-year-old mother still worked as an attorney for an international mining company—going through the motions of *habeas corpus* for the families of disappeared radicals in her spare time, a hobby her employers tolerated for the sake of cheap PR brownie points in the shareholder democracies. Guillermo had one elder brother, a retired surgeon, and one younger sister, a primary-school teacher, neither of them politically active.

Most of his education had taken place in Switzerland and the States; after his PhD, he'd held a succession of research posts in government institutes, the biotechnology industry, and academia—all with more or less the same real sponsors. Fifty-five, now, thrice divorced but still childless, he'd only ever returned to Lima for brief family visits.

After *three decades* working on the military applications of molecular genetics—unwittingly at first, but not for long—what could have triggered his sudden defection to El Nido? If he'd managed the cynical doublethink of reconciling defence research and pious liberal sentiments for so long, he must have got it down to a fine art. His latest psychological profile suggested as much: fierce pride in his scientific achievements balanced the self-loathing he felt when contemplating their ultimate purpose—with the conflict showing signs of decaying into comfortable indifference. A well-documented dynamic in the industry.

And he seemed to have acknowledged—deep in his heart, 30 years ago—that his "principles" were *less than chaff in a breeze.*

Perhaps he'd decided, belatedly, that if he was going to be a whore he might as well do it properly, and sell his skills to the highest bidder—even if that meant smuggling genetic weapons to a drugs cartel. I'd read his financial records, though: no tax fraud, no gambling debts, no evidence that he'd ever lived beyond his means. Betraying his employers, just as he'd betrayed his own youthful ideals to join them, might have seemed like an appropriately nihilistic gesture . . . but on a more pragmatic level, it was hard to imagine him finding the money, and the consequences, all that tempting. What could El Nido have offered him? A numbered satellite account, and a new identity in Paraguay? All the squalid pleasures of life on the fringes of the Third World plutocracy? He would have had everything to gain by living out his retirement in his adopted country, salving his conscience with one or two vitrolic essays on foreign policy in some unread left-wing netzine—and then finally convincing himself that any nation which granted him such unencumbered rights of free speech probably deserved everything he'd done to defend it.

Exactly what he *had* done to defend it, though—what tools he'd perfected, and stolen—I was not permitted to know.

As dusk fell, I locked the apartment and headed south down Wisconsin Avenue. Washington was coming alive, the streets already teeming with people looking for distraction from the heat. Nights in the cities were becoming hallucinatory. Teenagers sported bioluminescent symbionts, the veins in their temples, necks and pumped-up forearm muscles glowing electric blue, walking circulation diagrams who cultivated hypertension to improve the effect. Others used retinal symbionts to translate IR into visible light, their eyes flashing vampire red in the shadows.

And others, less visibly, had a skull full of White Knights.

Stem cells in the bone marrow infected with Mother—an engineered retrovirus—gave rise to something half-way between an embryonic neutron and a white blood cell. White Knights secreted the cytokines necessary to unlock the blood-brain barrier—and once through, cellular adhesion molecules guided them to their targets, where they could flood the site with a chosen neurotransmitter—or even form temporary quasi-synapses with genuine neurons. Users often had half a dozen or more sub-types in their bloodstream simultaneously, each one activated by a specific dietary additive: some cheap, harmless, and perfectly legitimate chemical not naturally present in the body. By ingesting the right mixture of innocuous artificial colorings, flavors and preservatives, they could modulate their neurochemistry in almost any fashion—until the White Knights died, as they were programmed to do, and a new dose of Mother was required.

Mother could be snorted, or taken intravenously . . . but the most efficient way to use it was to puncture a bone and inject it straight into the marrow—an excruciating, messy, dangerous business, even if the virus itself was uncontaminated and authentic. The good stuff came from El Nido. The bad stuff came from basement labs in California and Texas, where gene hackers tried to force cell cultures infected with Mother to reproduce a virus expressly designed to resist their efforts—and churned out batches of mutant strains ideal for inducing leukemia, astrocytomas, Parkinson's disease, and assorted novel phychoses.

Crossing the sweltering dark city, watching the heedlessly joyful crowds, I felt a penetrating, dreamlike clarity come over me. Part of me was numb, leaden, blank—but part of me was electrified, all-seeing. I seemed to be able to stare into the hidden landscapes of the people around me, to see deeper than the luminous rivers of blood; to pierce them with my vision right to the bone.

Right to the marrow.

I drove to the edge of a park I'd visited once before, and waited. I was already dressed for the part. Young people strode by, grinning, some glancing at the silver 2025 Ford Narcissus and whistling appreciatively. A teenaged boy danced on the grass, alone, tirelessly—blissed out on Coca-Cola, and not even getting paid to fake it.

Before too long, a girl approached the car, blue veins flashing on her bare arms. She leant down to the window and looked in, inquiringly.

"What you got?" She was 16 or 17, slender, dark-eyed, coffee-colored, with a faint Latino accent. She could have been my sister.

"Southern Rainbow." All twelve major genotypes of Mother, straight from El Nido, cut with nothing but glucose. Southern Rainbow—and a little fast food—could take you anywhere.

The girl eyed me sceptically, and stretched out her right

hand, palm down. She wore a ring with a large multifaceted jewel, with a pit in the centre. I took a sachet from the glove compartment, shook it, tore it open, and tipped a few specks of powder into the pit. Then I leant over and moistened the sample with saliva, holding her cool fingers to steady her hand. Twelve faces of the "stone" began to glow immediately, each one in a different colour. The immunoelectric sensors in the pit, tiny capacitors coated with antibodies, were designed to recognize several sites on the protein coats of the different strains of Mother—particularly the ones the bootleggers had the most trouble getting right.

With good enough technology, though, those proteins didn't have to bear the slightest relationship to the RNA inside.

The girl seemed to be impressed; her face lit up with anticipation. We negotiated a price. Too low by far; she should have been suspicious.

I looked her in the eye before handing over the sachet.

I said, "What do you need this shit for? The world is the world. You have to take it as it is. Accept it as it is: savage and terrible. Be strong. Never lie to yourself. That's the only way to survive."

She smirked at my apparent hypocrisy, but she was too pleased with her luck to turn nasty. "I hear what you're saying. It's a bad planet out there." She forced the money into my hand, adding, with wide-eyed mock-sincerity, "And this is the last time I do Mother, I promise."

I gave her the lethal virus, and watched her walk away across the grass and vanish into the shadows.

The Colombian air force pilot who flew me down from Bogotá didn't seem too thrilled to be risking his life for a DEA bureaucrat. It was 700 kilometres to the border, and five different guerrilla organizations held territory along the way: not a lot of towns, but several hundred possible sites for rocket launchers.

"My great-grandfather," he said sourly, "died in fucking Korea fighting for General Douglas fucking MacArthur." I wasn't sure if that was meant to be a declaration of pride, or an intimation of an outstanding debt. Both, probably.

The helicopter was eerily silent, fitted out with phased

sound absorbers, which looked like giant loudspeakers but swallowed most of the noise of the blades. The carbon-fiber fuselage was coated with an expensive network of chameleon polymers—although it might have been just as effective to paint the whole thing sky blue. An endothermic chemical mixture accumulated waste heat from the motor, and then discharged it through a parabolic radiator as a tightly focused skywards burst, every hour or so. The guerrillas had no access to satellite images, and no radar they dared use; I decided that we had less chance of dying than the average Bogotá commuter. Back in the capital, buses had been exploding without warning, two or three times a week.

Colombia was tearing itself apart; *La Violencia* of the 1950s, all over again. Although all of the spectacular terrorist sabotage was being carried out by organized guerrilla groups, most of the deaths so far had been caused by factions within the two mainstream political parties butchering each other's supporters, avenging a litany of past atrocities which stretched back for generations. The group who'd actually started the current wave of bloodshed had negligible support; *Ejército de Simón Bolívar* were lunatic right-wing extremists who wanted to "re-unite" with Panama, Venezuela and Ecuador—after two centuries of separation—and drag in Peru and Bolivia, to realize Bolívar's dream of *Gran Colombia.* By assassinating President Marín, though, they'd triggered a cascade of events which had nothing to do with their ludicrous cause. Strikes and protests, street battles, curfews, martial law. The repatriation of foreign capital by nervous investors, followed by hyperinflation, and the collapse of the local financial system. Then a spiral of opportunistic violence. Everyone, from the paramilitary death squads to the Maoist splinter groups, seemed to believe that their hour had finally come.

I hadn't seen so much as a bullet fired—but from the moment I'd entered the country, there'd been acid churning in my guts, and a heady, ceaseless adrenaline rush coursing through my veins. I felt wired, feverish . . . alive. Hypersensitive as a pregnant woman: I could smell blood, everywhere. When the hidden struggle for power which rules all human affairs finally breaks through to the surface, finally ruptures the skin, it's like witnessing some giant primordial creature rise up out of the ocean. Mesmerizing and appalling. Nauseating—and exhilarating.

Coming face to face with the truth is always exhilarating.

From the air, there was no obvious sign that we'd arrived; for the last 200 kilometres, we'd been passing over rain forest—cleared in patches for plantations and mines, ranches and timber mills, shot through with rivers like metallic threads—but most of it resembling nothing so much as an endless expanse of broccoli. El Nido permitted natural vegetation to flourish all around it—and then imitated it . . . which made sampling at the edges an inefficient way to gather the true genetic stock for analysis. Deep penetration was difficult, though, even with purpose-built robots—dozens of which had been lost—so edge samples had to suffice, at least until a few more members of Congress could be photographed committing statutory rape and persuaded to vote for better funding. Most of the engineered plant tissues self-destructed in the absence of regular chemical and viral messages drifting out from the core, reassuring them that they were still *in situ*—so the main DEA research facility was on the outskirts of El Nido itself, a collection of pressurized buildings and experimental plots in a clearing blasted out of the jungle on the Colombian side of the border. The electrified fences weren't topped with razor wire; they turned 90 degrees into an electrified roof, completing a chainlink cage. The heliport was in the center of the compound, where a cage within the cage could, temporarily, open itself to the sky.

Madelaine Smith, the research director, showed me around. In the open, we both wore hermetic biohazard suits—although if the modifications I'd received in Washington were working as promised, mine was redundant. El Nido's short-lived defensive viruses occasionally percolated out this far; they were never fatal, but they could be severely disabling to anyone who hadn't been inoculated. The forest's designers had walked a fine line between biological "self-defence" and unambiguously military applications. Guerrillas had always hidden in the engineered jungle—and raised funds by collaborating in the export of Mother—but El Nido's technology

had never been explicitly directed toward the creation of
lethal pathogens.

So far.

"Here, we're raising seedlings of what we hope will be a
stable El Nido phenotype, something we call beta seventeen."
They were unremarkable bushes with deep green foliage and
dark red berries; Smith pointed to an array of camera-like in-
struments beside them. "Real-time infrared microspec-
troscopy. It can resolve a medium-sized RNA transcript, if
there's a sharp surge in production in a sufficient number of
cells, simultaneously. We match up the data from these with
our gas chromatography records, which show the range of
molecules drifting out from the core. If we can catch these
plants in the act of sensing a cue from El Nido—and if their
response involves switching on a gene and synthesizing a protein—we may be able to elucidate the mechanism, and eventually short-circuit it."

"You can't just . . . sequence all the DNA, and work it out
from first principles?" I was meant to be passing as a newly
appointed administrator, dropping in at short notice to check
for gold-plated paper clips—but it was hard to decide exactly
how naive to sound.

Smith smiled politely. "El Nido DNA is guarded by enzymes which tear it apart at the slightest hint of cellular disruption. Right now, we'd have about as much of a chance of
sequencing it as I'd have of . . . reading your mind by autopsy.
And we still don't know how those enzymes work; we have a
lot of catching up to do. When the drug cartels started invest-
ing in biotechnology, 40 years ago, *copy protection* was their
first priority. And they lured the best people away from legitimate labs around the world—not just by paying more, but by
offering more creative freedom, and more challenging goals.
El Nido probably contains as many patentable inventions as
the entire agrotechnology industry produced in the same period. And all of them a lot more exciting."

Was that what had brought Largo here? *More challenging
goals?* But El Nido was complete, the challenge was over;
any further work was mere refinement. And at 55, surely he
knew that his most creative years were long gone.

I said, "I imagine the cartels got more than they bargained for; the technology transformed their business beyond recognition. All the old addictive substances became too easy to synthesize biologically—too cheap, too pure, and too readily available to be profitable. And addiction itself became bad business. The only thing that really sells now is novelty."

Smith motioned with bulky arms towards the towering forest outside the cage—turning to face south-east, although it all looked the same. "*El Nido* was more than they bargained for. All they really wanted was coca plants that did better at lower altitudes, and some gene-tailored vegetation to make it easier to camouflage their labs and plantations. They ended up with a small *de facto* nation full of gene hackers, anarchists, and refugees. The cartels are only in control of certain regions; half the original geneticists have split off and founded their own little jungle utopias. There are at least a dozen people who know how to program the plants—how to switch on new patterns of gene expression, how to tap into the communications networks—and with that, you can stake out your own territory."

"Like having some secret, shamanistic power to command the spirits of the forest?"

"Exactly. Except for the fact that it actually works."

I laughed. "Do you know what cheers me up the most? Whatever else happens . . . the *real* Amazon, the *real* jungle, will swallow them all in the end. It's lasted—what? Two million years? *Their own little utopias!* In 50 years' time, or a hundred, it will be as if El Nido had never existed."

Less than chaff in a breeze.

Smith didn't reply. In the silence, I could hear the monotonous click of beetles, from all directions. Bogotá, high on a plateau, had been almost chilly. Here, it was as sweltering as Washington itself.

I glanced at Smith; she said, "You're right, of course." But she didn't sound convinced at all.

In the morning, over breakfast, I reassured Smith that I'd found everything to be in order. She smiled warily. I think she suspected that I wasn't what I claimed to be, but that didn't really matter. I'd listened carefully to the gossip of the scientists, technicians and soldiers; the name *Guillermo Largo* hadn't been mentioned once. If they didn't even know about Largo, they could hardly have guessed my real purpose.

It was just after nine when I departed. On the ground, sheets of light, delicate as auroral displays, sliced through the trees around the compound. When we emerged above the canopy, it was like stepping from a mist-shrouded dawn into the brilliance of noon.

The pilot, begrudgingly, took a detour over the center of El Nido. "We're in Peruvian air space, now," he boasted. "You want to spark a diplomatic incident?" He seemed to find the possibility attractive.

"No. But fly lower."

"There's nothing to see. You can't even see the river."

"Lower." The broccoli grew larger, then suddenly snapped into focus; all that undifferentiated green turned into individual branches, solid and specific. It was curiously shocking, like looking at some dull familiar object through a microscope, and seeing its strange particularity revealed.

I reached over and broke the pilot's neck. He hissed through his teeth, surprised. A shudder passed through me, a mixture of fear and a twinge of remorse. The autopilot kicked in and kept us hovering; it took me two minutes to unstrap the man's body, drag him into the cargo hold, and take his seat.

I unscrewed the instrument panel and patched in a new chip. The digital log being beamed via satellite to an air force base to the north would show that we'd descended rapidly, out of control.

The truth wasn't much different. At a hundred meters, I hit a branch and snapped a blade on the front rotor; the computers compensated valiantly, modelling and remodelling the situation, trimming the active surfaces of the surviving blades—and no doubt doing fine for each five-second interval between bone-shaking impacts and further damage. The sound absorbers went berserk, slipping in and out of phase with the motors, blasting the jungle with pulses of intensified noise.

Fifty metres up, I went into a slow spin, weirdly smooth, showing me the thickening canopy as if in a leisurely cinematic pan. At 20 metres, free fall. Air bags inflated around me, blocking off the view. I closed my eyes, redundantly, and gritted my teeth. Fragments of prayers spun in my head—the detritus of childhood, afterimages burned into my brain, meaningless but unerasable. I thought: *If I die, the jungle will claim me. I am flesh, I am chaff. Nothing will remain to be judged.* By the time I recalled that this wasn't true jungle at all, I was no longer falling.

The airbags promptly deflated. I opened my eyes. There was water all around, flooded forest. A panel of the roof between the rotors blew off gently with a hiss like the dying pilot's last breath, and then drifted down like a slowly crashing kite, turning muddy silver, green and brown as it snatched at the colors around it.

The life raft had oars, provisions, flares—and a radio beacon. I cut the beacon loose and left it in the wreckage. I moved the pilot back into his seat, just as the water started flooding in to bury him.

Then I set off down the river.

El Nido had divided a once-navigable stretch of the Rio Putumayo into a bewildering maze. Sluggish channels of brown water snaked between freshly raised islands of soil, covered in palms and rubber plants, and the inundated banks where the oldest trees—chocolate-colored hardwood species (predating the geneticists, but not necessarily unmodified)—soared above the undergrowth and out of sight.

The lymph nodes in my neck and groin pulsed with heat, savage but reassuring; my modified immune system was dealing with El Nido's viral onslaught by generating thousands of new killer T-cell clones *en masse,* rather than waiting for a cautious antigen-mediated response. A few weeks in this state, and the chances were that a self-directed clone would slip through the elimination process and burn me up with a novel autoimmune disease—but I didn't plan on staying that long.

Fish disturbed the murky water, rising up to snatch surface-dwelling insects or floating seed pods. In the distance, the thick coils of an anaconda slid from an overhanging branch and slipped languidly into the water. Between the rubber plants, hummingbirds hovered in the maws of violet orchids. So far as I knew, none of these creatures had been tampered with; they had gone on inhabiting the prosthetic forest as if nothing had changed.

I took a stick of chewing gum from my pocket, rich in cyclamates, and slowly roused one of my own sets of White Knights. The stink of heat and decaying vegetation seemed to fade, as certain olfactory pathways in my brain were numbed, and others sensitized—a kind of inner filter coming into play, enabling any signal from the newly acquired receptors in my nasal membranes to rise above all the other, distracting odors of the jungle.

Suddenly, I could smell the dead pilot on my hands and clothes, the lingering taint of his sweat and feces—and the pheromones of spider monkeys in the branches around me, pungent and distinctive as urine. As a rehearsal, I followed the trail for 15 minutes, paddling the raft in the direction of the freshest scent, until I was finally rewarded with chirps of alarm and a glimpse of two skinny grey-brown shapes vanishing into the foliage ahead.

My own scent was camouflaged; symbionts in my sweat glands were digesting all the characteristic molecules. There were long-term side-effects from the bacteria, though, and the most recent intelligence suggested that El Nido's inhabitants didn't bother with them. There was a chance, of course, that Largo had been paranoid enough to bring his own.

I stared after the retreating monkeys, and wondered when I'd catch my first whiff of another living human. Even an illiterate peasant who'd fled the violence to the north would have valuable knowledge of the state of play between the factions in here, and some kind of crude mental map of the landscape.

The raft began to whistle gently, air escaping from one sealed compartment. I rolled into the water and submerged completely. A metre down, I couldn't see my own hands. I waited and listened, but all I could hear was the soft *plop* of fish breaking the surface. No rock could have holed the plastic of the raft; it had to have been a bullet.

I floated in the cool milky silence. The water would conceal my body heat, and I'd have no need to exhale for ten minutes. The question was whether to risk raising a wake by swimming away from the raft, or to wait it out.

Something brushed my cheek, sharp and thin. I ignored it. It happened again. It didn't feel like a fish, or anything living. A third time, and I seized the object as it fluttered past. It was a piece of plastic a few centimetres wide. I felt around the rim; the edge was sharp in places, soft and yielding in others. Then the fragment broke in two in my hand.

I swam a few metres away, then surfaced cautiously. The life raft was decaying, the plastic peeling away into the water like skin in acid. The polymer was meant to be cross-linked beyond any chance of biodegradation—but obviously some strain of El Nido bacteria had found a way.

I floated on my back, breathing deeply to purge myself of carbon dioxide, contemplating the prospect of completing the mission on foot. The canopy above seemed to waver, as if in a heat haze, which made no sense. My limbs grew curiously warm and heavy. It occurred to me to wonder exactly what I might be smelling, if I hadn't shut down 90 per cent of my olfactory range. I thought: *If I'd bred bacteria able to digest a substance foreign to El Nido, what else would I want them to do when they chanced upon such a meal? Incapacitate whoever had brought it in? Broadcast news of the event with a biochemical signal?*

I could smell the sharp odours of half a dozen sweat-drenched people when they arrived, but all I could do was lie in the water and let them fish me out.

After we left the river, I was carried on a stretcher, blindfolded and bound. No one talked within earshot. I might have judged the pace we set by the rhythm of my bearers' footsteps, or guessed the direction in which we travelled by hints of sunlight on the side of my face . . . but in the waking dream induced by the bacterial toxins, the harder I struggled to interpret those cues, the more lost and confused I became.

At one point, when the party rested, someone squatted beside me—and waved a scanning device over my body? That guess was confirmed by the pinpricks of heat where the polymer transponders had been implanted. Passive devices—but their resonant echo in a satellite microwave burst would have been distinctive. The scanner found, and fried, them all.

Late in the afternoon, they removed the blindfold. Certain that I was totally disoriented? Certain that I'd never escape? Or maybe just to rub my face in EL Nido's triumphant architecture.

The approach was a hidden path through swampland; I kept looking down to see my captors' boots not quite vanishing into the mud, while a dry, apparently secure stretch of high ground nearby was avoided.

Closer in, the dense thorned bushes blocking the way seemed to yield for us; the chewing gum had worn off enough for me to tell that we moved in a cloud of a sweet, ester-like compound. I couldn't see whether it was being sprayed into the air from a cylinder—or emitted bodily by a member of the party with symbionts in his skin, or lungs, or intestine.

The village emerged almost imperceptibly out of the imposter jungle. The ground—I could feel it—became, step by step, unnaturally firm and level. The arrangement of trees grew subtly ordered—defining no linear avenues, but increasingly *wrong* nonetheless. Then I started glimpsing "fortuitous" clearings to the left and right, containing "natural" wooden buildings, or shiny biopolymer sheds.

I was lowered to the ground outside one of the sheds. A man I hadn't seen before leaned over me, wiry and unshaven, holding up a gleaming hunting knife. He looked to me like the archetype of human as animal, human as predator, human as unself-conscious killer.

He said, "Friend, this is where we drain out all of your blood." He grinned and squatted down. I almost passed out from the stench of my own fear, as the glut overwhelmed the symbionts. He cut my hands free, adding, "And then put it all back in again." He slid one arm under me, around my ribs, raised me up from the stretcher, and carried me into the building.

Guillermo Largo said, "Forgive me if I don't shake your hand. I think we've almost cleaned you out, but I don't want to risk physical contact in case there's enough of a residue of the virus to make your own hyped-up immune system turn on you."

He was an unprepossessing, sad-eyed man; thin, short, slightly balding. I stepped up to the wooden bars between us and stretched my hand out towards him. "Make contact any time you like. I never carried a virus. Do you think I believe your *propaganda*?"

He shrugged, unconcerned. "It would have killed you, not me—although I'm sure it was meant for both of us. It may have been keyed to my genotype, but you carried far too much of it not to have been caught up in the response to my presence. That's history, though, not worth arguing about."

I didn't actually believe that he was lying; a virus to dispose of both of us made perfect sense. I even felt a begrudging respect for the Company, for the way I'd been used—there was a savage, unsentimental honesty to it—but it didn't seem politic to reveal that to Largo.

I said, "If you believe that I pose no risk to you now, though, why don't you come back with me? You're still considered valuable. One moment of weakness, one bad decision, doesn't have to mean the end of your career. Your employers are very pragmatic people; they won't want to punish you. They'll just need to watch you a little more closely in the future. Their problem, not yours; you won't even notice the difference."

Largo didn't seem to be listening, but then he looked straight at me and smiled. "Do you know what Victor Hugo said about Colombia's first constitution? He said it was written for a country of angels. It only lasted 23 years—and on the next attempt, the politicians lowered their sights. Considerably." He turned away, and started pacing back and forth in front of the bars. Two Mestizo peasants with automatic weapons stood by the door, looking on impassively. Both incessantly chewed what looked to me like ordinary coca leaves; there was something almost reassuring about their loyalty to tradition.

My cell was clean and well furnished, right down to the kind of bioreactor toilet that was all the rage in Beverly Hills. My captors had treated me impeccably, so far, but I had a feeling that Largo was planning something unpleasant. Handing me over to the Mother barons? I still didn't know what deal he'd done, what he'd sold them in exchange for a piece of El Nido and a few dozen bodyguards. Let alone why he thought this was better than an apartment in Bethesda and a hundred grand a year.

I said, "What do you think you're going to do, if you stay here? Build your own *country for angels*? Grow your own bioengineered utopia?"

"Utopia?" Largo stopped pacing, and flashed his crooked smile again. "No. How can there ever be a *utopia*? There is no *right way to live*, which we've simply failed to stumble upon. There is no set of rules, there is no system, there is no formula. Why should there be? Short of the existence of a creator—and a perverse one, at that—why should there be some blueprint for perfection, just waiting to be discovered?"

I said, "You're right. In the end, all we can do is be true to our nature. See through the veneer of civilization and hypocritical morality, and accept the real forces which shape us."

Largo burst out laughing. I actually felt my face burn at his response—if only because I'd misread him, and failed to get him on my side; not because he was laughing at the one thing I believed in.

He said, "Do you know what I was working on, back in the States?"

"No. Does it matter?" The less I knew, the better my chances of living.

Largo told me anyway. "I was looking for a way to render mature neurons *embryonic*. To switch them back into a less differentiated state, enabling them to behave the way they do in the fetal brain: migrating from site to site, forming new connections. Supposedly as a treatment for dementia and stroke . . . although the work was being funded by people who saw it as the first step towards viral weapons able to rewire parts of the brain. I doubt that the results could ever have been very sophisticated—no viruses for imposing political ideologies—but all kinds of disabling or docile behaviour might have been coded into a relatively small package."

"And you sold that to the cartels? So they can hold whole cities to ransom with it, next time one of their leaders is arrested? To save them the trouble of assassinating judges and politicians?"

Largo said mildly, "I sold it to the cartels, but not as a weapon. No infectious military version exists. Even the prototypes—which merely regress selected neurons, but make no programmed changes—are far too cumbersome and fragile to survive at large. And there are other technical problems. There's not much reproductive advantage for a virus in carrying out elaborate, highly specific modifications to its host's brain; unleashed on a real human population, mutants which simply ditched all of that irrelevant shit would soon predominate."

"Then . . . ?"

"I sold it to the cartels as *a product*. Or rather, I combined it with their own biggest seller, and handed over the finished hybrid. A new kind of Mother."

"Which does what?" He had me hooked, even if I was digging my own grave.

"Which turns a subset of the neurons in the brain into something like White Knights. Just as mobile, just as flexible. Far better at establishing tight new synapses, though, rather than just flooding the interneural space with a chosen substance. And not controlled by dietary additives; controlled by molecules they secrete themselves. Controlled by each other."

That made no sense to me. "*Existing neurons* become mobile? Existing brain structures . . . melt? You've made a version of Mother which turns people's brains to mush—and you expect them to pay for that?"

"Not mush. Everything's part of a tight feedback loop: the firing of these altered neurons influences the range of molecules they secrete—which in turn, controls the rewiring of nearby synapses. Vital regulatory centers and motor neurons are left untouched, of course. And it takes a strong signal to shift the Grey Knights; they don't respond to every random whim. You need at least an hour or two without distractions before you can have a significant effect on any brain structure.

"It's not altogether different from the way ordinary neurons end up encoding learned behaviour and memories—only faster, more flexible . . . and much more widespread. There are parts of the brain which haven't changed in 100,000 years, which can be remodelled completely in half a day."

He paused, and regarded me amiably. The sweat on the back of my neck went cold.

"You've used the virus—?"

"Of course. That's why I created it. For myself. That's why I came here in the first place."

"For do-it-yourself neurosurgery? Why not just slip a screwdriver under one eyeball and poke it around until the urge went away?" I felt physically sick. "At least . . . cocaine and heroin—and even White Knights—exploited *natural* receptors, *natural* pathways. You've taken a structure which evolution has honed over millions of years, and—"

Largo was greatly amused, but this time he refrained from laughing in my face. He said gently, "For most people, navigating their own psyche is like wandering in circles through a maze. That's what *evolution* has bequeathed us: a miserable, confusing prison. And the only thing crude drugs like cocaine or heroin or alcohol ever did was build short cuts to a few dead ends—or, like LSD, coat the walls of the maze with mirrors. And all that White Knights ever did was package the same effects differently.

"*Grey Knights* allow you to reshape the entire maze, at will. They don't confine you to some shrunken emotional repertoire; they empower you completely. They let you control *exactly who you are.*"

I had to struggle to put aside the overwhelming sense of revulsion I felt. Largo had decided to fuck himself in the head; that was his problem. A few users of Mother would do the same—but one more batch of poisonous shit to compete with all the garbage from the basement labs wasn't exactly a national tragedy.

Largo said affably, "I spent 30 years as someone I despised. I was too weak to change—but I never quite lost sight of what I wanted to become. I used to wonder if it would have been less contemptible, less hypocritical, to resign myself to the fact of my weakness, the fact of my corruption. But I never did."

"And you think you've erased your old personality, as easily as you erased your computer files? What are you now, then? A saint. *An angel?*"

"No. But I'm exactly what I want to be. With Grey Knights, you can't really be anything else."

I felt giddy for a moment, light-headed with rage; I steadied myself against the bars of my cage.

I said, "So you've scrambled your brain, and you feel better. And you're going to live in this fake jungle for the rest of your life, collaborating with drug pushers, kidding yourself that you've achieved redemption?"

"The rest of my life? Perhaps. But I'll be watching the world. And hoping."

I almost choked. "Hoping for *what*? You think your habit will ever spread beyond a few brain-damaged junkies? You think Grey Knights are going to sweep across the planet and transform it beyond recognition? Or were you lying—is the virus really infectious, after all?"

"No. But it gives people what they want. They'll seek it out, once they understand that."

I gazed at him, pityingly. "What people *want* is food, sex and power. That will never change. Remember the passage you marked in *Heart of Darkness*? What do you think that *meant*? Deep down, we're just animals with a few simple drives. Everything else is *less than chaff in a breeze.*"

Largo frowned, as if trying to recall the quote, then nodded slowly. He said, "Do you know how many different ways an ordinary human brain can be wired? Not an arbitrary neural network of the same size—but an actual, working *Homo sapiens* brain, shaped by real embryology and real experience? There are about ten-to-the-power-of-ten-million possibilities. A huge number: a lot of room for variation in personality and talents, a lot of space to encode the traces of different lives.

"But do you know what Grey Knights do to that number? They multiply it by the same again. They grant the part of us that was fixed, that was tied to 'human nature,' the chance to be as different from person to person as a lifetime's worth of memories.

"Of course Conrad was right. Every word of that passage

was true—when it was written. But now it doesn't go far enough. Because now, all of human nature is *less than chaff in a breeze*. 'The horror,' the heart of darkness, is *less than chaff in a breeze*. All the 'eternal verities'—all the sad and beautiful insights of all the great writers from Sophocles to Shakespeare—are *less than chaff in a breeze*."

I lay awake on my bunk, listening to the cicadas and frogs, wondering what Largo would do with me. If he didn't see himself as capable of murder, he wouldn't kill me—if only to reinforce his delusions of self-mastery. Perhaps he'd just dump me outside the research station—where I could explain to Madelaine Smith how the Colombian air force pilot had come down with an El Nido virus in midair, and I'd valiantly tried to take control.

I thought back over the incident, trying to get my story straight. The pilot's body would never be recovered; the forensic details didn't have to add up.

I closed my eyes and saw myself breaking his neck. The same twinge of remorse passed over me. I brushed it aside irritably. So I'd killed him—and the girl, a few days earlier—and a dozen others before that. The Company had very nearly disposed of me. Because it was expedient—and because it was possible. That was the way of the world: power would always be used, nation would subjugate nation, the weak would always be slaughtered. Everything else was pious self-delusion. A hundred kilometres away, Colombia's warring factions were proving the truth of that, one more time.

But if Largo had infected me with his own special brand of Mother? And if everything he'd told me about it was true?

Grey Knights only moved if you willed them to move. All I had to do in order to remain unscathed was to choose that fate. To wish only to be exactly who I was: a killer who'd always understood that he was facing the deepest of truths. Embracing savagery and corruption because, in the end, there was no other way.

I kept seeing them before me: the pilot, the girl.

I had to feel nothing . . . and wish to feel nothing—and keep on making that choice, again and again.

Or everything I was would disintegrate like a house of sand, and blow away.

One of the guards belched in the darkness, then spat.

The night stretched out ahead of me, like a river which had lost its way.

STABLE STRATEGIES
FOR MIDDLE
MANAGEMENT

Eileen Gunn

Eileen Gunn is not a prolific writer, but her stories are well worth waiting for, and are relished (and eagerly anticipated) by a small but select group of knowledgeable fans who know that she has a twisted perspective on life unlike anyone else's, and a strange and pungent sense of humor all her own. She has made several sales to Asimov's Science Fiction, *as well as to markets such as* Amazing, Proteus, Tales by Moonlight, *and* Alternate Presidents, *and has been a Nebula and Hugo finalist several times. She is currently at work on her first novel. Long involved in the administration of the Clarion West writers workshop, she was a resident of Seattle for many years, until moving to Brooklyn in 1998. Now, proving that once you set a stone to rolling it's hard to get it to stop, she's making plans to move to San Francisco sometime in the near future.*

In the strange and funny story that follows, a Hugo finalist, she shows us how bioscience may someday make possible career-advancement ploys far more bizarre than any that are possible today....

Our cousin the insect has an external skeleton made of shiny brown chitin, a material that is particularly responsive to the demands of evolution. Just as bioengineering has sculpted our bodies into new forms, so evolution has shaped the early insect's chewing mouthparts into her descendants' chisels, siphons, and stilettos, and has molded from the chitin special tools—pockets to carry pollen, combs to clean

her compound eyes, notches on which she can fiddle
a song.

> From the popular science
> program *Insect People!*

I awoke this morning to discover that bioengineering had
made demands upon me during the night. My tongue had
turned into a stiletto, and my left hand now contained a small
chitinous comb, as if for cleaning a compound eye. Since I
didn't have compound eyes, I thought that perhaps this pre-
saged some change to come.

I dragged myself out of bed, wondering how I was going
to drink my coffee through a stiletto. Was I now expected to
kill my breakfast, and dispense with coffee entirely? I hoped
I was not evolving into a creature whose survival depended on
early-morning alertness. My circadian rhythms would no
doubt keep pace with any physical changes, but my un-
evolved soul was repulsed at the thought of my waking cheerfully at dawn, ravenous for some wriggly little creature that
had arisen even earlier.

I looked down at Greg, still asleep, the edge of our red and
white quilt pulled up under his chin. His mouth had changed
during the night too, and seemed to contain some sort of a
long probe. Were we growing apart?

I reached down with my unchanged hand and touched his
hair. It was still shiny brown, soft and thick, luxurious. But
along his cheek, under his beard, I could feel patches of scle-
rotin, as the flexible chitin in his skin was slowly hardening to
an impermeable armor.

He opened his eyes, staring blearily forward without moving his head. I could see him move his mouth cautiously, ex-
amining its internal changes. He turned his head and looked
up at me, rubbing his hair slightly into my hand.

"Time to get up?" he asked. I nodded. "Oh, God," he said.
He said this every morning. It was like a prayer.

"I'll make coffee," I said. "Do you want some?"

He shook his head slowly. "Just a glass of apricot nectar,"

he said. He unrolled his long, rough tongue and looked at it, slightly cross-eyed. "This is real interesting, but it wasn't in the catalog. I'll be sipping lunch from flowers pretty soon. That ought to draw a second glance at Duke's."

"I thought account execs were expected to sip their lunches," I said.

"Not from the flower arrangements . . ." he said, still exploring the odd shape of his mouth. Then he looked up at me and reached up from under the covers. "Come here."

It had been a while, I thought, and I had to get to work. But he did smell terribly attractive. Perhaps he was developing aphrodisiac scent glands. I climbed back under the covers and stretched my body against his. We were both developing chitinous knobs and odd lumps that made this less than comfortable. "How am I supposed to kiss you with a stiletto in my mouth?" I asked.

"There are other things to do. New equipment presents new possibilities." He pushed the covers back and ran his unchanged hands down my body from shoulder to thigh. "Let me know if my tongue is too rough."

It was not.

Fuzzy-minded, I got out of bed for the second time and drifted into the kitchen.

Measuring the coffee into the grinder, I realized that I was no longer interested in drinking it, although it was diverting for a moment to spear the beans with my stiletto. What was the damn thing for, anyhow? I wasn't sure I wanted to find out.

Putting the grinder aside, I poured a can of apricot nectar into a tulip glass. Shallow glasses were going to be a problem for Greg in the future, I thought. Not to mention solid food.

My particular problem, however, if I could figure out what I was supposed to eat for breakfast, was getting to the office in time for my ten AM meeting. Maybe I'd just skip breakfast. I dressed quickly and dashed out the door before Greg was even out of bed.

• • •

Thirty minutes later, I was more or less awake and sitting in the small conference room with the new marketing manager, listening to him lay out his plan for the Model 2000 launch.

In signing up for his bioengineering program, Harry had chosen specialized primate adaptation, B-E Option No. 4. He had evolved into a text-book example: small and long-limbed, with forward-facing eyes for judging distances and long, grasping fingers to keep him from falling out of his tree.

He was dressed for success in a pin-striped three-piece suit that fit his simian proportions perfectly. I wondered what premium he paid for custom-made. Or did he patronize a ready-to-wear shop that catered especially to primates?

I listened as he leaped agilely from one ridiculous marketing premise to the next. Trying to borrow credibility from mathematics and engineering, he used wildly metaphoric bizspeak, "factoring in the need for pipeline throughout," "fine-tuning the media mix," without even cracking a smile.

Harry had been with the company only a few months, straight from business school. He saw himself as a much-needed infusion of talent. I didn't like him, but I envied his ability to root through his subconscious and toss out one half-formed idea after another. I know he felt it reflected badly on me that I didn't join in and spew forth a random selection of promotional suggestions.

I didn't think much of his marketing plan. The advertising section was a textbook application of theory with no practical basis. I had two options: I could force him to accept a solution that would work, or I could yes him to death, making sure everybody understood it was his idea. I knew which path I'd take.

"Yeah, we can do that for you," I told him. "No problem." We'd see which of us would survive and which was hurtling to an evolutionary dead end.

Although Harry had won his point, he continued to belabor it. My attention wandered—I'd heard it all before. His voice was the hum of an air conditioner, a familiar, easily ignored background noise. I drowsed and new emotions stirred in me, yearnings to float through moist air currents, to land on bright surfaces, to engorge myself with warm, wet food.

Adrift in insect dreams, I became sharply aware of the bare skin of Harry's arm, between his gold-plated watchband and his rolled-up sleeve, as he manipulated papers on the conference room table. He smelled greasily delicious, like a pepperoni pizza or a charcoal-broiled hamburger. I realized he probably wouldn't taste as good as he smelled, but I was hungry. My stiletto-like tongue was there for a purpose, and it wasn't to skewer cubes of tofu. I leaned over his arm and braced myself against the back of his hand, probing with my stylets to find a capillary.

Harry noticed what I was doing and swatted me sharply on the side of the head. I pulled away before he could hit me again.

"We were discussing the Model 2000 launch. Or have you forgotten?" he said, rubbing his arm.

"Sorry. I skipped breakfast this morning." I was embarrassed.

"Well, get your hormones adjusted, for chrissake." He was annoyed, and I couldn't really blame him. "Let's get back to the media allocation issue, if you can keep your mind on it. I've got another meeting at eleven in Building Two."

Inappropriate feeding behavior was not unusual in the company, and corporate etiquette sometimes allowed minor lapses to pass without pursuit. Of course, I could no longer hope that he would support me on moving some money out of the direct-mail budget. . . .

During the remainder of the meeting, my glance kept drifting through the open door of the conference room, toward a large decorative plant in the hall, one of those oases of generic greenery that dot the corporate landscape. It didn't look succulent exactly—it obviously wasn't what I would have preferred to eat if I hadn't been so hungry—but I wondered if I swung both ways?

I grabbed a handful of the broad leaves as I left the room and carried them back to my office. With my tongue, I probed a vein in the thickest part of a leaf. It wasn't so bad. Tasted green. I sucked them dry and tossed the husks in the waste-basket.

I was still omnivorous, at least—female mosquitoes don't eat plants. So the process wasn't complete. . . .

I got a cup of coffee, for company, from the kitchenette and sat in my office with the door closed and wondered what was happening. The incident with Harry disturbed me. Was I turning into a mosquito? If so, what the hell kind of good was that supposed to do me? The company didn't have any use for a whining loner.

There was a knock at the door, and my boss stuck his head in. I nodded and gestured him into my office. He sat down in the visitor's chair on the other side of my desk. From the look on his face, I could tell Harry had talked to him already.

Tom Samson was an older guy, pre-bioengineering. He was well versed in stimulus-response techniques, but had somehow never made it to the top job. I liked him, but then that was what he intended. Without sacrificing authority, he had pitched his appearance, his gestures, the tone of his voice, to the warm end of the spectrum. Even though I knew what he was doing, it worked.

He looked at me with what appeared to be sympathy, but was actually a practiced sign stimulus, intended to defuse any fight-or-flight response. "Is there something bothering you, Margaret?"

"Bothering me? I'm hungry, that's all. I get short-tempered when I'm hungry."

Watch it, I thought. He hasn't referred to the incident; leave it for him to bring up. I made my mind go blank and forced myself to meet his eyes. A shifty gaze is a guilty gaze.

Tom just looked at me, biding his time, waiting for me to put myself on the spot. My coffee smelt burnt, but I stuck my tongue in it and pretended to drink. "I'm just not human until I've had my coffee in the morning." Sounded phony. Shut up, I thought.

This was the opening that Tom was waiting for. "That's what I wanted to speak to you about, Margaret." He sat there, hunched over in a relaxed way, like a mountain gorilla, unthreatened by natural enemies. "I just talked to

Harry Winthrop, and he said you were trying to suck his blood during a meeting on marketing strategy." He paused for a moment to check my reaction, but the neutral expression was fixed on my face and I said nothing. His face changed to project disappointment. "You know, when we noticed you were developing three distinct body segments, we had great hopes for you. But your actions just don't reflect the social and organizational development we expected."

He paused, and it was my turn to say something in my defense. "Most insects are solitary, you know. Perhaps the company erred in hoping for a termite or an ant. I'm not responsible for that."

"Now, Margaret," he said, his voice simulating genial reprimand. "This isn't the jungle, you know. When you signed those consent forms, you agreed to let the B-E staff mold you into a more useful corporate organism. But this isn't nature, this is man reshaping nature. It doesn't follow the old rules. You can truly be anything you want to be. But you have to cooperate."

"I'm doing the best I can," I said, cooperatively. "I'm putting in eighty hours a week."

"Margaret, the quality of your work is not an issue. It's your interactions with others that you have to work on. You have to learn to work as part of the group. I just cannot permit such backbiting to continue. I'll have Arthur get you an appointment this afternoon with the B-E counselor." Arthur was his secretary. He knew everything that happened in the department and mostly kept his mouth shut.

"I'd be a social insect if I could manage it," I muttered as Tom left my office. "But I've never known what to say to people in bars."

For lunch I met Greg and our friend David Detlor at a health-food restaurant that advertises fifty different kinds of fruit nectar. We'd never eaten there before, but Greg knew he'd love the place. It was already a favorite of David's, and he still has all his teeth, so I figured it would be okay with me.

David was there when I arrived, but not Greg. David

works for the company too, in a different department. He, however, has proved remarkably resistant to corporate blandishment. Not only has he never undertaken B-E, he hasn't even bought a three-piece suit. Today he was wearing chewed-up blue jeans and a flashy Hawaiian shirt, of a type that was cool about ten years ago.

"Your boss lets you dress like that?" I asked.

"We have this agreement. I don't tell her she has to give me a job, and she doesn't tell me what to wear."

David's perspective on life is very different from mine. And I don't think it's just that he's in R&D and I'm in Advertising—it's more basic than that. Where he sees the world as a bunch of really neat but optional puzzles put there for his enjoyment, I see it as . . . well, as a series of SATs.

"So what's new with you guys?" he asked, while we stood around waiting for a table.

"Greg's turning into a goddamn butterfly. He went out last week and bought a dozen Italian silk sweaters. It's not a corporate look."

"He's not a corporate *guy*, Margaret."

"Then why is he having all this B-E done if he's not even going to use it?"

"He's dressing up a little. He just wants to look nice. Like Michael Jackson, you know?"

I couldn't tell whether David was kidding me or not. Then he started telling me about his music, this barbershop quartet that he sings in. They were going to dress in black leather for the next competition and sing Shel Silverstein's "Come to Me, My Masochistic Baby."

"It'll knock them on their tails," he said gleefully. "We've already got a great arrangement."

"Do you think it will win, David?" It seemed too weird to please the judges in that sort of a show.

"Who cares?" said David. He didn't look worried.

Just then Greg showed up. He was wearing a cobalt blue silk sweater with a copper green design on it. Italian. He was also wearing a pair of dangly earrings shaped like bright blue airplanes. We were shown to a table near a display of carved vegetables.

"This is great," said David. "Everybody wants to sit near

the vegetables. It's where you sit to be *seen* in this place." He nodded to Greg. "I think it's your sweater."

"It's the butterfly in my personality," said Greg. "Head-waiters never used to do stuff like this for me. I always got the table next to the espresso machine."

If Greg was going to go on about the perks that come with being a butterfly, I was going to change the subject.

"David, how come you still haven't signed up for B-E?" I asked. "The company pays half the cost, and they don't ask questions."

David screwed up his mouth, raised his hands to his face, and made small, twitching, insect gestures, as if grooming his nose and eyes. "I'm doing okay the way I am."

Greg chuckled at this, but I was serious. "You'll get ahead faster with a little adjustment. Plus you're showing a good attitude, you know, if you do it."

"I'm getting ahead faster than I want to right now—it looks like I won't be able to take the three months off that I wanted this summer."

"Three months?" I was astonished. "Aren't you afraid you won't have a job to come back to?"

"I could live with that," said David calmly, opening his menu.

The waiter took our orders. We sat for a moment in a companionable silence, the self-congratulation that follows ordering high-fiber foodstuffs. Then I told them the story of my encounter with Harry Winthrop.

"There's something wrong with me," I said. "Why suck his blood? What good is that supposed to do me?"

"Well," said David, "*you* chose this schedule of treatments. Where did you want it to go?"

"According to the catalog," I said, "the No. 2 Insect Option is supposed to make me into a successful competitor for a middle-management niche, with triggerable responses that can be useful in gaining entry to upper hierarchical levels. Unquote." Of course, that was just ad talk—I didn't really expect it to do all that. "That's what I want. I want to be in charge. I want to be the boss."

"Maybe you should go back to BioEngineering and try again," said Greg. "Sometimes the hormones don't do what you expect. Look at my tongue, for instance." He unfurled it gently and rolled it back into his mouth. "Though I'm sort of getting to like it." He sucked at his drink, making disgusting slurping sounds. He didn't need a straw.

"Don't bother with it, Margaret," said David firmly, taking a cup of rosehip tea from the waiter. "Bioengineering is a waste of time and money and millions of years of evolution. If human beings were intended to be managers, we'd have evolved pin-striped body covering."

"That's cleverly put," I said, "but it's dead wrong."

The waiter brought our lunches, and we stopped talking as he put them in front of us. It seemed like the anticipatory silence of three very hungry people, but was in fact the polite silence of three people who have been brought up not to argue in front of disinterested bystanders. As soon as he left, we resumed the discussion.

"I mean it," David said. "The dubious survival benefits of management aside, bioengineering is a waste of effort. Harry Winthrop, for instance, doesn't need B-E at all. Here he is, fresh out of business school, audibly buzzing with lust for a high-level management position. Basically he's just marking time until a presidency opens up somewhere. And what gives him the edge over you is his youth and inexperience, not some specialized primate adaptation."

"Well," I said with some asperity, "he's not constrained by a knowledge of what's failed in the past, that's for sure. But saying that doesn't solve my problem, David. Harry's signed up. I've signed up. The changes are under way and I don't have any choice."

I squeezed a huge glob of honey into my tea from a plastic bottle shaped like a teddy bear. I took a sip of the tea; it was minty and very sweet. "And now I'm turning into the wrong kind of insect. It's ruined my ability to deal with Product Marketing."

"Oh, give it a rest!" said Greg suddenly. "This is *so* boring. I don't want to hear any more about corporate hugger-mugger. Let's talk about something that's fun."

I had had enough of Greg's lepidopterate lack of concentration. "Something that's *fun?* I've invested all my time and most of my genetic material in this job. This is all the god-damn fun there is."

The honeyed tea made me feel hot. My stomach itched—I wondered if I was having an allergic reaction. I scratched, and not discreetly. My hand came out from under my shirt full of lit-tle waxy scales. What the hell was going on under there? I tasted one of the scales; it was wax all right. Worker bee changes? I couldn't help myself—I stuffed the wax into my mouth.

David was busying himself with his alfalfa sprouts, but Greg looked disgusted. "That's gross, Margaret," he said. He made a face, sticking his tongue part way out. Talk about gross. "Can't you wait until after lunch?"

I was doing what came naturally, and did not dignify his statement with a response. There was a side dish of bee pollen on the table. I took a spoonful and mixed it with the wax, chewing noisily. I'd had a rough morning, and bickering with Greg wasn't making the day more pleasant.

Besides, neither he nor David has any real respect for my position in the company. Greg doesn't take my job seriously at all. And David simply does what he wants to do, regardless of whether it makes any money, for himself or anyone else. He was giving me a back-to-nature lecture, and it was far too late for that.

This whole lunch was a waste of time. I was tired of lis-tening to them, and felt an intense urge to get back to work. A couple of quick stings distracted them both: I had the advan-tage of surprise. I ate some more honey and quickly waxed them over. They were soon hibernating side by side in two large octagonal cells.

I looked around the restaurant. People were rather ner-vously pretending not to have noticed. I called the waiter over and handed him my credit card. He signaled to several bus boys, who brought a covered cart and took Greg and David away. "They'll eat themselves out of that by Thursday after-noon," I told him. "Store them on their sides in a warm, dry place, away from direct heat." I left a large tip.

I walked back to the office, feeling a bit ashamed of myself. A couple days of hibernation weren't going to make Greg or

David more sympathetic to my problems. And they'd be real mad when they got out.

I didn't use to do things like that. I used to be more patient, didn't I? More appreciative of the diverse spectrum of human possibility. More interested in sex and television.

This job was not doing much for me as a warm, personable human being. At the very least, it was turning me into an unpleasant lunch companion. Whatever had made me think I wanted to get into management anyway?

The money, maybe.

But that wasn't all. It was the challenge, the chance to do something new, to control the total effort instead of just doing part of a project. . . .

The money too, though. There were other ways to get money. Maybe I should just kick the supports out from under the damn job and start over again.

I saw myself sauntering into Tom's office, twirling his visitor's chair around and falling into it. The words "I quit" would force their way out, almost against my will. His face would show surprise—feigned, of course. By then I'd have to go through with it. Maybe I'd put my feet up on his desk. And then—

But was it possible to just quit, to go back to being the person I used to be? No, I wouldn't be able to do it. I'd never be a management virgin again.

I walked up to the employee entrance at the rear of the building. A suction device next to the door sniffed at me, recognized my scent, and clicked the door open. Inside, a group of new employees, trainees, were clustered near the door, while a personnel officer introduced them to the lock and let it familiarize itself with their pheromones.

On the way down the hall, I passed Tom's office. The door was open. He was at his desk, bowed over some papers, and looked up as I went by.

"Ah, Margaret," he said. "Just the person I want to talk to. Come in for a minute, would you." He moved a large file folder onto the papers in front of him on his desk, and folded his hands on top of them. "So glad you were passing by." He nodded toward a large, comfortable chair. "Sit down.

"We're going to be doing a bit of restructuring in the de-

partment," he began, "and I'll need your input, so I want to fill
you in now on what will be happening."

I was immediately suspicious. Whenever Tom said "I'll
need your input," he meant everything was decided already.

"We'll be reorganizing the whole division, of course," he
continued, drawing little boxes on a blank piece of paper.
He'd mentioned this at the department meeting last week.

"Now, your group subdivides functionally into two separate areas, wouldn't you say?"

"Well—"

"Yes," he said thoughtfully, nodding his head as though in
agreement. "That would be the way to do it." He added a few
lines and a few more boxes. From what I could see, it meant
that Harry would do all the interesting stuff and I'd sweep up
afterwards.

"Looks to me as if you've cut the balls out of my area and
put them over into Harry Winthrop's," I said.

"Ah, but your area is still very important, my dear. That's
why I don't have you actually reporting to Harry." He gave
me a smile like a lie.

He had put me in a tidy little bind. After all, he was my
boss. If he was going to take most of my area away from me,
as it seemed he was, there wasn't much I could do to stop him.
And I would be better off if we both pretended that I hadn't
experienced any loss of status. That way I kept my title and
my salary.

"Oh, I see," I said. "Right."

It dawned on me that this whole thing had been decided already, and that Harry Winthrop probably knew all about it.
He'd probably even wangled a raise out of it. Tom had called
me in here to make it look casual, to make it look as though I
had something to say about it. I'd been set up.

This made me mad. There was no question of quitting now.
I'd stick around and fight. My eyes blurred, unfocused, refo-
cused again. Compound eyes! The promise of the small comb
in my hand was fulfilled! I felt a deep chemical understanding of the ecological system I was now a part of. I knew where
I fit in. And I knew what I was going to do. It was inevitable
now, hardwired in at the DNA level.

The strength of this conviction triggered another change in

the chitin, and for the first time I could actually feel the rearrangement of my mouth and nose, a numb tickling like inhaling seltzer water. The stiletto receded and mandibles jutted forth, rather like Katharine Hepburn. Form and function achieved an orgasmic synchronicity. As my jaw pushed forward, mantis-like, it also opened, and I pounced on Tom and bit his head off.

He leaped from his desk and danced headless about the office.

I felt in complete control of myself as I watched him and continued the conversation. "About the Model 2000 launch," I said. "If we factor in the demand for pipeline throughout and adjust the media mix just a bit, I think we can present a very tasty little package to Product Marketing by the end of the week."

Tom continued to strut spasmodically, making vulgar copulative motions. Was I responsible for evoking these mantid reactions? I was unaware of a sexual component in our relationship.

I got up from the visitor's chair and sat behind his desk, thinking about what had just happened. It goes without saying that I was surprised at my own actions. I mean, irritable is one thing, but biting people's heads off is quite another. But I have to admit that my second thought was, well, this certainly is a useful strategy, and should make a considerable difference in my ability to advance myself. Hell of a lot more productive than sucking people's blood.

Maybe there was something after all to Tom's talk about having the proper attitude.

And, of course, thinking of Tom, my third reaction was regret. He really had been a likeable guy, for the most part. But what's done is done, you know, and there's no use chewing on it after the fact.

I buzzed his assistant on the intercom. "Arthur," I said, "Mr. Samson and I have come to an evolutionary parting of the ways. Please have him re-engineered. And charge it to Personnel."

Now I feel an odd itching on my forearms and thighs. Notches on which I might fiddle a song?

GOOD WITH RICE

John Brunner

The late John Brunner was one of the most prolific and respected authors in the business, with more than fifty books to his credit, including, in addition to his science fiction, thrillers, contemporary novels, historical novels, and volumes of poetry. His massive and widely acclaimed novel Stand On Zanzibar *won him a Hugo Award and was one of the landmark books of the '60s, and he produced several of the most notable novels of the '70s as well with books like* The Jagged Orbit, The Sheep Look Up, *and the remarkably prescient* The Shockwave Rider—*which, in retrospect, cannot only be seen as an ancestor of cyberpunk, but which may have been the first serious fictional speculation about the workings of an "information economy" world; it even predicted computer viruses. In addition to the Hugo, Brunner won the British Fantasy Award, two British Science Fiction Awards, the Prix Apollo, two Cometa D'Argento awards, the Gilgamesh Award, and the Europa Award as Best Western European SF Writer. His many other books include the novels* The Squares of the City, The Atlantic Abomination, Polymath, Age of Miracles, The Crucible of Time, *and* The Tides of Time, *and the collections* The Book of John Brunner, The Fantastic Worlds of John Brunner, *and* The Best of John Brunner. *His last book was the novel* Children of the Thunder. *He died, an untimely death, in 1995.*

Brunner was always one of the most politically savvy of science fiction writers, and here, in a story that could have come out of this morning's headlines, he shows us how biological and genetic science might help solve some of the world's most pressing problems—at the cost of raising some unsettling new ones.

THE SUNSET DRAGON

. . . *crept the last* few hundred meters into Guangzhou Central station at less than walking pace. The train was so named because it hailed from about as far west as one could go without leaving the country. It was not, however, those of its thousand-odd passengers who had ridden it for the full two-and-a-half days that tried to open the doors before it halted, and on failing—because the rolling-stock was of the most modern design, with an interlock connected to the braking system—stuck their heads out of the windows to voice futile complaints. Rather, it was those who had joined it closer to this final destination, who had not yet had time to sink into the ancient lethargy of the long-distance traveler, so appropriate to a land whose very dust smeared one's skin with the powder of ancestral bones.

But their impatience was to meet a further check.

There must be some very influential people in the first carriage behind the locomotive. Where that car was to draw up, a section of the platform was isolated by metal barriers. Carpet had been laid. Railway officials in their smartest attire hung about expectantly. Two women fussed over a little girl in jacket and trousers of red silk who was to present a bouquet. Backs to the train, soldiers stood on guard bearing carbines at the port.

The exalted passengers should have emerged at once, accepted the flowers and the compliments, and been whisked to a waiting limousine. Instead, there was some sort of hitch. Had they been able to see why they were obliged to wait, perhaps even enjoy the little bit of spectacle, the passengers would have shrugged the matter off. Wherever one went in China nowadays, there always seemed to be Important People thrusting to the head of the line: politicians soliciting support for this or that school of opinion; businessmen involved (or claiming to be) in discussions with foreign corporations, Japanese, American, European; experts in a hundred disciplines seeking ways to mend the sick heart of the land. . . . As it was, though, the crowd quickly grew restive.

• • •

There are, of course, no such things as coincidence, and Policeman Wang was far too good a Taoist to imagine otherwise. When he looked back later, though, he could not help being struck by the number of preconditions necessary to set in motion the chain of events that was so soon to change the world—or rather, let the world find out how it was already being changed.

For instance, but for the delay in getting the Important Passengers away to their car, he might well not have spotted the old peasant as he hobbled by amid the throng, swept past like an autumn maple-leaf abob on a swollen stream. Or even if he had, which certainly was possible because in this thriving Special Economic Zone the fellow cut such an incongruous figure, would not have had the chance to act on his sudden inspiration—more properly called, he supposed, a hunch.

Being for the moment free of routine duties, such as discouraging peddlers anxious to fleece newly arrived countryfolk and noodle-cooks apt to overset their pushcarts in their eagerness to beat off competitors, he was able to take stock of his human surroundings in search of what had snagged his attention.

The passenger mix off the Sunset Dragon was typical for this time of a working day. There was a preponderance of men in suits and ties, clutching attaché cases and portfolios, fretting as though they were being conspired against and looking for someone to blame. There were merchants carrying craftwork, carpets, bales of cloth and skin rugs from non-endangered species such as pony and camel. There were a couple of priests in wide-brimmed conical hats, showing themselves openly again thanks to foreign insistence on religious toleration. There were a lot of elderly folk, remarkably spry because of their practice of *tai ch'i,* presumably here to visit relatives working in the city and thus allowed to live in it. There were virtually no children other than babes in arms, for it was during school hours, but Wang caught sight of three in a group, sickly and sad, presumably on their way to be examined at a hospital. There were several young people whom Wang would dearly have liked to accost, to find out why they weren't studying or at work, but they looked too well-dressed for him to risk it. Either they came from rich and influential families, untouchable by the police, or they were drug-dealers or black-marketeers, so he would be interfering in areas for which another branch of the force was responsible, or—in the case of the girls and possibly some of the boys as well—they were prostitutes who very probably had triad protectors. Sometimes Wang doubted whether the bosses in Beijing had understood what they were letting themselves in for when they insisted on reuniting Hong Kong with China.

But he didn't want to think about Hong Kong.

Heterogeneous though those around him were, the old peasant still stood out like a rock in a rice-bowl. (Old? Probably he was no more than fifty, but he had lost several teeth, the rest were stained with tobacco, and under his greasy blue cotton cap his face was so ingrained with dirt that every wrinkle, every line, was doubly overscored.) He was shabbily dressed in garb reminiscent of the Cultural Revolution, much repaired; only his shoes were new. Over one shoulder he balanced a bamboo pole, sagging at both ends for the weight of one bundle tied in cloth and one sack that failed to disguise its contents, an oblong hamper. He seemed unwilling to rest his load on the ground, though it must be tiring in the warmth of Guangdong. No doubt of it: rather than just being annoyed by the holdup, he was nervous. He kept glancing around in a totally different manner from his companions. When his gaze strayed to Wang, it darted away on the instant.

He's worried about the hamper. What's in it?

At Wang's side his partner Ho said sourly, "This lot look as though they could turn nasty. How much longer are they going to be kept hanging about?"

Wang disregarded the question. His eyes were still fixed on the old peasant.

"Not talking to me today, hm?" Ho said huffily. He had small liking for Wang, whom he regarded as an idiot. To have spent a year in Hong Kong and not come back rich—what a wasted chance! In many ways he reminded Wang of his wife, who seldom tired of saying the same.

But never mind him. The dignitaries had finally emerged from the train, the bouquet was being presented, there were bows and handshakes and official cordiality in progress. Wang reached a decision. Raising the aerial on his radio, he requested the co-operation of their squad commander, Inspector Chen.

Who was not a bad sort, Wang felt; at least he didn't share Ho's low opinion of him. He asked no questions and didn't even frown at being summoned by a subordinate. Together they closed on the peasant, with a scowling Ho in their wake.

Seeing police approach with batons drawn, the peasant panicked. He dropped his burden and would have fled, save that the crowd was not only too dense but also surging into motion as the barriers ahead were moved aside. Trapped, he turned through half a circle, closed his eyes, and pressed both hands against his chest, swaying as from a weak heart. A young man with a dark sly face reached for the fallen pole. Wang's baton cracked down one centimeter from his outstretched fingers. Mind changed, the fellow scurried away. By now Ho was steadying the peasant to save him from falling— vastly against his will, as was obvious from his expression of distaste.

"What do you suspect?" Inspector Chen muttered, with upraised baton directing the rest of the squad to hold back the crowd—rather like the conductor of a western orchestra.

There was a powerful smell of urine, more pungent even than the stench of humanity below the station roof. On the basis of that, plus the obvious fact that the peasant was of far-western stock, Wang said, positively, "A banned animal."

Chen stared for a moment. "Could anyone still be that stupid?" he demanded. Then he glanced at the peasant, who had recovered enough of his wits to glare daggers. "Let the fool sit down!" he called to Ho in passing, thus answering by implication his own question. With a gesture he indicated that Wang should fetch and open the sack.

Instead of consenting to sit, the peasant wrenched free of Ho's grip, fell to his knees and implored mercy with repeated kowtows. His accent was so thick they could barely grasp what he was saying, though it included some excuse about his wife being ill. But there was no mistaking the import of his actions.

Chen eyed Wang sardonically. Speaking clearly and slowly, with the intention of being understood, "You were right. He is a fool. Now let's find out what kind of animal it is. Better yet, why doesn't the fool tell us? You—what's-your-name!"

The old man was blubbering by now. Ho caught both his pipestem wrists in one hand and tugged a wad of greasy papers from the side pocket of his jacket—a stupid place to carry them in a crowded train, of course. Maybe he had got away with it because no one was much interested in stealing the identity of an old countryman.

"Name!" Chen snapped. When no reply was forthcoming he signalled to Ho.

"He's called Lin Yung-fei," the latter reported, having fumbled open the wad of papers. He added, punning on Lin's primary meaning of forest, "Perfect for a raw-food-eating barbarian!"

The insult cut short the peasant's sobs and he went back to glowering. It was a poor joke, though. Ignoring it, Chen indicated to Wang that he should proceed with his examination of the hamper. Circumspectly he complied: first untying the rope that attached the sack to the carrying-pole, then opening the sack and pushing it to ground-level on all sides, thus revealing that the hamper was made of wicker and that its lid was secured with rough wooden pegs.

The stink made it indisputable that his conclusion was correct.

The passengers from the arriving train had dispersed, but they were still surrounded by a score or more of onlookers. Wherever one went it seemed there were always people with nothing better to do, who veered to swarm like kites at every breath of an event. So long as they didn't try to meddle it was pointless to order them away. As many again would spring up, faster than mushrooms.

Lin recovered his voice long enough to curse: first his luck, then whoever the "friend" was who had told him he could make a lot of money by smuggling a rare animal to a big city, and thirdly the police. At that stage Ho's baton prodded him in the kidneys and he subsided.

The hamper-lid had holes around the fastening-pegs. Cautiously applying one eye, Wang confirmed that there was indeed an animal inside. It was brown, lithe and sleek; it had sharp white teeth in a wicked-looking jaw; and it had claws.

"It looks," he said slowly, "like a large ferret."

The peasant snorted. Apparently he had run out of lies and denials. "Just the sort of stupid remark you'd expect from a townie!" he rasped. "She's not a ferret, she's a marten!"

Wang nodded. He had heard the term and seen pictures.

"Is that a protected species?" Chen demanded, and didn't wait for an answer. "I guess it must be. If not, why is he bringing it here?"

Sadly Wang reflected that there had been a time when such a question could have been answered legitimately in more ways than one: *as a pet for my grandson, to be trained to rid our home of rats, to be bred so the pelts of her young can be made into hats and gloves. . . .*

That, though, had been before the tidal wave of humankind turned half of China into wasteland. He himself was married, to his cost, but he had not taken up his legal chance to become a father because he didn't want to be guilty of causing yet more desolation. To his wife, of course, he claimed it was because modern advances in biology would soon ensure a hundred percent guarantee that their sole child would be a son—and wasn't that what her mother had dreamed of all her life? Ho often taunted him for waiting, pointing out that there was always a fifty-fifty chance, but since his own child was a girl his gibes rang hollow.

"All right," Inspector Chen said after a pause, raising his radio. "I'll warn base that we're bringing this lot in. Ho, put handcuffs on the old fool. Wang, you carry the whatever-it's-called. You!"—more loudly, to the onlookers. "Move on! The fun's over, such as it was."

At that point Ho spoke up unexpectedly. Much as he claimed to look down on countryfolk as a rule, it wasn't the first time he had boasted of special knowledge due to rural ancestors. "Be careful!" he warned. "I know about martens. They can give you a nasty bite. This one's sure to be in a vile temper after being shut up hungry for so long. Matter of fact, I'm surprised it hasn't chewed its way out of the hamper!"

Wang hesitated. He was about to say that the animal didn't look very aggressive when he was forestalled by Lin.

"Who said I kept her hungry? I'm not so stupid that I'd

starve a valuable animal! She's worth much more alive than dead!"

He gave no indication of whether he wanted the marten alive because she was to be bred from, or for the more prosaic reason that no decent Chinese housewife would feed her family on flesh she herself had not seen killed.

"Is that true?" Chen demanded. Wang applied his eye to the hole in the hamper-lid again.

"Yes, it does seem to have something to eat. Some kind of fruit, by the look of it. Right?" he added to Lin.

Before the old man could reply, Ho interrupted. "Martens are carnivores," he scoffed. "They eat meat, not fruit."

"They eat that sort!" Lin snapped. "Same as we do!"

"What sort?" Chen demanded. Lin shrugged.

"That sort! We call it 'good-with-rice' because it is."

Wang felt a faint prickling on the back of his neck. He sensed something unfitting to the proper order of things. By his frown Chen did also. Having contacted base to warn of their arrival, the inspector added a request for someone to take charge of the marten, and then, after a brief hesitation, a further request, this time for information about kinds of fruit that carnivores might eat. The sense of bewilderment at the far end was almost audible.

That done, he returned his radio to its clip at his belt.

"Right!" he barked. "Let's go!"

THE TOWER OF STRENGTH

. . . pharmacy was typical of its kind: long dark wooden counters with many drawers below; more drawers in the cabinets that lined the walls, holding leaves, roots, stalks, flowers, seeds, bark, fungi; organs from animals, birds, reptiles, fish; dried blood, musk, gall, even dung, especially from birds; at intervals, work-stations where the staff weighed out these and other substances on shiny new electronic scales, then comminuted them in electric grinders—to the annoyance of many of the customers who thronged the premises, for they were as conservative as their devotion to traditional medicine indicated, and felt that some subtle essence might be lost from a drug if it were not pounded with an iron pestle in a marble mortar. But the only pestle and mortar to be seen reposed in the display window, gathering dust alongside a set of old-style balances with wide shallow pans of tarnished brass.

One thing, however, absolutely had not changed: the smell. From earliest childhood Wang could testify to that. Never the same yet never different, the aroma of a pharmacy was unique.

And it seemed to make people more than usually discourteous and pushful—or perhaps that stemmed from the anxiety due to being ill, or having someone ill in the family. Under most circumstances the citizens of Guangzhou retained some of their ancient respect for authority, and would move aside at the sight of a police uniform, but in here he could scarcely take two steps together.

Eventually he worked his way to the nearer of the two cash desks, whose occupant seemed harassed enough to be the manager or even the owner. This was one place where the wind of progress had not yet stirred the dust; his fingers were flickering across an abacus.

Leaning forward, Wang said sharply, "They told me at the university that I could find Dr. Soo Long here."

The manager, if such he were, looked as though he had bitten a sour fruit. He gave an inexact jerk of his head: *Over there!* Wang glanced around, but saw nothing but customers, staff, and a closed door.

"Where—?" he began. The other sighed.

"In the stock-room, being a nuisance as usual."

"Through that door?"

"Yes!" And back to counting, calculating, making change.

A senior clerk was supervising a junior one as they unpacked a box containing several jars and packets. They tensed as Wang entered, as though the box might contain something illegal, but if so it was none of his business, today at any rate. He stared around. Obviously this room's primary use was for checking and dividing up incoming supplies before transfer to the shop. At any rate the only other person visible—visible in the sense of giving a recognizable human shape to clothing, but in fact concealed head to toe by a green coverall and a black hood—was carrying out some kind of test on some kind of sample, using a machine that printed out density graphs on scaled paper.

"I'm looking for Dr. Soo Long," Wang announced. The third person turned, removing the black hood.

"I'm Sue Long. What do you want?"

The words were in good Cantonese, albeit with a Hong Kong accent. But the face was wrong—thin and pale under near-white hair cut very short—and so of course was the sex. For a long moment Wang could only stare.

"Well?" Dr. Long said impatiently. Wang recovered himself and fumbled in a pouch that hung at his belt.

"Uh . . . Sorry to bother you, Dr. Long, but—uh—your department at the university said I could find you here. It's about this."

He held out one of the partly gnawed fruits they had recovered from the marten's hamper.

The machine at Dr. Long's side uttered a beep and spilled ten extra centimeters of paper tape, unmarked; the end of a run. Excusing herself, she extracted a sample of what looked like tree-bark—there was a strong whiff of industrial solvent—sealed it in an envelope and clipped it to the paper tape before accepting the fruit. For a moment she didn't seem to know what to make of it: then the light dawned.

"Whose teeth? Some sort of cat—? No, that's not a feline dentition. What?"

"A marten."

"Really!" She raised the fruit to her nose and gave a cautious sniff. "That's a peculiar odor for a fruit, isn't it? But I guess it would have to be, to tempt a carnivore like a marten."

Wang felt a stir of relief at not having to explain why she ought to be interested. "You don't recognize it, then?" he ventured.

"No, I've never run across anything similar. How did you come by it?" She was turning it over in her hands—which, he suddenly noticed, were gloved.

He recounted the morning's events. With every moment of the narrative she grew tenser. At the end she burst out, "Where did you say this peasant hails from, this Lin?"

He repeated the address on the man's greasy ID papers.

"Is that so!" She whistled astonishment, by Chinese stan-

dards a most unwomanly act. But Wang had already begun to
suspect that he was dealing with a person who didn't fit pi-
geonholes. "Well!" she added after a moment. "I guess I'd
better pay your inspector a visit."

"Your work—?"

"Some of it's waited thousands of years. Another day or
two won't hurt."

She was peeling off her gloves as she spoke. Noticing his
eyes on them, she explained, "To make sure cells from my
skin don't contaminate the specimens. This too, of course"—
meaning the coverall which she now also discarded, revealing
an open-necked shirt and denim shorts appropriate for the
end-of-summer weather if not for the starchier citizens of
Guangzhou. With brisk, practiced motions she disconnected
her machine, which folded, gathered up her day's findings,
stowed the lot in a satchel and headed for a rear door.

"You don't need to tell the boss—?"

"He's not my boss, praise be! This way!"

In an alley beyond the door, chained to an iron grille, stood
a Kawasaki motorcycle. From the satchel she drew a crash-
helmet made of unilatrium, deformable in two dimensions but
rigid in the third. She didn't have a spare for Wang, but the
traffic police were unlikely to challenge a fellow officer. Be-
striding the machine, thumb poised over the starter, she interrupted herself.

"You do have more of those fruits?"

"Yes, the old man had a few left. He seems to have survived the whole trip on them. Plus rice and tea, of course."

He hesitated. Mistaking his reaction, Dr. Long said, "If
you don't fancy riding with me—"

"No, no! That's quite all right." He had to lick dry lips
nonetheless; the prospect of being a passenger on any motorbike in Guangzhou traffic would have been daunting. "No, I
was just wondering about something." He settled himself gingerly on the pillion.

"What?"

"Why you—uh—whistled when you were told where Lin
comes from."

They were under way with impressive smoothness. Also

quietness; they needed to raise their voices mostly because of the traffic.

"Where's the likeliest place in all of China to find an unknown fruit?"

Light dawned. "Green Phoenix Forest?"

"Where else?"

For a while she concentrated on driving while he pondered the implications. Then, while they were stopped at a red light, he ventured, "If you don't mind my asking, why did the university send me looking for you when I told them what we'd found?"

"Didn't they explain about my work?"

"No, I was expecting to meet some sort of specialist or consultant acting as an advisor to the pharmacy."

"That's not my line." The light changed; they hummed on, but only as far as the next. Walking would barely have been slower. "You know we're wiping out one species after another—plants, animals, insects?"

"Yes, of course. Aren't some of them supposed to be a terrible loss because they could have given us new drugs and even new types of food?"

"They're a terrible loss in any case, but you've got the idea. Well, using a technique I developed jointly with colleagues in America, I'm trying to recover the DNA, the germplasm, of plants so rare they may already be extinct. Obviously, the likeliest place to find them is a pharmacy like the Tower of Strength. They don't like me delving around in their expensive stock, but if there's the slightest chance we may catch a vanishing species before it's gone forever. . . . And whenever I get an opportunity—though this is mainly for my own interest—I also look for DNA in dragon-bones."

Those were an ingredient in many expensive traditional medicines: dinosaur bones occasionally, typically those of more ordinary animals inscribed with questions in ancient times, prior to divination and the casting of lots to foretell the future. Wang assumed she was referring more to the former.

"Most people say it's futile," she added. "But you never know."

•   •   •

Within five minutes of entering the police station Wang found out why the university had recommended calling in Dr. Long. She raked Lin with questions like a salvo of guided missiles, each striking to the heart of a new subject. She lost a few minutes being sidetracked by what Wang had half-grasped at the station: Lin's excuse was his wife's illness. What it might be was unclear—some form of cancer, possibly. However, since the lady wasn't here it seemed pointless to pursue the matter. Dr. Long was in any case far more interested in this curious fruit that appealed even to martens.

"And foxes, and cats, and dogs, and stoats and weasels!" Lin insisted, in hopes maybe of mitigating his inevitable punishment. A young man from the city zoo had turned up to claim the marten just before Dr. Long and Wang arrived, and was impatiently waiting for permission to remove it thither and go home.

"And humans," Wang said dryly.

Dr. Long glanced at him.

"Yes," she said in an indecipherable tone. "And humans . . . Tell me please"—to the young man from the zoo—"is this animal healthy?"

A shrug. "So far as I can tell without a full examination. It seems a bit lethargic, but that may just be because its belly is full."

"Yes." Dr. Long pondered, tapping one of her large white front teeth with a fingernail. "Keep it under observation for the time being," she continued at last. "Collect its urine, collect its droppings, above all preserve any vomitus. I want to hear of any unusual behavior the moment it happens. I'll give you my card."

Taking umbrage at being ordered about by a woman, and in particular a round-eye, the man from the zoo bridled and would have spoken but for intercepting a glare from Inspector Chen. Dr. Long either did not notice or successfully affected so.

"As to the fruit," she went on, glancing at the window (why, it was growing dark—where had the day gone?), "I need it at my lab. I want to run a sample through an analyzer, then beam the results to the States and have them checked against a database. If it's something already known, only I never heard of it, that'll be great. Otherwise. . . ."

Inspector Chen cleared his throat. "Otherwise?" he repeated.

"Otherwise, Inspector, we may have an international lawsuit on our hands. It wouldn't be the first time this country has released to the environment a genetically modified organism without proper safeguards, let alone FAO approval."

Wang reacted to her choice of words before he could stop himself.

"*We* may?"

Dr. Long glanced coolly at him. "I'm Chinese, Mr. Wang. For all that I was born in the States. I married a Chinese, moved here, took his nationality . . . And stayed on when he ran away. I trust that answers all your obvious questions?"

Wang wished very much he could vanish on a trapeze of clouds, like Monkey.

"Right! Now if you'll kindly let me have the fruit, I'll sign a pro-tem receipt. I'll fax you an official one when I get to the lab, on behalf of the university. Don't let the old man go, will you?"

"Of course not"—stoutly from Chen. "He'll be hauled up in court and duly sentenced for—"

"Oh, forget that! He's far too important to be sent to jail!"

Lin brightened visibly, like the sun emerging from a cloud.

"He's going to help us find the source of the fruit—*first!*"

The sun went in again.

Swinging her satchel with the remaining fruit in it, Dr. Long nodded to the company and headed for the door. Wang spoke up.

"Just a moment! I think I ought to come with you!"

Startled, Chen glanced at his watch. "You should have gone off shift half an hour ago," he objected. "Though you're quite right, of course. If this fruit is unique, at least around here—"

"Then if someone were to snatch Dr. Long's bag," Wang broke in, "it would be a disaster. I don't mind escorting her." (No mention of the real reason he would rather not go home). "To be honest, what she has told me about her work has sparked my interest. I'd like to find out more if she can spare the time."

Chen hesitated, but saw no way to object. He often commended his subordinates for displaying interest in unusual subjects that might one day prove relevant to police work, and who could say that this would not turn out useful in connection with protected animals and illegal plants? In any case, he was forestalled.

"That's very kind of you, Mr. Wang. I carry a teargas pistol, of course, but it's not a practical weapon on a motorbike. And you're absolutely right; it would be a disaster if we lost this fruit."

"You sound as though . . ." Chen began.

"As though I'm worried? Yes, Inspector, I am. I've lived in this country more than ten years. I've specialized in protected species of all kinds, animal and vegetable, terrestrial and aquatic. If there were anything in the literature about a fruit that not only humans but martens can thrive on, I'd know. I think. But I don't."

Handing Wang her satchel, retrieving from it her gauntlets and helmet before letting him sling it over his shoulder, she followed him back to the police-station parking lot.

THE UGLY TURTLE

. . . was the city-wide nickname for the floating extension to Guangzhou University, whose curving roof-plates bordered with guttering to catch precious rain did somewhat resemble a turtle's carapace. Pressure on living-space was not yet as intense as in Hong Kong or many cities in Japan, but rather than sacrifice more precious agricultural land for a new and badly needed biology laboratory it had been decided to moor it, along with a student dormitory and extra staff accommodation, to the bank of the Zhujiang, there being far less river traffic than formerly. Access to the area was restricted, at least in theory, but in practice there were so many people with a valid excuse to come and go that security was a joke. There wasn't even a guard on duty at the end of the gangway where they dismounted. Wang pushed the Kawasaki to the alcove where it was kept, frowning at such laxness.

At least the laboratory Dr. Long then led him to was properly protected. In a large room smelling faintly of ozone computer screens glowed and automatic machinery, somewhat like the device she had been using at the Tower of Strength, purred unattended. She began by transferring her day's findings to a university in America, via satellite, a process that took only moments. Then she chose from her satchel one of Lin's unbitten fruit and fed it to a machine that automatically cut sections off it, examined their macrostructure, triturated them, fractionated the pulp and peel separately using eight different solvents each at four temperatures, recording everything at every stage. . . . Used as he was to analyzers in police-work, for DNA comparison and the like, Wang could not help being impressed by the speed and compactness of Dr. Long's equipment.

"There," she said at length. "Now I could do with some tea. Do you have time for a cup before you leave?"

Suddenly Wang realized he was hungry, thirsty, and tired. He accepted gratefully, and she led him to her room, off a corridor beyond the lab. It was as spartan as the police barracks he had lived in before his marriage. Waving him to a chair, she filled a kettle, made tea, opened a box of crackers, and sat down with a barely suppressed yawn.

He did honestly want to learn more about her work, but now that he had the chance he felt too nervous. This self-assured young woman—she couldn't be more than five years older than his own count of thirty—was utterly different from anyone he had met before. He did at least manage to ask how long it would take to identify the fruit.

"Don't expect miracles," was the wry answer. "Amazing changes can be brought about by altering even a tiny sequence of DNA. You know we're more than 99 percent identical with chimpanzees? But there's quite a difference, isn't there?"

"Do you think it's a—a natural mutation?"

"How natural is natural? If it does come from Green Phoenix—well, admittedly they were desperate when they launched the project, but no one had the faintest idea how genes like those would react in the wild, especially the ones for accelerated growth. There are some which, if they got into bac-

teria. . . . Still, it hasn't happened yet. Maybe we'll be lucky.
Maybe Gaea is on our side again. More tea?"

"No, I must be going. Thank you very much." He rose, re-
signed to home, to the cramped flat always full of his wife's
complaints.

"Did you take the key out of my bike?"

"I'm sorry—I thought you had."

"No, I had to leave it in or the front wheel would have
locked and you couldn't have pushed it. I'll collect it now."

And at the point where he turned for shore and she toward
where the bike was kept, they wished each other good night.

Halfway down the gangway he heard her exclaim, and
glanced back. Barely visible in shadow, a man was bending
over her machine. Startled by her approach, he jerked upright.
Light flashed: a long-bladed knife.

Wang clawed for a grip on his baton, wishing he were allowed a gun, but before he had taken his first step in Dr.
Long's direction he was rushed by two other men from the
shore end of the gangway. Swinging wildly, he clouted the
first on the head hard enough to make him curse and sway, but
the second kicked his legs from under him and then kicked
him again in the belly, driving the wind out of him.

For a long moment all he could think of was that now he
would never know the truth about the marten and the Green
Phoenix fruit.

Then there was a scream, a shout, the noise of feet on the
steel floor. He felt something warmly wet splatter his bare
arms as a man stumbled past him, ordering the other two to
follow. But he had no chance to see what any of them looked
like.

He shut his eyes and spent a long and welcome moment
working his belly-muscles free of agony.

"Are you all right?"

It was Dr. Long's voice. Wang managed to drag himself to
his feet, using the rail for support. "How—?" he husked.

"You saved my life."

"What?"

"For official purposes!" she snapped. Feeling something
sticky on his skin, he glanced down. It looked black in the ar-

tificial light but it had to be blood. Shed by the man who had staggered past from the direction of where the bike was kept. . . . Comprehension dawned.

"Not his knife. Yours."

"Correct. I'd better lose it before your chums show up."

"They won't have been told yet," he objected.

"Of course not! Who likes getting mixed up in police business? Same everywhere, you know: in any American city you can be beaten to death with a hundred people in earshot . . . But you've got to radio in, haven't you?"

"I—uh—I suppose so."

"Go ahead, then. It'll look suspicious if you delay. Don't mention a knife. Say you came to the bike with me and when he jumped us you cracked him in the face and made his nose bleed, or split his lip, or something."

"But you actually cut him, didn't you? How deep?"

"How should I know?"—angrily. Then, relenting: "Yes, pretty deep. I don't suppose he'll get very far."

"Then the story won't hold water. If they find him alive—"

"It's *got* to hold water!" She turned blazing eyes on him. "I can't afford to be hamstrung by some petty criminal!"

He was on the point of saying something to the effect that robbery with violence wasn't so petty, when the look on her face prevented him. He said after a moment, "I'll do what I can."

"Good. Then I'd be obliged if you could stick around for a while." A quaver crept into her self-assured tone. "I never hurt anyone before. I mean not really meaning to hurt."

"He was going to steal your bike," Wang grunted, poising his radio.

"That's what he wanted me to think."

He checked as the implications sank in.

"What he wanted you to think?" he repeated slowly.

"The key was in. If all he was after was the bike he could have got away before I interrupted. I ride it down the gangplank all the time."

"What else, if not theft?"

"I don't know. But I can think of one peculiar thing that's happened today." She passed a weary hand across her hair. "Oh, maybe I'm paranoid, but a lot of high-ranking politicians staked their futures on Green Phoenix. And bioengineering has erupted from nowhere to become a multi-billion business. . . . Are you never going to call in?"

Wang came back to himself with a start. Her comments had brought to mind countless rumors he himself had heard ever since Green Phoenix was first announced. It was the most ambitious reclamation project in history—not just reforestation, but an attempt to create on ruined hills a unique, precisely calculated mix of trees, shrubs, grasses, epiphytes, saprophytes, fungi, every kind of plant, together with the micro-organisms necessary for their proper coexistence. All the plants were to be of proven benefit to humanity, whether by supplying food, or timber, or fibers, or drugs, or dyes; but all of them had been modified. That was what frightened people. Probably that was what was troubling Dr. Long. Though—the thought ran through Wang's mind as he whispered into his radio—how could anyone in Guangzhou have learned about the mysterious fruit so quickly, let alone where it was being taken? Could one of the regular traders in endangered animals have been waiting at the station? Unlikely; they were too recognizable. An agent, perhaps a new recruit, who had sneaked away baffled? How about the man who had tried to steal Lin's belongings? No, he would scarcely have been so blatant if he worked for one of the big traffickers . . .

Meantime he was uttering mechanical words.

There proved to be a patrol car within two blocks. It rounded the corner, siren wailing. He knew one of its crew by sight. They recorded statements, took samples of the drying blood, sighed over the unlikelihood of finding the culprit unless he was silly enough to get arrested on a different charge, and eventually gave Wang a lift to a stop on the bus-line serving his home district. Weary to the marrow, hungry and thirsty all over again, he returned to a note from his wife: since he hadn't turned up at the promised time she had gone to her mother's for the evening and might or might not be back.

He ate what he could find, stepped under a cool shower, and fell asleep as soon as he lay down. He dreamed about unwholesome creatures emerging from the Zhujiang and feeding on shiny metallic fruit that had erupted all over the Ugly Turtle like so many boils.

On arriving for work exactly one week later, he was summoned before Chief Superintendent Tan. Wondering what he might have done wrong, he obeyed at once. Others were already there. Inspector Chen's presence as his squad commander was no surprise, but with him was Dr. Long. She looked not just tired but exhausted, indeed visibly older, as though as many years had passed for her as days had for the rest of the world.

The chief spoke up without preamble. "Your report about last week's incident at the University Biological Department was incomplete," he rumbled. Wang felt a stir of apprehension, assuming that the man Dr. Long had stabbed must have been found and recounted his side of the story. But he was wrong.

"Dr. Long tells me your prompt intervention saved her life. You made no mention of the fact."

"Sir, I think—"

"There's no need to be modest," Dr. Long sighed. "I've said you deserve a commendation."

"Well, that's—uh . . ." His voice faltered from incredulity.

"It's too late to object," Tan said. "Sit down, by the way." Waving at a vacant chair, he leaned back in his own.

"Dr. Long has come with an unusual request," he went on, "but before I tell you what it is I gather there's something else she wants to say. Dr. Long?"

"Thank you." She rubbed her eyes, suppressing a yawn, and interpolated with a grimace, "Sorry, but I haven't had much sleep lately. I received a preliminary report from the States about that peculiar fruit not long after you went home, and it's kept me busy ever since. It's—uh—disturbing."

Wang tensed. "Is the fruit in fact from Green Phoenix?"

"That's the strangest aspect of the matter. They say not. That's to say, everyone except Lin says not."

Chen's eyes widened; Wang noticed from the corner of his own gaze. Tan was rather better at controlling his expression, but even he showed the ghost of a reaction.

"On the other hand," Dr. Long pursued, "I've traced reports of something similar from other places: Singapore, Hawaii, Australia. Not documented, not scientifically investigated. Not until now, that is."

"I'm afraid I don't quite follow," Wang admitted, sensing that the others would welcome a confession of ignorance.

"The fruit derives from a plum. As you must have noticed, though, it doesn't smell like a plum."

"No, it smells more like—well—raw meat. Like pork, maybe."

"To judge by the way the marten ate it, it must taste like pork as well. In fact that's exactly what Lin compared it to. When the report from America came through I made myself very unpopular by having him hauled out of his cell and carted off to City Hospital. I thought I'd had a bright idea. I was wrong." She rubbed her eyes again and this time failed to overrule a yawn.

"He's in pretty good health all things considered. On the other hand his wife is not likely to last out the year. She has a massive fibroid growth in her abdomen. It was discovered last month when she was undergoing a hysterectomy. Lin was able to tell me where the operation was performed, and even the name of the surgeon. I made myself unpopular with him too, by routing him out before breakfast."

She drew a deep breath.

"In the far west the incidence of this type of growth has shown an upsurge in the past few years. Commonest continues to be stomach cancer attributable to a diet high in spiced and salted food. Next commonest are cancer of the lung, mouth, and colon. However, in a remarkably short time this new one has achieved fifth place. Stranger yet, it's confined exclusively to adult women. What do you make of that?"

Wang licked his lips. "Something to do with the fruit?" he hazarded. "You're implying it's been modified to make its flesh more like animal tissue. But in that case the UN—"

"Quite right: the forest is nominally under UN supervision, though in practice that boils down to satellite inspections and an occasional guided tour for VIPs. However, they are supposed to receive details of all gene-modifying experiments, and there is no mention of any such project in records made available to FAO."

"Accidentally, then? It seems so unlikely . . ."

"Under normal circumstances I'd agree." Despite her fatigue, Dr. Long's tone was regaining some of its former crispness. "However, as I remember telling you, these circumstances aren't normal."

Wang nodded thoughtfully. He could well understand what lay behind Dr. Long's disquiet. There were political and economic factors, too. He recalled her reference to the powerful individuals who had staked their futures on the success of Green Phoenix. They wouldn't like it at all if it turned out that one of their creations—or rather one of the creations they had lent their blessing to—was responsible for an epidemic of cancer.

Maybe Dr. Long had not been so paranoid after all when she wondered whether the thieves had really come after her Kawasaki.

There was a short silence. Eventually Tan cleared his throat. "Dr. Long is planning to visit Green Phoenix," he said.

She nodded. "I expect permission any day. For once the UN's right of inspection is to be fully implemented. There have been misgivings about Green Phoenix right from the start, not just overseas but in this country too. The full-bellies have never approved, have they?"

It struck Wang as incongruous to hear this blonde round-eye refer so casually to one of the unofficial factions in the present Chinese government. Some held that a surplus of food allowed the leisure to plot subversion, so it was safer to keep the people hungry, others that shortages made them angry enough to rebel. In allusion to an ancient proverb they were nicknamed "full-bellies" and "empty-bellies." Obviously massive reclamation projects were anathematical to the former.

But what did all this have to do with Policeman Wang? He cast an inquiring look at Tan. "Dr. Long?" the chief superintendent invited.

"Mr. Wang, I hope you don't mind, but . . . well, I don't have to tell you that if this fruit does in fact originate from Green Phoenix sundry persons will find themselves in jeopardy. They may take steps to protect their reputations. The way you reacted the other night made me feel I can rely on you. I've asked for you to be detached on special assignment. I want you, in effect, to be my bodyguard."

"There's no need to decide at once," Tan began. "When permission comes through for the trip—Is something wrong?"

"No, sir." Wang straightened to full height. "Thank you, Dr. Long, for the suggestion. I'd like to volunteer straight away."

That added the near-theft of the Kawasaki to the necessary preconditions.

THE GREEN PHOENIX

. . . was indeed green. Brilliant viridian, searing emerald, acid lime, sprawled out of the five valleys where it had initially been seeded, that tapered in the manner of fingers—or claws—and now had surmounted all but the barest and rock-iest of the intervening ridges. Sight of it drove away the headache that had plagued Wang since undergoing, last evening, a whole battery of said-to-be-necessary immuniza-tions.

For it was wrong!

He had never traveled this far west before, never seen with his own eyes how valleys like these might have looked in olden time. He had never viewed the aboriginal firs and pines, breathed the electric scent of waterfalls, heard the clamor of uncounted birds. But images of them were part of the world he had been born to, immortalized in the work of long-dead artists, shadowed forth in poetry and legend, implicit to this day in the characters he had been taught to write with.

That was gone.

Instead, here loomed a mass like fungus, like pondweed, like moss, as crudely bright as though it had been painted, as stark as though it had been carved from plastic foam. Staring at it from the elderly twin-engined army plane Dr. Long had conjured up for the last stage of their journey, he felt horrified.

And more so yet when he looked elsewhere, for all the sur-rounding land bore testimony to the greed of humankind: scarps denuded of soil and vegetation; terraces ordained by far-off bureaucrats on the grounds that global warming had made it feasible to grow rice in this area, which squandered months of work and slumped at the first drop of rain, leaving cascades of mud to dry and blow away; felled logs by the hectare, last remnants of a noble forest, destined for sale abroad to the profit of parasitic middlemen, seized in the nick of time and kept back so that the local folk might warm their homes in winter, heat their food, and mulch their little plots with bark and sawdust before erosion stole the last trace of their fertile land. It had been a bold decision, much applauded. Even so, thousands of the starving had had to be relocated or allowed to emigrate.

Now the Green Phoenix provided work—better: a sharable ambition—for about a million who remained. Nonetheless the process of attrition still went on. Wang had never thought before how small a number a million really was. No one knew, no one had known since the nineties of last century, the population of his home city. He could only repeat what he had been told, that it was about twice as great as in the year of his birth: four million, then? Mexico City comprised, so it was said, more than thirty million, of whom most were doomed to starve, catch AIDS, or die by violence.

Guangzhou was a cosmopolitan place—had been since before Wang was born. Twice a year it was invaded by thousands of foreign visitors attending the great trade fairs, and in between there were countless minor cultural events. Since 1997 it had been as open to the world as any part of China and much more than most. But never before had Wang felt the reality of the world beyond the frontiers of the Middle Kingdom as keenly as when watching—there was small point in listening, for he spoke no language but his own—Dr. Long invoking the support of colleagues in country after country through computers at the Ugly Turtle. Now as the plane droned toward the edge of the Green Phoenix, toward the little landing-strip that served the headquarters town whence it had been directed since the forest's inception, he sensed the first impact of what she had achieved. Waiting for them at the head of a group that included soldiers was a man in a dark civilian overcoat whose very posture betrayed a wish to be anywhere but here, and not merely because it was a dank and misty afternoon. Wang wondered whether he dared pose a question, but was saved the need. Dr. Long spoke up.

"I knew they were taking me seriously, but I didn't realize *how* seriously!"

The third passenger glanced at her. Wang had only met Dr. Bin on the flight from Guangzhou: a greying bespectacled man of middle height, introduced by Dr. Long as a fellow biologist but manifestly more than just another scientist. He exuded a scent of politics.

"That's Project Director Pao, isn't it?" he grunted. "I didn't know you'd met."

"We haven't," was the composed reply. "But can you imagine someone like him sending a deputy with all these rumors flying around?"

"Are you sure they've reached this far?" Bin countered. "If so, the next thing we can look forward to is lunatic headlines like GOODBYE TO HUNGER and FAREWELL TO FAMINE!"

Wang started. Even though he had gathered, from what Dr. Long had told him about her discussions with colleagues, that people had been surprised and impressed by what he still thought of as "Lin's fruit," he hadn't pictured it as having such global consequences.

Surely, though, she had implied that it also gave people cancer—or had he misunderstood somewhere along the line? Quite possibly. He had a new problem on his mind. When first proposed the notion of this trip had seemed like a heaven-sent escape from the misery of home. Now, however, he couldn't help hearing over and over his wife's threat that if he didn't come back on the promised day, not even one day later, she would sue for divorce.

He suspected that was what she secretly wanted. In today's China, where so many parents of the last generation had opted for a boy in the traditional manner, there was a multimillion surplus of males and any girl less ugly than a water-buffalo could pick and choose. People didn't even object to divorcées any longer. So . . .

There was no actual control tower. Circling, their pilot was speaking to a man on the ground with a hand-held radio, confirming the identity of those on board. Dr. Bin scanned the area. "Do you see any sign of the equipment?" he inquired.

Dr. Long shrugged. "No, but I imagine the roads are pretty rough in this part of the world. Pilot!"

"Yes?" The woman at the controls glanced over her shoulder.

"Ask if there's any news of the trucks bringing our gear."

A brief half-heard exchange; then: "Yes, the lead driver called in not long ago. They're just the other side of that hill. Should come in sight any moment. . . . Okay, we're cleared to land."

And set them down ahead of a plume of dust.

Unstrapping as the plane halted, checking his gun, Wang demanded, "Doctor, should I go ahead and—?"

"And make like a bodyguard?" she countered wryly. "I guess you can skip it this time. We have had enough support from the level-heads."

He looked blank. Impatiently she rapped, "Not the full-bellies! Not the empty-bellies! The few politicians in this benighted land who sometimes worry about our whole species instead of just their chance of taking their hens and hogs and horses up to heaven! Don't bet on their ascendancy lasting, though. We're here chiefly because the pro-UN faction got the jump on the others, the people who stand to lose the most if we have to firebomb Green Phoenix. . . . In practice of course it would have to be nukes, and even they might not do the job properly."

Wang shook his head foggily. "Doctor, I—"

"Ah, I doubt it'll come to that. I think we may be in time. *Just* in time. . . . By the way, stop calling me doctor. My name's Sue. Sorry if you don't approve of such informality, but I prefer it. Put it down to my American upbringing."

Tossing aside her seat-straps, she advanced toward the exit. Wang had intended to precede her but instead followed in a daze. What in the name of the heaven of the Jade Emperor was happening? Green Phoenix might have to be nuked? But it was supposed to be the harbinger of a renaissance not merely here but all around the world! In the newspapers, on TV and radio, everyone had been told what a marvelous achievement it was!

Yet there had been no mention of fruit with a flavor of meat that could be eaten by humans, and martens too. What else had Lin cited? Dogs, cats—what about pigs? Ah, but pigs ate anything anyway. The notion of saying goodbye to hunger, though . . .

He snatched himself back to the present. The newcomers were being greeted by the man in the dark coat, whose manner made it clear how convinced he was of his own importance and whose words, though superficially polite, contrived to imply that no matter how distinguished his visitors they should have given him more notice. In fact, right now he was taking time off from urgent work he was obliged to return to. However, this evening he had arranged a banquet in their honor, and he looked forward to talking at more leisure then. For the present, here were members of "my" staff who would show them to their regrettably less than luxurious lodgings. Have a pleasant stay!

And was gone to a waiting jeep, leaving them in the care of subordinates.

It was clear Dr. Bin was affronted by this reception, and might have spoken his mind but that in the same moment Wang caught the sound of trucks grinding along in low gear. He turned in search of the source, and exclaimed:

"Your equipment's here!"

Three olive-drab trucks were gingerly breasting the final rise. But the going was rocky, and there was plenty of time before their actual arrival to sort out essential details. Wang tried to keep up with both Bin, who was talking about power-supplies and use of comms facilities, and Sue (he must remember to address her thus) who was discussing opportunities for visiting the forest and the nearby settlements, and in the upshot lost track of both. He was still floundering when—"Wang!"

He snatched himself back to attention.

"Yes, doctor? Uh . . . I mean: Sue?"

Through her tiredness, which an in-flight doze had done little to relieve, a sketch for a smile.

"This is Mr. Li. He'll show you where we're being quartered. Make sure we have decent ablutions. Stash our gear and rejoin me."

"Right away!"

She hesitated. "One more thing. You're married, aren't you?"

Swallowing hard, Wang nodded, trying not to think how hollow that partnership was. Of course, Sue's husband—hadn't she said he "ran away"? So she might sympathize.

"You'll want to tell your wife you're okay. I asked for a billet close to comms HQ so I can get an early crack at incoming data. Traffic isn't too heavy yet, not like it'll be when we start filing our reports. Just say you're with me and they'll let you call home."

She turned back to the person she had been talking to before Wang had time to explain that even nowadays, even in Guangzhou, the pay of a lowly policeman did not stretch to such luxuries as a private phone.

Thereafter Wand had to piece together what was happening as best he could. He lent a hand setting up the scientists' equipment; the technicians who accompanied it were Chinese themselves, but they spoke half the time in English and much of the rest in Japanese, the languages—Wang presumed—of their machines' instruction manuals. Even what he heard in *putonghua* baffled him because it was couched in such obscure technical terms. Sue noticed, and sympathized; however, she had no time to elucidate more than snatches. A sense of witnessing history in the making with scarcely a clue to its present import grew ever more frustrating.

Moreover, his conviction that there were no such things as coincidences was undermined still further. What if the thieves had chosen another night to target Sue's Kawasaki? The man she had stabbed had been located in the hospital. He had confessed to attempted robbery, other members of the gang he belonged to—specialists in stealing cars and motorcycles to order—had been arrested, a decision had been taken very high up not to prosecute Sue . . . but was "very high" high enough? Or might she suddenly be hauled back to Guangzhou to face a charge of assault? She had plenty of powerful friends, that was obvious. He had had no faintest notion how influential a person he had been directed to meet in the malodorous surroundings of the Tower of Strength. But a person like himself could not even begin to guess how much of her allies' power was liable to evaporate for secret reasons and without warning.

He hoped things would go well for her. He had respected her from the first. Now he was coming to like her, too.

Also he didn't want to be ordered home.

Officially Project Director Pao was in charge of the scientific and technical personnel at Green Phoenix. *De facto* he was the governor of the whole area. He was of a stamp Wang recognized on sight, wondering whether Sue did also: a loyal party hack who had engineered promotion to high rank at an early age and spent the rest of his career trying to make sure no one noticed how poorly qualified he was for his post. An incursion by scientists with UN backing, though it had always been a possibility, had caught him unawares. In a frantic attempt to make it appear as though he had been prepared for the visitors and was still in complete control, he had improvised for them and the project staff a dinner that he termed a banquet to be held in the little town's single large building. Known as the Refectory, it was a relic of the desert days when the local population numbered few enough for all to eat under the same roof.

"Sort of Maoist," Sue grunted when Wang asked what she thought of the invitation. "But I guess it shows willing."

"Won't we have to eat local food?"—thinking of Lin's wife and her abdominal growth.

"Oh, it can't be immediately poisonous. . . . Tell me, what do you make of Pao, or have you not had time to decide?" When he hesitated she added, "In confidence, of course!"

Baldly he expressed his opinion. Sue heard him out, then smiled. "I do agree! He reminds me of a woman I once heard about who drove into another car rounding a blind bend. She told the police in a hurt tone, 'But there's never been a car there before!' "

Wang chuckled. Yes, here was someone who could cope with China.

On the whole the dinner was good, though one had to suspect that much of its ferocious spicing was a disguise for inferior ingredients rather than a display of Far Western cuisine. At any rate the variety was impressive; there was even local carp, raised in rainwater ponded by tree- roots and water-weed. And there was plenty of wine. Grapevines had been among the plants first specified for inclusion in the mix.

This and other information was imparted as each course was delivered. Pao, sowing the seeds of future embarrassment, had jumped to conclusions on hearing that Sue Long hailed from America and assigned an interpreter who commentated in accordance with instructions. Disconcerted to find she was fluent in both Mandarin and Cantonese, he wound up talking to Wang instead.

Unfortunately most of what the guy had to say consisted of what he had been expecting to tell Sue. Wang's mind wandered. So did his eyes. Eventually they settled on a man with a straggly beard, standing near the door, who didn't look like a member of Pao's staff. In general the latter were presentably dressed, so it was surprising to see a person in muddy overalls. Moreover he was not Chinese—not Han, at any rate. Part of Wang's training had consisted of learning to recognize racial types. This man he guessed to be a Uighur. If so, he wasn't all that far from home. On the other hand, muddy overalls at a formal dinner . . .

He interrupted a disquisition about the way bees had integrated into the Green Phoenix complex.

"Who's that fellow in dirty clothes?"

The interpreter stumbletongued, but it was a sufficient definition. "A harmless simpleton," he answered with a shrug. "Director Pao being a generous man, he lets the fellow work here in return for his keep. Like many of his sort he does have a way with plants."

Sue had overheard these remarks, Wang realized. They exchanged wry glances. Director Pao was not the likeliest person one would expect to hear accused of generosity.

"What's his name?" Sue inquired. The interpreter smiled.

"Oh, no one knows. He's dumb. We call him Greenthumb—*Ah!*" He whipped out cigarettes. News of the dangers of smoking seemed not to have penetrated here; at some unnoticed signal half of those present were lighting up. And a microphone was being placed in front of Pao.

Speechifying time.

• • •

Pao matched Wang's stereotype perfectly. He was a classic devotee of statistics. Figure after number after figure flowed from his lips: so much barren land reclaimed, so many trees planted, so many non-tree species added, so much food supplied to towns and villages over so wide an area, especially mushrooms and nuts. . . . Incontestably it was an impressive achievement, even though Pao hadn't heard about the dangers of tobacco either and promised that Green Phoenix's next five-year plan would incorporate hectarage to supply a cigarette factory.

As the climax to his address he cited the fact that this was the sole part of China where there had been no difficulty enforcing the one-child policy. This proved that an adequate standard of living could outweigh people's traditional desire for descendants to worship them when they became ancestors, ha-ha! He sat down looking smug.

Then they called on Sue.

She was trembling as she stood up, but during the time it took to adjust her microphone she overcame her nervousness. Her first words provoked a ripple of amusement that lasted just long enough.

"My apologies to the interpreters who were looking forward to a hard evening's work. . . . Project Director Pao, members of the Green Phoenix staff, no one could fail to acknowledge your ambition, your sincerity and your dedication. It has been well said that one should not waste breath on repeating what must be known to everyone already. In compliance with that principle I'll confine myself to asking why, Director, you omitted from your account of Green Phoenix's achievements what people hereabouts have nicknamed 'good-with-rice.' It's astonishing: a fruit containing as much protein as high-quality meat, even smelling and tasting like it, edible by humans and even wild carnivores. This is something the world has long been waiting for. . . . Director?"

A hushed and hurried consultation was in progress. At length not Pao but someone beside him declared, "You are mistaken! This has nothing to do with us! We know nothing about it!"

The hiss of indrawn breath was almost a gale. Scattered

voices framed confused questions, tailing away amid a welter of second thoughts. Wang tensed, staring around the broad low-ceilinged room.

Sue, still on her feet, was perspiring visibly although it was cooler here than in Guangzhou. Plainly she had anticipated this reaction, for she was rehearsing words under her breath, but now that confrontation was upon her she was having difficulty uttering them.

During this hiatus, a distracting movement. Visibly bored, Greenthumb was sidling toward the door. On the way he groped in a pocket, produced something Wang could not see clearly, made to lob it toward the head table—

Bodyguard. They make bombs so small now. A grenade?

"Wang!" Sue cried his name. Too late. His gun was leveled. Had gone off. He saw red in the distance. Time shrank. The thing thrown had fallen to the floor. He hurled himself atop it and awaited death.

Cries of terror were replaced with nervous laughter. Bewildered, he rolled over and sat up, feeling an utter fool.

The "grenade" was a fruit the size of a turkey egg. His falling on it had burst the skin and it was leaking juice the way Greenthumb was leaking blood from his chest. It smelt no less like meat.

In the meantime Pao and his associates had fled like panicked pigs.

THE UNSEEN OCTOPUS

. . . of modern communications twitched its tentacles on every continent in response to the reports from China. Hitherto, though, there had been no such grand public reaction as Bin had sourly predicted, with sensational headlines announcing the abolition of hunger. Merely, certain scientists and politicians who had earlier decided against visiting Green Phoenix reconsidered on learning that what to those few who had heard about it seemed a promising new food might have undesirable side-effects—worse, was not as might have been assumed the end product of a rigorously supervised research program: the former sensing the chance of a paper for a prestigious journal, the latter in search of re-election clout.

It being a time of relative quiet on the international scene, the shooting of Greenthumb provided an extra impulse that translocated Pao's domain from the science to the general news pages. Suddenly reporters from twenty countries were clamoring for Chinese visas.

There would have to be an inquiry, of course. Pao wanted to mount it himself and at once, perhaps in hope of getting rid of an inconvenient intruder; however, the prospect of it being in progress during an influx of still more influential visitors proved daunting. In the end he was instructed to await a lawyer from Beijing, pending whose arrival Wang was to be released in Sue's custody—a reversal of roles that might have been amusing had the situation not been so explosive.

Explosive. . . . How could I have mistaken a fruit for a bomb?

More embarrassed than he would have thought possible— in a sense, in shock himself—Wang begged Sue to accompany him to the infirmary where Greenthumb was awaiting transfer to a proper hospital where they would remove the bullet. They were allowed to see him, but he had been given massive doses of painkiller and his meager response was a blank, hurt expression: why?

There must be something I can do to make amends. . . .

As they were leaving Wang checked in mid-stride. "Sue!" he burst out. "Can you get someone to take a photograph of Greenthumb?"

"I guess so. Why?"

"I can't help wondering what he's doing here. A dumb simpleton that Pao gives work to out of charity? How much charity can you imagine Pao displaying in an average year? And he was the one who not only knew what you meant but had evidence to—to throw at you. Maybe you should have his picture scanned and circulated."

Even as he uttered them Wang found his words unconvincing. With so many people in the world . . .

Yet Sue was nodding. "You're no fool, are you?" she said cordially. "I'd been wondering about Greenthumb too, but that didn't occur to me. Now where do we find a Polaroid?"

And by the time pictures of the Uighur had been transmitted to the world's police agencies along with his fingerprints and DNA type, just in case, they were due to explore the body of the Phoenix.

On the hillsides mist had lingered well past dawn, but it cleared soon after Sue and Wang set forth in a convoy of three cross-country vehicles, leaving Bin to monitor incoming messages at the comms center. Their group included one of Pao's staff as a guide and a platoon of soldiers escorting technical equipment and the day's rations.

At first their route took them through small towns that had sprung up because of the new forest. Not long ago they had been mere villages, but despite the success hereabouts of the one-child policy their population had ballooned thanks to reverse emigration; unhappy in strange cities, thousands of local people who had moved away had applied to return, and permission had in general been granted. So many trees having been felled, most of their homes were burrowed into hillsides.

Inevitably hordes of the curious attended the visitors wherever they went. Inevitably that included markets, of which there was one in each little town. Inevitably Sue decided in the end to ask why she saw no "good-with-rice" on sale, risking a rebuff from their guide who would inevitably declare that it wasn't one of the Green Phoenix projects.

Wang saved her from embarrassment. He tapped her arm and pointed left, right, ahead, behind: low bushes, branches laden, before every house, thriving equally in the ground or in pottery tubs.

She whistled as she had back in Guangzhou. Why pay for what—as their guide grumpily admitted under pressure—grew anywhere and everywhere faster than a weed, yet, astonishingly, never seeded itself but needed to be planted by human hand?

Several late risers were emerging from their homes and culling the fruit for breakfast. No charge.

"Don't they know about the risk of cancer?" Wang whispered. "There must have been enough cases by now for someone to make a connection."

"False sago," was Sue's reply.

He shook his head uncomprehendingly.

"The starchy food we call sago comes from a palm-tree. There are other plants that yield something similar but aren't palms. They're cycads, a kind of giant fern. If you eat the wrong sort you fall ill, become paralyzed and finally die. That's been known for years. Yet people go on eating the stuff."

"Because they're starving?"

"More because they don't think it will happen to them."

"I see. . . . We're a short-sighted species, aren't we?"

"Yes."

Beyond that point their route took them deeper and deeper into the forest. There were no more villages or even settlements, only isolated buildings where half-trained "scientists" strove to keep track of the biological explosion taking place around them. Their equipment was old and ill maintained; they reminded Sue, she said, of priests rehearsing rituals whose purpose was forgotten. No wonder something like "good-with-rice" could emerge without anybody grasping its significance . . . although oddly enough they saw no sign of it within the forest.

Wang would have wished to inquire further. By now, however, he had been overwhelmed by the majesty of their improbable surroundings, and he was not alone. Earlier the soldiers had been arguing via the radio, the subject being why strangers were suddenly making such a fuss about "good-with-rice," which they had so long been accustomed to, but at length even the most talkative of them had been shamed into silence by the monstrous actuality of the Green Phoenix. He had had it in mind to make a good impression by commenting intelligently on what they were seeing—the intertwined branches that screened the sky, the creepers and mosses draping them, the birds, the insects, the snakes, the fungi, that polluted deliriously amid moist heavy-scented air a good five degrees warmer than at their starting-point. Sue, however, ignored him and everyone else, ordering the soldiers to take samples of this, that and the other, meantime recording comments of her own.

In the upshot Wang wasn't sorry. Passing trivial remarks about this amazing achievement would have seemed blasphe-

mous. No matter how artificial, how grafted-on, Green
Phoenix might look from afar, once you entered it there was
no doubt this was in a sense rebellion against the destructive-
ness of humankind—as though the clock had been turned
back by millions of years, to a time when the biosphere
teemed with unrealized potential.

Empty chatter in such a setting would have been like
drunken ballads on a temple altar.

On their return to base, shortly before sundown, they found
gangs of men lackadaisically mending potholes in the landing-strip, as though Pao had realized he must make preparations for a flood of visitors but so far had not yet thought of
anything more practical to do.

"Protective magic!" Sue said dismissively, and gave orders
for the care of the samples they had brought back before has-
tening, with Wang in tow, to rejoin Bin at the communications
center. By now it was so crowded with the additional equipment he had helped install yesterday that one had to sidle between a double row of monitors reporting incomprehensible
data. Without a word Bin handed Sue a wad of faxes. She rif-
fled through them, her near-white eyebrows rising higher and
higher.

"This is incredible!" she burst out as she finished the last.
"But there's one point these messages don't cover."

"You mean: is 'good-with-rice' really not part of the Green
Phoenix program?"

"Yes!"

"Apparently that's true." Bin, suddenly sounding very old,
leaned back and stretched as far as the press of equipment
would allow.

"Yet it can't possibly be an accident!" Sue clenched her
fists. "I can't believe in the sort of voluntary mutation that
would let a plant choose to become dependent on human intervention. Did you know it doesn't spread by itself, but always needs to be planted, whereupon it just erupts even in the
poorest of soils?"

"That fits with the predictions Allard has been making
about it in Paris. You saw."

Face the palest Wang had seen, she nodded. "He spent time

in Indo-China, didn't he? Knows a bit about Asian plants. . . . Any ideas about its origins?"

"You've got everything there is so far." Bin stretched again and this time dissolved into a frank yawn.

Sue re-read some of the faxes. Eventually, not looking up, she said, "I think I ought to take pity on Wang. It'll help to clarify my mind if I spell things out to someone. . . . Wang, has it struck you as odd that 'good-with-rice' has turned up in several countries—obviously spread by emigrés or sent to friends and relatives—yet not attracted much attention and certainly not the sort it deserves?"

Wang hesitated, then drew a deep breath.

"I don't think it's odd anymore," he declared. "I did at first, but now I've seen how quickly and easily you can make it grow. No one needs to raise it commercially—"

"But you'd expect people to try," Sue stabbed. "It's something you could take to market, sell for a good price—"

"More and more of us Chinese," Wang said, letting his voice dwell a moment on the last word, "have turned our backs on farming because our peasant ancestors led such hard lives. Yet there's something symbolic about making things grow. I feel it. Dr. Bin, do you see what I mean?"

The older man had been studying him curiously. "You're an unusual type for a policeman," he grunted now. "It was smart of Sue to pick you out. Yes, I can well believe that in Singapore and Australia and the other places where 'good-with-rice' has turned up it's been largely treated as a private treasure for the Chinese community. Do you have any inkling just what a treasure it may become?"

Wang hesitated anew. He said at last, "If it causes cancer—"

"Oh, that can probably be tailored out," Sue said with a shrug. "In spite of what Allard says."

"That being—?"

She was momentarily embarrassed. "Sorry! He thinks the carcinogenic factor is so integrated with its total genetic makeup that there's no way of isolating it. But he's only had samples for just over a week. I think he's being pessimistic. Don't you?"—handing back the faxes.

"In principle I have to agree," Bin acknowledged.

"Fine. Now I need a shower and something to eat before I—"

"Just a moment." Bin stretched for another sheet of paper. "Over in the States and Europe they set some of the search parameters extremely wide, and there's a phrase that keeps cropping up right on the fringes. Does the term 'peasant's son' mean anything to you?"

"I don't think so," Sue said, staring. "Origin?"

"Maybe the old USSR. But it's deep stuff from multiply encrypted databanks."

She frowned. "For a moment I seemed to recall. . . . No, it's gone. Maybe it'll come back to me when I'm less tired. Coming with us?"

"No, I'm not hungry yet. I had a good lunch."

"As you like. Come on, Wang! By the way, I don't suppose 'peasant's son' means anything to you, does it? No? Pity!"

During the meal Sue's enthusiasm got the better of her fatigue. She enlarged on the possibilities inherent in "good-with-rice." According to her it represented a credible solution to famine, and despite reservations Allard and other foreign scientists were coming to agree. Over and over she harked back to the astonishing circumstances that it had been under everybody's nose certainly for several years without its significance being appreciated. She talked so much Wang dared to remind her that she needed to eat, as well, and eventually she remembered to.

Just as they were finishing their meal a girl brought a folded note from Bin. Sue erupted to her feet, oversetting her chair, and ran off. Perforce Wang followed. He caught up with her in the command center, leaning over Bin's shoulder as he tapped at a keyboard beneath a monitor that showed . . .

Greenthumb's face. Younger, clean-shaven, but unmistakable. And a name. Not a Chinese one.

A-er Mu.

"An inspiration, Wang," Sue whispered softly. "Thank *you!*"

And promptly forgot him as, together with Bin, she embarked on the second extraordinary journey of today, this time through an electronic jungle as rife with strange amazing growths as was Green Phoenix.

"Amnesium! I didn't know they'd perfected it!"

Wang snapped back to wakefulness. He had been leaning against a stack of computers just the right height to support him, luckily without doing any harm. What had Sue just said? He struggled to gather scraps of sense from Bin's reply. The two of them were staring at a screenful of forking lines dense and various as the canopy of Green Phoenix. Under her breath Sue whispered, "God, look how it ramifies!"

"Leave it," Bin said incisively. "Now we have a lead to 'peasant's son' we'd better follow through."

"Sure, go ahead. . . . It was staring us in the face! I'd heard of it—even I had!—and I thought it was KGB disinformation!" Sue clenched her fists. "No wonder there's no record of 'good-with-rice' in the Green Phoenix files!"

Wang could contain himself no longer. He burst out, "You've found out who Greenthumb is?"

"Just a moment!" Sue rapped, eyes fixed on a new display. It was in alphabet, not character, and it took Wang a moment to recognize it as *puthonghua* in pinyin, not some mysterious foreign tongue. But what could an ancient Russian legend have to do with the Green Phoenix?

Oh. Of course. It doesn't. "Good-with-rice" wasn't part of the Green Phoenix program. . . .

"That fits," Sue sighed, turning away from the screen. "To think I was making all those wild predictions over dinner! Wang, I'm sorry! Bin has dug up the truth, and it's not pleasant!"

Taking a deep breath, she drew herself to full height and turned to confront him.

"The old USSR boasted some of the world's finest biologists. It also boasted some of the most paranoid politicians, ignorant of science but convinced that by threats they could force their scientists to produce any desired result. Given the speed with which the Soviets came up with an atom-bomb and then an H-bomb they did have grounds. . . .

"In the early days of bioengineering a group of enthusiastic young biologists volunteered to work at a base in Siberia where the dream was to develop organisms that could survive on Mars. This was the heyday of space exploration; their greatest hero was Gagarin.

"But that was under Khrushchev. Following his downfall the project was canceled. However, the scientists were not allowed to disperse. They were set to work on something new.

"On the Soviet Union's eastern frontier loomed not so much an enemy as a rival. A political rival, certainly, but more importantly a rival for *land*. Never mind what politicians might say, sooner or later population pressure in China was bound to force an invasion to the west.

"If it wasn't stopped."

She passed a weary hand over her short hair. "Sorry if I don't make perfect sense," she interpolated. "Bin has found the way to such amazing data that I haven't digested them yet."

Forcing tension out of her limbs by sheer willpower, she resumed.

"And the way they settled on to stop that invasion was brilliant. What drives people to migrate? They are too numerous for the land to support. So a research program was decreed. Find a means, the orders said, both to feed these Chinese hordes despite the way they're ruining their land, *and at the same time to stop them breeding*.

"And they did it."

Wang hadn't noticed, but several "good-with-rice" rested on a dish in reach of Bin, who now passed one to Sue.

"This," she said, hefting it, "is the result. And I'm prepared to believe Allard now. Now that I know Greenthumb was once A-er Mu. That was a famous name in certain circles, last century. He was director of the research station where this stuff was designed. The estimate was that it would take about thirty years to do its work. Someone recalled the legend of the Russian hero who couldn't walk till he was thirty-three and then became the greatest defender of his people: Ilya Mouromets. His surname means 'peasant's son.' So that was what they called the research station—sited near the Chinese border, in Uighur country, which is where A-er Mu hails from.

"When the Soviet Union collapsed, the project was still incomplete. But it had progressed amazingly. Not only was the artificial fruit viable—it tasted good, it was genuinely nour-ishing, *and* it incorporated carcinogenic genes capable of sur-viving the digestive process."

"And triggered in the host," said Bin in a rusty-sounding voice, "by the hormones associated with pregnancy—any pregnancy, even one that doesn't go to term. No wonder Pao can boast about the success of the one-child program in this area! All mothers develop carcinoma of the ovaries!"

"There were many ultra-secret projects," Sue resumed, "that the ex-bosses of the USSR didn't want to come to world attention. Prudently they had made preparations. I imag-ined—along with practically everybody else—that not only was 'peasant's son' a disinformation exercise, but amnesium as well. Having found out who Greenthumb used to be, I now believe they had created exactly what they claimed: a drug to wipe the memory of higher faculties including speech while leaving intact basic ones like walking and eating. In the twi-light of Soviet power they allegedly sent out KGB poisoners to administer it by force, lest research they had conducted on political prisoners might be exposed. It all sounds very Russ-ian, hmm?"

Wang shook his head confusedly. This was too far beyond his everyday world. All he could think of was that he had shot the man they were talking about and no one had yet told him whether he had done wrong.

Suddenly Sue sounded bitter. "You were right," she con-cluded, tossing up and catching the fruit Bin had passed her.

Wang shook his head in bafflement.

"This is not the cure for famine. It's exactly what you took it for, exactly what you might expect from our sick species.

"It's a weapon."

THE HARE

. . . dwells in the moon and guards the elixir of immortality. But it was traded for the right to father sons; hence he is the patron of inverts, and only women celebrate his feast.

Wang thought about the hare for a while. Then he husked, "People are going to go on eating it, aren't they?"

Sober nods. With feigned cheerfulness Bin said, "Yes, it's

spread too far to call it back. But there's a chance that some day, *pace* Dr. Allard, we may eliminate the carcinogenic genes. Or invent a better version! And, you know, something that sterilizes people only after they have had the chance to breed . . . it could be no bad thing."

But Sue wasn't listening. She was turning "good-with-rice" over and over in her hands, much as she had the gnawed one Wang had shown her at the Tower of Strength, and whispering, "It's a weapon. It's a weapon, and we poor fools imagined it was food."

SUNKEN GARDENS

Bruce Sterling

*One of the most powerful and innovative new talents to
enter SF in recent years, a man with a rigorously worked-
out and aesthetically convincing vision of what the future
may have in store for humanity, Bruce Sterling as yet may
still be better known to the cognoscente than to the SF-read-
ing population at large, in spite of recent Hugo wins. If you
look behind the scenes, though, you will find him everywhere, and he had almost as much to do (as writer, critic,
propagandist, aesthetic theorist, and tireless polemicist)
with the shaping and evolution of SF in the '80s and '90s as
Michael Moorcock did with the shaping of SF in the '60s; it
is not for nothing that many of his peers refer to him, half
ruefully, half admiringly, as "Chairman Bruce."*

*Sterling sold his first story in 1976. By the end of the
'80s, he had established himself, with a series of stories set
in his exotic "Shaper/Mechanist" future, with novels such
as the complex and Stapeldonian* Schismatrix *and the well-
received* Islands in the Net *(as well as with his editing of the
influential anthology* Mirrorshades: The Cyberpunk Anthology *and the infamous critical magazine* Cheap Truth*),
as perhaps the prime driving force behind the revolutionary
"cyberpunk" movement in science fiction, and also as one
of the best new hard science writers to enter the field in
some time. His other books include a critically acclaimed
nonfiction study of First Amendment issues in the world of
computer networking,* The Hacker Crackdown: Law and
Disorder on the Electronic Frontier, *the novels* The Artificial Kid, Involution Ocean, Heavy Weather, *and* Holy Fire,
a novel in collaboration with William Gibson, The Difference Engine, *and the landmark collections* Crystal Express
and Globalhead. *His most recent books include the omnibus
collection (it contains the novel* Schismatrix *as well as most
of his Shaper/Mechanist stories)* Schismatrix Plus, *a new*

novel, Distraction, *and a new collection,* A Good Old-Fashioned Future. *His story "Bicycle Repairman" earned him a long-overdue Hugo in 1997, and he won another Hugo in 1997 for his story "Taklamakan." He lives with his family in Austin, Texas.*

Here he gives us a ringside seat for a strange and deadly biotech contest between competing ecosystems, a literal battle of worlds, in which the stakes are life itself. . . .

Mirasol's crawler loped across the badlands of the Mare Hadriacum, under a tormented Martian sky. At the limits of the troposphere, jet streams twisted, dirty streaks across pale lilac. Mirasol watched the winds through the fretted glass of the control bay. Her altered brain suggested one pattern after another: nests of snakes, nets of dark eels, maps of black arteries.

Since morning the crawler had been descending steadily into the Hellas Basin, and the air pressure was rising. Mars lay like a feverish patient under this thick blanket of air, sweating buried ice.

On the horizon thunderheads rose with explosive speed below the constant scrawl of the jet streams.

The basin was strange to Mirasol. Her faction, the Patternists, had been assigned to a redemption camp in northern Syrtis Major. There, two-hundred-mile-an-hour surface winds were common, and their pressurized camp had been buried three times by advancing dunes.

It had taken her eight days of constant travel to reach the equator.

From high overhead, the Regal faction had helped her navigate. Their orbiting city-state, Terraform-Fluster, was a nexus of monitor satellites. The Regals showed by their helpfulness that they had her under closer surveillance.

The crawler lurched as its six picklike feet scrabbled down the slopes of a deflation pit. Mirasol suddenly saw her own face reflected in the glass, pale and taut, her dark eyes dreamily self-absorbed. It was a bare face, with the anonymous

beauty of the genetically Reshaped. She rubbed her eyes with
nail-bitten fingers.

To the west, far overhead, a gout of airborne topsoil surged
aside and revealed the Ladder, the mighty anchor cable of the
Terraform-Kluster.

Above the winds the cable faded from sight, vanishing
below the metallic glitter of the Kluster, swinging aloofly in
orbit.

Mirasol stared at the orbiting city with an uneasy mix of
envy, fear and reverence. She had never been so close to the
Kluster before, or to the all-important Ladder that linked it to
the Martian surface. Like most of her faction's younger generation, she had never been into space. The Regals had carefully kept her faction quarantined in the Syrtis redemption
camp.

Life had not come easily to Mars. For one hundred years
the Regals of Terraform-Kluster had bombarded the Martian
surface with giant chunks of ice. This act of planetary engineering was the most ambitious, arrogant, and successful of
all the works of man in space.

The shattering impacts had torn huge craters in the Martian crust, blasting tons of dust and steam into Mars's thread-
bare sheet of air. As the temperature rose, buried oceans of
Martian permafrost roared forth, leaving networks of twisted
badlands and vast expanses of damp mud, smooth and sterile
as a television. On these great playas and on the frost-caked
walls of channels, cliffs, and calderas, transplanted lichen had
clung and leapt into devouring life. In the plains of Eridania,
in the twisted megacanyons of the Coprates Basin, in the
damp and icy regions of the dwindling poles, vast clawing
thickets of its sinister growth lay upon the land—massive disaster areas for the inorganic.

As the terraforming project had grown, so had the power
of Terraform-Kluster.

As a neutral point in humanity's factional wars, T-K was
crucial to financiers and bankers of every sect. Even the alien
Investors, those star-traveling reptiles of enormous wealth,
found T-K useful, and favored it with their patronage.

And as T-K's citizens, the Regals, increased their power,
smaller factions faltered and fell under their sway. Mars was

dotted with bankrupt factions, financially captured and transported to the Martian surface by the T-K plutocrats.

Having failed in space, the refugees took Regal charity as ecologists of the sunken gardens. Dozens of factions were quarantined in cheerless redemption camps, isolated from one another, their lives pared to a grim frugality.

And the visionary Regals made good use of their power. The factions found themselves trapped in the arcane bioaesthetics of Posthumanist philosophy, subverted constantly by Regal broadcasts, Regal teaching, Regal culture. With time even the stubbornest faction would be broken down and digested into the cultural blood-stream of T-K. Faction members would be allowed to leave their redemption camp and travel up the Ladder.

But first they would have to prove themselves. The Patternists had awaited their chance for years. It had come at last in the Ibis Crater competition, an ecological struggle of the factions that would prove the victors' right to Regal status. Six factions had sent their champions to the ancient Ibis Crater, each one armed with its group's strongest biotechnologies. It would be a war of the sunken gardens, with the Ladder as the prize.

Mirasol's crawler followed a gully through a chaotic terrain of rocky permafrost that had collapsed in karsts and sinkholes. After two hours, the gully ended abruptly. Before Mirasol rose a mountain range of massive slabs and boulders, some with the glassy sheen of impact melt, others scabbed over with lichen.

As the crawler started up the slope, the sun came out, and Mirasol saw the crater's outer rim jigsawed in the green of lichen and the glaring white of snow.

The oxygen readings were rising steadily. Warm, moist air was drooling from within the crater's lip, leaving a spittle of ice. A half-million-ton asteroid from the Rings of Saturn had fallen here at fifteen kilometers a second. But for two centuries rain, creeping glaciers, and lichen had gnawed at the crater's rim, and the wound's raw edges had slumped and scarred.

The crawler worked its way up the striated channel of an empty glacier bed. A cold alpine wind keened down the channel, where flourishing patches of lichen clung to exposed veins of ice.

Some rocks were striped with sediment from the ancient Martian seas, and the impact had peeled them up and thrown them on their backs.

It was winter, the season for pruning the sunken gardens. The treacherous rubble of the crater's rim was cemented with frozen mud. The crawler found the glacier's root and clawed its way up the ice face. The raw slope was striped with winter snow and storm-blown summer dust, stacked in hundreds of red-and-white layers. With the years the stripes had warped and rippled in the glacier's flow.

Mirasol reached the crest. The crawler ran spiderlike along the crater's snowy rim. Below, in a bowl-shaped crater eight kilometers deep, lay a seething ocean of air.

Mirasol stared. Within this gigantic airsump, twenty kilometers across, a broken ring of majestic rain clouds trailed their dark skirts, like duchesses in quadrille, about the ballroom floor of a lens-shaped sea.

Thick forests of green-and-yellow mangroves rimmed the shallow water and had overrun the shattered islands at its center. Pinpoints of brilliant scarlet ibis spattered the trees. A flock of them suddenly spread kitelike wings and took to the air, spreading across the crater in uncounted millions. Mirasol was appalled by the crudity and daring of this ecological concept, its crass and primal vitality.

This was what she had come to destroy. The thought filled her with sadness.

Then she remembered the years she had spent flattering her Regal teachers, collaborating with them in the destruction of her own culture. When the chance at the Ladder came, she had been chosen. She put her sadness away, remembering her ambitions and her rivals.

The history of mankind in space had been a long epic of ambitions and rivalries. From the very first, space colonies had struggled for self-sufficiency and had soon broken their ties with the exhausted Earth. The independent life-support systems had given them the mentality of city-states. Strange ideologies had bloomed in the hot-house atmosphere of the o'neills, and breakaway groups were common.

Space was too vast to police. Pioneer elites burst forth, defying anyone to stop their pursuit of aberrant technologies. Quite suddenly the march of science had become an insane, headlong scramble. New sciences and technologies had shattered whole societies in waves of future shock.

The shattered cultures coalesced into factions, so thoroughly alienated from one another that they were called humanity only for lack of a better term. The Shapers, for instance, had seized control of their own genetics, abandoning mankind in a burst of artificial evolution. Their rivals, the Mechanists, had replaced flesh with advanced prosthetics.

Mirasol's own group, the Patternists, was a breakaway Shaper faction.

The Patternists specialized in cerebral asymmetry. With grossly expanded right-brain hemispheres, they were highly intuitive, given to metaphors, parallels, and sudden cognitive leaps. Their inventive minds and quick, unpredictable genius had given them a competitive edge at first. But with these advantages had come grave weaknesses: autism, fugue states, and paranoia. Patternists grew out of control and became grotesque webs of fantasy.

With these handicaps their colony had faltered. Patternist industries went into decline, outpaced by industrial rivals. Competition had grown much fiercer. The Shaper and Mechanist cartels had turned commercial action into a kind of endemic warfare. The Patternist gamble had failed, and the day came when their entire habitat was bought out from around them by Regal plutocrats. In a way it was a kindness. The Regals were suave and proud of their ability to assimilate refugees and failures.

The Regals themselves had started as dissidents and defectors. Their Posthumanist philosophy had given them the moral power and the bland assurance to dominate and absorb factions from the fringes of humanity. And they had the support of the Investors, who had vast wealth and the secret techniques of star travel.

The crawler's radar alerted Mirasol to the presence of a landcraft from a rival faction. Leaning forward in her pilot's couch, she put the craft's image on screen. It was a lumpy sphere, balanced uneasily on four long, spindly legs. Silhouetted against the horizon, it moved with a strange wobbling speed along the opposite lip of the crater, then disappeared down the outward slope.

Mirasol wondered if it had been cheating. She was tempted to try some cheating herself—to dump a few frozen packets of aerobic bacteria or a few dozen capsules of insect eggs down the slope—but she feared the orbiting monitors of the T-K supervisors. Too much was at stake—not only her own career but that of her entire faction, huddled bankrupt and despairing in their cold redemption camp. It was said that T-K's ruler, the Posthuman being they called the Lobster King, would himself watch the contest. To fail before his black abstracted gaze would be a horror.

On the crater's outside slope, below her, a second rival craft appeared, lurching and slithering with insane, aggressive grace. The craft's long supple body moved with a sidewinder's looping and coiling, holding aloft a massive shining head, like a faceted mirror ball.

Both rivals were converging on the rendezvous camp, where the six contestants would receive their final briefing from the Regal Adviser. Mirasol hurried forward.

When the camp first flashed into sight on her screen, Mirasol was shocked. The place was huge and absurdly elaborate: a drug dream of paneled geodesics and colored minarets, sprawling in the lichenous desert like an abandoned chandelier. This was a camp for Regals.

Here the arbiters and sophists of the BioArts would stay and judge the crater as the newly planted ecosystems struggled among themselves for supremacy.

The camp's airlocks were surrounded with shining green thickets of lichen, where the growth feasted on escaped humidity. Mirasol drove her crawler through the yawning airlock and into a garage. Inside the garage, robot mechanics were scrubbing and polishing the coiled hundred-meter length of the snake craft and the gleaming black abdomen of an eight-legged crawler. The black crawler was crouched with its periscoped head sunk downward, as if ready to pounce. Its swollen belly was marked with a red hourglass and the corporate logos of its faction.

The garage smelled of dust and grease overlaid with floral perfumes. Mirasol left the mechanics to their work and walked stiffly down a long corridor, stretching the kinks out of her back and shoulders. A latticework door sprang apart into filaments and resealed itself behind her.

She was in a dining room that clinked and rattled with the high-pitched repetitive sound of Regal music. Its walls were paneled with tall display screens showing startlingly beautiful garden panoramas. A pulpy-looking servo, whose organo-metallis casing and squat, smiling head had a swollen and almost diseased appearance, showed her to a chair.

Mirasol sat, denting the heavy white tablecloth with her knees. There were seven places at the table. The Regal Adviser's tall chair was at the table's head. Mirasol's assigned position gave her a sharp idea of her own status. She sat at the far end of the table, on the Adviser's left.

Two of her rivals had already taken their places. One was a tall, red-haired Shaper with long, thin arms, whose sharp face and bright, worried eyes gave him a querulous birdlike look. The other was a sullen, feral Mechanist with prosthetic hands and a paramilitary tunic marked at the shoulders with a red hourglass.

Mirasol studied her two rivals with silent, sidelong glances. Like her, they were both young. The Regals favored the young, and they encouraged captive factions to expand their populations widely.

This strategy cleverly subverted the old guard of each faction in a tidal wave of their own children, indoctrinated from birth by Regals.

The birdlike man, obviously uncomfortable with his place directly at the Adviser's right, looked as if he wanted to speak but dared not. The piratical Mech sat staring at his artificial hands, his ears stoppered with headphones.

Each place setting had a squeezebulb of liqueur. Regals, who were used to weightlessness in orbit, used these bulbs by habit, and their presence here was both a privilege and a humiliation.

The door fluttered open again, and two more rivals burst in, almost as if they had raced. The first was a flabby Mech, still not used to gravity, whose sagging limbs were supported

by an extraskeletal framework. The second was a severely
mutated Shaper whose elbowed legs terminated in grasping
hands. The pedal hands were gemmed with heavy rings that
clicked against each other as she waddled across the parquet
floor.

The woman with the strange legs took her place across
from the birdlike man. They began to converse haltingly in a
language that none of the others could follow. The man in the
framework, gasping audibly, lay in obvious pain in the chair
across from Mirasol. His plastic eyeballs looked as blank as
chips of glass. His sufferings in the pull of gravity showed
that he was new to Mars, and his place in the competition
meant that his faction was powerful. Mirasol despised him.

Mirasol felt a nightmarish sense of entrapment. Everything
about her competitors seemed to proclaim their sickly unfit-
ness for survival. They had a haunted, hungry look, like starving men in a lifeboat who wait with secret eagerness for the
first to die.

She caught a glimpse of herself reflected in the bowl of a
spoon and saw with a flash of insight how she must appear to
the others. Her intuitive right brain was swollen beyond
human bounds, distorting her skull. Her face had the blank
prettiness of her genetic heritage, but she could feel the bleak
strain of her expression. Her body looked shapeless under her
quilted pilot's vest and dun-drab, general-issue blouse and
trousers. Her fingertips were raw from biting. She saw in herself the fey, defeated aura of her faction's older generation,
those who had tried and failed in the great world of space, and
she hated herself for it.

They were still waiting for the sixth competitor when the
plonking music reached a sudden crescendo and the Regal
Adviser arrived. Her name was Arkadya Sorienti, Incorporated. She was a member of T-K's ruling oligarchy, and she
swayed through the bursting door with the careful steps of a
woman not used to gravity.

She wore the Investor-style clothing of a high-ranking
diplomat. The Regals were proud of their diplomatic ties with
the alien Investors, since Investor patronage proved their own
vast wealth. The Sorienti's knee-high boots had false birdlike
toes, scaled like Investor hide. She wore a heavy skirt of gold

cords braided with jewels, and a stiff wrist-length formal jacket with embroidered cuffs. A heavy collar formed an arching multicolored frill behind her head. Her blonde hair was set in an interlaced style as complex as computer wiring. The skin of her bare legs had a shiny, glossy look, as if freshly enameled. Her eyelids gleamed with soft reptilian pastels.

One of her corporate ladyship's two body-servos helped her to her seat. The Sorienti leaned forward brightly, interlacing small, pretty hands so crusted with rings and bracelets that they resembled gleaming gauntlets.

"I hope the five of you have enjoyed this chance for an informal talk," she said sweetly, just as if such a thing were possible. "I'm sorry I was delayed. Our sixth participant will not be joining us."

There was no explanation. The Regals never publicized any action of theirs that might be construed as a punishment. The looks of the competitors, alternately stricken and calculating, showed that they were imagining the worst.

The two squat servos circulated around the table, dishing out courses of food from trays balanced on their flabby heads. The competitors picked uneasily at their plates.

The display screen behind the Adviser flicked into a schematic diagram of the Ibis Crater. "Please notice the revised boundary lines," the Sorienti said. "I hope that each of you will avoid trespassing—not merely physically but biologically as well." She looked at them seriously. "Some of you may plan to use herbicides. This is permissible, but the spreading of spray beyond your sector's boundaries is considered crass. Bacteriological establishment is a subtle art. The spreading of tailored disease organisms is an aesthetic distortion. Please remember that your activities here are a disruption of what should ideally be a natural process. Therefore the period of biotic seeding will last only twelve hours. Thereafter, the new complexity level will be allowed to stabilize itself without any other interference at all. Avoid self-aggrandizement, and confine yourselves to a primal role, as catalysts."

The Sorienti's speech was formal and ceremonial. Mirasol studied the display screen, noting with much satisfaction that her territory had been expanded.

Seen from overhead, the crater's roundness was deeply marred.

Mirasol's sector, the southern one, showed the long flattened scar of a major landslide, where the crater wall had slumped and flowed into the pit. The simple ecosystem had recovered quickly, and mangroves festooned the rubble's lowest slopes. Its upper slopes were gnawed by lichen and glaciers.

The sixth sector had been erased, and Mirasol's share was almost twenty square kilometers of new land.

It would give her faction's ecosystem more room to take root before the deadly struggle began in earnest.

This was not the first such competition. The Regals had held them for decades as an objective test of the skills of rival factions. It helped the Regals' divide-and-conquer policy, to set the factions against one another.

And in the centuries to come, as Mars grew more hospitable to life, the gardens would surge from their craters and spread across the surface. Mars would become a warring jungle of separate creations. For the Regals the competitions were closely studied simulations of the future.

And the competitions gave the factions motives for their work. With the garden wars to spur them, the ecological sciences had advanced enormously. Already, with the progress of science and taste, many of the oldest craters had become ecoaesthetic embarrassments.

The Ibis Crater had been an early, crude experiment. The faction that had created it was long gone, and its primitive creation was now considered tasteless.

Each gardening faction camped beside its own crater, struggling to bring it to life. But the competitions were a shortcut up the Ladder. The competitors' philosophies and talents, made into flesh, would carry out a proxy struggle for supremacy. The sine-wave curves of growth, the rallies and declines of expansion and extinction, would scroll across the monitors of the Regal judges like stock-market reports. This complex struggle would be weighed in each of its aspects: technological, philosophical, biological, and aesthetic. The winners would abandon their camps to take on Regal wealth and power. They would roam T-K's jeweled corridors and revel in its perquisites: extended life spans, corporate titles, cosmopolitan tolerance, and the interstellar patronage of the Investors.

When red dawn broke over the landscape, the five were poised around the Ibis Crater, awaiting the signal. The day was calm, with only a distant nexus of jet streams marring the sky. Mirasol watched pink-stained sunlight creep down the inside slope of the crater's western wall. In the mangrove thickets birds were beginning to stir.

Mirasol waited tensely. She had taken a position on the upper slopes of the landslide's raw debris. Radar showed her rivals spaced along the interior slopes: to her left, the hourglass crawler and the jewel-headed snake; to her right, a mantislike crawler and the globe on stilts.

The signal came, sudden as lightning: a meteor of ice shot from orbit and left a shock-wave cloud plume of ablated steam. Mirasol charged forward.

The Patternists' strategy was to concentrate on the upper slopes and the landslide's rubble, a marginal niche where they hoped to excel. Their cold crater in Syrtis Major had given them some expertise in alpine species, and they hoped to exploit this strength. The landslide's long slope, far above sea level, was to be their power base. The crawler lurched downslope, blasting out a fine spray of lichenophagous bacteria.

Suddenly the air was full of birds. Across the crater, the globe on stilts had rushed down to the waterline and was laying waste the mangroves. Fine wisps of smoke showed the slicing beam of a heavy laser.

Burst after burst of birds took wing, peeling from their nests to wheel and dip in terror. At first, their frenzied cries came as a high-pitched whisper. Then, as the fear spread, the screeching echoed and reechoed, building to a mindless surf of pain. In the crater's dawn-warmed air, the scarlet motes hung in their millions, swirling and coalescing like drops of blood in free-fall.

Mirasol scattered the seeds of alpine rock crops. The crawler picked its way down the talus, spraying fertilizer into cracks and crevices. She pried up boulders and released a scattering of invertebrates: nematodes, mites, sowbugs, altered millipedes. She splattered the rocks with gelatin to feed them until the mosses and ferns took hold.

The cries of the birds were appalling. Downslope the other factions were thrashing in the muck at sea level, wreaking havoc, destroying the mangroves so that their own creations could take hold. The great snake looped and ducked through the canopy, knotting itself, ripping up swathes of mangroves by the roots. As Mirasol watched, the top of its faceted head burst open and released a cloud of bats.

The mantis crawler was methodically marching along the borders of its sector, its saw-edged arms reducing everything before it into kindling. The hourglass crawler had slashed through its territory, leaving a mussy network of fire zones. Behind it rose a wall of smoke.

It was a daring ploy. Sterilizing the sector by fire might give the new biome a slight advantage. Even a small boost could be crucial as exponential rates of growth took hold. But the Ibis Crater was a closed system. The use of fire required great care. There was only so much air within the bowl.

Mirasol worked grimly. Insects were next. They were often neglected in favor of massive sea beasts or flashy predators, but in terms of biomass, gram by gram, insects could overwhelm. She blasted a carton downslope to the shore, where it melted, releasing aquatic termites. She shoved aside flat shelves of rock, planting egg cases below their sunwarmed surfaces. She released a cloud of leaf-eating midges, their tiny bodies packed with bacteria. Within the crawler's belly, rack after automatic rack was thawed and fired through nozzles, dropped through spiracles or planted in the holes jabbed by picklike feet.

Each faction was releasing a potential world. Near the water's edge, the mantis had released a pair of things like giant black sail planes. They were swooping through the clouds of ibis, opening great sieved mouths. On the islands in the center of the crater's lake, scaled walruses clambered on the rocks, blowing steam. The stilt ball was laying out an orchard in the mangroves' wreckage. The snake had taken to the water, its faceted head leaving a wake of V-waves.

In the hourglass sector, smoke continued to rise. The fires were spreading, and the spider ran frantically along its network of zones. Mirasol watched the movement of the smoke as she released a horde of marmots and rock squirrels.

A mistake had been made. As the smoky air gushed upward in the feeble Martian gravity, a fierce valley wind of cold air from the heights flowed downward to fill the vacuum. The mangroves burned fiercely. Shattered networks of flaming branches were flying into the air.

The spider charged into the flames, smashing and trampling. Mirasol laughed, imagining demerits piling up in the judges' data banks. Her talus slopes were safe from fire. There was nothing to burn.

The ibis flock had formed a great wheeling ring above the shore. Within their scattered ranks flitted the dark shapes of airborne predators. The long plume of steam from the meteor had begun to twist and break. A sullen wind was building up.

Fire had broken out in the snake's sector. The snake was swimming in the sea's muddy waters, surrounded by bales of bright-green kelp. Before its pilot noticed, fire was already roaring through a great piled heap of the wreckage it had left on shore. There were no windbreaks left. Air poured down the denuded slope. The smoke column guttered and twisted, its black clouds alive with sparks.

A flock of ibis plunged into the cloud. Only a handful emerged; some of them were flaming visibly. Mirasol began to know fear. As smoke rose to the crater's rim, it cooled and started to fall outward and downward. A vertical whirlwind was forming, a torus of hot smoke and cold wind.

The crawler scattered seed-packed hay for pygmy mountain goats. Just before her an ibis fell from the sky with a dark squirming shape, all claws and teeth, clinging to its neck. She rushed forward and crushed the predator, then stopped and stared distractedly across the crater.

Fires were spreading with unnatural speed. Small puffs of smoke rose from a dozen places, striking large heaps of wood with uncanny precision. Her altered brain searched for a pattern. The fires springing up in the mantic sector were well beyond the reach of any falling debris.

In the spider's zone, flames had leapt the firebreaks without leaving a mark. The pattern felt wrong to her, eerily wrong, as if the destruction had a force all its own, a raging synergy that fed upon itself.

The pattern spread into a devouring crescent. Mirasol felt the dread of lost control—the sweating fear an orbiter feels at the hiss of escaping air or the way a suicide feels at the first bright gush of blood.

Within an hour the garden sprawled beneath a hurricane of hot decay. The dense columns of smoke had flattened like thunderheads at the limits of the garden's sunken troposphere. Slowly a spark-shot gray haze, dripping ash like rain, began to ring the crater. Screaming birds circled beneath the foul torus, falling by tens and scores and hundreds. Their bodies littered the garden's sea, their bright plumage blurred with ash in a steel-gray sump.

The landcraft of the others continued to fight the flames, smashing unharmed through the fire's charred borderlands. Their efforts were useless, a pathetic ritual before the disaster.

Even the fire's malicious purity had grown tired and tainted. The oxygen was failing. The flames were dimmer and spread more slowly, releasing a dark nastiness of half-combusted smoke.

Where it spread, nothing that breathed could live. Even the flames were killed as the smoke billowed along the crater's crushed and smoldering slopes.

Mirasol watched a group of striped gazelles struggle up the barren slopes of the talus in search of air. Their dark eyes, fresh from the laboratory, rolled in timeless animal fear. Their coats were scorched, their flanks heaved, their mouths dripped foam. One by one they collapsed in convulsions, kicking at the lifeless Martian rock as they slid and fell. It was a vile sight, the image of a blighted spring.

An oblique flash of red downslope to her left attracted her attention. A large red animal was skulking among the rocks. She turned the crawler and picked her way toward it, wincing as a dark surf of poisoned smoke broke across the fretted glass.

She spotted the animal as it broke from cover. It was a scorched and gasping creature like a great red ape. She dashed forward and seized it in the crawler's arms. Held aloft, it clawed and kicked, hammering the crawler's arms with a smoldering branch. In revulsion and pity, she crushed it. Its bodice of tight-sewn ibis feathers tore, revealing blood-slicked human flesh.

Using the crawler's grips, she tugged at a heavy tuft of feathers on its head. The tight-fitting mask ripped free, and the dead man's head slumped forward. She rolled it back, revealing a face tattooed with stars.

The ornithopter sculled above the burned-out garden, its long red wings beating with dreamlike fluidity. Mirasol watched the Sorienti's painted face as her corporate ladyship stared into the shining viewscreen.

The ornithopter's powerful cameras cast image after image onto the tabletop screen, lighting the Regal's face. The tabletop was littered with the Sorienti's elegant knickknacks: an inhaler case, a half-empty jeweled squeezebulb, lorgnette binoculars, a stack of tape cassettes.

"An unprecedented case," her ladyship murmured. "It was not a total dieback after all but merely the extinction of everything with lungs. There must be strong survivorship among the lower orders: fish, insects, annelids. Now that the rain's settled the ash, you can see the vegetation making a strong comeback. Your own section seems almost undamaged."

"Yes," Mirasol said. "The natives were unable to reach it with torches before the fire storm had smothered itself."

The Sorienti leaned back into the tasseled arms of her couch. "I wish you wouldn't mention them so loudly, even between ourselves."

"No one would believe me."

"The others never saw them," the Regal said. "They were too busy fighting the flames." She hesitated briefly. "You were wise to confide in me first."

Mirasol locked eyes with her new patroness, then looked away. "There was no one else to tell. They'd have said I built a pattern out of nothing but my own fears."

"You have your faction to think of," the Sorienti said with an air of sympathy. "With such a bright future ahead of them, they don't need a renewed reputation for paranoid fantasies."

She studied the screen. "The Patternists are winners by default. It certainly makes an interesting case study. If the new garden grows tiresome we can have the whole crater sterilized from orbit. Some other faction can start again with a clean slate."

"Don't let them build too close to the edge," Mirasol said.

Her corporate ladyship watched her attentively, tilting her head.

"I have no proof," Mirasol said, "but I can see the pattern behind it all. The natives had to come from somewhere. The colony that stocked the crater must have been destroyed in that huge landslide. Was that your work? Did your people kill them?"

The Sorienti smiled. "You're very bright, my dear. You will do well, up the Ladder. And you can keep secrets. Your office as my secretary suits you very well."

"They were destroyed from orbit," Mirasol said. "Why else would they hide from us? You tried to annihilate them."

"It was a long time ago," the Regal said. "In the early days, when things were shakier. They were researching the secret of starflight, techniques only the Investors know. Rumor says they reached success at last, in their redemption camp. After that, there was no choice."

"Then they were killed for the Investors' profit," Mirasol said. She stood up quickly and walked around the cabin, her new jeweled skirt clattering around the knees. "So that the aliens could go on toying with us, hiding their secret, selling us trinkets."

The Regal folded her hands with a clicking of rings and bracelets. "Our Lobster King is wise," she said. "If humanity's efforts turned to the stars, what would become of terraforming? Why should we trade the power of creation itself to become like the Investors?"

"But think of the people," Mirasol said. "Think of them losing their technologies, degenerating into human beings. A handful of savages, eating bird meat. Think of the fear they felt for generations, the way they burned their own home and killed themselves when they saw us come to smash and destroy their world. Aren't you filled with horror?"

"For humans?" the Sorienti said. "No!"

"But can't you see? You've given this planet life as an art form, as an enormous game. You force us to play in it, and those people were killed for it! Can't you see how that blights everything?"

"Our game is reality," the Regal said. She gestured at the viewscreen. "You can't deny the savage beauty of destruction."

"You defend this catastrophe?"

The Regal shrugged. "If life worked perfectly, how could things evolve? Aren't we Posthuman? Things grow; things die. In time the cosmos kills us all. The cosmos has no meaning, and its emptiness is absolute. That's pure terror, but it's also pure freedom. Only our ambitions and our creations can fill it."

"And that justifies your actions?"

"We act for life," the Regal said. "Our ambitions have become this world's natural laws. We blunder because life blunders. We go on because life must go on. When you've taken the long view, from orbit—when the power we wield is in your own hands—then you can judge us." She smiled. "You will be judging yourself. You'll be Regal."

"But what about your captive factions? Your agents, who do your will? Once we had our own ambitions. We failed, and now you isolate us, indoctrinate us, make us into rumors. We must have something of our own. Now we have nothing."

"That's not so. You have what we've given you. You have the Ladder."

The vision stung Mirasol: power, light, the hint of justice, this world with its sins and sadness shrunk to a bright arena far below. "Yes," she said at last. "Yes, we do."

THE OTHER SHORE

J. R. Dunn

Here's one of the most harrowing potentialities of genetic technology, a nightmare scenario that, thank God, hasn't yet come to pass—but one that could, any day now.

A former political reporter, J. R. Dunn has made sales to Omni, Asimov's Science Fiction, Amazing, The Magazine of Fantasy & Science Fiction, *and other markets. His books include* This Side of Judgment.

"**What do they** call their lawyers over there?" Dave glanced at Bedford, unable to make out his features in the darkness. A blank silhouette against the passing outside lights and no more. "It's the British system," he said. "Solicitors and barristers. One prepares the case, the other argues it. I forget which is which. . . ."

"That's okay," Bedford said. "Long as I see justice." The words were followed by a short laugh.

Dave made no reply. Bedford had been saying that continually over the past weeks, as if the words were a kind of mantra. He usually made a joke of it, as he did most things, but Dave had stopped laughing. There was no such thing as justice where Arthur Bedford was headed.

It was well past midnight—closer to one, in fact; they'd started late. He looked out the rear window at the tail car, twenty feet behind. Four men in that one, the same in the car ahead, and two in this one aside from Dave himself. All armed. Dave with his service revolver, the rest with MP-5s or Ingrams. There were people who thought Bedford didn't need a trial.

They were taking the back roads to the airport instead of the main highway. Another convoy drove that route, a decoy with a lot more cars, shepherded by lifters and helicopters. A bit obvious, Dave thought; it wouldn't fool many, but everything helped. He looked down at his watch. Another fifteen minutes and they'd be airborne and he could relax.

Words blurred by static sounded from the radio. In the front seat Wolfe lifted the headset and held it to one ear. He muttered into the mike and tossed it on the dash. "Goddammit," he said. He turned to face Dave. "There's a riot brewing at the airport. Word leaked out somehow. At least fifteen hundred maniacs in front of the terminal."

Dave felt Bedford stiffen. "Who is it?" he said.

"Everybody," Wolfe replied. "Black Justice Coalition, CORE, Remembrance, the Klan, that nut cult claims Satan made 'em do it, the goddamn Nazis, for Chrissake. All about to go for each other's throats." He shook his head in disgust. "How they found out, I don't know."

"Could have been anybody," Dave said. "There's always some jackass who's got to tell his old lady. Never fails." He turned to Bedford. "Don't worry about it," he said quietly. "A company of federal troops are there. It'll be okay." There was no reply so he turned back to Wolfe. "Any changes in the route?"

"Yeah," Wolfe said. "They're taking out a piece of runway fence half mile north of the terminal." He looked over at the driver. "They'll drop it as soon as we show, Al." The driver nodded wordlessly.

They drove on in silence for a few minutes, then Dave heard Bedford sigh. He looked over inquiringly, forgetting that he was invisible himself. Bedford spoke nonetheless. "I don't know why they can't hold the trial in the U.S.," he said. "Instead of flying all the way over there. You'd think they'd want to save their money."

"Symbolism," Dave said. "Lets them feel they've got some control over the process. After all, they're the ones who suffered." He paused before going on. "Doesn't sound like much, but it means a lot to them."

"Well," Bedford said, louder now. "As long as I get my day in court." Another tattered laugh.

Dave stared at the black patch that was Bedford and sank lower in the seat. There was no question that Bedford had been in touch with the Porter Group. He was a geneticist, his specialty was DNA charting, he'd known them all and had met with at least three of them in the months prior to the Plague.

But Dave had his doubts. He was far from convinced that Bedford was guilty, that he'd had anything to do with the Greening. During the interrogation he'd had an answer for everything. Why had he gone to Cozumel? He'd retired. He'd made plenty of money off of phages and didn't have to work anymore. Why had he met with Olbers and the others? Shop talk. The biotech field was pretty small; everybody knew everybody else. Why had he stayed in Mexico all these years? Well, biotechs weren't too popular after the Plague; he'd been scared. He even had an explanation for those articles he'd written, the ones about eliminating excess biomass.

But it wasn't that he hadn't confessed or that there was no concrete evidence. The problem was that Dave liked Art Bedford.

He'd been assigned to Bedford during the interrogation, not to question him, but simply to be there: to keep him company, be his pal, talk to him, cheer him up—and to listen when and if he decided to talk about what he'd been doing those last days of May eight years ago.

The buddy program had begun after Hollis hanged himself in his cell. The papers had gone wild over that: screaming headlines, speculations about conspiracies, pious editorials on the massive guilt that had forced him to suicide. That may have been part of it, but it had been the conditions as much as anything else: the paper prison uniform, the eight-hour interrogation sessions, the bad food, the unutterable loneliness of being a man hated by most of the world. Things had changed after Hollis—better food, normal clothing, but more important, simple human contact, somebody they didn't have to be afraid of, someone to lean on as they walked the mile. That the somebody also doubled as a bodyguard mattered not at all.

Dave had been through it four times now, and each time he'd ended up, more or less against his will, liking the man he'd been assigned to—even Olbers, weird as he'd been. He knew what they were and what they'd done, but their human qualities touched him regardless. It was hard to hate a man after you'd broken bread with him.

But Bedford was different. He was a funny man, with a vast supply of stories and jokes about everything imaginable. He was able to see the humor in anything, no matter what the situation, even the one that had made him the sole prisoner on the top floor of Leavenworth. Beyond that, he'd been as careful of Dave's feelings as Dave had been of his. The others had snapped at him at one time or another as the pressure got to them, cursing him as a plant, asking if he got a kick out of watching them, but not Art. He'd taught Dave to play chess, and had even explained genetics to him, not that he understood it even now.

Dave would have liked Art no matter how they'd met. The fact that he was probably innocent had nothing to do with it.

He'd had it out with Wills, the agent in charge, earlier that evening. Wills had called Dave down to his office to talk about Bedford: how he hadn't slipped once, hadn't given one sign of guilt, how his story had held together so well. Then Wills had gotten to the point: "You like him, don't you?"

"Yeah, I do. He's what we used to call a noble bro."

Wills smiled. "So do I," he said, fiddling with a pen. "And you don't think he had anything to do with it."

His tone was flat, deliberately so. Dave shut his eyes and shook his head.

Wills sat quietly, tapping the pen on the desktop, his lips pursed. "I hear you were rough on the Japanese delegation last week," he said finally.

Dave shifted uncomfortably. He'd been wondering when that would come up. "They were threatening him," he said.

"Well, you should have come to me. I got some flack on it from upstairs. But," he waved his hand, "that's past." He paused once again, then went on, his voice quiet. "Is this one getting to you?"

"They all do."

"All of them?"

"Almost," Dave said, giving him a thin smile.

"Right." Wills nodded. He stared at the wall as if deeply

interested in the institutional green paint of the room. "You don't think he should go."

"I'd like to hold him a month or so, see what turns up. . . ."

"Can't do it, Dave," Wills said, shaking his head. "Delhi wants him. It's been two years since the last—"

Dave cut him off. "So that's it? We're on a deadline now? Maybe we should start sending over the guys who sold them the equipment. There are quite a few of them." He fell silent, surprised at his own vehemence.

Wills dropped his head. "I know it's tough," he said heavily, "and this one's tougher than most." He raised his eyes. "Do you want to be relieved?"

Dave hesitated. He'd been anticipating the trial with more dread than he cared to admit. He could be out now, no problem—Wills wouldn't hold it against him. . . . But it wouldn't be fair to Art. He shook his head.

"You just have to say the word."

"No," Dave said. "But what I do want is this: I want to know that this thing isn't becoming an automatic process, that we aren't sending people over there just to keep the wheels turning. Anyone who goes to Delhi is a dead man—the trial is just a formality. Art Bedford wouldn't be convicted in this country on what we've got on him."

Lighting another of his never-ending string of cigarettes, Wills stared thoughtfully at the coal. Dave knew he was mulling it over and he was tempted to say something, a remark about the court maybe, that would tip the balance and get him out of it, but he remained silent.

"You know, Dave," Wills said finally, "you'd have made a good small-town cop. There's something about you makes people want to confess. You remember Reed sat here screaming he was innocent, he had his rights, every other damn thing, and then. . . ."

"On the plane he tells me everything."

"Right. Even Olbers came around in the end."

Dave nodded. Olbers had been one who hadn't bothered him. He'd sat through interrogation with utter disinterest, saying nothing even though they had him nailed—his thumbprint had been found on a flask in Mombasa. The trial had gone the same way, Olbers acting as if the whole business was a boring duty that required his presence but not his attention. Yet at the end, as he was led out of the cell, he'd turned to Dave and said, "Three billion for one, Novak—not a bad trade, eh?" and had walked off between his guards with a slight smile that hadn't changed even when the gas hit the acid.

"You think the same will happen with Bedford?"

"Be nice," Wills said.

"What if he's got nothing to tell?"

Wills butted the cigarette out and lit another. "Do what you can," he said quietly. "Some of us have our doubts, too." He lifted his eyes to Dave. "I think you know what I'm saying."

"Yeah," Dave said.

"All right," Wills said. "Now go on and get some sleep."

He'd gone back to the cellblock, but sleep was another matter. After two hours spent tossing on the bed, an ordinary one, not a prison cot, he'd gotten up and spent the rest of the evening walking the corridor, thinking about what Wills had said. Quite a character, Wills. Dave had heard he'd once studied to be a priest. He should sit down with him sometime, get to know him, find out how he'd ended up in the FBI.

As the hours passed he picked up the phone more than once to call Wills, but each time he had a vision of Bedford's face and changed his mind. He felt oddly relieved when the guard appeared to tell him to get ready. He'd have to see it through now. Take Art over there, be his last friend. He smiled mirthlessly as he pulled on a clean shirt. Charon . . .

"Okay," Wolfe said. "Should be right along here."

Dave leaned forward. They were on the airport service road, driving parallel to the fence. The terminal, brightly lit, was a short distance ahead. He narrowed his eyes, trying to make out the crowd, but the lights were too bright.

"Goddammit," the driver said. "Look where those idiots are." They'd slowed down, and the lead car was now fifty feet ahead. "Get on the horn and tell those yohabs to close it up."

Wolfe was reaching for the headset when the lead car suddenly turned onto the grass strip next to the road. As it did a section of the fence sagged and shadowy figures quickly pulled it away. Dousing their headlights, they drove through the gap and onto the runway. A lifter hovering over the field turned toward them and thrummed overhead, vulcans hunting aimlessly, the dull green of the army rondels barely visible against the black of the hull. A moment later they were beneath the wing of a big 828B Starclipper parked a hundred yards from the terminal.

A squad of soldiers running double-time surrounded the car. Gun at ready, Wolfe got out to inspect the scene. A moment later he leaned back inside. "Clear," he said.

Pushing the door open, Dave stepped out and paused to look things over for himself. The troops were in good order, facing away from the car, guns at chest level. He turned to gesture Bedford out and discovered that he was standing beside him, gazing at the terminal over the car roof. The shouts of the mob rang out clearly. Bedford frowned, then reached up to fiddle with the knot of his tie. "Think I should go out and calm 'em down?"

Behind Dave somebody laughed, and Wolfe said, "Art, get on the goddamn airplane." Bedford shrugged and with a smile began to walk toward the plane. Dave followed him.

Halfway there Dave slowed momentarily then quickened his pace to catch up with Bedford. An army officer stood just ahead, visor up, and Dave could see that he was black. He hesitated, wondering if he should grab Bedford's arm to pull him farther away, but then they were upon the soldier. Dave glanced up as they went by. Whoever the officer was, he was a pro; his expression didn't even change as they passed.

Dave stayed right behind Bedford as they climbed the steps. At the top Sheehan and his squad parted to let Bedford through then followed him aboard.

Dave glanced into the rear cabin, which was reserved for Bedford and himself. Art was just sitting down two seats back, talking to Sheehan and a couple of the others. Turning, Dave looked into the forward section, where the delegates were. He felt the muscles of his face tighten as he saw them. There were more than usual, and for a moment he wondered why until he remembered that it had been a while since the last flight. A couple of Latins in black suits, beyond them a small Asian, perhaps a Malay, talking to an African in tribal robes. But his eyes were caught by the two Hindus. Sheehan's men were just completing their search, going over a plump brown man in a tan suit. He was speaking angrily to a figure in uniform, who answered in quiet but firm tones. To his surprise, Dave recognized him: Paresh Naqui, a colonel he'd met on a previous mission. As the search ended and the plump man walked huffily away Naqui caught sight of Dave and raised his hand. Forcing himself to smile, Dave nodded back and walked out of the hatch.

He leaned against the gasket lining the doorway, shivering in spite of the warm night air. An officer was ordering the troops to form a line around the plane, but Dave paid them no attention. He was thinking of India, eight years ago: the fires glowing on the horizon, the wrecked towns, the constant, sweet-smelling smoke. . . .

Sensing someone next to him, he turned to see that Sheehan had joined him. He looked quizzically at Dave. "You okay?"

"What?" Dave unconsciously rubbed his hands on his chest. "Yeah . . . I'm fine. What's holding things up? You didn't search 'em until just now?"

Sheehan grimaced. "Ahh, some mechanic came back to the plane looking for a tool. They didn't catch him until he was walking away, so we had to do it all over. Weiner took advantage to go make some calls. Now we're waiting for him to get his ass aboard. . . ."

"Nate? What the hell's he doing here?"

"Who knows. If he ain't back in five minutes, though, this bird is flying regardless." He nodded toward the terminal. The shouts of the demonstrators had gotten louder, as if they were somehow aware that Bedford had arrived. "That bunch won't leave until they know he's gone, and we sure as hell don't need a riot." He glanced at his watch, then back up at Dave. "Why don't you go find Weiner?"

"I don't want to leave Art. . . ."

"Hey, I'm in charge until the plane rolls. Sooner you track down that silly bastard, sooner you'll get out of here."

Dave thought it over, then shrugged. "Okay."

"Good enough," Sheehan said. He turned back to the hatch. "I'll keep an eye on the package."

Dave clattered down the steps and went across the concrete to the terminal. At the entrance a soldier checked his ID before waving him on. Inside, the departure lounge was nearly empty; at the window a news team was filming the plane, staring intently at it as if they had been told it was going to go into a dance any minute now. They were being watched in turn by a pair of men in civilian clothes; he recognized neither of them.

There were plenty of phones in the corridor but no Nate. He walked on, the shouts of the protesters echoing down the hallway. He passed a car rental office, lights on but counter empty, then turned the corner to the waiting room.

It was probably his imagination, but he could have sworn that the crowd got louder as he came into sight. They were just past the big plate-glass windows, divided into two groups by a squad of soldiers. The largest was right outside, a varied bunch, some looking like professional demonstrators but the majority ordinary people. He studied their signs as he neared the windows: the standard symbol, a green swastika overlaying the globe, others reading DEATH TO ECONAZIS and a few with HITLER, STALIN AND POL POT in small letters with a huge BEDFORD in red underneath. There were others, crude and homemade, but they were being shaken so much that he couldn't read them.

A much smaller group stood in the parking lot. No signs—they'd probably been confiscated—but this crew didn't need them; what they were wearing said plenty. About half were in Klan robes or storm trooper gear: brown shirts, jackboots, and of course the armband. They were chanting, fists pushing forward in ragged unison, easily heard above the roar of the larger crowd: ". . . finish the job, finish the job, finish the job. . . ."

He looked around but saw no sign of Nate. Outside, the nearer mob had spotted him and were leaning over the crowd barrier, waving their signs. As he was turning away one of them ducked beneath the barrier and ran toward the window: a middle-aged black woman, well-dressed, somewhat plump. As she reached the curb she stumbled, catching herself and lifting the poster she was holding.

It wasn't a sign. It was a blown-up photo of a girl, a teenager, hair cut short and waved in a style popular ten years ago. The woman raised it high and shook it at Dave, shouting, her mouth open wide. He couldn't make out the words.

Two suits raced up to her. For a moment she struggled against them, dropping the photo as the taller cop leaned close to speak to her. She collapsed against him, body wracked with sobs, and they led her out of sight, the shorter man stooping to retrieve the picture.

Dave turned and walked across the terminal, shaking his head. There had been plenty of plague deaths in the U.S., too. Not as bad as the rest of the world, but enough.

Ahead of him a loose gaggle of cops and army officers stood around a coffee stand, staring at him in open suspicion. He ignored them and went on past. He'd just spotted Nate at the other side of the terminal.

He was at a phone bank, receiver cradled on his shoulder. He had a finger in his other ear and was gesturing broadly with a plastic cup, nearly shouting into the phone: "I just wish the whole defense team wasn't American . . . I know nobody wants to touch it, but it was an international crime. Two of them were European, dammit. . . ."

Dave tapped him on the shoulder, pointing to his watch as he swung around. Nate frowned, then closed his eyes and nodded. "I know it's too late for this round, but see what we can do next time. Ask the Swedes; they like to get involved . . . Listen, Maggie, the plane's leaving. Call you from Delhi."

He hung up, took a swig from the cup, and sputtered. "Ahh . . . cold." Crumpling it, he tossed it into a trash can.

"Come on, let's move," Dave said, grabbing his arm. "What are you doing in the States anyway?"

Nate took off his glasses to polish them, peering at Dave nearsightedly. He was a virtual caricature of a trial lawyer, hair a horseshoe, glasses porthole thick, suit a tailored masterpiece. "Got called back to Washington. They're confused about a witness, somebody supposed to have known our boy in Mexico. I had to hold their hands and explain it five times. Knew Bedford, alright, but never been south of the border." He slipped the glasses back on and smiled. "So how you doing? Been a while."

They walked through the terminal talking about nothing in

particular. The crowd, backs turned to listen to someone speak, paid them no attention.

Sheehan was waiting at the top of the steps. "Hallelujah," he bellowed at them, then stepped inside. "Okay, let's get this wagon in the air."

There was a rush of voices as Dave entered the plane. In back the guards stood around Bedford, shaking his hand and clapping him on the shoulder. He said something and they laughed then turned to make their way to the stairs. Bedford stood watching them, smiling broadly but unable to keep a look of desperation out of his eyes. One of them hollered good luck as he left; Art raised his hand slightly, then his smile vanished and he sat back down.

Dave turned to Sheehan, who was checking his watch. "Okay," he said. "One forty-seven and it's all yours."

"You check everything?"

"Yeah. All buttoned up. . . ."

The bathroom door opened behind Dave and he swung toward it, hand automatically rising to his holster. He let it drop as Wolfe emerged, tucking in his shirt. "Wolfe, for Chrissake. . . . Will you get out of here?"

"You're leaving, man?" Wolfe rushed past them, still fiddling with his belt. "I don't wanna go to India. They kill people there."

Shaking his head, Dave looked over at Sheehan, who shrugged and vanished down the steps. A moment later the door slid shut, a low whine sounded as the engines started and Dave went into the rear compartment.

Bedford was sitting back with his eyes closed. As Dave sat down he opened them and smiled wanly. "Knight to bishop three," he said quietly.

"What?"

"The game we were playing this afternoon," Bedford said, his smile broadening.

"Ah, come on, Art. You know I can't play in my head."

"Neither can I, usually, but my mind's been wonderfully concentrated." He chuckled, and Dave was about to ask him what he meant when they started moving.

The plane was windowless, but there was a screen up forward and two in the walls that served the same purpose. He

looked at the one above the door. The army troops had retreated to the terminal and stood watching. They slid across
the screen, vanishing as the plane taxied toward the runway.
Dave noticed two lifters hovering to the west, watching for
somebody with a stinger or, for that matter, even a shotgun:
one nick in the skin of this bird at mach 8 and it'd be all over.

The screen switched to the nose camera. The lifters drifted
apart, opening a path for them. There was a buzz and he realized that he hadn't buckled his seat belt. He reached down and
did so, and a moment later the plane was rolling.

As the thrust of takeoff pushed him back, he reviewed the
flight in his mind. An hour to the coast, two hours hypersonic
over the Pacific, another hour to New Delhi. That made it six
central time, which would be what in India . . . ? He tried to
work it out in his head but gave up. He'd check a schedule
later.

Bedford was sitting with his eyes half-closed. A good-
looking man, face craggy and weathered from a lot of time
spent outdoors, blue eyes, wavy hair left long in what Dave
called the scientist's cut. It was the kind of face women
trusted, and Bedford had been a ladies' man, never married,
always running with a different woman. Dave knew that, as
he knew everything else. He'd read virtually everything written by or about Bedford before he'd ever met him.

"What are you thinking about, Dave?" Bedford said without changing his expression.

Dave paused a moment before answering. If he was ever
going to get the truth out of him—even a small piece of it—
he'd better start now. "I was just remembering what Olbers
kept calling me when I flew over with him."

"Hmm?"

"Charon. He called me Charon. Said I was taking him to
the other shore. I didn't know what the hell he was talking
about. Had to look it up."

Bedford chuckled quietly. "I can't say I agree. Charon was
a pretty cold SOB."

"Lot like Olbers himself."

Bedford's eyebrows rose. "Couldn't say, Dave. I barely
knew the man."

He closed his eyes and shifted in the seat. Dave sat back,

feeling vaguely ashamed, as if he'd been taking advantage.
Well, there was plenty of time. The trial would last at least a
month, with every affected nation trying to get its word in,
and the pressure on Bedford wouldn't lessen any.

They'd never spoken much about the Plague or its after-
math, and then only in the abstract, as if it had nothing to do
with them personally. Bedford referred to it only as a technical problem: the difficulty of creating a microorganism that
would infect only select populations. Concerning reasons or
purpose he'd said nothing, even though he'd thought about
it—his own writings were proof of that.

Dave glanced over at him, lying back, his eyes closed. He
hadn't even told Bedford about India. . . .

The plane reached cruising altitude and the seat belt sign
went off. He glanced at his watch. Another half-hour before
they boosted. He decided to take a look around. Unfastening
the belt, he got up, walking quietly so as not to disturb Bedford. As he was about to go through the door something
made him look back. Bedford had awakened, if he'd ever
been asleep at all, and was staring at him with a look of sick
fear. As Dave met his glance the expression vanished, replaced by a weak smile. He stood there uncertainly, wondering whether to go back, but Bedford shut his eyes once
again so he went on.

Just past the bathroom he came upon Nate in the small alcove that was the plane's excuse for a galley. He was pouring
himself a cup of coffee out of an urn sitting in the place of
honor above the microwave. He looked up at Dave inquiringly. "Want one?"

Dave mulled it over. "Guess I'd better."

Pouring another, Nate handed it to him. Dave took a sip
and grimaced—the stuff had evidently been brewing for the
past week. He usually took it black, but. . . . He leaned past
Nate for a packet of creamer and dumped it in.

He studied Nate as he finished preparing his own, an
elaborate ritual involving two and a half sugars and two
packets of creamer. He took a gulp and smiled at the cup—
Dave couldn't help laughing. Frowning at him, Nate took
another sip.

"So where are you sitting?" Dave said.

"Oh, I sat up front for takeoff," Nate said, gesturing with his cup. "They didn't bite me. How's our boy?"

"About how you'd expect. Hiding it well, though, I've got to admit. He's sleeping now."

Draining his cup, Nate turned to the urn. "Sleep of the just," he muttered, so low that Dave barely heard him. Cup filled, he drew himself up and eyed Dave. "I hear you think he's innocent."

"I never said that . . ."

Nate grabbed a couple of packs of sugar. "You said the evidence against him was shit."

"I said it wouldn't stand up in an American court."

Nate's eyes narrowed. "So what the hell do you think that means?" he said, his voice harsh.

Openmouthed, Dave stared at him. Nate had never acted like this before, not even with Olbers, when he'd had good reason. "I'm just keeping an open mind."

"An open mind," Nate said. He tore at a packet of creamer and shook it over the cup, scattering half of it on the counter. "Must be an awful nice thing to have. You, Wills, the AG, all open minds. It must feel pretty good."

"What are you, Nate, switching to the prosecution now?"

Nate ignored him while he stirred the coffee. When he looked up his face was red, his eyes slits behind the thick lenses. "You like that son of a bitch, don't you?"

Dave looked away and shrugged. Nate nodded to himself as if he'd encountered a great truth. "Yeah," he said. "Well, I think he's got the mark of Cain on him."

Wordlessly he pushed past. Still facing the galley, Dave noticed that he'd left his work case. The top flap was open and he could see that the system was up. He turned to call out and saw Nate standing a few feet into the rear compartment. He walked back slowly as Dave picked up the case. Grasping the handle, he stood there fiddling with his glasses. "Sorry, Dave," he said finally. "Jet lag, I guess."

Dave smiled. "It's never easy, man."

"In truth." Nate headed toward the rear. Dave noticed he didn't look down as he passed Bedford's sleeping form.

He considered another cup of coffee but decided the hell with it. Tossing the empty cup away, he walked into the forward compartment. Conversation ceased as he entered; dark heads turned to inspect him before going on in lower tones. The plump Indian, wearing bifocals, was working on some papers. He glanced up as Dave passed, sneered and went back to work.

A few feet on he saw Naqui, sitting in a sort of truncated lounge area. He rose as Dave approached, giving him a firm handshake. "How are you, old man?" Naqui said as he sat back down, hitching his pants up at the knees.

Naqui was a colonel—general now, it seemed, by the new stars on his jacket—attached to the Indian government. He'd been educated in England and had the air of a British officer of the old school. His English was perfect, with none of the singsong qualities common among Hindus, and was one of the few who didn't act as if every last American was responsible for the Greening. Dave liked him.

Smiling, Dave sat back. "Now you get asked the question of the day: What were you doing on our side of the water?"

"Oh, a dustup with your new administration," Naqui said, waving a languid hand. "They've been a bit trying about our not holding elections, so I was sent to see to them. An entirely different lot with not the vaguest idea of where the subcontinent is, much less the conditions there." He shook his head. "And it happens every four years. I don't see how you manage."

"How are things, anyway?"

Naqui eyed him appraisingly. "Oh, that's right, you've had a full plate, haven't you? Not very good, frankly. We had an enormous riot in Kashmir two months ago, quite a number killed. The governor tried to close the camps and force the poor wretches back to the fields. Moving ahead on his own, I'm afraid. Needless to say it wasn't on, and when they weren't fed they ran wild. Took us weeks to restore order. But you wouldn't have heard that in any case—we thought it best to keep the lid on."

"They're still refusing to go back to the villages."

"Yes. Of course, one can't blame them. Most of them are living better than they possibly could anywhere else." He sighed. "I suppose we'll have to put our hopes in the younger generation."

Dave merely shrugged; there was nothing that could be said to that. It was the same throughout the Southern Hemisphere; the survivors were simply refusing to take up their lives again. It was a new form of mass neurosis, a type of survivor's shock: Quite simply, they had endured the end of the world and saw no reason for going on.

Naqui was still speaking. "Aside from that, it's the usual thing. Banditry, petty corruption, speculation in food supplies and so forth. It seems a typhoid epidemic broke out in Bangladesh this past week. I'll have to look into that as soon as we get back." He shrugged. "We're managing, at least. It could be far worse. We're better off than the Chinese, the poor devils."

Dave nodded in silent agreement. China was everybody's bad conscience. It had collapsed totally in the wake of the Plague. The Russians had taken over the northern quarter, for humanitarian reasons, they said, and there was some semblance of order there. But the rest was hell on earth. It was just too big, too enormous a task for anyone to take up. There were whole cities in the interior that would not see a human being for generations, if ever, provinces virtually empty of life. More relief teams were working there than anywhere else on the planet, but it was futile. The only thing that would heal China was time.

He realized that Naqui had spoken again. "I asked how the defendant was doing," Naqui said, hands clasped in front of him.

Dave grimaced. "As well as they all do."

Leaning forward, Naqui touched him on the knee. "I understand that there's some doubt about this man Bedford."

Wordlessly, Dave blinked at him, wondering how he could possibly have heard. Naqui gazed back a moment before settling into the seat. "Yes," he said quietly.

Naqui frowned at the cabin floor before going on. "There's something you should know," he said in a low voice. "Under the rose, of course. There seems to be a conviction in Nationalist Party circles that your government has sent in a ringer who can be proven innocent in order to halt the trial process. . . ."

"Bullshit," Dave said.

"Ludicrous, I agree. Utterly paranoid, but there you are. We're doing our best to put a stop to it, but we haven't made much headway. We do know that there will be an attempt on your man sometime before the trial begins."

"Great," Dave said. "Just what we need."

"Probably be wise to change the spot where he'll be held . . . but I won't tell you how to do your job." Naqui glanced over his shoulder then went on quickly. "We'll give you what help we can, needless to say. Our problem, after all. We'll discuss it further after we land."

Dave started to reply, but Naqui was getting up. Looking past him Dave saw a young Pakistani in uniform coming down the aisle. He halted and spoke to Naqui in high-pitched Urdu. Naqui turned back to Dave. "Some bother at home," he said. "We'll speak later."

"Right," Dave said. "And thanks, Paresh."

Leaning back against the seat, Dave looked up at the screen, wondering where they were. It was totally black, not even any stars—the cameras weren't sensitive enough to pick them up. Well out over the Pacific, most likely. He noticed that the boost warning light beneath the screen was lit up. Strange, he hadn't even heard the buzzer.

He felt a stab of irritation at Naqui but suppressed it. Normal reaction, blaming the messenger, but he had no time to indulge himself, and besides, Paresh had done him a favor. There was a hollow feeling at the pit of his stomach as he thought of what awaited them. It was different, somehow, knowing it was coming. And the government involved, too. Jesus, it was going to be rough.

He let his head rest against the cabin wall. A distant thrumming came through the metal; no sound, they were traveling too fast for that. He closed his eyes. India. He was going back once more, eight years after he'd sworn never to set foot there again, never to so much as think about it. The place of nightmares . . .

He'd been twenty, in his second year of college, when he'd volunteered for one of the relief teams. They sent him to Bombay.

Of course, he'd known what was happening, he'd seen all the news reports, but it hadn't prepared him for what he'd found. Nothing could have: the constant stench of death, the piles of corpses, the pyres burning day and night that the *Liberty* crew said were visible from orbit. He hadn't foreseen how it would affect him, either. After the first week he'd taken to going off by himself so that no one could see him crying. He didn't know why he bothered—most of the others were in far worse shape. There had been two suicides the first month, one of them the team psychiatrist. It was Dave who had discovered her, floating in a tub of pink-dyed water, red splotches printed on the wall above that must have meant something, though no sense could be made of them.

He reached his limit the fifth week, while immunizing the survivors against cholera—a small gift from fate thrown in to keep things interesting. The tent had been mobbed—there were so many of them: starved, sick, covered with sores. Three died while waiting for the shots, and sometime after that he'd lost it completely and had run off, still holding the injector. He couldn't remember much but they told him later that he'd been screaming.

He ran aimlessly for what seemed like hours, stumbling through the wreckage in the streets, smashing into abandoned cars, falling over bodies that seethed with maggots in the tropical sun, the faces, where there were faces, mottled with black, at times to a point where they resembled masks.

It had seemed to him then that he could run those streets forever and not reach the end, that the zone of death had expanded to swallow the world, and that he, Dave, was the final witness, the last shrieking remnant of a failed race.

Finally he collapsed before one of the camps ringing the city, injector clutched in his hand. The refugees gathered about him, staring expressionlessly. After a time he drew himself up on his knees, seeking, he thought now, some unimaginable kind of expiation. They could have murdered him then, and nobody would have known—it had happened to plenty of Americans in the preceding months—but they did not. Perhaps it was the injector that stopped them, perhaps just the look on his face. Whatever it had been, two of them—an old man and a boy whose thinness showed that he had just recovered himself—had taken his arms and led him out of the camp. They left him at relief headquarters, the old man saying a few words that Dave hadn't understood. He flew home the next day.

They'd had different names for it: the Salvaging, the Greening, as if giving it an innocuous label could excuse what they'd done. A simple concept: that half or more of the human race had to be eliminated to avert environmental catastrophe. Half or more—the "excess biomass" of the planet Earth. What a phrase; they had phrases for everything.

They'd tried to justify it later, after they'd been caught, but there was no justifying it. The population explosion had fizzled. The rate of increase had been dropping worldwide for decades. Everyone was being fed, not well, but enough. Environmental problems were under control. A reprieve, at the very least, though there had been plenty of debate.

But the Porter Group hadn't had time for debate. They knew better. They had made their plans, had done their work, and had cast it into the winds blowing east of Eden.

And there had been the final twist: that the bacillus had been tailored to infect only non-Caucasians. Dave had asked Reed about that, after he'd broken down on the plane. Reed had answered immediately: "Because they were the largest population reservoir, of course."

But that wasn't the answer. It hadn't exactly been racism either, as so many had said since. The truth was much simpler, far more basic, as basic as blood itself: because they'd lacked the guts to let the thing run its course, to take its portion of the whole race. Their own would have been at risk then.

It must have been so easy, working in isolation, insulated from any voice that would have questioned them on grounds of logic, of ethics, of decency. Starting out with an idea that grew into a scenario that took on a life of its own as they realized that they had the power to do a thing unimagined in history.

Someday you'll thank us, Reed had said, as he'd left the cell for the last time. Not me, Dave told himself, as he had told Reed. Not me.

He grew aware that someone was staring at him. Across the aisle the overweight Hindu sat, hand poised above the pocket printer—but he was not looking at it. Instead his head was turned toward Dave, eyes fixed on him, mouth twisted in a rictus that on his round face looked like childish petulance but that Dave knew was anything but. Startled, he jerked up in the seat, looking away instinctively. When he turned back the man was tapping the keys, face as blank as if he had nothing beyond that on his mind. Dave studied him for a moment then got up and made his way down the aisle toward the rear cabin.

There was a burst of laughter behind him as he reached the door. He looked back over his shoulder. They were staring at him, smiling maliciously, the African, the Latins, all but the Hindu, who remained bent over his paperwork. He felt a sudden rush of fury and swung toward them, but caught himself and halted halfway. "Steady," he muttered aloud, then turned back and went on through the door. They began laughing again as he left the cabin, but he gave no sign that he'd heard.

He looked into the rear. Nate was sitting at the far end, staring down at something in front of him, lips moving. Dave frowned, wondering what he was up to, but then Nate raised the mike high enough for him to see it and he realized that he was dictating. Turning his eyes to Bedford he saw he was asleep. Dave shook his head, wondering once again if Art had been with them, and what part he had played, and if so how he had reconciled himself to the results, what he had told himself, in his deepest heart, to make it possible to live on afterward. To go on knowing that the wretched of the earth had been annihilated in a manner beyond belief, that the survivors were living in even greater misery than before, that his own people would be servants to them for a hundred years.

He had half a mind to go over and shake him awake and ask him . . . Ask him what? If he needed a blanket?

Rubbing the back of his neck, he turned away. He glanced at the coffee urn. No, tired as he was, he had no more use for that nasty stuff. Besides, the last cup was working on him. . . . He looked down the length of the plane then stepped to the rest room.

The room was minuscule; he was able to rest his head on his arm as he leaned over the bowl. He finished and went to the sink to wash his hands. Plenty of hot water, anyway. Bending over, he splashed some on his face. There was a small mirror above the sink and as he straightened up he saw himself in it, water dripping from nose and chin. His eyes were sunken, with black circles around them. He grimaced and was shocked to see the result: a slack-lipped, vicious leer that he never would have pictured. He dropped his head. Might as well face it: He was through.

He took some paper towels from the dispenser, coarse brown stuff that started to tear the minute it was damp. Nice, he thought as he dried his face. A hundred-million-dollar spaceplane and they put this crap in the bathroom.

Wadding the towels, he tossed them and looked back in the mirror, straightening his tie and running a hand over his hair. He tried smiling at himself, but he didn't much like that effect either.

Wills had been right. He had no business being on this mission the state he was in. It wasn't fair to anybody for him to try to stagger through it at this point. He'd call from the cockpit and let Wills know, so that he could arrange things with the team in Delhi.

That still left Art. He closed his eyes, wishing he'd never gotten on the plane. It was going to be twice as hard now. What could he do, tell him, "They're going to take a pop at you, buddy, best of luck, I'm gone"? Maybe he could ask Nate . . . no, that was no good.

He was working up the nerve to break it to him when he heard a shout.

He pushed the door open, but it rebounded against something and he kicked it wide. Stepping out into the aisle he saw the African, stunned and off balance against the wall where the door had flung him. Dave gave him only a quick glance before heading to the rear.

It was the Hindu, as he'd guessed it would be. He was standing with his back to the aisle, waving something with one hand while he shook Bedford with the other, lifting him bodily out of the seat, screaming in a mixture of Hindi and English that Dave couldn't make any sense of. Bedford was staring up at him, eyes wide.

Dave reached for his gun but dropped his hand as he touched the grip. He ran down the aisle and as he was reaching for him the Hindu dropped the thing he was waving, grabbing the lapel of Bedford's coat to shake him harder; Dave could see Art's head bobbing uncontrollably.

He slipped his hands underneath the man's arms and reached up to cup them behind his head. He could smell him, a combination of sweat and some kind of shaving lotion, as he yanked him into the aisle. The Hindu kept his grip on Bedford, dragging him after them. "Get off him," Dave yelled, inches away from the man's ear. "Let him go or I'll snap it."

The man hesitated, then released Bedford, who flopped half in the aisle and half in the seat. The Hindu struggled for a moment as Dave pulled him away then went limp, nearly knocking them both flat. "He killed them," he cried out, his voice thick, then, sobbing, began mumbling in his own language.

Dave got him turned about and started pushing him down the aisle. They were all standing in the doorway: the African, the Latins, the unidentifiable little Asian. As Dave reached them they parted to let through the orderly, followed by Naqui. The soldier grabbed the man's arm as Dave released him. Naqui had already waved the others back; he nodded to Dave then turned to help the orderly. As they went through the doorway the Hindu pulled them to a halt and turned back to Bedford. His face was streaked with tears. "You are a very wicked man," he shouted, then let them lead him away.

At the other end of the cabin Nate was on his feet, his mouth open. He set the mike down and hurried up the aisle. Turning to Bedford, Dave saw that he had got back into the seat and was lodged against the side, staring wild-eyed at the front cabin. As Dave went over Bedford looked down at the seat next to him and reached out to something lying atop it. He pushed at it, hesitantly, as if afraid to touch it, until it fell into the aisle. Dave picked it up. It was a photograph, wrinkled and split, showing the Hindu man, much thinner and with more hair, sitting next to a young woman in a sari. On their laps was a boy in a sailor suit, his black hair combed forward in bangs. They were smiling.

He felt Nate come up beside him and handed it to him without a word. Bedford was still crouched in the corner, eyes fixed on the now-empty doorway. As Dave watched his lips drew back from his teeth. "Fucking raghead," Bedford spat out. "Fucking dot bastard."

His eyes swung toward them, focused on Nate. "What are you looking at?"

Turning to Nate, Dave saw that he was gazing down at Bedford with no expression at all on his face. For a moment he just stood there, saying nothing, then he stepped back and walked toward the front cabin, holding the picture before him.

Dave turned to Bedford. "You all right?" he said quietly.

Bedford looked away. "What's his problem?" he said finally.

"You wouldn't know, would you?" Dave settled into the opposite seat and studied the carpet for a few seconds. "Nate's wife was a sansei, a Japanese-American. Katherine Iroku Weiner. I never met her, but. . . ." He stopped speaking and raised his head.

Bedford was staring into space, his eyes empty. He lifted his hands to his face and pressed himself harder against the cushioned bulkhead as if that would shelter him. A shudder went through him, then he stiffened as if by act of will and slowly pushed himself up in the seat. He dropped his hands and gazed at Dave, his face totally calm. Dave looked back in silence, trying to control his features as Nate had, knowing it was futile; he'd never been any good at hiding what he felt.

Bedford smiled. "Game of chess?" he said, his voice husky. He eyed Dave for a moment, then laughed, deep in his throat. "No."

He got up and stepped into the aisle. "Maybe later, Dave," he said, and walked to the back of the cabin.

Dave watched him go. Bedford the good guy, Bedford the scapegoat, Bedford the sacrifice.

The file could be closed now. No more kidding himself, no more pretending that there was an end to it. Even if Bedford was the last of them, there was no exit, no way to lay that burden down. Not for the fat Hindu, not for Nate, not for Dave himself. He would run those dead streets for all the years he had left.

Bedford had reached the last seat. There he hesitated, raising his head slightly as if to look back at Dave, but instead he merely sat down where he could be seen by no one. Bedford the damned soul.

I will be your Charon, Dave told him silently. I'll lead you through it. The demonstrations, the riots, the attempts to kill you before your time, the trial, the undying hatred of the brown people. I'll be with you every step of the way. I will take you to the other shore.

He'd have to call Delhi, to tell them what changes to make. As he got up the screen caught his eye. It was no longer totally dark; there was a line of light in the center, red and gold, and he realized that they had caught up with the day. The sky lightened, the clouds taking color far below. He watched until the sun peered over the horizon and, rising quickly with the swiftness of their passage, loomed over the sea. Then he walked to the front of the plane and all the work that lay ahead.

WRITTEN IN BLOOD

Chris Lawson

Here's an elegant and incisive look at some of the unex-pected effects of high-tech bioscience, some of which may reach all the way down to the very marrow of your bones . . .

New writer Chris Lawson grew up in Papua New Guinea, and now lives in Melbourne, Australia, with his wife, Andrea. While studying medicine, he earned extra money as a computer programmer, and has worked as a medical practitioner and as a consultant to the pharmaceu-tical industry. He's made short fiction sales to Asimov's, Dreaming Down-Under, Eidolon, *and* Event Horizon.

CTA TAA CAG TGT AGC GAC GAA TGT CTA
CAG AAA CAA GAA TGT CAT GAG TGT CTA
GAT CAT AAC CGA TGT AGC GAC GAA TGT
CTA CAA GAA AGG AAT TAA GAG GGA TAC
CGA TGT AGC GAC GAA TGT CTA AAT CAT
CAA CAC AAA AGT AGT TAA CAT CAG AAA
AGC GAA TGC TTC TTT

In the Name of God, the Merciful, the Compassionate.

These words open the Qur'an. They were written in my fa-ther's blood. After Mother died, and Da recovered from his chemotherapy, we went on a pilgrimage together. In my usual eleven-year-old curious way, I asked him why we had to go to the Other End of the World to pray when we could do it just fine at home.

"Zada," he said, "there are only five pillars of faith. It is easier than any of the other pillars because you only need to do it once in a lifetime. Remember this during Ramadan, when you are hungry and you know you will be hungry again the next day, but your *haj* will be over."

Da would brook no further discussion, so we set off for the Holy Lands. At eleven, I was less than impressed. I expected to find Paradise filled with thousands of fountains and birds and orchids and blooms. Instead, we huddled in cloth tents with hundreds of thousands of sweaty pilgrims, most of whom spoke other languages, as we tramped across a cramped and dirty wasteland. I wondered why Allah had made his Holy Lands so dry and dusty, but I had the sense even then not to ask Da about it.

Near Damascus, we heard about the bloodwriting. The pilgrims were all speaking about it. Half thought it blasphemous, the other half thought it a path to Heaven. Since Da was a biologist, the pilgrims in our troop asked him what he thought. He said he would have to go to the bloodwriters directly and find out.

On a dusty Monday, after morning prayer, my father and I visited the bloodwriter's stall. The canvas was a beautiful white, and the man at the stall smiled as Da approached. He spoke some Arabic, which I could not understand.

"I speak English," said my father.

The stall attendant switched to English with the ease of a juggler changing hands. "Wonderful, sir! Many of our customers prefer English."

"I also speak biology. My pilgrim companions have asked me to review your product." I thought it very forward of my father, but the stall attendant seemed unfazed. He exuded confidence about his product.

"An expert!" he exclaimed. "Even better. Many pilgrims are distrustful of Western science. I do what I can to reassure them, but they see me as a salesman and not to be trusted. I welcome your endorsement."

"Then earn it."

The stall attendant wiped his mustache, and began his spiel. "Since the Dawn of Time, the Word of Allah has been read by mullahs. . . ."

"Stop!" said Da. "The Qur'an was revealed to Mohammed fifteen centuries ago; the Dawn of Time predates it by several billion years. I want answers, not portentous falsehoods."

Now the man was nervous. "Perhaps you should see my uncle. He invented the bloodwriting. I will fetch him." Soon he returned with an older, infinitely more respectable man with grey whiskers in his mustache and hair.

"Please forgive my nephew," said the old man. "He has watched too much American television and thinks the best way to impress is to use dramatic words, wild gestures, and where possible, a toll-free number." The nephew bowed his head and slunk to the back of the stall, chastened.

"May I answer your questions?" the old man asked.

"If you would be so kind," said Da, gesturing for the man to continue.

"Bloodwriting is a good word, and I owe my nephew a debt of gratitude for that. But the actual process is something altogether more mundane. I offer a virus, nothing more. I have taken a hypo-immunogenic strain of adeno-associated virus and added a special code to its DNA."

Da said, "The other pilgrims tell me that you can write the Qur'an into their blood."

"That I can, sir," said the old man. "Long ago I learned a trick that would get the adeno-associated virus to write its code into bone marrow stem cells. It made me a rich man. Now I use my gift for Allah's work. I consider it part of my *zakât.*"

Da suppressed a wry smile. *Zakât,* charitable donation, was one of the five pillars. This old man was so blinded by avarice that he believed selling his invention for small profit was enough to fulfill his obligation to God.

The old man smiled and raised a small ampoule of red liquid. He continued, "This, my friend, is the virus. I have stripped its core and put the entire text of the Qur'an into its DNA. If you inject it, the virus will write the Qur'an into your myeloid precursor cells, and then your white blood cells will carry the Word of Allah inside them."

I put my hand up to catch his attention. "Why not red blood cells?" I asked. "They carry all the oxygen."

The old man looked at me as if he noticed me for the first time. "Hello, little one. You are very smart. Red blood cells carry oxygen, but they have no DNA. They cannot carry the Word."

It all seemed too complicated to an eleven-year-old girl.

My father was curious. "DNA codes for amino acid sequences. How can you write the Qur'an in DNA?"

"DNA is just another alphabet," said the old man. He handed my father a card. "Here is the crib sheet."

My father studied the card for several minutes, and I saw his face change from skeptical to awed. He passed the card to me. It was filled with Arabic squiggles, which I could not understand. The only thing I knew about Arabic was that it was written right-to-left, the reverse of English.

"I can't read it," I said to the man. He made a little spinning gesture with his finger, indicating that I should flip the card over. I flipped the card and saw the same crib sheet, only with Anglicized terms for each Arabic letter. Then he handed me another crib sheet, and said: "This is the sheet for English text."

AAA	a	AGA	q	ATA	[—] dash	ACA	
AAG	b	AGG	r	ATG	{/} slash	ACG	
AAT	c	AGT	s	ATT	**{stop}**	ACT	
AAC	d	AGC	t	ATC	**{stop}**	ACC	
GAA	e	GGA	u	GTA	['] apostrophe	GCA	**{stop}**
GAG	f	GGG	v	GTG	["] quotation mark	GCG	
GAT	g	GGT	w	GTT	[(] open bracket	GCT	0
GAC	h	GGC	x	GTC	[)] close bracket	GCC	1
TAA	i	TGA	y	TTA	[?] question mark	TCA	2
TAG	j	TGG	z	TTG	[!] exclamation	TCG	3
TAT	k	TGT	[ ] space	TTT	[*] end verse	TCT	4
TAC	l	TGC	[.] period	TTC	[¶] paragraph	TCC	5
CAA	m	CGA	[,] comma	CTA	{cap} capital	CCA	6
CAG	n	CGG	[:] colon	CTG		CCG	7
CAT	o	CGT	[;] semi-colon	CTT		CCT	8
CAC	p	CGC	[-] hyphen	CTC		CCC	9

"The Arabic alphabet has 28 letters. Each letter changes form depending on its position in the word. But the rules are rigid, so there is no need to put each variation in the crib sheet. It is enough to know that the letter is *aliph* or *bi,* and whether it is at the start, at the end, or in the middle of the word.

"The [stop] commands are also left in their usual places. These are the body's natural commands and they tell ribosomes when to stop making a protein. It only cost three spots and there were plenty to spare, so they stayed in."

My father asked, "Do you have an English translation?"

"Your daughter is looking at the crib sheet for the English language," the old man explained, "and there are other texts one can write, but not the Qur'an."

Thinking rapidly, Da said, "But you could write the Qur'an in English?"

"If I wanted to pursue secular causes, I could do that," the old man said. "But I have all the secular things I need. I have copyrighted crib sheets for all the common alphabets, and I make a profit on them. For the Qur'an, however, translations are not acceptable. Only the original words of Mohammed can be trusted. It is one thing for *dhimmis* to translate it for their own curiosity, but if you are a true believer you must read the word of God in its unsullied form."

Da stared at the man. The old man had just claimed that millions of Muslims were false believers because they could not read the original Qur'an. Da shook his head and let the matter go. There were plenty of imams who would agree with the old man.

"What is the success rate of the inoculation?"

"Ninety-five percent of my trial subjects had identifiable Qur'an text in their blood after two weeks, although I cannot guarantee that the entire text survived the insertion in all of those subjects. No peer-reviewed journal would accept the paper." He handed my father a copy of an article from *Modern Gene Techniques*. "Not because the science is poor, as you will see for yourself, but because Islam scares them."

Da looked serious. "How much are you charging for this?"

"Aha! The essential question. I would dearly love to give it away, but even a king would grow poor if he gave a grain of rice to every hungry man. I ask enough to cover my costs, and no haggling. It is a hundred US dollars or equivalent."

Da looked into the dusty sky, thinking. "I am puzzled," he said at last. "The Qur'an has one hundred and fourteen suras, which comes to tens of thousands of words. Yet the adeno-associated virus is quite small. Surely it can't all fit inside the viral coat?"

At this the old man nodded. "I see you are truly a man of wisdom. It is a patented secret, but I suppose that someday a greedy industrialist will lay hands on my virus and sequence the genome. So, I will tell you on the condition that it goes no further than this stall."

Da gave his word.

"The code is compressed. The original text has enormous redundancy, and with advanced compression, I can reduce the amount of DNA by over 80 percent. It is still a lot of code."

I remember Da's jaw dropping. "That must mean the viral code is self-extracting. How on Earth do you commandeer the ribosomes?"

"I think I have given away enough secrets for today," said the old man.

"Please forgive me," said Da. "It was curiosity, not greed, that drove me to ask." Da changed his mind about the blood-writer. This truly was fair *zakât*. Such a wealth of invention for only a hundred US dollars.

"And the safety?" asked my father.

The old man handed him a number of papers, which my father read carefully, nodding his head periodically, and humming each time he was impressed by the data.

"I'll have a dose," said Da. "Then no one can accuse me of being a slipshod reviewer."

"Sir, I would be honored to give a complimentary blood-writing to you and your daughter."

"Thank you. I am delighted to accept your gift, but only for me. Not for my daughter. Not until she is of age and can make her own decision." Da took a red ampoule in his hands and held it up to the light, as if he was looking through an envelope for the letters of the Qur'an. He shook his head at the marvel and handed it back to the old man, who drew it up in a syringe.

That night, our fellow pilgrims made a fire and gathered around to hear my father talk. As he spoke, four translators whispered their own tongues to the crowd. The scene was like a great theater from the Arabian Nights. Scores of people wrapped in white robes leaned into my father's words, drinking up his excitement. It could have been a meeting of princes.

Whenever Da said something that amazed the gathered masses, you could hear the inbreath of the crowd, first from the English-speakers, and then in patches as the words came out in the other languages. He told them about DNA, and how it told our bodies how to live. He told them about introns, the long stretches of human DNA that are useless to our bodies, but that we carry still from viruses that invaded our distant progenitors, like ancestral scars. He told them about the DNA code, with its triplets of adenine, guanine, cytosine, and thymine, and he passed around copies of the bloodwriter's crib sheet. He told them about blood, and the white cells that fought infection. He talked about the adeno-associated virus and how it injected its DNA into humans. He talked about the bloodwriter's injection and the mild fever it had given him. He told them of the price.

And he answered questions for an hour.

The next day, as soon as the morning prayers were over, the bloodwriting stall was swamped with customers. The old man ran out of ampoules by mid-morning, and only avoided a riot by promising to bring more the following day.

I had made friends with another girl. She was two years younger than I was, and we did not share a language, but we still found ways to play together to relieve the boredom.

One day, I saw her giggling and whispering to her mother, who looked furtively at me and at Da. The mother waved over her companions, and spoke to them in solemn tones. Soon a very angry-looking phalanx of women descended on my unsuspecting father. They stood before him, hands on hips, and the one who spoke English pointed a finger at me.

"Where is her mother?" asked the woman. She was taller than the others, a weather-beaten woman who looked like she was sixty, but must have been younger because she had a child only two years old. "This is no place for a young girl to be escorted by a man."

"Zada's mother died in a car accident back home. I am her father, and I can escort her without help, thank you."

"I think not," said the woman.

"What right have you to say such a thing?" asked Da. "I am her father."

The woman pointed again. "Ala says she saw your daughter bathing, and she has not had the *khitan*. Is this true?"

"It is none of your business," said Da.

The woman screamed at him. "I will not allow my daughter to play with harlots. Is it true?"

"It is none of your business."

The woman lurched forward and pulled me by my arm. I squealed and twisted out of her grasp and ran behind my father for protection. I wrapped my arms around his waist and held on tightly.

"Show us," demanded the woman. "Prove she is clean enough to travel with this camp."

Da refused, which made the woman lose her temper. She slapped him so hard she split his lip. He tasted the blood, but stood resolute. She reached around and tried to unlock my arms from Da's waist. He pushed her away.

"She is not fit to share our camp. She should be cut, or else she will be shamed in the sight of Allah," the woman screamed. The other women were shouting and shaking their fists, but few of them knew English, so it was as much in confusion as anger.

My father fixed the woman with a vicious glare. "You call my daughter shameful in the sight of Allah? I am a servant of Allah. Prove to me that Allah is shamed and I will do what I can to remove the shame. Fetch a mullah."

The woman scowled. "I will fetch a mullah, although I doubt your promise is worth as much as words in the sand."

"Make sure the mullah speaks English," my father demanded as she slipped away. He turned to me and wiped away tears. "Don't worry, Zada. No harm will come to you."

"Will I be allowed to play with Ala?"

"No. Not with these old vultures hanging around."

By the evening, the women had found a mullah gullible enough to mediate the dispute. They tugged his sleeves as he walked toward our camp, hurrying him up. It was obvious that his distaste had grown with every minute in the company of the women, and now he was genuinely reluctant to speak on the matter.

The weathered woman pointed us out to the mullah and spat some words at him that we did not understand."

"Sir, I hear that your daughter is uncircumcised. Is this true?"

"It is none of your business," said Da.

The mullah's face dropped. You could almost see his heart sinking. "Did you not promise . . . ?"

"I promised to discuss theology with you and that crone. My daughter's anatomy is not your affair."

"Please, sir . . ."

Da cut him off abruptly. "Mullah, in your considered opinion, is it necessary for a Muslim girl to be circumcised?"

"It is the accepted practice," said the mullah.

"I do not care about the accepted practice. I ask what Mohammed says."

"Well, I'm sure that Mohammed says something on the matter," said the mullah.

"Show me where."

The mullah coughed, thinking of the fastest way to extract himself. "I did not bring my books with me," he said.

Da laughed, not believing that a mullah would travel so far to mediate a theological dispute without a book. "Here, have mine," Da said as he passed the Qur'an to the mullah. "Show me where Mohammed says such a thing."

The mullah's shoulders slumped. "You know I cannot. It is not in the Qur'an. But it is *sunnah*."

"*Sunnah*," said Da, "is very clear on the matter. Circumcision is *makrumah* for women. It is honorable but not compulsory. There is no requirement for women to be circumcised."

"Sir, you are very learned. But there is more to Islam than a strict reading of the Qur'an and *sunnah*. There have even been occasions when the word of Mohammed has been overturned by later imams. Mohammed himself knew that he was not an expert on all things, and he said that it was the responsibility of future generations to rise above his imperfect knowledge."

"So, you are saying that even if it was recorded in the Qur'an, that would not make it compulsory." Da gave a smile—the little quirk of his lips that he gave every time he had laid a logical trap for someone.

The mullah looked grim. The trap had snapped shut on his leg, and he was not looking forward to extricating himself.

"Tell these women so we can go back to our tents and sleep," said Da.

The mullah turned to the women and spoke to them. The weathered woman became agitated and started waving her hands wildly. Her voice was an overwrought screech. The mullah turned back to us.

"She refuses to share camp with you, and insists you leave."

Da fixed the mullah with his iron gaze. "Mullah, you are a learned man in a difficult situation, but surely you can see the woman is half-mad. She complains that my daughter has not been mutilated, and would not taint herself with my daughter's presence. Yet she is tainted herself. Did she tell you that she tried to assault my daughter and strip her naked in public view? Did she tell you that she inflicted this wound on me when I stood between her and my daughter? Did she tell you that I have taken the bloodwriting, so she spilled the Word of God when she drew blood?"

The mullah looked appalled. He went back to the woman, who started screeching all over again. He cut her off and began berating her. She stopped talking, stunned that the mullah had turned on her. He kept berating her until she showed a sign of humility. When she bowed her head, the mullah stopped his tirade, but as soon as the words stopped she sent a dagger-glance our way.

That night, three families pulled out of our camp. Many of the others in camp were pleased to see them go. I heard one of the grandmothers mutter "Taliban" under her breath, making a curse of the words.

The mood in camp lifted, except for mine. "It's my fault Ala left," I said.

"No, it is not your fault," said Da. "It was her family's fault. They want the whole world to think the way they think and to do what they do. This is against the teaching of the Qur'an, which says that there shall be no coercion in the matter of faith. I can find the sura if you like."

"Am I unclean?"

"No," said Da. "You are the most beautiful girl in the world."

By morning, the camp had been filled by other families. The faces were more friendly, but Ala was gone. It was my first lesson in tolerance, and it came from my own faith.

In Sydney, we sat for hours, waiting to be processed. By the third hour, Da finally lost patience and approached the customs officer.

"We are Australian citizens, you know?" Da said.

"Please be seated. We are still waiting for cross-checks."

"I was born in Brisbane, for crying out loud! Zada was born in Melbourne. My family is Australian four generations back."

His protests made no difference. Ever since the Saladin Outbreak, customs checked all Muslims thoroughly. Fifty residents of Darwin had died from an outbreak of a biological weapon that the Saladins had released. Only a handful of Saladins had survived, and they were all in prison, and it had been years ago, but Australia still treated its Muslims as if every single one of us was a terrorist waiting for the opportunity to go berserk.

We were insulted, shouted at, and spat on by men and women who then stepped into their exclusive clubs and talked about how uncivilized we were. Once it had been the Aborigines, then it had been the Italian and Greek immigrants; a generation later it was the Asians; now it was our turn. Da thought that we could leave for a while, go on our pilgrimage and return to a more settled nation, but our treatment by the customs officers indicated that little had changed in the year we were away.

They forced Da to strip for a search, and nearly did the same for me, until Da threatened them with child molestation charges. They took blood samples from both of us. They went through our luggage ruthlessly. They X-rayed our suitcases from so many angles that Da joked they would glow in the dark.

Then they made us wait, which was the worst punishment of all.

Da leaned over to me and whispered, "They are worried about my blood. They think that maybe I am carrying a deadly virus like a Saladin. And who knows? Maybe the Qur'an *is* a deadly virus." He chuckled.

"Can they read your blood?" I asked.

"Yes, but they can't make sense of it without the code sheet."

"If they knew it was just the Qur'an texts, would they let us go?"

"Probably," said Da.

"Why don't you give it to them, then?"

He sighed. "Zada, it is hard to understand, but many people hate us for no reason other than our faith. I have never killed or hurt or stolen from anyone in my life, and yet people hate me because I pray in a church with a crescent instead of a cross."

"But I want to get out of here," I pleaded.

"Listen to me, daughter. I could show them the crib sheet and explain it to them, but then they would know the code, and that is a terrifying possibility. There are people who have tried to design illnesses that attack only Jews or only blacks, but so far they have failed. The reason why they have failed is that there is no serological marker for black or Jewish blood. Now we stupid Muslims, and I count myself among the fools, have identified ourselves. In my blood is a code that says that I am a Muslim, not just by birth, but by active faith. I have marked myself. I might as well walk into a neo-Nazi rally wearing a Star of David."

"Maybe I am just a pessimist," he continued. "Maybe no one will ever design an anti-Muslim virus, but it is now technically possible. The longer it takes the *dhimmis* to find out how, the better."

I looked up at my father. He had called himself a fool. "Da, I thought you were smart."

"Most of the time, darling. But sometimes faith means you have to do the dumb thing."

"I don't want to be dumb," I said.

Da laughed. "You know you can choose whatever you want to be. But there is a small hope I have for you. To do it you would need to be very, *very* smart."

"What?" I asked.

"I want you to grow up to be smart enough to figure out how to stop the illnesses I'm talking about. Mark my words, racial plagues will come one day, unless someone can stop them."

"Do you think I could?"

Da looked at me with utter conviction. "I have never doubted it."

Da's leukemia recurred a few years later. The chemotherapy had failed to cure him after all, although it had given him seven good years: just long enough to see me to adulthood, and enrolled in genetics. I tried to figure out a way to cure Da, but I was only a freshman. I understood less than half the words in my textbooks. The best I could do was hold his hand as he slowly died.

It was then that I finally understood what he meant when he said that sometimes it was important not to be smart. At the climax of our *haj* we had gone around the Kaabah seven times, moving in a human whirlpool. It made no sense at all intellectually. Going around and around a white temple in a throng of strangers was about as pointless a thing as you could possibly do, and yet I still remember the event as one of the most moving in my life. For a brief moment I felt a part of a greater community, not just of Muslims, but of the Universe. With that last ritual, Da and I became *haji* and *hajjah,* and it felt wonderful.

But I could not put aside my thoughts the way Da could. I had to be smart. Da had *asked* me to be smart. And when he died, after four months and two failed chemo cycles, I no longer believed in Allah. I wanted to maintain my faith, as much for my father as for me, but my heart was empty.

The event that finally tipped me, although I did not even realize it until much later, was seeing his blood in a sample tube. The oncology nurse had drawn 8 mls from his central line, then rolled the sample tube end over end to mix the blood with the anticoagulant. I saw the blood darken in the tube as it deoxygenated, and I thought about the blood cells in there. The white cells contained the suras of the Qur'an, but they also carried the broken code that turned them into cancer cells.

Da had once overcome leukemia years before. The doctors told me it was very rare to have a relapse after seven years. And this relapse seemed to be more aggressive than the first one. The tests, they told me, indicated this was a new mutation.

Mutation: a change in genetic code. Mutagen: an agent that promotes mutation.

Bloodwriting, by definition, was mutagenic. Da had injected one hundred and fourteen suras into his own DNA. The designer had been very careful to make sure that the bloodwriting virus inserted itself somewhere safe so it would not disrupt a tumor suppressor gene or switch on an oncogene— but that was for normal people. Da's DNA was already damaged by leukemia and chemotherapy. The virus had written a new code over the top, and I believe the new code switched his leukemia back on.

The Qur'an had spoken to his blood, and said: "He it is Who created you from dust, then from a small lifegerm, then from a clot, then He brings you forth as a child, then that you may attain your maturity, then that you may be old—and of you there are some who are caused to die before—and that you may reach an appointed term, and that you may understand. / He it is who gives life and brings death, so when He decrees an affair, He only says to it: *Be,* and it is."

I never forgave Allah for saying "*Be!*" to my father's leukemia.

An educated, intelligent biologist, Da must have suspected that the Qur'an had killed him. Still, he never missed a prayer until the day he died. My own faith was not so strong. It shattered like fine china on concrete. Disbelief is the only possible revenge for omnipotence.

An infidel I was by then, but I had made a promise to my father, and for my postdoc I solved the bloodwriting problem. He would have been proud.

I abandoned the crib sheet. In my scheme the codons were assigned randomly to letters. Rather than preordaining *TAT* to mean *zen* in Arabic or "k" in English, I designed a process that shuffled the letters into a new configuration every time. Because there are 64 codons, with three {stop} marks and eight blanks, that comes to about 5×10^{83} or 500,000,000,000,000,000,000,000,000,000,000,000,000,000, 000,000,000,000,000,000,000,000,000,000,000,000,000,000 combinations. No one could design a virus specific to the Qur'an suras anymore. The *dhimmi* bastards would need to design a different virus for every Muslim on the face of the Earth. The faith of my father was safe to bloodwrite.

In my own blood I have written the things important to me. There is a picture of my family, a picture of my wedding, and a picture of my parents from when they were both alive. Pictures can be encoded just as easily as text.

There is some text: Crick and Watson's original paper describing the double-helix of DNA, and Martin Luther King's "I Have a Dream" speech. I also transcribed Cassius's words from *Julius Caesar*:

> The fault, dear Brutus, is not in our stars,
> But in ourselves, that we are underlings.

For the memory of my father, I included a Muslim parable, a *sunnah* story about Mohammed: One day, a group of farmers asked Mohammed for guidance on improving their crop. Mohammed told the farmers not to pollinate their date trees. The farmers recognized Mohammed as a wise man, and did as he said. That year, however, none of the trees bore any dates. The farmers were angry, and they returned to Mohammed demanding an explanation. Mohammed heard their complaints, then pointed out that he was a religious man, not a farmer, and his wisdom could not be expected to encompass the sum of human learning. He said, "You know your worldly business better."

It is my favorite parable from Islam, and is as important in its way as Jesus' Sermon on the Mount.

At the end of my insert, I included a quote from the *dhimmi* Albert Einstein, recorded the year after the atomic bombing of Japan.

He said, "The release of atom power has changed everything but our way of thinking," then added, "The solution of this problem lies in the heart of humankind."

I have paraphrased that last sentence into the essence of my new faith. No God was ever so succinct.

My artificial intron reads:

8 words, 45 codons, 135 base pairs that say:

    CTA AGC GAC GAA TGT AGT CAT TAC GGA
    AGC TAA CAT CAG TGT TAC TAA GAA AGT
    TGT TAA CAG TGT AGC GAC GAA TGT GAC
    GAA AAA AGG AGC TGT CAT GAG TGT GAC
    GGA CAA AAA CAG TAT TAA CAG AAC TGC

The solution lies in the heart of humankind.

I whisper it to my children every night.

THE PIPES OF PAN

Brian Stableford

Here's a quiet but disturbing story that suggests that even in a world where high-tech genetic science enables you to create your offspring to order, sooner or later children grow up. Whether you try to stop them or not . . .

Critically acclaimed British "hard science" writer Brian Stableford is the author of more than thirty books, including Cradle of the Sun, The Blind Worm, Days of Glory, In the Kingdom of the Beasts, Day of Wrath, The Halcyon Drift, The Paradox of the Sets, The Realms of Tartarus, *and the renowned trilogy consisting of* The Empire of Fear, The Angel of Pain, *and* The Carnival of Destruction. *His most recent novels are* Serpent's Blood, *the start of another projected trilogy, and a new hard science novel,* Inherit the Earth. *His short fiction has been collected in* Sexual Chemistry: Sardonic Tales of the Genetic Revolution. *His nonfiction books include* The Sociology of Science Fiction *and, with David Langford,* The Third Millennium: A History of the World A.D. 2000–3000. *His acclaimed novella "Les Fleurs Du Mal" was a finalist for the Hugo Award in 1994. A biologist and sociologist by training, Stableford lives in Reading, England.*

In her dream Wendy was a pretty little girl living wild in a magical wood where it never rained and never got cold. She lived on sweet berries of many colors, which always tasted wonderful, and all she wanted or needed was to be happy.

There were other girls living wild in the dream-wood but they all avoided one another, because they had no need of company. They had lived there, untroubled, for a long time—far longer than Wendy could remember.

Then, in the dream, the others came: the shadow-men with horns on their brows and shaggy legs. They played strange music on sets of pipes which looked as if they had been made from reeds—but Wendy knew, without knowing how she knew or what sense there was in it, that those pipes had been fashioned out of the blood and bones of something just like her, and that the music they played was the breath of her soul.

After the shadow-men came, the dream became steadily more nightmarish, and living wild ceased to be innocently joyful. After the shadow-men came, life was all hiding with a fearful, fluttering heart, knowing that if ever she were found she would have to run and run and run, without any hope of escape—but wherever she hid, she could always hear the music of the pipes.

When she woke up in a cold sweat, she wondered whether the dreams her parents had were as terrible, or as easy to understand. Somehow, she doubted it.

There was a sharp rat-a-tat on her bedroom door.

"Time to get up, Beauty." Mother didn't bother coming in to check that Wendy responded. Wendy always responded. She was a good girl.

She climbed out of bed, took off her night-dress, and went to sit at the dressing-table, to look at herself in the mirror. It had become part of her morning ritual, now that her awakenings were indeed awakenings. She blinked to clear the sleep from her eyes, shivering slightly as an image left over from the dream flashed briefly and threateningly in the depths of her emergent consciousness.

Wendy didn't know how long she had been dreaming. The dreams had begun before she developed the sense of time which would have allowed her to make the calculation. Perhaps she had always dreamed, just as she had always got up in the morning in response to the summoning rat-a-tat, but she had only recently come by the ability to remember her dreams. On the other hand, perhaps the beginning of her dreams had been the end of her innocence.

She often wondered how she had managed not to give herself away in the first few months, after she first began to remember her dreams but before she attained her present level of waking self-control, but any anomalies in her behavior must have been written off to the randomizing factor. Her parents were always telling her how lucky she was to be thirteen, and now she was in a position to agree with them. At thirteen, it was entirely appropriate to be a little bit inquisitive and more than a little bit odd. It was even possible to get away with being too clever by half, as long as she didn't overdo it.

It was difficult to be sure, because she didn't dare interrogate the house's systems too explicitly, but she had figured out that she must have been thirteen for about thirty years, in mind and body alike. She was thirteen in her blood and her bones, but not in the privacy of her head.

Inside, where it counted, she had now been unthirteen for at least four months.

If it would only stay inside, she thought, *I might keep it a secret forever. But it won't. It isn't. It's coming out. Every day that passes is one day closer to the moment of truth.*

She stared into the mirror, searching the lines of her face for signs of maturity. She was sure that her face looked thinner, her eyes more serious, her hair less blonde. All of that might be mostly imagination, she knew, but there was no doubt about the other things. She was half an inch taller, and her breasts were getting larger. It was only a matter of time before that sort of thing attracted attention, and as soon as it was noticed the truth would be manifest. Measurements couldn't lie. As soon as they were moved to measure her, her parents would know the horrid truth.

Their baby was growing up.

"Did you sleep well, dear?" Mother said, as Wendy took her seat at the breakfast-table. It wasn't a trick question; it was just part of the routine. It wasn't even a matter of pretending, although her parents certainly did their fair share of that. It was just a way of starting the day off. Such rituals were part and parcel of what they thought of as *everyday life.* Parents had their innate programming too.

"Yes thank you," she replied, meekly.

"What flavor manna would you like today?"

"Coconut and strawberry please." Wendy smiled as she spoke, and Mother smiled back. Mother was smiling because

Wendy was smiling. Wendy was supposed to be smiling because she was a smiley child, but in fact she was smiling because saying "strawberry and coconut" was an authentic and honest *choice,* an exercise of freedom which would pass as an expected manifestation of the randomizing factor.

"I'm afraid I can't take you out this morning, Lovely," Father said, while Mother punched out the order. "We have to wait in for the house-doctor. The waterworks still aren't right."

"If you ask me," Mother said, "the real problem's the water table. The taproots are doing their best but they're having to go down too far. The system's fine just so long as we get some good old-fashioned rain once in a while, but every time there's a dry spell the whole estate suffers. We ought to call a meeting and put some pressure on the landscape engineers. Fixing a water table shouldn't be too much trouble in this day and age."

"There's nothing wrong with the water table, dear," Father said, patiently. "It's just that the neighbors have the same indwelling systems that we have. There's a congenital weakness in the root-system; in dry weather the cell-terminal conduits in the phloem tend to get gummed up. It ought to be easy enough to fix—a little elementary somatic engineering, probably no more than a single-gene augment in the phloem—but you know what doctors are like; they never want to go for the cheap and cheerful cure if they can sell you something more complicated."

"What's phloem?" Wendy asked. She could ask as many questions as she liked, to a moderately high level of sophistication. That was a great blessing. She was glad she wasn't an eight-year-old, reliant on passive observation and a restricted vocabulary. At least a thirteen-year-old had the right equipment for thinking all set up.

"It's a kind of plant tissue," Father informed her, ignoring the tight-lipped look Mother was giving him because he'd contradicted her. "It's sort of equivalent to your veins, except of course that plants have sap instead of blood."

Wendy nodded, but contrived to look as if she hadn't really understood the answer.

"I'll set the encyclopedia up on the system," Father said.

"You can read all about it while I'm talking to the house-doctor."

"She doesn't want to spend the morning reading what the encyclopedia has to say about phloem," Mother said, peevishly. "She needs to get out into the fresh air." That wasn't mere ritual, like asking whether she had slept well, but it wasn't pretense either. When Mother started talking about Wendy's supposed wants and needs she was usually talking about her own wants and supposed needs. Wendy had come to realize that talking that way was Mother's preferred method of criticizing Father; she was paying him back for disagreeing about the water table.

Wendy was fully conscious of the irony of the fact that she really did want to study the encyclopedia. There was so much to learn and so little time. Maybe she didn't *need* to do it, given that it was unlikely to make any difference in the long run, but she wanted to understand as much as she could before all the pretense had to end and the nightmare of uncertainty had to begin.

"It's okay, Mummy," she said. "Honest." She smiled at them both, attempting to bring off the delicate trick of pleasing Father by taking his side while simultaneously pleasing Mother by pretending to be as heroically long-suffering as Mother liked to consider herself.

They both smiled back. All was well, for now. Even though they listened to the news every night, they didn't seem to have the least suspicion that it could all be happening in their own home, to their own daughter.

It only took a few minutes for Wendy to work out a plausible path of icon selection which got her away from translocation in plants and deep into the heart of child physiology. Father had set that up for her by comparing phloem to her own circulatory system. There was a certain danger in getting into recent reportage regarding childhood diseases, but she figured that she could explain it well enough if anyone took the trouble to consult the log to see what she'd been doing. She didn't think anyone was likely to, but she simply couldn't help being anxious about the possibility—there were, it seemed, a lot of things one simply couldn't help being anxious about, once it was possible to be anxious at all.

"I wondered if I could get sick like the house's roots," she would say, if asked. "I wanted to know whether my blood could get clogged up in dry weather." She figured that she would be okay as long as she pretended not to have understood what she'd read, and conscientiously avoided any mention of the word *progeria*. She already knew that progeria was what she'd got, and the last thing she wanted was to be taken to a child-engineer who'd be able to confirm the fact.

She called up a lot of innocuous stuff about blood, and spent the bulk of her time pretending to study elementary material of no real significance. Every time she got hold of a document she really wanted to look at she was careful to move on quickly, so it would seem as if she hadn't even bothered to look at it if anyone did consult the log to see what she'd been doing. She didn't dare call up any extensive current affairs information on the progress of the plague or the fierce medical and political arguments concerning the treatment of its victims.

It must be wonderful to be a parent, she thought, *and not have to worry about being found out—or about anything at all, really.*

At first, Wendy had thought that Mother and Father really did have worries, because they talked as if they did, but in the last few weeks she had begun to see through the sham. In a way, they *thought* that they did have worries, but it was all just a matter of habit, a kind of innate restlessness left over from the olden days. Adults must have had authentic anxieties at one time, back in the days when everybody could expect to die young and a lot of people never even reached seventy, and she presumed that they hadn't quite got used to the fact that they'd changed the world and changed themselves. They just hadn't managed to lose the habit. They probably would, in the fullness of time. Would they still need children then, she wondered, or would they learn to do without? Were children just another habit, another manifestation of innate restlessness? Had the great plague come just in time to seal off the redundant umbilical cord which connected mankind to its evolutionary past?

We're just betwixts and betweens, Wendy thought, as she rapidly scanned a second-hand summary of a paper in the latest issue of *Nature* which dealt with the pathology of progeria. *There'll soon be no place for us, whether we grow older or not. They'll get rid of us all.*

The article which contained the summary claimed that the development of an immunoserum was just a matter of time, although it wasn't yet clear whether anything much might be done to reverse the aging process in children who'd already come down with it. She didn't dare access the paper itself, or even an abstract—that would have been a dead giveaway, like leaving a bloody thumbprint at the scene of a murder.

Wendy wished that she had a clearer idea of whether the latest news was good or bad, or whether the long-term prospects had any possible relevance to her now that she had started to show physical symptoms as well as mental ones. She didn't know what would happen to her once Mother and Father found out and notified the authorities; there was no clear pattern in the stories she glimpsed in the general newsbroadcasts, but whether this meant that there was as yet no coherent social policy for dealing with the rapidly escalating problem she wasn't sure.

For the thousandth time she wondered whether she ought simply to tell her parents what was happening, and for the thousandth time, she felt the terror growing within her at the thought that everything she had might be placed in jeopardy, that she might be sent back to the factory or handed over to the researchers or simply cut adrift to look after herself. There was no way of knowing, after all, what really lay behind the rituals which her parents used in dealing with her, no way of knowing what would happen when their thirteen-year-old daughter was no longer thirteen.

Not yet, her fear said. *Not yet. Hang on. Lie low . . . because once you can't hide, you'll have to run and run and run and there'll be nowhere to go. Nowhere at all.*

She left the workstation and went to watch the house-doctor messing about in the cellar. Father didn't seem very glad to see her, perhaps because he was trying to talk the house-doctor round to his way of thinking and didn't like the way the house-doctor immediately started talking to her in-

stead of him, so she went away again, and played with her
toys for a while. She still enjoyed playing with her toys—
which was perhaps as well, all things considered.

"We can go out for a while now," Father said, when the house-
doctor had finally gone. "Would you like to play ball on the
back lawn?"

"Yes please," she said.

Father liked playing ball, and Wendy didn't mind. It was
better than the sedentary pursuits which Mother preferred. Father had more energy to spare than Mother, probably because
Mother had a job that was more taxing physically. Father only
played with software; his clever fingers did all his work.
Mother actually had to get her hands inside her remote-gloves
and her feet inside her big red boots and get things moving.
"Being a ghost in a machine," she would often complain,
when she thought Wendy couldn't hear, "can be bloody hard
work." She never swore in front of Wendy, of course.

Out on the back lawn, Wendy and Father threw the ball
back and forth for half an hour, making the catches more difficult as time went by, so that they could leap about and dive
on the bone-dry carpet-grass and get thoroughly dusty.

To begin with, Wendy was distracted by the ceaseless
stream of her insistent thoughts, but as she got more involved in the game she was able to let herself go a little. She
couldn't quite get back to being thirteen, but she could get
to a state of mind which wasn't quite so fearful. By the time
her heart was pounding and she'd grazed both her knees and
one of her elbows she was enjoying herself thoroughly, all
the more so because Father was evidently having a good
time. He was in a good mood anyhow, because the house-
doctor had obligingly confirmed everything he'd said about
the normality of the water table, and had then backed down
gracefully when he saw that he couldn't persuade Father that
the house needed a whole new root-system.

"Those somatic transformations don't always take," the
house-doctor had said, darkly but half-heartedly, as he left.
"You might have trouble again, three months down the line."

"I'll take the chance," Father had replied, breezily.
"Thanks for your time."

Given that the doctor was charging for his time, Wendy had thought, it should have been the doctor thanking Father, but she hadn't said anything. She already understood that kind of thing well enough not to have to ask questions about it. She had other matters she wanted to raise once Father collapsed on the baked earth, felled by healthy exhaustion, and demanded that they take a rest.

"I'm not as young as you are," he told her, jokingly. "When you get past a hundred and fifty you just can't take it the way you used to." He had no idea how it affected her to hear him say *you* in that careless fashion, when he really meant *we:* a *we* which didn't include her and never would.

"I'm bleeding," she said, pointing to a slight scratch on her elbow.

"Oh dear," he said. "Does it hurt?"

"Not much," she said, truthfully. "If too much leaks out, will I need injections, like the house's roots?"

"It won't come to that," he assured her, lifting up her arm so that he could put on a show of inspecting the wound. "It's just a drop. I'll kiss it better." He put his lips to the wound for a few seconds, then said: "It'll be as good as new in the morning."

"Good," she said. "I expect it'd be very expensive to have to get a whole new girl."

He looked at her a little strangely, but it seemed to Wendy that he was in such a light mood that he was in no danger of taking it too seriously.

"Fearfully expensive," he agreed, cheerfully, as he lifted her up in his arms and carried her back to the house. "We'll just have to take very good care of you, won't we?"

"Or do a somatic whatever," she said, as innocently as she possibly could. "Is that what you'd have to do if you wanted a boy for a while?"

He laughed, and there appeared to be no more than the merest trace of unease in his laugh. "We love you just the way you are, Lovely," he assured her. "We wouldn't want you to be any other way."

She knew that it was true. That was the problem.

She had ham and cheese manna for lunch, with real greens homegrown in the warm cellar-annex under soft red lights.

She would have eaten heartily had she not been so desperately anxious about her weight, but as things were she felt it better to peck and pretend, and she surreptitiously discarded the food she hadn't consumed as soon as Father's back was turned.

After lunch, judging it to be safe enough, she picked up the thread of the conversation again. "Why did you want a girl and not a boy?" she asked. "The Johnsons wanted a boy." The Johnsons had a ten-year-old named Peter. He was the only other child Wendy saw regularly, and he had not as yet exhibited the slightest sign of disease to her eager eye.

"We didn't want *a girl*," Father told her, tolerantly. "We wanted *you*."

"Why?" she asked, trying to look as if she were just fishing for compliments, but hoping to trigger something a trifle more revealing. This, after all, was *the* great mystery. Why her? Why anyone? Why did adults think they needed children?

"Because you're beautiful," Father said. "And because you're Wendy. Some people are Peter people, so they have Peters. Some people are Wendy people, so they have Wendys. Your Mummy and I are definitely Wendy people—probably the Wendiest people in the world. It's a matter of taste."

It was all baby-talk, all gobbledygook, but she felt that she had to keep trying. Some day, surely, one of them would let a little truth show through their empty explanations.

"But you have different kinds of manna for breakfast, lunch and dinner," Wendy said, "and sometimes you go right off one kind for weeks on end. Maybe some day you'll go off me, and want a different one."

"No we won't, darling," he answered, gently. "There are matters of taste and matters of taste. Manna is fuel for the body. Variety of taste just helps to make the routine of eating that little bit more interesting. Relationships are something else. It's a different kind of need. We love you, Beauty, more than anything else in the world. Nothing could ever replace you."

She thought about asking about what would happen if Father and Mother ever got divorced, but decided that it would

be safer to leave the matter alone for now. Even though time
was pressing, she had to be careful.

They watched TV for a while before Mother came home. Father had a particular fondness for archive film of extinct animals—not the ones which the engineers had re-created but
smaller and odder ones: weirdly shaped sea-dwelling creatures. He could never have seen such creatures even if they
had still existed when he was young, not even in an aquar-
ium; they had only ever been known to people as things on
film. Even so, the whole tone of the tapes which documented
their one-time existence was nostalgic, and Father seemed
genuinely affected by a sense of personal loss at the thought
of the sterilization of the seas during the last ecocatastrophe
but one.

"Isn't it beautiful?" he said, of an excessively tentacled sea
anemone which sheltered three vivid clown-fish while un-
gainly shrimps passed by. "Isn't it just *extraordinary*?"

"Yes," she said, dutifully, trying to inject an appropriate
reverence into her tone. "It's lovely." The music on the sound-
track was plaintive; it was being played on some fluty wind-
instrument, possibly by a human player. Wendy had never
heard music like it except on TV sound-tracks; it was as if the
sound were the breath of the long-lost world of nature, teeming with undesigned life.

"Next summer," Father said, "I want us to go out in one of
those glass-bottomed boats that take sight-seers out to the new
barrier reef. It's not the same as the original one, of course,
and they're deliberately setting out to create something modern, something new, but they're stocking it with some truly
weird and wonderful creatures."

"Mother wants to go up the Nile," Wendy said. "She wants
to see the sphinx, and the tombs."

"We'll do that the year after," Father said. "They're just
ruins. They can wait. Living things . . ." He stopped. "Look at
those!" he said, pointing at the screen. She looked at a host of
jellyfish swimming close to the silvery surface, their bodies
pulsing like great translucent hearts.

It doesn't matter, Wendy thought. *I won't be there. I won't
see the new barrier reef or the sphinx and the tombs. Even if*

they find a cure, and even if you both want me cured, I won't be there. Not the real me. The real me will have died, one way or another, and there'll be nothing left except a girl who'll be thirteen forever, and a randomizing factor which will make it seem that she has a lively mind.

Father put his arm around her shoulder, and hugged her fondly.

Father must really love her dearly, she thought. After all, he had loved her for thirty years, and might love her for thirty years more, if only she could stay the way she was . . . if only she could be returned to what she had been before. . . .

The evening TV schedules advertised a documentary on progeria, scheduled for late at night, long after the nation's children had been put to bed. Wendy wondered if her parents would watch it, and whether she could sneak downstairs to listen to the sound-track through the closed door. In a way, she hoped that they wouldn't watch it. It might put ideas into their heads. It was better that they thought of the plague as a distant problem: something that could only affect other people; something with which they didn't need to concern themselves.

She stayed awake, just in case, and when the luminous dial of her bedside clock told her it was time she silently got up, and crept down the stairs until she could hear what was going on in the living room. It was risky, because the randomizing factor wasn't really supposed to stretch to things like that, but she'd done it before without being found out.

It didn't take long to ascertain that the TV wasn't even on, and that the only sound to be heard was her parents' voices. She actually turned around to go back to bed before she suddenly realized what they were talking about.

"Are you *sure* she isn't affected mentally?" Mother was saying.

"Absolutely certain," Father replied. "I watched her all afternoon, and she's perfectly normal."

"Perhaps she hasn't got it at all," Mother said, hopefully.

"Maybe not the worst kind," Father said, in a voice that was curiously firm. "They're not sure that even the worst cases are manifesting authentic self-consciousness, and there's a strong contingent which argues that the vast majority of cases are relatively minor dislocations of programming. But there's no doubt about the physical symptoms. I picked her up to carry her indoors and she's a stone heavier. She's got hair growing in her armpits and she's got tangible tits. We'll have to be careful how we dress her when we take her to public places."

"Can we do anything about her food—reduce the calorific value of her manna or something?"

"Sure—but that'd be hard evidence if anyone audited the house records. Not that anyone's likely to, now that the doctor's been and gone, but you never know. I read an article which cites a paper in the latest *Nature* to demonstrate that a cure is just around the corner. If we can just hang on until then . . . she's a big girl anyhow, and she might not put on more than an inch or two. As long as she doesn't start behaving oddly, we might be able to keep it secret."

"If they do find out," said Mother, ominously, "there'll be hell to pay."

"I don't think so," Father assured her. "I've heard that the authorities are quite sympathetic in private, although they have to put on a sterner face for publicity purposes."

"I'm not talking about the bloody bureaucrats," Mother retorted, "I'm talking about the estate. If the neighbors find out we're sheltering a center of infection . . . well, how would you feel if the Johnsons' Peter turned out to have the disease and hadn't warned us about the danger to Wendy?"

"They're not certain how it spreads," said Father, defensively. "They don't know what kind of vector's involved—until they find out there's no reason to think that Wendy's endangering Peter just by living next door. It's not as if they spend much time together. We can't lock her up—that'd be suspicious in itself. We have to pretend that things are absolutely normal, at least until we know how this thing is going to turn out. I'm not prepared to run the risk of their taking her away—not if there's the slightest chance of avoiding it. I don't care what they say on the newstapes—this thing is getting out of control and I really don't know how it's going to turn out. I'm not letting Wendy go anywhere, unless I'm absolutely forced. She may be getting heavier and hairier, but *in-*

side she's still Wendy, and *I'm not letting them take her away.*"

Wendy heard Father's voice getting louder as he came toward the door, and she scuttled back up the stairs as fast as she could go. Numb with shock, she climbed back into bed. Father's words echoed inside her head: "I watched her all afternoon, and she's perfectly normal . . . *inside* she's still Wendy. . . ."

They were putting on an act too, and she hadn't known. She hadn't been able to tell. She'd been watching them, and they'd seemed perfectly normal . . . but *inside,* where it counted . . .

It was a long time before she fell asleep, and when she finally did, she dreamed of shadow-men and shadow-music, which drew the very soul from her even as she fled through the infinite forest of green and gold.

The men from the Ministry of Health arrived next morning, while Wendy was finishing her honey and almond manna. She saw Father go pale as the man in the gray suit held up his identification card to the door camera. She watched Father's lip trembling as he thought about telling the man in the gray suit that he couldn't come in, and then realized that it wouldn't do any good. As Father got up to go to the door he exchanged a bitter glance with Mother, and murmured: "That bastard house-doctor."

Mother came to stand behind Wendy, and put both of her hands on Wendy's shoulders. "It's all right, darling," she said. Which meant, all too clearly, that things were badly wrong.

Father and the man in the gray suit were already arguing as they came through the door. There was another man behind them, dressed in less formal clothing. He was carrying a heavy black bag, like a rigid suitcase.

"I'm sorry," the man in the gray suit was saying. "I understand your feelings, but this is an epidemic—a national emergency. We have to check out all reports, and we have to move swiftly if we're to have any chance of containing the problem."

"If there'd been any cause for alarm," Father told him, hotly, "I'd have called you myself." But the man in the gray suit ignored him; from the moment he had entered the room his eyes had been fixed on Wendy. He was smiling. Even though Wendy had never seen him before and didn't know the first thing about him, she knew that the smile was dangerous.

"Hello, Wendy," said the man in the gray suit, smoothly. "My name's Tom Cartwright. I'm from the Ministry of Health. This is Jimmy Li. I'm afraid we have to carry out some tests."

Wendy stared back at him as blankly as she could. In a situation like this, she figured, it was best to play dumb, at least to begin with.

"You can't do this," Mother said, gripping Wendy's shoulders just a little too hard. "You can't take her away."

"We can complete our initial investigation here and now," Cartwright answered, blandly. "Jimmy can plug into your kitchen systems, and I can do my part right here at the table. It'll be over in less than half an hour, and if all's well we'll be gone in no time." The way he said it implied that he didn't really expect to be gone in no time.

Mother and Father blustered a little more, but it was only a gesture. They knew how futile it all was. While Mr. Li opened up his bag of tricks to reveal an awesome profusion of gadgets forged in metal and polished glass Father came to stand beside Wendy, and like Mother he reached out to touch her.

They both assured her that the needle Mr. Li was preparing wouldn't hurt when he put it into her arm, and when it did hurt—bringing tears to her eyes in spite of her efforts to blink them away—they told her the pain would go away in a minute. It didn't, of course. Then they told her not to worry about the questions Mr. Cartwright was going to ask her, although it was as plain as the noses on their faces that they were terrified by the possibility that she would give the wrong answers.

In the end, though, Wendy's parents had to step back a little, and let her face up to the man from the Ministry on her own.

I mustn't play too dumb, Wendy thought. *That would be just as much of a giveaway as being too clever. I have to try to make my mind blank, let the answers come straight out*

*without thinking at all. It ought to be easy. After all, I've been
thirteen for thirty years, and unthirteen for a matter of
months . . . it should be easy.*

She knew that she was lying to herself. She knew well
enough that she had crossed a boundary that couldn't be re-
crossed just by stepping backward.

"How old are you, Wendy?" Cartwright asked, when
Jimmy Li had vanished into the kitchen to play with her
blood.

"Thirteen," she said, trying to return his practiced smile
without too much evident anxiety.

"Do you know *what* you are, Wendy?"

"I'm a girl," she answered, knowing that it wouldn't wash.

"Do you know what the difference between children and
adults is, Wendy? Apart from the fact that they're smaller."

There was no point in denying it. At thirteen, a certain
amount of self-knowledge was included in the package, and
even thirteen-year-olds who never looked at an encyclopedia
learned quite a lot about the world and its ways in the course
of thirty years.

"Yes," she said, knowing full well that she wasn't going to
be allowed to get away with minimal replies.

"Tell me what you know about the difference," he said.

"It's not such a big difference," she said, warily. "Children
are made out of the same things adults are made of—but
they're made so they stop growing at a certain age, and never
get any older. Thirteen is the oldest—some stop at eight."

"Why are children made that way, Wendy?" Step by inex-
orable step he was leading her toward the deep water, and she
didn't know how to swim. She knew that she wasn't clever
enough—yet—to conceal her cleverness.

"Population control," she said.

"Can you give me a more detailed explanation, Wendy?"

"In the olden days," she said, "there were catastrophes.
Lots of people died, because there were so many of them.
They discovered how not to grow old, so that they could live
for hundreds of years if they didn't get killed in bad accidents.
They had to stop having so many children, or they wouldn't
be able to feed everyone when the children kept growing up,
but they didn't want to have a world with no children in it.

Lots of people still wanted children, and couldn't stop wanting them—and in the end, after more catastrophes, those people who really wanted children a lot were able to have them . . . only the children weren't allowed to grow up and have more children of their own. There were lots of arguments about it, but in the end things calmed down."

"There's another difference between children and adults, isn't there?" said Cartwright, smoothly.

"Yes," Wendy said, knowing that she was supposed to have that information in her memory and that she couldn't refuse to voice it. "Children can't think very much. They have *limited self-consciousness.*" She tried hard to say it as though it were a mere formula, devoid of any real meaning so far as she was concerned.

"Do you know why children are made with limited self-consciousness?"

"No." She was sure that *no* was the right answer to that one, although she'd recently begun to make guesses. It was so they wouldn't know what was happening if they were ever sent back, and so that they didn't *change* too much as they learned things, becoming un-childlike in spite of their appearance.

"Do you know what the word *progeria* means, Wendy?"

"Yes," she said. Children watched the news. Thirteen-year-olds were supposed to be able to hold intelligent conversations with their parents. "It's when children get older even though they shouldn't. It's a disease that children get. It's happening a lot."

"Is it happening to you, Wendy? Have you got progeria?"

For a second or two she hesitated between *no* and *I don't know,* and then realized how bad the hesitation must look. She kept her face straight as she finally said: "I don't think so."

"What would you think if you found out you *had* got progeria, Wendy?" Cartwright asked, smug in the knowledge that she must be out of her depth by now, whatever the truth of the matter might be.

"You can't ask her that!" Father said. "She's thirteen! Are you trying to scare her half to death? Children can be scared, you know. They're not *robots.*"

"No," said Cartwright, without taking his eyes off Wendy's face. "They're not. Answer the question, Wendy."

"I wouldn't like it," Wendy said, in a low voice. "I don't want anything to happen to me. I want to be with Mummy and Daddy. I don't want anything to happen."

While she was speaking, Jimmy Li had come back into the room. He didn't say a word and his nod was almost imperceptible, but Tom Cartwright wasn't really in any doubt.

"I'm afraid it has, Wendy," he said, softly. "It *has* happened, as you know very well."

"*No she doesn't!*" said Mother, in a voice that was halfway to a scream. "She doesn't know any such thing!"

"It's a very mild case," Father said. "We've been watching her like hawks. It's purely physical. Her behavior hasn't altered at all. She isn't showing any mental symptoms whatsoever."

"You can't take her away," Mother said, keeping her shrillness under a tight rein. "We'll keep her in quarantine. We'll join one of the drug-trials. You can monitor her *but you can't take her away*. She doesn't understand what's happening. She's just a little girl. It's only slight, only her body."

Tom Cartwright let the storm blow out. He was still looking at Wendy, and his eyes seemed kind, full of concern. He let a moment's silence endure before he spoke to her again.

"Tell them, Wendy," he said, softly. "Explain to them that it isn't slight at all."

She looked up at Mother, and then at Father, knowing how much it would hurt them to be told. "I'm still Wendy," she said, faintly. "I'm still your little girl. I . . ."

She wanted to say *I always will be,* but she couldn't. She had always been a good girl, and some lies were simply too difficult to voice.

I wish I was a randomizing factor, she thought, fiercely wishing that it could be true, that it might be true. *I wish I was . . .*

Absurdly, she found herself wondering whether it would have been more grammatical to have thought *I wish I were . . .*

It was so absurd that she began to laugh, and then she began to cry, helplessly. It was almost as if the flood of tears could wash away the burden of thought—almost, but not quite.

Mother took her back into her bedroom, and sat with her, holding her hand. By the time the shuddering sobs released her—long after she had run out of tears—Wendy felt a new sense of grievance. Mother kept looking at the door, wishing that she could be out there, adding her voice to the argument, because she didn't really trust Father to get it right. The sense of duty which kept her pinned to Wendy's side was a burden, a burning frustration. Wendy didn't like that. Oddly enough, though, she didn't feel any particular resentment at being put out of the way while Father and the Ministry of Health haggled over her future. She understood well enough that she had no voice in the matter, no matter how unlimited her self-consciousness had now become, no matter what progressive leaps and bounds she had accomplished as the existential fetters had shattered and fallen away.

She was still a little girl, for the moment.

She was still Wendy, for the moment.

When she could speak, she said to Mother: "Can we have some music?"

Mother looked suitably surprised. "What kind of music?" she countered.

"Anything," Wendy said. The music she was hearing in her head was soft and fluty music, which she heard as if from a vast distance, and which somehow seemed to be the oldest music in the world, but she didn't particularly want it duplicated and brought into the room. She just wanted something to fill the cracks of silence which broke up the muffled sound of arguing.

Mother called up something much more liquid, much more upbeat, much more modern. Wendy could see that Mother wanted to speak to her, wanted to deluge her with reassurances, but couldn't bear to make any promises she wouldn't be able to keep. In the end, Mother contented herself with hugging Wendy to her bosom, as fiercely and as tenderly as she could.

When the door opened it flew back with a bang. Father came in first.

"It's all right," he said, quickly. "They're not going to take her away. They'll quarantine the house instead."

Wendy felt the tension in Mother's arms. Father could work entirely from home much more easily than Mother, but there was no way Mother was going to start protesting on those grounds. While quarantine wasn't exactly *all right* it was better than she could have expected.

"It's not generosity, I'm afraid," said Tom Cartwright. "It's necessity. The epidemic is spreading too quickly. We don't have the facilities to take tens of thousands of children into state care. Even the quarantine will probably be a short-term measure—to be perfectly frank, it's a panic measure. The simple truth is that the disease can't be contained no matter what we do."

"How could you let this happen?" Mother said, in a low tone bristling with hostility. "How could you let it get this far out of control? With all modern technology at your disposal you surely should be able to put the brake on a simple virus."

"It's not so simple," Cartwright said, apologetically. "If it really had been a freak of nature—some stray strand of DNA which found a new ecological niche—we'd probably have been able to contain it easily. We don't believe that anymore."

"It was *designed*," Father said, with the airy confidence of the well-informed—though even Wendy knew that this particular item of wisdom must have been news to him five minutes ago. "Somebody cooked this thing up in a lab and let it loose *deliberately*. It was all planned, in the name of liberation . . . in the name of chaos, if you ask me."

Somebody did this to me! Wendy thought. *Somebody actually set out to take away the limits, to turn the randomizing factor into . . . into what, exactly?*

While Wendy's mind was boggling, Mother was saying: "Who? How? Why?"

"You know how some people are," Cartwright said, with a fatalistic shrug of his shoulders. "Can't see an apple-cart without wanting to upset it. You'd think the chance to live for a thousand years would confer a measure of maturity even on the meanest intellect, but it hasn't worked out that way.

Maybe someday we'll get past all that, but in the meantime . . ."

Maybe someday, Wendy thought, *all the things left over from the infancy of the world will go. All the craziness, all the disagreements, all the diehard habits.* She hadn't known that she was capable of being quite so sharp, but she felt perversely proud of the fact that she didn't have to spell out—even to herself, in the brand new arena of her private thoughts—the fact that one of those symptoms of craziness, one of the focal points of those disagreements, and the most diehard of all those habits, was keeping children in a world where they no longer had any biological function—or, rather, keeping the *ghosts* of children, who weren't really children at all because they were *always* children.

"They call it liberation," Father was saying, "but it really is a disease, a terrible affliction. It's the destruction of *innocence.* It's a kind of mass murder." He was obviously pleased with his own eloquence, and with the righteousness of his wrath. He came over to the bed and plucked Wendy out of Mother's arms. "It's all right, Beauty," he said. "We're all in this together. We'll face it together. You're absolutely right. You're still our little girl. You're still Wendy. Nothing terrible is going to happen."

It was far better, in a way, than what she'd imagined—or had been too scared to imagine. There was a kind of relief in not having to pretend anymore, in not having to keep the secret. That boundary had been crossed, and now there was no choice but to go forward.

Why didn't I tell them before? Wendy wondered. *Why didn't I just tell them, and trust them to see that everything would be all right?* But even as she thought it, even as she clutched at the straw, just as Mother and Father were clutching, she realized how hollow the thought was, and how meaningless Father's reassurances were. It was all just sentiment, and habit, and pretense. Everything couldn't and wouldn't be "all right," and never would be again, unless . . .

Turning to Tom Cartwright, warily and uneasily, she said: "Will I be an adult now? Will I live for a thousand years, and have my own house, my own job, my own . . . ?"

She trailed off as she saw the expression in his eyes, realizing that she was still a little girl, and that there were a thousand questions adults couldn't and didn't want to hear, let alone try to answer.

It was late at night before Mother and Father got themselves into the right frame of mind for the kind of serious talk that the situation warranted, and by that time Wendy knew perfectly well that the honest answer to almost all the questions she wanted to ask was: "Nobody knows."

She asked the questions anyway. Mother and Father varied their answers in the hope of appearing a little wiser than they were, but it all came down to the same thing in the end. It all came down to desperate pretense.

"We have to take it as it comes," Father told her. "It's an unprecedented situation. The government has to respond to the changes on a day-by-day basis. We can't tell how it will all turn out. It's a mess, but the world has been in a mess before—in fact, it's hardly ever been out of a mess for more than a few years at a time. We'll cope as best we can. *Everybody* will cope as best they can. With luck, it might not come to violence—to war, to slaughter, to ecocatastrophe. We're entitled to hope that we really are past all that now, that we really are capable of handling things *sensibly* this time."

"Yes," Wendy said, conscientiously keeping as much of the irony out of her voice as she could. "I understand. Maybe we won't just be sent back to the factories to be scrapped . . . and maybe if they find a cure, they'll ask us whether we want to be cured before they use it." *With luck,* she added, silently, *maybe we can all be* adult *about the situation.*

They both looked at her uneasily, not sure how to react. From now on, they would no longer be able to grin and shake their heads at the wondrous inventiveness of the randomizing factor in her programming. From now on, they would actually have to try to figure out what she *meant,* and what unspoken thoughts might lie behind the calculated wit and hypocrisy of her every statement. She had every sympathy for them; she had only recently learned for herself what a difficult, frustrating and thankless task that could be.

This happened to their ancestors once, she thought. *But not as quickly. Their ancestors didn't have the kind of head-*

start you can get by being thirteen for thirty years. It must have been hard, to be a thinking ape among unthinkers. Hard, but . . . well, they didn't ever want to give it up, did they?

"Whatever happens, Beauty," Father said, "we love you. Whatever happens, you're our little girl. When you're grown up, we'll still love you the way we always have. We always will."

He actually believes it, Wendy thought. He actually believes that the world can still be the same, in spite of everything. He can't let go of the hope that even though everything's changing, it will all be the same underneath. But it won't. Even if there isn't a resource crisis—after all, grown-up children can't eat much more than un-grown-up ones—the world can never be the same. This is the time in which the adults of the world have to get used to the fact that there can't be any more families, because from now on children will have to be rare and precious and strange. This is the time when the old people will have to recognize that the day of their silly stopgap solutions to imaginary problems is over. This is the time when we all have to grow up. If the old people can't do that by themselves, then the new generation will simply have to show them the way.

"I love you too," she answered, earnestly. She left it at that. There wasn't any point in adding: "I always have," or "I can mean it now," or any of the other things which would have underlined rather than assuaged the doubts they must be feeling.

"And we'll be all right," Mother said. "As long as we love one another, and as long as we face this thing together, we'll be all right."

What a wonderful thing true innocence is, Wendy thought, rejoicing in her ability to think such a thing freely, without shame or reservation. I wonder if I'd be able to cultivate it, if I ever wanted to.

That night, bedtime was abolished. She was allowed to stay up as late as she wanted to. When she finally did go to bed she was so exhausted that she quickly drifted off into a deep and peaceful sleep—but she didn't remain there indefinitely. Eventually, she began to dream.

In her dream Wendy was living wild in a magical wood

where it never rained. She lived on sweet berries of many colors. There were other girls living wild in the dream-wood but they all avoided one another. They had lived there for a long time but now the others had come: the shadow-men with horns on their brows and shaggy legs who played strange music, which was the breath of souls.

Wendy hid from the shadow-men, but the fearful fluttering of her heart gave her away, and one of the shadow-men found her. He stared down at her with huge baleful eyes, wiping spittle from his pipes onto his fleecy rump.

"Who are you?" she asked, trying to keep the tremor of fear out of her voice.

"I'm the devil," he said.

"There's no such thing," she informed him, sourly.

He shrugged his massive shoulders. "So I'm the Great God Pan," he said. "What difference does it make? And how come you're so smart all of a sudden?"

"I'm not thirteen anymore," she told him, proudly. "I've been thirteen for thirty years, but now I'm growing up. The whole world's growing up—for the first and last time."

"Not me," said the Great God Pan. "I'm a million years old and I'll *never* grow up. Let's get on with it, shall we? I'll count to ninety-nine. You start running."

Dream-Wendy scrambled to her feet, and ran away. She ran and she ran and she ran, without any hope of escape. Behind her, the music of the reed-pipes kept getting louder and louder, and she knew that whatever happened, her world would never fall silent.

When Wendy woke up, she found that the nightmare hadn't really ended. The meaningful part of it was still going on. But things weren't as bad as all that, even though she couldn't bring herself to pretend that it was all just a dream which might go away.

She knew that she had to take life one day at a time, and look after her parents as best she could. She knew that she had to try to ease the pain of the passing of their way of life, to which they had clung a little too hard and a little too long. She knew that she had to hope, and to trust, that a cunning combination of intelligence and love would be enough to see her and the rest of the world through—at least until the next catastrophe came along.

She wasn't absolutely sure that she could do it, but she was determined to give it a bloody good try.

And whatever happens in the end, she thought, *to live will be an awfully big adventure.*

WHIPTAIL

Robert Reed

*Robert Reed sold his first story in 1986, and quickly estab-
lished himself as a frequent contributor to* The Magazine of
Fantasy and Science Fiction *and* Asimov's Science Fiction,
as well as selling many stories to Science Fiction Age, Universe, New Destinies, Tomorrow, Synergy, Starlight, *and
elsewhere. Reed is almost as prolific as a novelist as he is as
a short story writer, having produced eight novels to date,
including* The Lee Shore, The Hormone Jungle, Black Milk,
The Remarkables, Down the Bright Way, Beyond the Veil of
Stars, An Exaltation of Larks, *and* Beneath the Gated Sky.
His most recent book is his long-overdue first collection,
The Dragons of Springplace. *He lives in Lincoln, Nebraska,
where he's at work on a novel-length version of his 1997
novella, "Marrow."*

*Here, in a story that was a Hugo Finalist in 1999, he
shows us how the societies of a distant future world may be
turned upside down forever by the revolutionary biological
lessons to be learned from a humble little lizard. . . .*

"**W**hat a beautiful morning," I was singing. "And so
strange! Isn't it? This incredible, wonderful fog, and how the
frost clings everywhere. Lovely, lovely, just lovely. Is this
how it always is, Chrome . . . ?"

"Always," she joked, laughing quietly. Patiently. "All year
long, practically."

She was teasing. I knew that, and I didn't care. A river of
words just kept pouring out of me: I was talking about the
scenery and the hour, and goodness, we were late and her poor
mother would be waiting, and God on her throne, I was hungry. Sometimes I told my Chrome to drive faster, and she

would, and then I would find myself worrying, and I'd tell her, "Slow down a little." I'd say, "This road doesn't look all that dry."

Chrome smiled the whole time, not minding my prattle.

At least I hoped she didn't.

I can't help what I am. Dunlins, by nature, are small and electric. Nervous energy always bubbling. Particularly when they're trying not to be nervous. Particularly when their lover is taking them to meet her family for the first time.

"Have you ever seen a more magical morning, Chrome?"

"Never," she promised, her handsome face smiling at me.

It was the morning of the Solstice, which helped that sense of magic. But mostly it was because of the weather. A powerful cold front had fallen south from the chilly Arctic Sea, smashing into the normally warm winter air. The resulting fog was luscious thick, except in sudden little patches where it was thin enough to give us a glimpse of the pale northern sun. Wherever the fog touched a cold surface, it froze, leaving every tree limb and bush branch and tall blade of grass coated with a glittering hard frost. Whiteness lay over everything. Everything wore a delicate, perishable whiteness born of degrees. A touch colder, and there wouldn't have been any fog. Warmed slightly, and everything white would have turned to vapor and an afternoon's penetrating dampness.

The road had its own magic. A weathered charm, I'd call it. Old and narrow, its pavement was rutted by tires and cracked in places, and the potholes were marked with splashes of fading yellow paint. Chrome explained that it had been thirty years since the highway association had touched it. "Not enough traffic to bother with," she said. We were climbing up a long hillside, and at the top, where the road flattened, there was a corner and a weedy graveled road that went due south.

"Our temple's down there," she told me.

I looked and looked, but all I saw was the little road flanked by the white farm fields, both vanishing into the thickest fog yet.

For maybe the fiftieth time, I asked, "How do I look?"

"Awful," she joked.

Then she grabbed my knee, and with a laughing voice, Chrome said, "No, you look gorgeous, darling. Just perfect."

I just hoped that I wasn't too ugly. That's all.

We started down a long hillside, passing a small weathered sign that quietly announced that we were entering Chromatella. I read the name aloud, twice. Then came the first of the empty buildings, set on both sides of the little highway. My Chrome had warned me, but it was still a sad shock. There were groceries and hardware stores and clothing stores and gas stations, and all of them were slowly collapsing into their basements, old roofs pitched this way and that. One block of buildings had been burned down. A pair of Chrome's near-daughters had been cooking opossum in one of the abandoned kitchens. At least that was the official story. But my Chrome gave me this look, confessing, "When I was their age, I wanted to burn all of this. Every night I fought the urge. It wasn't until I was grown up that I understood why Mother left these buildings alone."

I didn't understand why, I thought. But I managed not to admit it.

A big old mothering house halfway filled the next block. Its roof was in good repair, and its white walls looked like they'd been painted this year. Yet the house itself seemed dark and drab compared to the whiteness of the frost. Even with the OPEN sign flashing in the window, it looked abandoned. Forgotten. And awfully lonely.

"Finally," my Chrome purred. "She's run out of things to say."

Was I that bad? I wondered.

We pulled up to the front of the house, up under the verandah, and I used the mirror, checking my little Dunlin face before climbing out.

There was an old dog and what looked like her puppies waiting for us. They had long wolfish faces and big bodies, and each of them wore a heavy collar, each collar with a different colored tag. "Red Guard!" Chrome shouted at the mother dog. Then she said, "Gold. Green. Pink. Blue. Hello, ladies. Hello!"

The animals were bouncing, and sniffing. And I stood like a statue, trying to forget how much dogs scare me.

Just then the front door crashed open, and a solid old voice was shouting, "Get away from her, you bitches! Get!"

Every dog bolted.

Thankfully.

I looked up at my savior, then gushed, "Mother Chromatella. I'm *so* glad to meet you, finally!"

"A sweet Dunlin," she said. "And my first daughter, too."

I shook the offered hand, trying to smile as much as she smiled. Then we pulled our hands apart, and I found myself staring, looking at the bent nose and the rounded face and the gray spreading through her short black hair. That nose was shattered long ago by a pony, my Chrome had told me. Otherwise the face was the same, except for its age. And for the eyes, I noticed. They were the same brown as my Chrome's, but when I looked deep, I saw something very sad lurking in them.

Both of them shivered at the same moment, saying, "Let's go inside."

I said, "Fine."

I grabbed my suitcase, even though Mother Chromatella offered to carry it. Then I followed her through the old door with its cut-glass and its brass knob and an ancient yellow sign telling me, "Welcome."

The air inside was warm, smelling of bacon and books. There was a long bar and maybe six tables in a huge room that could have held twenty tables. Bookshelves covered two entire walls. Music was flowing from a radio, a thousand voices singing about the Solstice. I asked where I should put my things, and my Chrome said, "Here," and wrestled the bag from me, carrying it and hers somewhere upstairs.

Mother Chrome asked if it was a comfortable trip.

"Very," I said. "And I adore your fog!"

"My fog." That made her laugh. She set a single plate into the sink, then ran the tap until the water was hot. "Are you hungry, Dunlin?"

I said, "A little, yes," when I could have said, "I'm starving."

My Chrome came downstairs again. Without looking her way, Mother Chrome said, "Daughter, we've got plenty of eggs here."

My Chrome pulled down a clean skillet and spatula, then asked, "The others?"

Her sisters and near-daughters, she meant.

"They're walking up. Now, or soon."

To the Temple, I assumed. For their Solstice service.

"I don't need to eat now," I lied, not wanting to be a burden.

But Mother Chrome said, "Nonsense," while smiling at me. "My daughter's hungry, too. Have a bite to carry you over to the feast."

I found myself dancing around the main room, looking at the old neon beer signs and the newly made bookshelves. Like before, I couldn't stop talking. Jabbering. I asked every question that came to me, and sometimes I interrupted Mother Chrome's patient answers.

"Have you ever met a Dunlin before?"

She admitted, "Never, no."

"My Chrome says that this is the oldest mothering house in the district? Is that so?"

"As far as I know—"

"Neat old signs. I bet they're worth something, if you're a collector."

"I'm not, but I believe you're right."

"Are these shelves walnut?"

"Yes."

"They're beautiful," I said, knowing that I sounded like a brain-damaged fool. "How many books do you have here?"

"Several thousand, I imagine."

"And you've read all of them?"

"Once, or more."

"Which doesn't surprise me," I blurted. "Your daughter's a huge reader, too. In fact, she makes me feel a little stupid sometimes."

From behind the bar, over the sounds of cooking eggs, my Chrome asked, "Do I?"

"Nonsense," said Mother Chrome. But I could hear the pride in her voice. She was standing next to me, making me feel small—in so many ways, Chromatellas are big strong people—and she started to say something else. Something else kind, probably. But her voice got cut off by the soft *bing-bing-bing* of the telephone.

"Excuse me," she said, picking up the receiver.

I looked at my Chrome, then said, "It's one of your sisters. She's wondering what's keeping us."

"It's not." My Chrome shook her head, saying, "That's the out-of-town ring." And she looked from the eggs to her mother and back again, her brown eyes curious but not particularly excited.

Not then, at least.

The eggs got cooked and put on plates, and I helped pour apple juice into two clean glasses. I was setting the glasses on one of the empty tables when Mother Chrome said, "Good-bye. And thank you." Then she set down the receiver and leaned forward, resting for a minute. And her daughter approached her, touching her on the shoulder, asking, "Who was it? Is something wrong?"

"Corvus," she said.

I recognized that family name. Even then.

She said, "My old instructor. She was calling from the Institute . . . to warn me. . . ."

"About what?" my Chrome asked. Then her face changed, as if she realized it for herself. "Is it done?" she asked. "Is it?"

"And it's been done for a long time, apparently. In secret." Mother Chrome looked at the phone again, as if she still didn't believe what she had just heard. That it was a mistake, or someone's silly joke.

I said nothing, watching them.

My Chrome asked, "When?"

"Years ago, apparently."

Mine asked, "And they kept it a secret?"

Mother Chrome nodded and halfway smiled. Then she said, "Today," and took a huge breath. "Dr. Corvus and her staff are going to hold a press conference at noon. She wanted me to be warned. And thank me, I guess."

My Chrome said, "Oh, my."

I finally asked, "What is it? What's happening?"

They didn't hear me.

I got the two plates from the bar and announced, "These eggs smell *gorgeous*."

The Chromatellas were trading looks, saying everything with their eyes.

Just hoping to be noticed, I said, "I'm awfully hungry, really. May I start?"

With the same voice, together, they told me, "Go on."

But I couldn't eat alone. Not like that. So I walked up to my Chrome and put an arm up around her, saying, "Join me, darling."

She said, "No."

Smiling and crying at the same time, she confessed, "I'm not hungry anymore."

She was the first new face in an entire week.

Even in Boreal City, with its millions from everywhere, there are only so many families and so many faces. So when I saw the doctor at the clinic, I was a little startled. And interested, of course. Dunlins are very social people. We love diversity in our friends and lovers, and everywhere in our daily lives.

"Dunlins have weak lungs," I warned her.

She said, "Quiet," as she listened to my breathing. Then she said, "I know about you. Your lungs are usually fine. But your immune system has a few holes in it."

I was looking at her face. Staring, probably.

She asked if I was from the Great Delta. A substantial colony of Dunlins had built that port city in that southern district, its hot climate reminding us of our homeland back on Mother's Land.

"But I live here now," I volunteered. "My sisters and I have a trade shop in the new mall. Have you been there?" Then I glanced at the name on her tag, blurting out, "I've never heard of the Chromatella's before."

"That's because there aren't many of us," she admitted.

"In Boreal?"

"Anywhere," she said. Then she didn't mention it again.

In what for me was a rare show of self-restraint, I said nothing. For as long as we were just doctor and patient, I managed to keep my little teeth firmly planted on my babbling tongue. But I made a point of researching her name, and after screwing up my courage and asking her to dinner, I confessed what I knew and told her that I was sorry. "It's just so tragic," I told her, as if she didn't know. Then desperate to say anything that might help, I said, "In this day and age, you just don't think it could ever happen anywhere."

Which was, I learned, a mistake.

My Chrome regarded me over her sweet cream dessert, her beautiful eyes dry and her strong jaw pushed a little forward. Then she set down her spoon and calmly, quietly told me all of those dark things that doctors know, and every Chromatella feels in her blood:

Inoculations and antibiotics have put an end to the old plagues. Families don't have to live in isolated communities, in relative quarantine, fearing any stranger because she might bring a new flu bug, or worse. People today can travel far, and if they wish, they can live and work in the new cosmopolitan cities, surrounded by an array of faces and voices and countless new ideas.

But the modern world only seems stable and healthy.

Diseases mutate. And worse, new diseases emerge every year. As the population soars, the margin for error diminishes. "Something horrible will finally get loose," Dr. Chromatella promised me. "And when it does, it'll move fast and it'll go everywhere, and the carnage is going to dwarf all of the famous old epidemics. There's absolutely no doubt in my mind."

I am such a weakling. I couldn't help but cry into my sweet cream.

A strong hand reached across and wiped away my tears. But instead of apologizing, she said, "Vulnerability," and smiled in a knowing way.

"What do you mean?" I sniffled.

"I want my daughters to experience it. If only through their mother's lover."

How could I think of love just then?

I didn't even try.

Then with the softest voice she could muster, my Chrome told me, "But even if the worst does happen, you know what we'll do. We'll pick ourselves up again. We always do."

I nodded, then whispered, "We do, don't we?"

"And I'll be there with you, my Dunnie."

I smiled at her, surprising myself.

"Say that again," I told her.

"I'll be with you. If you'll have me, of course."

"No, that other part—"

"My Dunnie?"

I felt my smile growing and growing.

"Call up to the temple," my Chrome suggested.

"Can't," her mother replied. "The line blew down this summer, and nobody's felt inspired to put it up again."

Both of them stared at the nearest clock.

I stared at my cooling eggs, waiting for someone to explain this to me.

Then Mother Chrome said, "There's that old television in the temple basement. We have to walk there and set it up."

"Or we could eat," I suggested. "Then drive."

My Chrome shook her head, saying, "I feel like walking."

"So do I," said her mother. And with that both of them were laughing, their faces happier than even a giddy Dunlin's.

"Get your coat, darling," said my Chrome.

I gave up looking at my breakfast.

Stepping out the back door, out into the chill wet air, I realized that the fog had somehow grown thicker. I saw nothing of the world but a brown yard with an old bird feeder set out on a tree stump, spilling over with grain, dozens of brown sparrows and brown-green finches eating and talking in soft cackles. From above, I could hear the ringing of the temple bells. They sounded soft and pretty, and suddenly I remembered how it felt to be a little girl walking between my big sisters, knowing that the Solstice ceremony would take forever, but afterward, if I was patient, there would come the feast and the fun of opening gifts.

Mother Chrome set the pace. She was quick for a woman of her years, her eyes flipping one way, then another. I knew that expression from my Chrome. She was obviously thinking hard about her phone call.

We were heading south, following an empty concrete road. The next house was long and built of wood, three stories tall and wearing a steeply pitched roof. People lived there. I could tell by the roof and the fresh coat of white paint, and when we were close, I saw little tractors for children to ride and old dolls dressed in farmer clothes, plus an antique dollhouse that was the same shape and color as the big house.

I couldn't keep myself from talking anymore.

I admitted, "I don't understand. What was that call about?" Neither spoke, at first.

On the frosty sidewalk I could see the little shoeprints of children, and in the grass, their mothers' prints. I found myself listening for voices up ahead, and giggles. Yet I heard nothing but the bells. Suddenly I wanted to be with those children, sitting in the temple, nothing to do but sing for summer's return.

As if reading my mind, Mother Chrome said, "We have a beautiful temple. Did you see it in all *my* fog?"

I shook my head. "No."

"Beautiful," she repeated. "We built it from the local sandstone. More than a hundred and fifty years ago."

"Yes, ma'am," I muttered.

Past the long house, tucked inside a grove of little trees, was a pig pen. There was a strong high fence, electrified and barbed. The shaggy brown adults glared at us, while their newest daughters, striped and halfway cute, came closer, begging for scraps and careless fingers.

I asked again, "What about that call? What's so important?"

"We were always a successful family," said Mother Chrome. "My daughter's told you, I'm sure."

"Yes, ma'am."

"Mostly we were farmers, but in the last few centuries, our real talents emerged. We like science and the healing arts most of all."

My Chrome had told me the same thing. In the same words and tone.

We turned to the west, climbing up the hill toward the temple. Empty homes left empty for too long lined both sides of the little street. They were sad and sloppy, surrounded by thick stands of brown weeds. Up ahead of us, running from thicket to thicket, was a flock of wild pheasants, dark brown against the swirling fog.

"Chromatellas were a successful family," she told me, "and relatively rich, too."

Just before I made a fool of myself, I realized that Mother Chrome was trying to answer my questions.

"Nearly forty years ago, I was awarded a student slot at the Great Western Institute." She looked back at me, then past me. "It was such a wonderful honor and a great opportunity. And of course my family threw a party for me. Complete with a parade. With my mother and my grand, I walked this route. This ground. My gown was new, and it was decorated with ribbons and flower blossoms. Everyone in Chromatella stood in two long lines, holding hands and singing to me. My sisters. My near-sisters. Plus travelers at the mother house, and various lovers, too."

I was listening, trying hard to picture the day.

"A special feast was held in the temple. A hundred fat pigs were served. People got drunk and stood up on their chairs and told the same embarrassing stories about me, again and again. I was drunk for the first time. Badly. And when I finished throwing up, my mother and sisters bundled me up, made certain that my inoculation records were in my pocket, then they put me on the express train racing south."

We were past the abandoned homes, and the bells were louder. Closer.

"When I woke, I had a premonition. I realized that I would never come home again. Which is a common enough premonition. And silly. Of course your family will always be there. Always, always. Where else can they be?"

Mother Chrome said those last words with a flat voice and strange eyes.

She was walking slower now, and I was beside her, the air tingling with old fears and angers. And that's when the first of the tombstones appeared: Coming out of the cold fog, they were simple chunks of fieldstone set on end and crudely engraved.

They looked unreal at first.

Ready to dissolve back into the fog.

But with a few more steps, they turned as real as any of us, and a breath of wind began blowing away the worst of the fog, the long hillside suddenly visible, covered with hundreds and thousands of crude markers, the ground in front of each slumping and every grave decorated with wild flowers: Easy to seed, eager to grow, requiring no care and perfectly happy in this city of ghosts.

When my great was alive, she loved to talk about her voyage from Mother's Land. She would describe the food she ate, the fleas in her clothes, the hurricane that tore the sails from the ship's masts, and finally the extraordinary hope she felt when the New Lands finally passed into view.

None of it ever happened to her, of course.

The truth is that she was born on the Great Delta. It was her grand who had ridden on the immigrant boat, and what she remembered were her grand's old stories. But isn't that the way with families? Surrounded by people who are so much like you, you can't help but have their large lives bleed into yours, and yours, you can only hope, into theirs.

Now the Chromatellas told the story together.

The older one would talk until she couldn't anymore, then her daughter would effortlessly pick up the threads, barely a breath separating their two voices.

Like our great cities, they said, the Institutes are recent inventions.

Even four decades ago, the old precautions remained in effect. Students and professors had to keep their inoculation records on hand. No one could travel without a doctor's certificate and forms to the Plague Bureau. To be given the chance to actually live with hundreds and thousands of people who didn't share your blood—who didn't even know you a little bit—was an honor and an astonishment for the young Chromatella.

After two years, she earned honors and new opportunities. One of her professors hired her as a research assistant, and after passing a battery of immunological tests, the two of them were allowed up into the wild mountain country. Aboriginals still lived the old ways. Most kept their distance. But a brave young person came forward, offering to be their guide and provider and very best friend. Assuming, of course, that they would pay her and pay her well.

She was a wild creature, said Mother Chrome.

She hunted deer for food and made what little clothing she needed from their skins. And to make herself more beautiful to her sister-lover, she would rub her body and hair with the fresh fat of a bear.

In those days, those mountains were barely mapped.

Only a handful of biologists had even walked that ground, much less made a thorough listing of its species.

As an assistant, Mother Chrome was given the simple jobs: She captured every kind of animal possible, by whatever means, measuring them and marking their location on the professor's maps, then killing them and putting them away for future studies. To catch lizards, she used a string noose. Nooses worked well enough with the broad-headed, slow-witted fence lizards. But not with the swift, narrow-headed whiptails. They drove her crazy. She found herself screaming and chasing after them, which was how she slipped on rocks and tumbled to the rocky ground below.

The guide came running.

Her knee was bleeding and a thumb was jammed. But the Chromatella was mostly angry, reporting what had happened, cursing the idiot lizards until she realized that her hired friend and protector was laughing wildly.

"All right," said Mother Chrome. "You do it better!"

The guide rose and strolled over to the nearest rock pile, and after waiting forever with a rock's patience, she easily snatched up the first whiptail that crawled out of its crevice.

A deal was soon struck: One copper for each whiptail captured.

The guide brought her dozens of specimens, and whenever there was a backlog, she would sit in the shade and watch Mother Chrome at work. After a while, with genuine curiosity, the guide asked, "Why?" She held up a dull brown lizard, then asked, "Why do you put this one on that page, while the one in your hand goes on that other page?"

"Because they're different species," Mother Chrome explained. Then she flipped it on its back, pointing and saying, "The orange neck is the difference. And if you look carefully, you can tell that they're not quite the same size."

But the guide remained stubbornly puzzled. She shook her head and blew out her cheeks as if she was inflating a balloon.

Mother Chrome opened up her field guide. She found the right page and pointed. "There!" At least one field biologist had come to the same easy conclusion: Two whiptails, two species. Sister species, obviously. Probably separated by one or two million years of evolution, from the looks of it.

The guide gave a big snort.

Then she calmly put the orange neck into her mouth and bit off the lizard's head, and with a small steel blade, she opened up its belly and groin, telling Mother Chrome, "Look until you see it. Until you can."

Chromatellas have a taste for details. With a field lens and the last of her patience, she examined the animal's internal organs. Most were in their proper places, but a few were misplaced, or they were badly deformed.

The guide had a ready explanation:

"The colorful ones are lazy ladies," she claimed. "They lure in the drab ones with their colors, and they're the aggressors in love. But they never lay any eggs. What they do, I think, is slip their eggs inside their lovers. Then their lovers have to lay both hers and the mate's together, in a common nest."

It was an imaginative story, and wrong.

But it took the professor and her assistant another month to be sure it was wrong, and then another few months at the Institute to realize what was really happening.

And at that point in the story, suddenly, the two Chromatellas stopped talking. They were staring at each other, talking again with their eyes.

We were in the oldest, uppermost end of the cemetery. The tombstones there were older and better made, polished and pink and carefully engraved with nicknames and birthdates and deathdates. The temple bells were no longer ringing. But we were close now. I saw the big building looming over us for a moment, then it vanished as the fog thickened again. And that's when I admitted, "I don't understand." I asked my Chrome, "If the guide was wrong, then what's the right explanation?"

"The lizard is one species. But it exists in two forms." She sighed and showed an odd little smile. "One form lays eggs.

While the other one does nothing. Nothing but donate half of its genetic information, that is."

I was lost.

I felt strange and alone, and lost, and now I wanted to cry, only I didn't know why. How could I know?

"As it happens," said Mother Chrome, "a team of biologists working near the south pole were first to report a similar species. A strange bird that comes in two forms. It's the eggless form that wears the pretty colors."

Something tugged at my memory.

Had my Chrome told me something about this, or did I read about it myself? Maybe from my days in school . . . maybe . . . ?

"Biologists have found several hundred species like that," said my Chrome. "Some are snakes. Some are mice. Most of them are insects." She looked in my direction, almost smiling. "Of course flowering plants do this trick, too. Pollen is made by the stamen, and the genetics in the seeds are constantly mixing and remixing their genes. Which can be helpful. If your conditions are changing, you need to make new models to keep current. To evolve."

Again, the temple appeared from the fog.

I had been promised something beautiful, but the building only looked tall and cold to me. The stone was dull and simple and sad, and I hated it. I had to chew on my tongue just to keep myself from saying what I was thinking.

What was I thinking?

Finally, needing to break up all this deep thinking, I turned to Mother Chrome and said, "It must have been exciting, anyway. Being one of the first to learn something like that."

Her eyes went blind, and she turned and walked away.

I stopped, and my Chrome stopped. We watched the old woman marching toward the big doors of the temple, and when she was out of earshot, I heard my lover say, "She wasn't there when Dr. Corvus made the breakthrough."

I swallowed and said, "No?"

"She was called home suddenly. In the middle of the term." My Chrome took me by the shoulder and squeezed too hard, telling me, "Her family here, and everywhere else . . .

all the Chromatellas in the world were just beginning to die. . . ."

A stupid pesticide was to blame.

It was sold for the first time just after Mother Chrome left for school. It was too new and expensive for most farmers, but the Chromatellas loved it. I can never remember its name: Some clumsy thing full of ethanes and chlorines and phenyl-somethings. Her sisters sprayed it on their fields and their animals, and they ate traces of it on their favorite foods, and after the first summer, a few of the oldest Chromes complained of headaches that began to turn into brain tumors, which is how the plague showed itself.

At first, people considered the tumors to be bad luck.

When Mother Chrome's great and grand died in the same winter, it was called a coincidence, and it was sad. Nothing more.

Not until the next summer did the Plague Bureau realize what was happening. Something in the Chromatella blood wasn't right. The pesticide sneaked into their bodies and brains, and fast-growing tumors would flare up. First in the old, then the very young. The Bureau banned the poison immediately. Whatever was left unused was buried or destroyed. But almost every Chromatella had already eaten and breathed too much of it. When Mother Chrome finally came home, her mother met her at the train station, weeping uncontrollably. Babies were sick, she reported, and all the old people were dying. Even healthy adults were beginning to suffer headaches and tremors, which meant it would be all over by spring. Her mother said that several times. "Over by spring," she said. Then she wiped at her tears and put on a brave Chromatella face, telling her daughter, "Dig your grave now. That's my advice. And find a headstone you like, before they're all gone."

But Mother Chrome never got ill.

"The Institute grew their own food," my Chrome told me.

We were in bed together, warm and happy and in love, and she told the story because it was important for me to know what had happened, and because she thought that I was curious. Even though I wasn't. I knew enough already, I was telling myself.

"They grew their own food," she repeated, "and they used different kinds of pesticides. Safer ones, it turns out."

I nodded, saying nothing.

"Besides," she told me, "Mother spent that summer in the wilderness. She ate clean deer and berries and the like."

"That helped too?" I asked.

"She's never had a sick day in her life," my Chrome assured me. "But after she came home, and for those next few months, she watched everyone else get sicker and weaker. Neighbor communities sent help when they could, but it was never enough. Mother took care of her dying sisters and her mother, then she buried them. And by spring, as promised, it was over. The plague had burnt itself out. But instead of being like the old plagues, where a dozen or fifty of us would survive . . . instead of a nucleus of a town, there was one of us left. In the entire world, there was no one exactly like my mother."

I was crying. I couldn't help but sob and sniffle.

"Mother has lived at home ever since." My Chrome was answering the question that she only imagined I would ask. "Mother felt it was her duty. To make a living, she reopened the old mothering house. A traveler was her lover, for a few nights, and that helped her conceive. Which was me. Until my twin sisters were born, I was the only other Chromatella in the world."

And she was my Chrome.

Unimaginably rare, and because of it, precious.

Five sisters and better than a dozen children were waiting inside the temple, sitting together up front, singing loudly for the Solstice.

But the place felt empty nonetheless.

We walked up the long, long center aisle. After a few steps, Mother Chrome was pulling away from us. She was halfway running, while I found myself moving slower. And between us was my Chrome. She looked ahead, then turned and stared at me. I could see her being patient. I could hear her patience.

She asked, "What?" Then she drifted back to me, asking again, "What?"

I felt out of place.

Lonely, and lost.

But instead of confessing it, I said, "I'm stupid. I know."

"You are not stupid," she told me. Her patience was fraying away. Too quietly, she said, "What don't you understand? Tell me."

"How can those lizards survive? If half of them are like you say, how do they ever lay enough eggs?"

"Because the eggs they lay have remixed genes," she told me, as if nothing could be simpler. "Every whiptail born is different from every other one. Each is unique. A lot of them are weaker than their parents, sure. But if their world decides to change around them—which can happen in the mountains—then a few of them will thrive."

But the earth is a mild place, mostly. Our sun has always been steady, and our axis tilts only a few degrees. Which was why I had to point out, "God knew what she was doing, making us the way we are. Why would anyone need to change?"

My Chrome almost spoke. Her mouth came open, then her face tilted, and she slowly turned away from me, saying nothing.

The singing had stopped.

Mother Chrome was speaking with a quick quiet voice, telling everyone about the telephone call. She didn't need to explain it to her daughters for them to understand. Even the children seemed captivated, or maybe they were just bored with singing and wanted to play a new game.

My Chrome took one of her sisters downstairs to retrieve the old television.

I sat next to one of the twins, waiting.

There was no confusing her for my Chrome. She had a farmer's hands and solid shoulders, and she was six months pregnant. With those scarred hands on her belly, she made small talk about the fog and the frost. But I could tell that her mind was elsewhere, and after a few moments, our conversation came to a halt.

The television was set up high on the wooden altar, between Winter's haggard face and Spring's swollen belly.

My Chrome found an electrical cord and a channel, then fought with the antenna until we had a clear picture and sound. The broadcast was from Boreal City, from one of the giant All-Family temples. For a moment, I thought there was a mistake. My Chrome was walking toward me, finally ready to sit, and I was thinking that nothing would happen. We would watch the service from Boreal, then have our feast, and everyone would laugh about this very strange misunderstanding.

Then the temple vanished.

Suddenly I was looking at an old person standing behind a forest of microphones, and beside her, looking young and strange, was a very homely girl.

Huge, she was.

She had a heavy skull, and thick hair sprouted from both her head and her face.

But I didn't say one word about her appearance. I sat motionless, feeling more lost than ever, and my Chrome slid in beside me, and her mother sat beside her.

Everyone in the temple said, "Oh my!" when they saw that ugly girl.

They sounded very impressed and very silly, and I started laughing, then bit down on my tongue.

To the world, the old woman announced, "My name is Corvus. This is my child. Today is her sixteenth birthday."

The pregnant sister leaned and asked her mother, "How soon till we get ours?"

Mother Chrome leaned, and loud enough for everyone to hear, she said, "Very soon. It's already sent."

I asked my Chrome, "What's sent?"

"The pollen," she whispered. "We're supposed to get one of the very first shipments. Corvus promised it to Mother years ago."

What pollen? I wondered.

"I'll need help with the fertilizations," said her mother. "And a physician's hands would be most appreciated."

She was speaking to my Chrome.

On television, the woman was saying, "My child represents a breakthrough. By unlocking ancient, unused genes, then modifying one of her nuclear bodies, we have produced the first of what should be hundreds, perhaps thousands of special children whose duty and honor it will be to prepare us for our future!"

"I'll stay here with you," I promised my Chrome. "As long as necessary."

Then the hairy girl was asked to say something. Anything. So she stepped up to the microphones, gave the world this long, strange smile, then with the deepest, slowest voice that I had ever heard, she said, "Bless us all. I am pleased to serve."

I had to laugh.

Finally.

My Chrome's eyes stabbed at me.

"I'm sorry," I said, not really meaning it. Then I was laughing harder, admitting, "I expected *it* to look prettier. You know? With a nice orange neck, or some brightly colored hair."

My Chrome was staring.

Like never before, she was studying me.

"What's wrong?" I finally asked.

Then I wasn't laughing. I sat up straight, and because I couldn't help myself, I told all the Chromatellas, "I don't care how smart you know you are. What you're talking about here is just plain stupid!"

I said, "Insane."

Then I said, "It's my world, too. Or did you forget that?"

And that's when my Chrome finally told me, "Shut up," with the voice that ended everything. "Will you please, for once, you idiot-bitch, think and *shut up!*"

A PLANET
NAMED SHAYOL

Cordwainer Smith

The late Cordwainer Smith—in real life Dr. Paul M.A. Linebarger, scholar, statesman, and author of the definitive text (still taught today) on the art of psychological warfare—was a writer of enormous talents who, from 1948 until his untimely death in 1966, produced a double-handful of some of the best short fiction this genre has ever seen— "Alpha Ralpha Boulevard," "A Planet Named Shayol," "On the Storm Planet," "The Ballad of Lost C'Mell," "The Dead Lady of Clown Town," "The Game of Rat and Dragon," "The Lady Who Sailed the Soul," "Under Old Earth," "Scanners Live in Vain"—as well as a large number of lesser, but still fascinating, stories, all twisted and blended and woven into an interrelated tapestry of incredible lushness and intricacy. Smith created a baroque cosmology unrivaled even today for its scope and complexity: a millennia-spanning future history, logically outlandish and elegantly strange, set against a vivid, richly colored, mythically intense universe where animals assume the shape of men, vast planoform ships whisper through multidimensional space, immense sick sheep are the most valuable objects in the universe, immortality can be bought, and the mysterious Lords of the Instrumentality rule a hunted Earth too old for history. . . .

It is a cosmology that looks as evocative and bizarre today in the '00s as it did in the '60s; certainly for sheer sweep and daring of conceptualization, in its vision of how different and strange the future will be, it rivals any contemporary vision conjured up by Young Turks such as Bruce Sterling and Greg Bear, and I suspect that it is timeless.

In the nightmarish and yet hallucinatorially beautiful

story that follows, decades ahead of its time both stylistically and conceptually, he takes us to one of the strangest worlds ever imagined in science fiction, a literal hell where the sufferings of the damned themselves are turned to a socially useful function by the most sophisticated of genetic technologies, for a vivid lesson in sin, redemption, and transfiguration. . . .

Cordwainer Smith's books include the novel Norstrilia *and the collections* Space Lords—*one of the landmark collections of the genre*—The Best of Cordwainer Smith, Quest of the Three Worlds, Stardreamer, You Will Never Be The Same, *and* The Instrumentality of Mankind. *As Felix C. Forrest, he wrote two mainstream novels,* Ria *and* Carola, *and as Carmichael Smith he wrote the thriller* Atomsk.

His most recent book is the posthumous collection The Rediscovery of Man: The Complete Short Science Fiction of Cordwainer Smith (*NESFA Press, P.O. Box 809, Framingham, MA 07101-0203, $24.95*), *a huge book that collects almost all of his short fiction, and which will certainly stand as one of the very best collections of the decade—and a book that belongs in every complete science fiction collection.*

1

There was a tremendous difference between the liner and the ferry in Mercer's treatment. On the liner, the attendants made gibes when they brought him his food.

"Scream good and loud," said one rat-faced steward, "and then we'll know it's you when they broadcast the sounds of punishment on the Emperor's birthday."

The other, fat steward ran the tip of his wet, red tongue over his thick, purple-red lips one time and said, "Stands to reason, man. If you hurt all the time, the whole lot of you would die. Something pretty good must happen, along with the—whatchamacallit. Maybe you turn into a woman. Maybe you turn into two people. Listen, cousin, if it's real crazy fun, let me know . . ." Mercer said nothing. Mercer had enough troubles of his own not to wonder about the daydreams of nasty men.

At the ferry it was different. The biopharmaceutical staff was deft, impersonal, quick in removing his shackles. They took off all his prison clothes and left them on the liner. When he boarded the ferry, naked, they looked him over as if he were a rare plant or a body on the operating table. They were almost kind in the clinical deftness of their touch. They did not treat him as a criminal, but as a specimen.

Men and women, clad in their medical smocks, they looked at him as though he were already dead.

He tried to speak. A man, older and more authoritative than the others, said firmly and clearly, "Do not worry about talking. I will talk to you myself in a very little time. What we are having now are the preliminaries, to determine your physical condition. Turn around, please."

Mercer turned around. An orderly rubbed his back with a very strong antiseptic.

"This is going to sting," said one of the technicians, "but it is nothing serious or painful. We are determining the toughness of the different layers of your skin."

Mercer, annoyed by this impersonal approach, spoke up just as a sharp little sting burned him above the sixth lumbar vertebra. "Don't you know who I am?"

"Of course we know who you are," said a woman's voice. "We have it all in a file in the corner. The chief doctor will talk about your crime later, if you want to talk about it. Keep quiet now. We are making a skin test, and you will feel much better if you do not make us prolong it."

Honesty forced her to add another sentence: "And we will get better results as well."

They had lost no time at all in getting to work.

He peered at them sidewise to look at them. There was nothing about them to indicate that they were human devils in the antechambers of hell itself. Nothing was there to indicate that this was the satellite of Shayol, the final and uttermost place of chastisement and shame. They looked like medical people from his life before he committed the crime without a name.

They changed from one routine to another. A woman, wearing a surgical mask, waved her hand at a white table.

"Climb up on that, please."

No one had said "please" to Mercer since the guards had seized him at the edge of the palace. He started to obey her and then he saw that there were padded handcuffs at the head of the table. He stopped.

"Get along, please," she demanded. Two or three of the others turned around to look at both of them.

The second "please" shook him. He had to speak. These were people, and he was a person again. He felt his voice rising, almost cracking into shrillness as he asked her, "Please, Ma'am, is the punishment going to begin?"

"There's no punishment here," said the woman. "This is the satellite. Get on the table. We're going to give you your first skin-toughening before you talk to the head doctor. Then you can tell him all about your crime—"

"You know my crime?" he said, greeting it almost like a neighbor.

"Of course not," said she, "but all the people who come through here are believed to have committed crimes. Somebody thinks so or they wouldn't be here. Most of them want to talk about their personal crimes. But don't slow me down. I'm a skin technician, and down on the surface of Shayol you're going to need the very best work that any of us can do for you. Now get on that table. And when you are ready to talk to the chief you'll have something to talk about besides your crime."

He complied.

Another masked person, probably a girl, took his hands in cool, gentle fingers and fitted them to the padded cuffs in a way he had never sensed before. By now he thought he knew every interrogation machine in the whole empire, but this was nothing like any of them.

The orderly stepped back. "All clear, Sir and Doctor."

"Which do you prefer?" said the skin technician. "A great deal of pain or a couple of hours' unconsciousness?"

"Why should I want pain?" said Mercer.

"Some specimens do," said the technician, "by the time they arrive here. I suppose it depends on what people have done to them before they got here. I take it you did not get any of the dream-punishments."

"No," said Mercer. "I missed those." He thought to himself, I didn't know that I missed anything at all.

He remembered his last trial, himself wired and plugged in to the witness stand. The room had been high and dark. Bright blue light shone on the panel of judges, their judicial caps a fantastic parody of the episcopal mitres of long, long ago. The judges were talking, but he could not hear them. Momentarily the insulation slipped and he heard one of them say, "Look at that white, devilish face. A man like that is guilty of everything. I vote for Pain Terminal." "Not Planet Shayol?" said a second voice. "The dromozoa place," said a third voice. "That should suit him," said the first voice. One of the judicial engineers must then have noticed that the prisoner was listening illegally. He was cut off. Mercer then thought that he had gone through everything which the cruelty and intelligence of mankind could devise.

But this woman said he had missed the dream-punishments. Could there be people in the universe even worse off than himself? There must be a lot of people down on Shayol. They never came back.

He was going to be one of them; would they boast to him of what they had done, before they were made to come to this place?

"You asked for it," said the woman technician. "It is just an ordinary anesthetic. Don't panic when you awaken. Your skin is going to be thickened and strengthened chemically and biologically."

"Does it hurt?"

"Of course," said she. "But get this out of your head. We're not punishing you. The pain here is just ordinary medical pain. Anybody might get it if they needed a lot of surgery. The punishment, if that's what you want to call it, is down on Shayol. Our only job is to make sure that you are fit to survive after you are landed. In a way, we are saving your life ahead of time. You can be grateful for that if you want to be. Meanwhile, you will save yourself a lot of trouble if you realize that your nerve endings will respond to the change in the skin. You had better expect to be very uncomfortable when you recover. But then, we can help that, too." She brought down an enormous lever and Mercer blacked out.

When he came to, he was in an ordinary hospital room, but he did not notice it. He seemed bedded in fire. He lifted his hand to see if there were flames on it. It looked the way it always had, except that it was a little red and a little swollen. He tried to turn in the bed. The fire became a scorching blast which stopped him in mid-turn. Uncontrollably, he moaned.

A voice spoke. "You are ready for some pain-killer."

It was a girl nurse. "Hold your head still," she said, "and I will give you half an amp of pleasure. Your skin won't bother you then."

She slipped a soft cap on his head. It looked like metal but it felt like silk.

He had to dig his fingernails into his palms to keep from thrashing about on the bed.

"Scream if you want to," she said. "A lot of them do. It will just be a minute or two before the cap finds the right lobe in your brain."

She stepped to the corner and did something which he could not see.

There was the flick of a switch.

The fire did not vanish from his skin. He still felt it; but suddenly it did not matter. His mind was full of delicious pleasure which throbbed outward from his head and seemed to pulse down through his nerves. He had visited the pleasure palaces, but he had never felt anything like this before.

He wanted to thank the girl, and he twisted around in the bed to see her. He could feel his whole body flash with pain as he did so, but the pain was far away. And the pulsating pleasure which coursed out of his head, down his spinal cord and into his nerves was so intense that the pain got through only as a remote, unimportant signal.

She was standing very still in the corner.

"Thank you, nurse," said he.

She said nothing.

He looked more closely, though it was hard to look while

enormous pleasure pulsed through his body like a symphony written in nerve-messages. He focused his eyes on her and saw that she too wore a soft metallic cap.

He pointed at it.

She blushed all the way down to her throat.

She spoke dreamily. "You looked like a nice man to me. I didn't think you'd tell on me . . ."

He gave her what he thought was a friendly smile, but with the pain in his skin and the pleasure bursting out of his head, he really had no idea of what his actual expression might be. "It's against the law," he said. "It's terribly against the law. But it is nice."

"How do you think *we* stand it here?" said the nurse. "You specimens come in here talking like ordinary people and then you go down to Shayol. Terrible things happen to you on Shayol. Then the surface station sends up parts of you, over and over again. I may see your head ten times, quick-frozen and ready for cutting up, before my two years are up. You prisoners ought to know how we suffer," she crooned, the pleasure-charge still keeping her relaxed and happy. "You ought to die as soon as you get down there and not pester us with your torments. We can hear you screaming, you know. You keep on sounding like people even after Shayol begins to work on you. Why do you do it, Mr. Specimen?" She giggled sillily. "You hurt our feelings so. No wonder a girl like me has to have a little jolt now and then. It's real, real dreamy and I don't mind getting you ready to go down on Shayol." She staggered over to his bed. "Pull this cap off me, will you? I haven't got enough will power left to raise my hands."

Mercer saw his hand tremble as he reached for the cap.

His fingers touched the girl's soft hair through the cap. As he tried to get his thumb under the edge of the cap, in order to pull it off, he realized this was the loveliest girl he had ever touched. He felt that he had always loved her, that he always would. Her cap came off. She stood erect, staggering a little before she found a chair to hold to. She closed her eyes and breathed deeply.

"Just a minute," she said in her normal voice. "I'll be with you in just a minute. The only time I can get a jolt of this is when one of you visitors gets a dose to get over the skin trouble."

She turned to the room mirror to adjust her hair. Speaking with her back to him, she said, "I hope I didn't say anything about downstairs."

Mercer still had the cap on. He loved this beautiful girl who had put it on him. He was ready to weep at the thought that she had had the same kind of pleasure which he still enjoyed. Not for the world would he say anything which could hurt her feelings. He was sure she wanted to be told that she had not said anything about "downstairs"—probably shop talk for the surface of Shayol—so he assured her warmly, "You said nothing. Nothing at all."

She came over to the bed, leaned, kissed him on the lips. The kiss was as far away as the pain; he felt nothing; the Niagara of throbbing pleasure which poured through his head left no room for more sensation. But he liked the friendliness of it. A grim, sane corner of his mind whispered to him that this was probably the last time he would ever kiss a woman, but it did not seem to matter.

With skilled fingers she adjusted the cap on his head. "There, now. You're a sweet guy. I'm going to pretend-forget and leave the cap on you till the doctor comes."

With a bright smile she squeezed his shoulder.

She hastened out of the room.

The white of her skirt flashed prettily as she went out the door. He saw that she had very shapely legs indeed.

She was nice, but the cap . . . ah, it was the cap that mattered! He closed his eyes and let the cap go on stimulating the pleasure centers of his brain. The pain in his skin was still there, but it did not matter any more than did the chair standing in the corner. The pain was just something that happened to be in the room.

A firm touch on his arm made him open his eyes.

The older, authoritative-looking man was standing beside the bed, looking down at him with a quizzical smile.

"She did it again," said the old man.

Mercer shook his head, trying to indicate that the young nurse had done nothing wrong.

"I'm Doctor Vomact," said the older man, "and I am going

to take this cap off you. You will then experience the pain
again, but I think it will not be so bad. You can have the cap
several more times before you leave here."

With a swift, firm gesture he snatched the cap off Mercer's
head.

Mercer promptly doubled up with the inrush of fire from
his skin. He started to scream and then saw that Doctor Vomact was watching him calmly.

Mercer gasped, "It is—easier now."

"I knew it would be," said the doctor. "I had to take the cap
off to talk to you. You have a few choices to make."

"Yes, Doctor," gasped Mercer.

"You have committed a serious crime and you are going
down to the surface of Shayol."

"Yes," said Mercer.

"Do you want to tell me your crime?"

Mercer thought of the white palace walls in perpetual sunlight, and the soft mewing of the little things when he reached
them. He tightened his arms, legs, back and jaw. "No," he
said, "I don't want to talk about it. It's the crime without a
name. Against the Imperial family . . ."

"Fine," said the doctor, "that's a healthy attitude. The
crime is past. Your future is ahead. Now, I can destroy your
mind before you go down—if you want me to."

"That's against the law," said Mercer.

Doctor Vomact smiled warmly and confidently. "Of course
it is. A lot of things are against human law. But there are laws
of science, too. Your body, down on Shayol, is going to serve
science. It doesn't matter to me whether the body has Mercer's mind or the mind of a low-grade shellfish. I have to
leave enough mind in you to keep the body going, but I can
wipe out the historic you and give your body a better chance
of being happy. It's your choice, Mercer. Do you want to be
you or not?"

Mercer shook his head back and forth. "I don't know."

"I'm taking a chance," said Doctor Vomact, "in giving you
this much leeway. I'd have it done if I were in your position.
It's pretty bad down there."

Mercer looked at the full, broad face. He did not trust the
comfortable smile. Perhaps this was a trick to increase his

punishment. The cruelty of the Emperor was proverbial. Look at what he had done to the widow of his predecessor, the Dowager Lady Da. She was younger than the Emperor himself, and he had sent her to a place worse than death. If he had been sentenced to Shayol, why was this doctor trying to interfere with the rules? Maybe the doctor himself had been conditioned, and did not know what he was offering.

Doctor Vomact read Mercer's face. "All right. You refuse. You want to take your mind down with you. It's all right with me. I don't have you on my conscience. I suppose you'll refuse the next offer too. Do you want me to take your eyes out before you go down? You'll be much more comfortable without vision. I *know* that, from the voices that we record for the warning broadcasts. I can sear the optic nerves so that there will be no chance of your getting vision again."

Mercer rocked back and forth. The fiery pain had become a universal itch, but the soreness of his spirit was greater than the discomfort of his skin.

"You refuse that, too?" said the doctor.

"I suppose so," said Mercer.

"Then all I have to do is to get ready. You can have the cap for a while, if you want."

Mercer said, "Before I put the cap on, can you tell me what happens down there?"

"Some of it," said the doctor. "There is an attendant. He is a man, but not a human being. He is a homunculus fashioned out of cattle material. He is intelligent and very conscientious. You specimens are turned loose on the surface of Shayol. The dromozoa are a special lifeform there. When they settle in your body, B'dikkat—that's the attendant—carves them out with an anesthetic and sends them up here. We freeze the tissue cultures, and they are compatible with almost any kind of oxygen-based life. Half the surgical repair you see in the whole universe comes out of buds that we ship from here. Shayol is a very healthy place, so far as survival is concerned. You won't die."

"You mean," said Mercer, "that I am getting perpetual punishment."

"I didn't say that," said Doctor Vomact. "Or if I did, I was wrong. You won't die soon. I don't know how long you will live down there. Remember, no matter how uncomfortable you get, the samples which B'dikkat sends up will help thousands of people in all the inhabited worlds. Now take the cap."

"I'd rather talk," said Mercer. "It may be my last chance."

The doctor looked at him strangely. "If you can stand that pain, go ahead and talk."

"Can I commit suicide down there?"

"I don't know," said the doctor. "It's never happened. And to judge by the voices, you'd think they wanted to."

"Has anybody ever come back from Shayol?"

"Not since it was put off limits about four hundred years ago."

"Can I talk to other people down there?"

"Yes," said the doctor.

"Who punishes me down there?"

"Nobody does, you fool," cried Doctor Vomact. "It's not punishment. People don't like it down on Shayol, and it's better, I guess, to get convicts instead of volunteers. But there isn't anybody *against* you at all."

"No jailers?" asked Mercer, with a whine in his voice.

"No jailers, no rules, no prohibitions. Just Shayol, and B'dikkat to take care of you. Do you still want your mind and your eyes?"

"I'll keep them," said Mercer. "I've gone this far and I might as well go the rest of the way."

"Then let me put the cap on you for your second dose," said Doctor Vomact.

The doctor adjusted the cap just as lightly and delicately as had the nurse; he was quicker about it. There was no sign of his picking out another cap for himself.

The inrush of pleasure was like a wild intoxication. His burning skin receded into distance. The doctor was near in space, but even the doctor did not matter. Mercer was not afraid of Shayol. The pulsation of happiness out of his brain was too great to leave room for fear or pain.

Doctor Vomact was holding out his hand.

Mercer wondered why, and then realized that the wonder-

ful, kindly cap-giving man was offering to shake hands. He
lifted his own. It was heavy, but his arm was happy, too.

They shook hands. It was curious, thought Mercer, to feel
the handshake beyond the double level of cerebral pleasure
and dermal pain.

"Goodbye, Mr. Mercer," said the doctor. "Goodbye and a
good night . . ."

2

The ferry satellite was a hospitable place. The hundreds of
hours that followed were like a long, weird dream.

Twice again the young nurse sneaked into his bedroom
with him when he was being given the cap and had a cap with
him. There were baths which calloused his whole body. Under
strong local anesthetics, his teeth were taken out and stainless
steel took their place. There were irradiations under blazing
lights which took away the pain of his skin. There were special treatments for his fingernails and toenails. Gradually they
changed into formidable claws; he found himself stropping
them on the aluminum bed one night and saw that they left
deep marks.

His mind never became completely clear.

Sometimes he thought he was home with his mother, that
he was little again, and in pain. Other times, under the cap, he
laughed in his bed to think that people were sent to this place
for punishment when it was all so terribly much fun. There
were no trials, no questions, no judges. Food was good, but he
did not think about it much; the cap was better. Even when he
was awake, he was drowsy.

At last, with the cap on him, they put him into an adiabatic
pod—a one-body missile which could be dropped from the
ferry to the planet below. He was all closed in, except for his
face.

Doctor Vomact seemed to swim into the room. "You are
strong, Mercer," the doctor shouted, "you are very strong!
Can you hear me?"

Mercer nodded.

"We wish you well, Mercer. No matter what happens, remember you are helping other people up here."

"Can I take the cap with me?" said Mercer.

For an answer, Doctor Vomact removed the cap himself. Two men closed the lid of the pod, leaving Mercer in total darkness. His mind started to clear, and he panicked against his wrappings.

There was the roar of thunder and the taste of blood.

The next thing that Mercer knew, he was in a cool, cool room, much chillier than the bedrooms and operating rooms of the satellite. Someone was lifting him gently onto a table.

He opened his eyes.

An enormous face, four times the size of any human face Mercer had ever seen, was looking down at him. Huge brown eyes, cowlike in their gentle inoffensiveness, moved back and forth as the big face examined Mercer's wrappings. The face was that of a handsome man of middle years, clean-shaven, hair chestnut-brown, with sensual, full lips and gigantic but healthy yellow teeth exposed in a half-smile. The face saw Mercer's eyes open, and spoke with a deep friendly roar.

"I'm your best friend. My name is B'dikkat, but you don't have to use that here. Just call me Friend, and I will always help you."

"I hurt," said Mercer.

"Of course you do. You hurt all over. That's a big drop," said B'dikkat.

"Can I have a cap, please," begged Mercer. It was not a question; it was a demand; Mercer felt that his private inward eternity depended on it.

B'dikkat laughed. "I haven't any caps down here. I might use them myself. Or so they think. I have other things, much better. No fear, fellow, I'll fix you up."

Mercer looked doubtful. If the cap had brought him happiness on the ferry, it would take at least electrical stimulation of the brain to undo whatever torments the surface of Shayol had to offer.

B'dikkat's laughter filled the room like a bursting pillow.

"Have you ever heard of condamine?"

"No," said Mercer.

"It's a narcotic so powerful that the pharmacopoeias are not allowed to mention it."

"You have that?" said Mercer hopefully.

"Something better. I have super-condamine. It's named after the New French town where they developed it. The chemists hooked in one more hydrogen molecule. That gave it a real jolt. If you took it in your present shape, you'd be dead in three minutes, but those three minutes would seem like ten thousand years of happiness to the inside of your mind." B'dikkat rolled his brown cow eyes expressively and smacked his rich red lips with a tongue of enormous extent.

"What's the use of it, then?"

"*You* can take it," said B'dikkat. "You can take it after you have been exposed to the dromozoa outside this cabin. You get all the good effects and none of the bad. You want to see something?"

What answer is there except *yes*, thought Mercer grimly; does he think I have an urgent invitation to a tea party?

"Look out the window," said B'dikkat, "and tell me what you see."

The atmosphere was clear. The surface was like a desert, ginger-yellow with streaks of green where lichen and low shrubs grew, obviously stunted and tormented by high, dry winds. The landscape was monotonous. Two or three hundred yards away there was a herd of bright pink objects which seemed alive, but Mercer could not see them well enough to describe them clearly. Farther away, on the extreme right of his frame of vision, there was the statue of an enormous human foot, the height of a six-story building. Mercer could not see what the foot was connected to. "I see a big foot," said he, "but—"

"But what?" said B'dikkat, like an enormous child hiding the denouement of a hugely private joke. Large as he was, he would have been dwarfed by any one of the toes on that tremendous foot.

"But it can't be a real foot," said Mercer.

"It is," said B'dikkat. "That's Go-Captain Alvarez, the man who found this planet. After six hundred years he's still in fine shape. Of course, he's mostly dromozootic by now, but I think there is some human consciousness inside him. You know what I do?"

"What?" said Mercer.

"I give him six cubic centimeters of super-condamine and he snorts for me. Real happy little snorts. A stranger might think it was a volcano. That's what super-condamine can do. And you're going to get plenty of it. You're a lucky, lucky man, Mercer. You have me for a friend, and you have my needle for a treat. I do all the work and you get all the fun. Isn't that a nice surprise?"

Mercer thought, You're lying! Lying! Where do the screams come from that we have all heard broadcast as a warning on Punishment Day? Why did the doctor offer to cancel my brain or to take out my eyes?

The cow-man watched him sadly, a hurt expression on his face. "You don't believe me," he said, very sadly.

"It's not quite that," said Mercer, with an attempt at heartiness, "but I think you're leaving something out."

"Nothing much," said B'dikkat. "You jump when the dromozoa hit you. You'll be upset when you start growing new parts—heads, kidneys, hands. I had one fellow in here who grew thirty-eight hands in a single session outside. I took them all off, froze them and sent them upstairs. I take good care of everybody. You'll probably yell for a while. But remember, just call me Friend, and I have the nicest treat in the universe waiting for you. Now, would you like some fried eggs? I don't eat eggs myself, but most true men like them."

"Eggs?" said Mercer. "What have eggs got to do with it?"

"Nothing much. It's just a treat for you people. Get something in your stomach before you go outside. You'll get through the first day better."

Mercer, unbelieving, watched as the big man took two precious eggs from a cold chest, expertly broke them into a little pan and put the pan in the heat-field at the center of the table Mercer had awakened on.

"Friend, eh?" B'dikkat grinned. "You'll see I'm a good friend. When you go outside, remember that."

An hour later, Mercer did go outside.

Strangely at peace with himself, he stood at the door. B'dikkat pushed him in a brotherly way, giving him a shove which was gentle enough to be an encouragement.

"Don't make me put on my lead suit, fellow." Mercer had seen a suit, fully the size of an ordinary space-ship cabin, hanging on the wall of an adjacent room. "When I close this door, the outer one will open. Just walk on out."

"But what will happen?" said Mercer, the fear turning around in his stomach and making little grabs at his throat from the inside.

"Don't start that again," said B'dikkat. For an hour he had fended off Mercer's questions about the outside. A map? B'dikkat had laughed at the thought. Food? He said not to worry. Other people? They'd be there. Weapons? What for, B'dikkat had replied. Over and over again, B'dikkat had insisted that he was Mercer's friend. What would happen to Mercer? The same that happened to everybody else.

Mercer stepped out.

Nothing happened. The day was cool. The wind moved gently against his toughened skin.

Mercer looked around apprehensively.

The mountainous body of Captain Alvarez occupied a good part of the landscape to the right. Mercer had no wish to get mixed up with that. He glanced back at the cabin. B'dikkat was not looking out the window.

Mercer walked slowly, straight ahead.

There was a flash on the ground, no brighter than the glitter of sunlight on a fragment of glass. Mercer felt a sting in the thigh, as though a sharp instrument had touched him lightly. He brushed the place with his hand.

It was as though the sky fell in.

A pain—it was more than a pain; it was a living throb—ran from his hip to his foot on the right side. The throb reached up to his chest, robbing him of breath. He fell, and the ground hurt him. Nothing in the hospital-satellite had been like this. He lay in the open air, trying not to breathe, but he did breathe anyhow. Each time he breathed, the throb moved with his thorax. He lay on his back, looking at the sun. At last he noticed that the sun was violet-white.

It was no use even thinking of calling. He had no voice. Tendrils of discomfort twisted within him. Since he could not stop breathing, he concentrated on taking air in the way that hurt him least. Gasps were too much work. Little tiny sips of air hurt him least.

The desert around him was empty. He could not turn his head to look at the cabin. Is this it? he thought. Is an eternity of this the punishment of Shayol?

There were voices near him.

Two faces, grotesquely pink, looked down at him. They might have been human. The man looked normal enough, except for having two noses side by side. The woman was a caricature beyond belief. She had grown a breast on each cheek and a cluster of naked baby-like fingers hung limp from her forehead.

"It's a beauty," said the woman, "a new one."

"Come along," said the man.

They lifted him to his feet. He did not have strength enough to resist. When he tried to speak to them a harsh cawing sound, like the cry of an ugly bird, came from his mouth.

They moved with him efficiently. He saw that he was being dragged to the herd of pink things.

As they approached, he saw that they were people. Better, he saw that they had once been people. A man with the beak of a flamingo was picking at his own body. A woman lay on the ground; she had a single head, but beside what seemed to be her original body, she had a boy's naked body growing sidewise from her neck. The boy-body, clean, new, paralytically helpless, made no movement other than shallow breathing. Mercer looked around. The only one of the group who was wearing clothing was a man with his overcoat on sidewise. Mercer stared at him, finally realizing that the man had two—or was it three?—stomachs growing on the outside of his abdomen. The coat held them in place. The transparent peritoneal wall looked fragile.

"New one," said his female captor. She and the two-nosed man put him down.

The group lay scattered on the ground.

Mercer lay in a state of stupor among them.

An old man's voice said, "I'm afraid they're going to feed us pretty soon."

"Oh, no!" "It's too early!" "Not again!" Protests echoed from the group.

The old man's voice went on, "Look, near the big toe of the mountain!"

The desolate murmur in the group attested their confirmation of what he had seen.

Mercer tried to ask what it was all about, but produced only a caw.

A woman—was it a woman?—crawled over to him on her hands and knees. Beside her ordinary hands, she was covered with hands all over her trunk and halfway down her thighs. Some of the hands looked old and withered. Others were as fresh and pink as the baby-fingers on his captress' face. The woman shouted at him, though it was not necessary to shout.

"The dromozoa are coming. This time it hurts. When you get used to the place, you can dig in—"

She waved at a group of mounds which surrounded the herd of people.

"They're dug in," she said.

Mercer cawed again.

"Don't you worry," said the hand-covered woman, and gasped as a flash of light touched her.

The lights reached Mercer too. The pain was like the first contact but more probing. Mercer felt his eyes widen as odd sensations within his body led to an inescapable conclusion: these lights, these things, these whatever they were, were feeding him and building him up.

Their intelligence, if they had it, was not human, but their motives were clear. In between the stabs of pain he felt them fill his stomach, put water in his blood, draw water from his kidneys and bladder, massage his heart, move his lungs for him.

Every single thing they did was well meant and beneficent in intent.

And every single action hurt.

Abruptly, like the lifting of a cloud of insects, they were gone. Mercer was aware of a noise somewhere outside—a brainless, bawling cascade of ugly noise. He started to look around. And the noise stopped.

It had been himself, screaming. Screaming the ugly screams of a psychotic, a terrified drunk, an animal driven out of understanding or reason.

When he stopped, he found he had his speaking voice again.

A man came to him, naked like the others. There was a spike sticking through his head. The skin had healed around it on both sides. "Hello, fellow," said the man with the spike.

"Hello," said Mercer. It was a foolishly commonplace thing to say in a place like this.

"You can't kill yourself," said the man with the spike through his head.

"Yes, you can," said the woman covered with hands.

Mercer found that his first pain had disappeared. "What's happening to me?"

"You got a part," said the man with the spike. "They're always putting parts on us. After a while B'dikkat comes and cuts most of them off, except for the ones that ought to grow a little more. Like her," he added, nodding at the woman who lay with the boy-body growing from her neck.

"And that's all?" said Mercer. "The stabs for the new parts and the stinging for the feeding?"

"No," said the man. "Sometimes they think we're too cold and they fill our insides with fire. Or they think we're too hot and they freeze us, nerve by nerve."

The woman with the boy-body called over, "And sometimes they think we're unhappy, so they try to force us to be happy. *I* think that's the worst of all."

Mercer stammered, "Are you people—I mean—are you the only herd?"

The man with the spike coughed instead of laughing. "Herd! That's funny. The land is full of people. Most of them dig in. We're the ones who can still talk. We stay together for company. We get more turns with B'dikkat that way."

Mercer started to ask another question, but he felt the strength run out of him. The day had been too much.

The ground rocked like a ship on water. The sky turned black. He felt someone catch him as he fell. He felt himself being stretched out on the ground. And then, mercifully and magically, he slept.

3

Within a week, he came to know the group well. They were an absent-minded bunch of people. Not one of them ever knew when a dromozoon might flash by and add another part. Mercer was not stung again, but the incision he had obtained just outside the cabin was hardening. Spike-head looked at it when Mercer modestly undid his belt and lowered the edge of his trouser-top so they could see the wound.

"You've got a head," he said. "A whole baby head. They'll be glad to get that one upstairs when B'dikkat cuts it off you."

The group even tried to arrange his social life. They introduced him to the girl of the herd. She had grown one body after another, pelvis turning into shoulders and the pelvis below that turning into shoulders again until she was five people long. Her face was unmarred. She tried to be friendly to Mercer.

He was so shocked by her that he dug himself into the soft dry crumbly earth and stayed there for what seemed like a hundred years. He found later that it was less than a full day. When he came out, the long many-bodied girl was waiting for him.

"You didn't have to come out just for me," said she.

Mercer shook the dirt off himself.

He looked around. The violet sun was going down, and the sky was streaked with blues, deeper blues and trails of orange sunset.

He looked back at her. "I didn't get up for you. It's no use lying there, waiting for the next time."

"I want to show you something," she said. She pointed to a low hummock. "Dig that up."

Mercer looked at her. She seemed friendly. He shrugged and attacked the soil with his powerful claws. With tough skin and heavy digging-nails on the ends of his fingers, he found it was easy to dig like a dog. The earth cascaded beneath his busy hands. Something pink appeared down in the hole he had dug. He proceeded more carefully.

He knew what it would be.

It was. It was a man, sleeping. Extra arms grew down one

side of his body in an orderly series. The other side looked
normal.

Mercer turned back to the many-bodied girl, who had
writhed closer.

"That's what I think it is, isn't it?"

"Yes," she said. "Doctor Vomact burned his brain out for
him. And took his eyes out, too."

Mercer sat back on the ground and looked at the girl. "You
told me to do it. Now tell me what for."

"To let you see. To let you know. To let you think."

"That's all?" said Mercer.

The girl twisted with startling suddenness. All the way
down her series of bodies, her chests heaved. Mercer wondered how the air got into all of them. He did not feel sorry
for her; he did not feel sorry for anyone except himself. When
the spasm passed the girl smiled at him apologetically.

"They just gave me a new plant."

Mercer nodded grimly.

"What now, a hand? It seems you have enough."

"Oh, those," she said, looking back at her many torsos. "I
promised B'dikkat that I'd let them grow. He's *good*. But that
man, stranger. Look at that man you dug up. Who's better off,
he or we?"

Mercer stared at her. "Is that what you had me dig him
up for?"

"Yes," said the girl.

"Do you expect me to answer?"

"No," said the girl, "not now."

"Who are you?" said Mercer.

"We never ask that here. It doesn't matter. But since you're
new, I'll tell you. I used to be the Lady Da—the Emperor's
stepmother."

"You!" he exclaimed.

She smiled, ruefully. "You're still so fresh you think it
matters! But I have something more important to tell you."
She stopped and bit her lip.

"What?" he urged. "Better tell me before I get another bite.
I won't be able to think or talk then, not for a long time. Tell
me now."

She brought her face close to his. It was still a lovely face, even in the dying orange of this violet-sunned sunset. "People never live forever."

"Yes," said Mercer. "I knew that."

"*Believe* it," ordered the Lady Da.

Lights flashed across the dark plain, still in the distance. Said she, "Dig in, dig in for the night. They may miss you."

Mercer started digging. He glanced over at the man he had dug up. The brainless body, with motions as soft as those of a starfish under water, was pushing its way back into the earth.

Five or seven days later, there was a shouting through the herd.

Mercer had come to know a half-man, the lower part of whose body was gone and whose viscera were kept in place with what resembled a translucent plastic bandage. The half-man had shown him how to lie still when the dromozoa came with their inescapable errands of doing good.

Said the half-man, "You can't fight them. They made Alvarez as big as a mountain, so that he never stirs. Now they're trying to make us happy. They feed us and clean us and sweeten us up. Lie still. Don't worry about screaming. We all do."

"When do we get the drug?" said Mercer.

"When B'dikkat comes."

B'dikkat came that day, pushing a sort of wheeled sled ahead of him. The runners carried it over the hillocks; the wheels worked on the surface.

Even before he arrived, the herd sprang into furious action. Everywhere, people were digging up the sleepers. By the time B'dikkat reached their waiting place, the herd must have uncovered twice their own number of sleeping pink bodies— men and women, young and old. The sleepers looked no better and no worse than the waking ones.

"Hurry!" said the Lady Da. "He never gives any of us a shot until we're all ready."

B'dikkat wore his heavy lead suit.

He lifted an arm in friendly greeting, like a father returning home with treats for his children. The herd clustered around him but did not crowd him.

He reached into the sled. There was a harnessed bottle which he threw over his shoulders. He snapped the locks on the straps. From the bottle there hung a tube. Midway down the tube there was a small pressure-pump. At the end of the tube there was a glistening hypodermic needle.

When ready, B'dikkat gestured for them to come closer. They approached him with radiant happiness. He stepped through their ranks and past them, to the girl who had the boy growing from her neck. His mechanical voice boomed through the loudspeaker set in the top of his suit.

"Good girl. Good, good girl. You get a big, big present." He thrust the hypodermic into her so long that Mercer could see an air bubble travel from the pump up to the bottle.

Then he moved back to the others, booming a word now and then, moving with improbable grace and speed amid the people. His needle flashed as he gave them hypodermics under pressure. The people dropped to sitting positions or lay down on the ground as though half-asleep.

He knew Mercer. "Hello, fellow. Now you can have the fun. It would have killed you in the cabin. Do you have anything for me?"

Mercer stammered, not knowing what B'dikkat meant, and the two-nosed man answered for him. "I think he has a nice baby-head, but it isn't big enough for you to take yet."

Mercer never noticed the needle touch his arm.

B'dikkat had turned to the next knot of people when the super-condamine hit Mercer.

He tried to run after B'dikkat, to hug the lead space suit, to tell B'dikkat that he loved him. He stumbled and fell, but it did not hurt.

The many-bodied girl lay near him. Mercer spoke to her.

"Isn't it wonderful? You're beautiful, beautiful, beautiful. I'm so happy to be here."

The woman covered with growing hands came and sat beside them. She radiated warmth and good fellowship. Mercer thought that she looked very distinguished and charming. He struggled out of his clothes. It was foolish and snobbish to wear clothing when none of these nice people did.

The two women babbled and crooned at him.

With one corner of his mind he knew that they were saying nothing, just expressing the euphoria of a drug so powerful that the known universe had forbidden it. With most of his mind he was happy. He wondered how anyone could have the good luck to visit a planet as nice as this. He tried to tell the Lady Da, but the words weren't quite straight.

A painful stab hit him in the abdomen. The drug went after the pain and swallowed it. It was like the cap in the hospital, only a thousand times better. The pain was gone, though it had been crippling the first time.

He forced himself to be deliberate. He rammed his mind into focus and said to the two ladies who lay pinkly nude beside him in the desert. "That was a good bite. Maybe I will grow another head. That would make B'dikkat happy!"

The Lady Da forced the foremost of her bodies in an upright position. Said she, "I'm strong, too. I can talk. Remember, man, remember. People never live forever. We can die, too, we can die like real people. I do so believe in death!"

Mercer smiled at her through his happiness.

"Of course you can. But isn't this nice . . ."

With this he felt his lips thicken and his mind go slack. He was wide awake, but he did not feel like doing anything. In that beautiful place, among all those companionable and attractive people, he sat and smiled.

B'dikkat was sterilizing his knives.

Mercer wondered how long the super-condamine had lasted him. He endured the ministrations of the dromozoa without screams or movement. The agonies of nerves and itching of skin were phenomena which happened somewhere near him, but meant nothing. He watched his own body with remote, casual interest. The Lady Da and the handcovered woman stayed near him. After a long time the half-man dragged himself over to the group with his powerful arms. Having arrived he blinked sleepily and friendlily at them, and lapsed back into the restful stupor from which he had emerged. Mercer saw the sun rise on occasion, closed his eyes briefly, and opened them to see stars shining. Time had no meaning. The dromozoa fed him in their mysterious way; the drug canceled out his needs for cycles of the body.

At last he noticed a return of the inwardness of pain.

The pains themselves had not changed; he had.

He knew all the events which could take place on Shayol.

He remembered them well from his happy period. Formerly he had noticed them—now he felt them.

He tried to ask the Lady Da how long they had had the drug, and how much longer they would have to wait before they had it again. She smiled at him with benign, remote happiness; apparently her many torsos, stretched out along the ground, had a greater capacity for retaining the drug than did his body. She meant him well, but was in no condition for articulate speech.

The half-man lay on the ground, arteries pulsating prettily behind the half-transparent film which protected his abdominal cavity.

Mercer squeezed the man's shoulder.

The half-man woke, recognized Mercer and gave him a healthily sleepy grin.

"'A good morrow to you, my boy.' That's out of a play. Did you ever see a play?"

"You mean a game with cards?"

"No," said the half-man, "a sort of eye-machine with real people doing the figures."

"I never saw that," said Mercer, "but I—"

"But you want to ask me when B'dikkat is going to come back with the needle."

"Yes," said Mercer, a little ashamed of his obviousness.

"Soon," said the half-man. "That's why I think of plays. We all know what is going to happen. We all know when it is going to happen. We all know what the dummies will do—" he gestured at the hummocks in which the decorticated men were cradled—"and we all know what the new people will ask. But we never know how long a scene is going to take."

"What's a 'scene'?" asked Mercer. "Is that the name for the needle?"

The half-man laughed with something close to real humor. "No, no, no. You've got the lovelies on the brain. A scene is just part of a play. I mean we know the order in which things happen, but we have no clocks and nobody cares enough to count days or to make calendars and there's not much climate here, so none of us know how long anything takes. The pain seems short and the pleasure seems long. I'm inclined to think that they are about two Earth-weeks each."

Mercer did not know what an "Earth-week" was, since he had not been a well-read man before his conviction, but he got nothing more from the half-man at that time. The half-man received a dromozootic implant, turned red in the face, shouted senselessly at Mercer, "Take it out, you fool! Take it out of me!"

While Mercer looked on helplessly, the half-man twisted over on his side, his pink dusty back turned to Mercer, and wept hoarsely and quietly to himself.

Mercer himself could not tell how long it was before B'dikkat came back. It might have been several days. It might have been several months.

Once again B'dikkat moved among them like a father; once again they clustered like children. This time B'dikkat smiled pleasantly at the little head which had grown out of Mercer's thigh—a sleeping child's head, covered with light hair on top and with dainty eyebrows over the resting eyes. Mercer got the blissful needle.

When B'dikkat cut the head from Mercer's thigh, he felt the knife grinding against the cartilage which held the head to his own body. He saw the child-face grimace as the head was cut; he felt the far, cool flash of unimportant pain, as B'dikkat dabbed the wound with a corrosive antiseptic which stopped all bleeding immediately.

The next time it was two legs growing from his chest.

Then there had been another head beside his own.

Or was that after the torso and legs, waist to toe-tips, of the little girl which had grown from his side?

He forgot the order.

He did not count time.

Lady Da smiled at him often, but there was no love in this place. She had lost the extra torsos. In between teratologies, she was a pretty and shapely woman; but the nicest thing about their relationship was her whisper to him, repeated some thousands of times, repeated with smiles and hope, "People never live forever."

She found this immensely comforting, even though Mercer did not make much sense out of it.

Thus events occurred, and victims changed in appearance, and new ones arrived. Sometimes B'dikkat took the new ones,

resting in the everlasting sleep of their burned-out brains, in a
ground-truck to be added to other herds. The bodies in the
truck thrashed and bawled without human speech when the
dromozoa struck them.

Finally, Mercer did manage to follow B'dikkat to the door
of the cabin. He had to fight the bliss of super-condamine to
do it. Only the memory of the previous hurt, bewilderment
and perplexity made him sure that if he did not ask B'dikkat
when he, Mercer, was happy, the answer would no longer be
available when he needed it. Fighting pleasure itself, he
begged B'dikkat to check the records and to tell him how long
he had been there.

B'dikkat grudgingly agreed, but he did not come out of the
doorway. He spoke through the public address box built into the
cabin, and his gigantic voice roared out over the empty plain,
so that the pink herd of talking people stirred gently in their
happiness and wondered what their friend B'dikkat might be
wanting to tell them. When he said it, they thought it exceed-
ingly profound, though none of them understood it, since it was
simply the amount of time that Mercer had been on Shayol:

"Standard years—eighty-four years, seven months, three
days, two hours, eleven and one half minutes. Good luck,
fellow."

Mercer turned away.

The secret little corner of his mind, which stayed sane
through happiness and pain, made him wonder about
B'dikkat. What persuaded the cow-man to remain on Shayol?
What kept him happy without super-condamine? Was
B'dikkat a crazy slave to his own duty or was he a man who
had hopes of going back to his own planet some day, surrounded by a family of little cow-people resembling himself?
Mercer, despite his happiness, wept a little at the strange fate
of B'dikkat. His own fate he accepted.

He remembered the last time he had eaten—actual eggs
from an actual pan. The dromozoa kept him alive, but he did
not know how they did it.

He staggered back to the group. The Lady Da, naked in the
dusty plain, waved a hospitable hand and showed that there
was a place for him to sit beside her. There were unclaimed

square miles of seating space around them, but he appreciated the kindliness of her gesture nonetheless.

4

The years, if they were years, went by. The land of Shayol did not change.

Sometimes the bubbling sound of geysers came faintly across the plain to the herd of men; those who could talk declared it to be the breathing of Captain Alvarez. There was night and day, but no setting of crops, no change of season, no generations of men. Time stood still for these people, and their load of pleasure was so commingled with the shocks and pains of the dromozoa that the words of the Lady Da took on very remote meaning.

"People never live forever."

Her statement was a hope, not a truth in which they could believe. They did not have the wit to follow the stars in their courses, to exchange names with each other, to harvest the experience of each for the wisdom of all. There was no dream of escape for these people. Though they saw the old-style chemical rockets lift up from the field beyond B'dikkat's cabin, they did not make plans to hide among the frozen crop of transmuted flesh.

Far long ago, some other prisoner than one of these had tried to write a letter. His handwriting was on a rock. Mercer read it, and so had a few of the others, but they could not tell which man had done it. Nor did they care.

The letter, scraped on stone, had been a message home. They could still read the opening: "Once, I was like you, stepping out of my window at the end of day, and letting the winds blow me gently toward the place I lived in. Once, like you, I had one head, two hands, ten fingers on my hands. The front part of my head was called a face, and I could talk with it. Now I can only write, and that only when I get out of pain. Once, like you, I ate foods, drank liquid, had a name. I cannot remember the name I had. You can stand up, you who get this letter. I cannot even stand up. I just wait for the lights to put my food in me molecule by molecule, and to take it out again.

Don't think that I am punished anymore. This place is not a punishment. It is something else."

Among the pink herd, none of them ever decided what was "something else."

Curiosity had died among them long ago.

Then came the day of the little people.

It was a time—not an hour, not a year: a duration somewhere between them—when the Lady Da and Mercer sat wordless with happiness and filled with the joy of supercondamine. They had nothing to say to one another; the drug said all things for them.

A disagreeable roar from B'dikkat's cabin made them stir mildly.

Those two, and one or two others, looked toward the speaker of the public address system.

The Lady Da brought herself to speak, though the matter was unimportant beyond words. "I do believe," said she, "that we used to call that the War Alarm."

They drowsed back into their happiness.

A man with two rudimentary heads growing beside his own crawled over to them. All three heads looked very happy, and Mercer thought it delightful of him to appear in such a whimsical shape. Under the pulsing glow of supercondamine, Mercer regretted that he had not used times when his mind was clear to ask him who he had once been. He answered it for them. Forcing his eyelids open by sheer will power, he gave the Lady Da and Mercer the lazy ghost of a military salute and said, "Suzdal, Ma'am and Sir, former cruiser commander. They are sounding the alert. Wish to report that I am . . . I am . . . I am not quite ready for battle."

He dropped off to sleep.

The gentle peremptorinesses of the Lady Da brought his eyes open again.

"Commander, why are they sounding it here? Why did you come to us?"

"You, Ma'am, and the gentleman with the ears seem to think best of our group. I thought you might have orders."

Mercer looked around for the gentleman with the ears. It was himself. In that time his face was almost wholly obscured with a crop of fresh little ears, but he paid no attention to them, other than expecting that B'dikkat would cut them all off in due course and that the dromozoa would give him something else.

The noise from the cabin rose to a higher, ear-splitting intensity.

Among the herd, many people stirred.

Some opened their eyes, looked around, murmured. "It's a noise," and went back to the happy drowsing with super-condamine.

The cabin door opened.

B'dikkat rushed out, *without his suit*. They had never seen him on the outside without his protective metal suit.

He rushed up to them, looked wildly around, recognized the Lady Da and Mercer, picked them up, one under each arm, and raced with them back to the cabin. He flung them into the double door. They landed with bone-splitting crashes, and found it amusing to hit the ground so hard. The floor tilted them into the room. Moments later, B'dikkat followed.

He roared at them, "You're people, or you were. You understand people; I only obey them. But this I will not obey. Look at that!"

Four beautiful human children lay on the floor. The two smallest seemed to be twins, about two years of age. There was a girl of five and a boy of seven or so. All of them had slack eyelids. All of them had thin red lines around their temples and their hair, shaved away, showed how their brains had been removed.

B'dikkat, heedless of danger from dromozoa, stood beside the Lady Da and Mercer, shouting.

"You're real people. I'm just a cow. I do my duty. My duty does not include this. These are *children*."

The wise, surviving recess of Mercer's mind registered shock and disbelief. It was hard to sustain the emotion, because the super-condamine washed at his consciousness like a great tide, making everything seem lovely. The forefront of his mind, rich with the drug, told him, "Won't it be nice to have some children with us!" But the undestroyed interior of his mind, keeping the honor he knew before he came to Shayol, whispered, "This is a crime worse than any crime we have committed! *And the Empire has done it.*"

"What have you done?" said the Lady Da. "What can we do?"

"I tried to call the satellite. When they knew what I was talking about, they cut me off. After all, I'm not people. The head doctor told me to do my work."

"Was it Doctor Vomact?" Mercer asked.

"Vomact?" said B'dikkat. "He died a hundred years ago, of old age. No, a new doctor cut me off. I don't have people-feeling, but I am Earth-born, of Earth blood. I have emotions myself. Pure cattle emotions! *This* I cannot permit."

"What have you done?"

B'dikkat lifted his eyes to the window. His face was illuminated by a determination which, even beyond the edges of the drug which made them love him, made him seem like the father of this world—responsible, honorable, unselfish.

He smiled. "They will kill me for it, I think. But I have put in the Galactic Alert—*all ships here.*"

The Lady Da, sitting back on the floor, declared, "But that's only for new invaders! It is a false alarm." She pulled herself together and rose to her feet. "Can you cut these things off me, right now, in case people come? And get me a dress. And do you have anything which will counteract the effect of the super-condamine?"

"That's what I wanted!" cried B'dikkat. "I will not take these children. You give me leadership."

There and then, on the floor of the cabin, he trimmed her down to the normal proportions of mankind.

The corrosive antiseptic rose like smoke in the air of the cabin. Mercer thought it all very dramatic and pleasant, and dropped off in catnaps part of the time. Then he felt B'dikkat trimming him too. B'dikkat opened a long, long drawer and put the specimens in; from the cold in the room it must have been a refrigerated locker.

He sat them both up against the wall.

"I've been thinking," he said. "There is no antidote for super-condamine. Who would want one? But I can give you the hypos from my rescue boat. They are supposed to bring a person back, no matter what has happened to that person out in space."

There was a whining over the cabin roof. B'dikkat

knocked a window out with his fist, stuck his head out of the window and looked up.

"Come on in," he shouted.

There was the thud of a landing craft touching ground quickly. Doors whirred. Mercer wondered, mildly, why people dared to land on Shayol. When they came in he saw that they were not people; they were Customs Robots, who could travel at velocities which people could never match. One wore the insigne of an inspector.

"Where are the invaders?"

"There are no—" began B'dikkat.

The Lady Da, imperial in her posture though she was completely nude, said in a voice of complete clarity, "I am a former Empress, the Lady Da. Do you know me?"

"No, ma'am," said the robot inspector. He looked as uncomfortable as a robot could look. The drug made Mercer think that it would be nice to have robots for company, out on the surface of Shayol.

"I declare this Top Emergency, in the ancient words. Do you understand? Connect me with the Instrumentality."

"We can't—" said the Inspector.

"You can ask," said the Lady Da.

The inspector complied.

The Lady Da turned to B'dikkat. "Give Mercer and me those shots now. Then put us outside the door so the dromozoa can repair these scars. Bring us in as soon as a connection is made. Wrap us in cloth if you do not have clothes for us. Mercer can stand the pain."

"Yes," said B'dikkat, keeping his eyes away from the four soft children and their collapsed eyes.

The injection burned like no fire ever had. It must have been capable of fighting the super-condamine, because B'dikkat put them through the open window, so as to save time going through the door. The dromozoa, sensing that they needed repair, flashed upon them. This time the super-condamine had something else fighting it.

Mercer did not scream but he lay against the wall and wept for ten thousand years; in objective time, it must have been several hours.

The Customs robots were taking pictures. The dromozoa

were flashing against them too, sometimes in whole swarms, but nothing happened.

Mercer heard the voice of the communicator inside the cabin calling loudly for B'dikkat. "Surgery Satellite calling Shayol. B'dikkat, get on the line!"

He obviously was not replying.

There were soft cries coming from the other communicator, the one which the customs officials had brought into the room. Mercer was sure that the eye-machine was on and that people in other worlds were looking at Shayol for the first time.

B'dikkat came through the door. He had torn navigation charts out of his lifeboat. With these he cloaked them.

Mercer noted that the Lady Da changed the arrangement of the cloak in a few minor ways and suddenly looked like a person of great importance.

They re-entered the cabin door.

B'dikkat whispered, as if filled with awe, "The Instrumentality has been reached, and a lord of the Instrumentality is about to talk to you."

There was nothing for Mercer to do, so he sat back in a corner of the room and watched. The Lady Da, her skin healed, stood pale and nervous in the middle of the floor.

The room filled with an odorless intangible smoke. The smoke clouded. The full communicator was on.

A human figure appeared.

A woman, dressed in a uniform of radically conservative cut, faced the Lady Da.

"This is Shayol. You are the Lady Da. You called me."

The Lady Da pointed to the children on the floor. "This must not happen," she said. "This is a place of punishments, agreed upon between the Instrumentality and the Empire. No one said anything about children."

The woman on the screen looked down at the children.

"This is the work of insane people!" she cried.

She looked accusingly at the Lady Da, "Are you imperial?"

"I was an Empress, madam," said the Lady Da.

"And you permit this!"

"Permit it?" cried the Lady Da. "I had nothing to do with

it." Her eyes widened. "I am a prisoner here myself. Don't you understand?"

The image-woman snapped, "No, I don't."

"I," said the Lady Da, "am a specimen. Look at the herd out there. I came from them a few hours ago."

"Adjust me," said the image-woman to B'dikkat. "Let me see that herd."

Her body, standing upright, soared through the wall in a flashing arc and was placed in the very center of the herd.

The Lady Da and Mercer watched her. They saw even the image lose its stiffness and dignity. The image-woman waved an arm to show that she should be brought back into the cabin. B'dikkat tuned her back into the room.

"I owe you an apology," said the image. "I am the Lady Johanna Gnade, one of the lords of the Instrumentality."

Mercer bowed, lost his balance and had to scramble up from the floor. The Lady Da acknowledged the introduction with a royal nod.

The two women looked at each other.

"You will investigate," said the Lady Da, "and when you have investigated, please put us all to death. You know about the drug?"

"Don't mention it," said B'dikkat, "don't even say the name into a communicator. It is a secret of the Instrumentality!"

"I am the Instrumentality," said the Lady Johanna. "Are you in pain? I did not think that any of you were alive. I had heard of the surgery banks on your off-limits planet, but I thought that robots tended parts of people and sent up the new grafts by rocket. Are there any people with you? Who is in charge? Who did this to the children?"

B'dikkat stepped in front of the image. He did not bow. "I'm in charge."

"You're underpeople!" cried the Lady Johanna. "You're a cow!"

"A bull, Ma'am. My family is frozen back on Earth itself, and with a thousand years' service I am earning their freedom and my own. Your other questions, Ma'am. I do all the work. The dromozoa do not affect me much, though I have to cut a part off myself now and then. I throw those away. They don't go into the bank. Do you know the secret of this place?"

The Lady Johanna talked to someone behind her on another world. Then she looked at B'dikkat and commanded, "Just don't name the drug or talk too much about it. Tell me the rest."

"We have," said B'dikkat very formally, "thirteen hundred and twenty-one people who can still be counted on to supply parts when the dromozoa implant them. There are about seven hundred more, including Go-Captain Alvarez, who have been so thoroughly absorbed by the planet that it is no use trimming them. The Empire set up this place as a point of uttermost punishment. But the Instrumentality gave secret orders for *medicine*—" he accented the word strangely, meaning super-condamine—"to be issued so that the punishment would be counteracted. The Empire supplies our convicts. The Instrumentality distributes the surgical material."

The Lady Johanna lifted her right hand in a gesture of silence and compassion. She looked around the room. Her eyes came back to the Lady Da. Perhaps she guessed what effort the Lady Da had made in order to remain standing erect while the two drugs, the super-condamine and the lifeboat drug, fought within her veins.

"You people can rest. I will tell you now that all things possible will be done for you. The Empire is finished. The Fundamental Agreement, by which the Instrumentality surrendered the Empire a thousand years ago, has been set aside. We did not know that you people existed. We would have found out in time, but I am sorry we did not find out sooner. Is there anything we can do for you right away?"

"Time is what we all have," said the Lady Da. "Perhaps we cannot ever leave Shayol, because of the domozoa and the *medicine*. The one could be dangerous. The other must never be permitted to be known."

The Lady Johanna Gnade looked around the room. When her glance reached him, B'dikkat fell to his knees and lifted his enormous hands in complete supplication.

"What do you want?" said she.

"These," said B'dikkat, pointing to the mutilated children. "Order a stop on children. Stop it now!" He commanded her with the last cry, and she accepted his command. "And Lady—" he stopped as if shy.

"Yes? Go on."

"Lady, I am unable to kill. It is not in my nature. To work, to help, but not to kill. What do I do with these?" He gestured at the four motionless children on the floor.

"Keep them," she said. "Just keep them."

"I can't," he said. "There's no way to get off this planet alive. I do not have food for them in the cabin. They will die in a few hours. And governments," he added wisely, "take a long, long time to do things."

"Can you give them the *medicine?*"

"No, it would kill them if I give them that stuff first before the dromozoa have fortified their bodily processes."

The Lady Johanna Gnade filled the room with tinkling laughter that was very close to weeping. "Fools, poor fools, and the more fool I! If super-condamine works only *after* the dromozoa, what is the purpose of the secret?"

B'dikkat rose to his feet, offended. He frowned, but he could not get the words with which to defend himself.

The Lady Da, ex-empress of a fallen empire, addressed the other lady with ceremony and force: "Put them outside, so they will be touched. They will hurt. Have B'dikkat give them the drug as soon as he thinks it safe. I beg your leave, my Lady . . ."

Mercer had to catch her before she fell.

"You've all had enough," said the Lady Johanna. "A storm ship with heavily armed troops is on its way to your ferry satellite. They will seize the medical personnel and find out who committed this crime against children."

Mercer dared to speak. "Will you punish the guilty doctor?"

"*You* speak of punishment," she cried. "You!"

"It's fair. I was punished for doing wrong. Why shouldn't he be?"

"Punish—punish!" she said to him. "We will cure that doctor. And we will cure you too, if we can."

Mercer began to weep. He thought of the oceans of happiness which super-condamine had brought him, forgetting the hideous pain and the deformities on Shayol. Would there be no next needle? He could not guess what life would be like off

Shayol. Was there to be no more tender, fatherly B'dikkat coming with his knives?

He lifted his tear-stained face to the Lady Johanna Gnade and choked out the words. "Lady, we are all insane in this place. I do not think we want to leave."

She turned her face away, moved by enormous compassion. Her next words were to B'dikkat. "You are wise and good, even if you are not a human being. Give them all of the drug they can take. The Instrumentality will decide what to do with all of you. I will survey your planet with robot soldiers. Will the robots be safe, cow-man?"

B'dikkat did not like the thoughtless name she called him, but he held no offense. "The robots will be all right, Ma'am, but the dromozoa will be excited if they cannot feed them and heal them. Send as few as you can. We do not know how the dromozoa live or die."

"As few as I can," she murmured. She lifted her hand in command to some technician unimaginable distances away. The odorless smoke rose about her and the image was gone.

A shrill cheerful voice spoke up. "I fixed your window," said the customs pilot. B'dikkat thanked him absentmindedly. He helped Mercer and the Lady Da into the doorway. When they had gotten outside, they were promptly stung by the dromozoa. It did not matter.

B'dikkat himself emerged, carrying the four children in his two gigantic, tender hands. He lay the slack bodies on the ground near the cabin. He watched as the bodies went into spasm with the onset of the dromozoa. Mercer and the Lady Da saw that his brown cow eyes were rimmed with red and that his huge cheeks were dampened by tears.

Hours or centuries.

Who could tell them apart?

The herd went back to its usual life, except that the intervals between needles were much shorter. The once-commander, Suzdal, refused the needle when he heard the news. Whenever he could walk, he followed the customs robots around as they photographed, took soil samples, and made a count of the bodies. They were particularly interested in the mountain of the Go-Captain Alvarez and professed themselves uncertain as to whether there was organic life or not. The mountain did

appear to react to super-condamine, but they could find no
blood, no heart-beat. Moisture, moved by the dromozoa,
seemed to have replaced the once-human bodily processes.

5

And then, early one morning, the sky opened.

Ship after ship landed. People emerged, wearing clothes.

The dromozoa ignored the newcomers. Mercer, who was
in a state of bliss, confusedly tried to think this through until
he realized that the ships were loaded to their skins with communications machines; the "people" were either robots or images of persons in other places.

The robots swiftly gathered together the herd. Using
wheelbarrows, they brought the hundreds of mindless people
to the landing area.

Mercer heard a voice he knew. It was the Lady Johanna
Gnade. "Set me high," she commanded.

Her form rose until she seemed one-fourth the size of Alvarez. Her voice took on more volume.

"Wake them all," she commanded.

Robots moved among them, spraying them with a gas
which was both sickening and sweet. Mercer felt his mind go
clear. The super-condamine still operated in his nerves and
veins, but his cortical area was free of it. He thought clearly.

"I bring you," cried the compassionate feminine voice of
the gigantic Lady Johanna, "the judgment of the Instrumentality on the planet Shayol.

"Item: the surgical supplies will be maintained and the
dromozoa will not be molested. Portions of human bodies will
be left here to grow, and the grafts will be collected by robots.
Neither man nor homunculus will live here again.

"Item: the underman B'dikkat, of cattle extraction, will be
rewarded by an immediate return to Earth. He will be paid
twice his expected thousand years of earnings."

The voice of B'dikkat, without amplification, was almost
as loud as hers through the amplifier. He shouted his protest,
"Lady, Lady!"

She looked down at him, his enormous body reaching to

ankle height on her swirling gown, and said in a very informal tone, "What do you want?"

"Let me finish my work first," he cried, so that all could hear. "Let me finish taking care of these people."

The specimens who had minds all listened attentively. The brainless ones were trying to dig themselves back into the soft earth of Shayol, using their powerful claws for the purpose. Whenever one began to disappear, a robot seized him by a limb and pulled him out again.

"Item: cephalactomies will be performed on all persons with irrecoverable minds. Their bodies will be left here. Their heads will be taken away and killed as pleasantly as we can manage, probably by an overdosage of super-condamine."

"The last big jolt," murmured Commander Suzdal, who stood near Mercer. "That's fair enough."

"Item: the children have been found to be the last heirs of the Empire. An over-zealous official sent them here to prevent their committing treason when they grew up. The doctor obeyed orders without questioning them. Both the official and the doctor have been cured and their memories of this have been erased, so that they need have no shame or grief for what they have done."

"It's unfair," cried the half-man. "They should be punished as we were!"

The Lady Johanna Gnade looked down at him. "Punishment is ended. We will give you anything you wish, but not the pain of another. I shall continue.

"Item: since none of you wish to resume the lives which you led previously, we are moving you to another planet nearby. It is similar to Shayol, but much more beautiful. There are no dromozoa."

At this an uproar seized the herd. They shouted, wept, cursed, appealed. They all wanted the needle, and if they had to stay on Shayol to get it, they would stay.

"Item," said the gigantic image of the lady, overriding their babble with her great but feminine voice, "you will not have super-condamine on the new planet, since without dromozoa it would kill you. But there will be caps. *Remember the caps.* We will try to cure you and to make people of you again. But if you give up, we will not force you. Caps are very powerful; with medical help you can live under them many years."

A hush fell on the group. In their various ways, they were trying to compare the electrical caps which had stimulated their pleasure-lobes with the drug which had drowned them a thousand times in pleasure. Their murmur sounded like assent.

"Do you have any questions?" said the Lady Johanna.

"When do we get the caps?" said several. They were human enough that they laughed at their own impatience.

"Soon," said she reassuringly, "very soon."

"Very soon," echoed B'dikkat, reassuring his charges even though he was no longer in control.

"Question," cried the Lady Da.

"My Lady . . . ?" said the Lady Johanna, giving the ex-empress her due courtesy.

"Will we be permitted marriage?"

The Lady Johanna looked astonished. "I don't know." She smiled. "I don't know any reason why not—"

"I claim this man Mercer," said the Lady Da. "When the drugs were deepest, and the pain was greatest, he was the one who always tried to think. May I have him?"

Mercer thought the procedure arbitrary but he was so happy that he said nothing. The Lady Johanna scrutinized him and then she nodded. She lifted her arms in a gesture of blessing and farewell.

The robots began to gather the pink herd into two groups. One group was to whisper in a ship over to a new world, new problems and new lives. The other group, no matter how much its members tried to scuttle into the dirt, was gathered for the last honor which humanity could pay their manhood.

B'dikkat, leaving everyone else, jogged with his bottle across the plain to give the mountain-man Alvarez an especially large gift of delight.